SEARCHING FOR KHLOE

Eagle Point Search & Rescue, Book 7

SUSAN STOKER

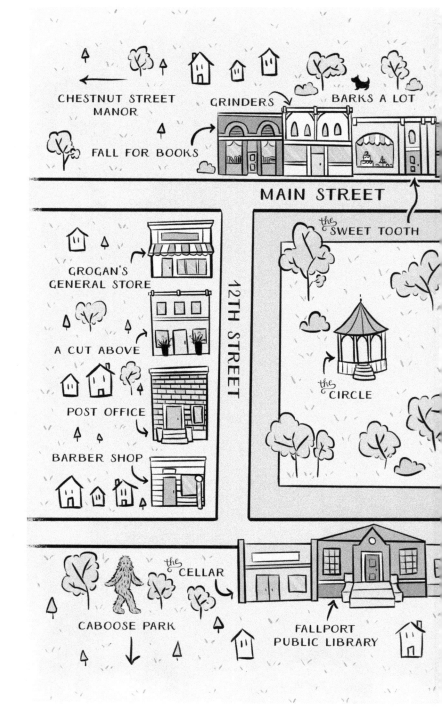

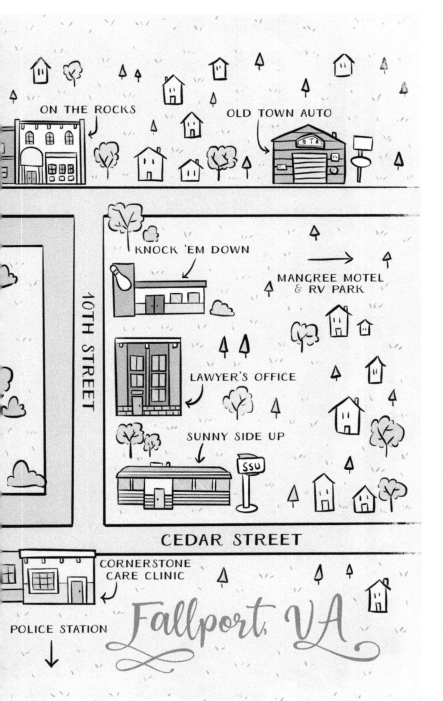

DEDICATION

To "Uncle" Mike
Thanks for sharing your love of D&D
May Anise and Bjorn live on forever

CHAPTER ONE

Raiden Walker stared in disbelief at the woman who'd upended his life. This wasn't the same woman he'd hired to work with him at the Fallport Public Library. She was a completely different person. If it wasn't his dog, his beloved Duke, whose life was in danger, he probably would've pulled Khloe Moore aside right then and insisted she tell him who the hell she really was.

But as Duke's life *was* in danger, and Khloe was currently doing everything in her power to save him, Raid stood back and observed.

Thirty minutes ago, she'd burst into his office at the library and told him to call Simon, Fallport's police chief, and Doc Snow. Then she'd driven like a bat out of hell to the only vet clinic in town. Doctor Ziegler, the veterinarian, was out of town, but that hadn't slowed Khloe down.

She'd wanted the police chief there so she didn't get in trouble for breaking into the vet clinic, and apparently Doc Snow was there to assist her in surgery.

Duke had bloated. Gastric Dilation Volvulus, GDV, was when the stomach of a dog, usually a deep-chested breed like a bloodhound, twists either a hundred and eighty degrees, all the way around, or somewhere in between. Once twisted, the stomach fills with fluid and gas and expands. Because of the twist, the dog can't vomit, as the entrance to the stomach is blocked, and nothing can leave the stomach via the intestines either. Blood vessels can rupture and lead to hemorrhage. The huge stomach pushes on the diaphragm, making it hard for the dog to breathe.

Raid also heard Khloe explaining to Doc Snow that the stomach can also put pressure on the caudal vena cava, a large vein that transports blood to the heart, which can throw the animal into shock.

Raiden knew the longer the stomach was twisted, the more damage was done. If it wasn't repaired, the stomach tissue would die and rupture, leading to death. The thought of losing Duke was unimaginable.

Yes, Raid knew the time would come when his faithful companion would die, but he'd thought that would be years in the future. He wasn't ready to lose another dog before his time.

Blocking out memories of another time, and another dog, Raiden forced himself to concentrate on the here and now.

"Raid! I need you over here," Khloe barked out.

He'd been standing back, giving Khloe room to work. But at her order, he rushed over to where she was standing next to a tall table. Duke was lying on his side, panting, looking completely miserable.

"I need you to keep him calm while I perform a trocarization. He'll relax more if you're touching him and talking to him."

Raid had no idea what a trocarization was, but he didn't argue. He immediately went to Duke's head and squatted down so he was eye-to-eye with the bloodhound. "Hey, buddy. You're okay. I know it hurts, but Khloe's gonna make it better. Hang in there."

He continued to speak gently to Duke while watching Khloe work. She quickly shaved a patch of hair from Duke's leg then inserted a catheter. She'd broken into Doctor Ziegler's drug cabinet earlier—under Simon's watchful eye—and now she administered fentanyl and fluids to help Duke's pain and keep him from going into shock. She then took a large-gauge needle and inserted it into Duke's stomach to try to relieve the buildup of air.

As Raiden watched, Duke's belly visibly shrunk. Khloe breathed out a sigh of relief, then lifted her gaze to meet his.

"He's not out of the woods. I need to do surgery."

Raid nodded without hesitation. As he stared into Khloe's hazel eyes, he saw nothing but confidence in her own abilities. She was stressed, and the concern for Duke was there too, but it was the assurance that she had this crisis handled that made Raid relax a fraction. "Okay," he said simply.

Khloe stared at him for a beat before asking, "You aren't going to ask me about my credentials?"

"Can you save him?" Raid asked.

"Yes."

"Then no, I'm not going to ask any useless questions

that would take time away from you doing what needs to be done to save my dog's life. You obviously know what you're doing. But that doesn't mean we aren't going to have a talk later."

Khloe winced, but nodded.

Raid's admiration for the woman went up several notches. He and Khloe had a complicated relationship. She was the most frustrating woman he'd ever met. Just when Raiden thought he was getting to know her, she'd do or say something that would have him questioning everything he thought he knew. He also regularly found himself sniping at her and being twice as hard on her than he would anyone else.

The truth was...she got under his skin more than any woman ever had. He wanted her to talk to him. Tell him what was bothering her, because it was obvious she had some serious weight on her shoulders. But from the moment they met, she'd refused to let him deepen their friendship. Insisted on keeping him at arm's length.

This was his first glimpse of what he instinctively knew was the *real* Khloe...and Raid had to admit that he liked it. She was strong and confident here in this world. It was no wonder she'd never seemed fully comfortable working at the library. She was used to interacting with animals, not humans.

All the times he'd seen her with Duke, and the kittens she'd rescued, and every other animal she'd come across, made a lot more sense now.

Yeah, he and Khloe needed to sit down and have a heart to heart...but first she needed to save Duke's life.

A commotion at the door made Raid stiffen, and he stood and took a step to the side, putting himself between

Khloe and whoever was trying to get past Simon and enter the small operating room.

It was instinctive. Wanting to protect Khloe from anyone and anything that might want to hurt her. But typical of the woman he'd gotten to know over the last few months, she wasn't having any of that. She brushed past him and went to the door.

"I'm sorry, Khloe, she insisted on speaking with you," Simon said apologetically as he pushed open the door.

"My name's Afton. I'm a vet tech here," the woman explained. She was around five-eight or so, had her black hair up in a bun and off her face and was wearing a pair of light blue scrubs. "I help Doctor Ziegler with surgeries. I live across the street, so it's my job to check on the animals who stay overnight after procedures. I knew he was supposed to be gone for another few days, so when I saw all the cars over here, I had to come see what was going on." She paused when her eyes fell on the exam table. "Oh no—is that Duke? What's wrong? Can I help?"

Khloe eyed the woman for a long moment. "Yes, he's got a GDV."

"Crap! Was it caught soon enough?" she asked.

"Yes, although I need to get this surgery started if I'm going to save him."

The vet tech straightened. "Let me help."

"Yeah, let her help," Doc Snow echoed. "My specialty is humans, not dogs."

Khloe glanced at him. "I'm sure you'll be fine," she told him, then faced Afton once again. "Ziegler's gonna be pissed that I broke in. If you stay and help me, I wouldn't be surprised if you found yourself without a job."

Afton shrugged. "He's a jerk," she said firmly. "I've

already been trying to find something else. He's technically good at what he does, but he has absolutely no compassion for the animals he treats. He's more interested in how much money he can make than actually caring for the pets. I mean, case in point—he closed down the office for two weeks to go on one of those canned hunts. You know, where a bear or moose or something is penned into an area and hunted down by tourists? It's disgusting, yet he was so excited to go. He didn't even try to get anyone in to cover his business either. When I asked what the residents were supposed to do if there was an emergency with their pets while he was gone, he shrugged and said they'd have to go to the emergency vet in Christiansburg."

Khloe scowled. "I wish I could say I'm surprised, but I'm not. If you want to stay and help, I'd appreciate it. But I'll also understand if you turn around and leave and we can both pretend you weren't here and know nothing."

"I'll go get gowned up," Afton said, turning and rushing down the hall.

Khloe returned to Duke. Raid saw the bloodhound's eyes were partially closed. The painkillers had done their thing, and that, along with the release of pressure in his belly, clearly had him feeling drowsy.

"You can go out and hang with Simon now," Khloe told him.

"I'm staying."

"No, you aren't," Khloe countered. "Look, I know you're worried, but I've got this. It's better if you don't see this part. I'll call you back in when I'm done. You can be there while he's recovering."

Raid wanted to protest. But the steely determination

6

in Khloe's eyes made it clear he wasn't going to get his way. Besides...he trusted her.

He was about to agree, but his hesitation must've made her assume he would protest.

"I know this is confusing for you, and I'm sorry. I have my reasons for why I haven't said anything about being a vet. But I'm qualified. I've kept my license current and stayed up to date on new procedures and done my continuing education requirements. I've never lost a dog to bloat, and I'm not going to start now."

"I trust you." Raid might be confused about why Khloe was in Fallport, and why she was a librarian's assistant instead of a veterinarian, but he had the utmost confidence that she'd do everything she could to help Duke. Hell, if it wasn't for her, it probably would've been several hours before Raiden even noticed something was wrong. And then he would've had to drive to the closest emergency vet, which would've wasted *more* valuable time.

His words must've surprised Khloe, because he saw her visible reaction. She blinked rapidly and inhaled sharply. "Thanks," she said.

"I'll make sure no one disturbs you while you're operating," he told her. "If you need anything, anything at all, just let me know and I'll get it for you."

"I think I'll be good. Now that Afton is here to help me find stuff when I need it, we should be fine. But I have to warn you, Raymond *really* isn't going to like that I broke into his clinic."

"No shit," Raid said. "We can worry about that after Duke's on the mend."

She nodded. "Right. I need to go scrub up."

Raiden couldn't stop himself from stepping toward

7

Khloe. She stood her ground and didn't back away. He reached a hand out and wrapped it around the back of her neck. He was almost a foot and a half taller than the fascinating woman in front of him, her head coming only to his chest. He stared down at her for a beat...then did what he'd dreamed about for months.

He leaned down and kissed her.

It was a short kiss. Merely a brushing of his lips against hers. But even that small contact sent lightning bolts shooting down his extremities, making his toes and fingers tingle.

Khloe stared up at him with wide eyes. Her light brown hair was pulled back in a low bun at the base of her neck and he could feel the soft strands against his fingers. Her hand came up to grip his forearm as she blinked slowly. Probably wondering what the hell he thought he was doing, taking such liberties.

All his life, Raiden had felt like an outsider. He was too tall. His ears were too pointy. He was too nerdy. His red hair and pale skin stood out. Even when he was a member of the Coast Guard canine handler team, he didn't fit in with his fellow handlers, despite being as skilled as anyone else.

It was extremely difficult to qualify to even be considered for the prestigious position, and Raid had worked his butt off to excel. The amount of trust a dog must have in his handler wasn't something that could easily be achieved, and Raid found himself hating every second he had to put his dog in danger, even though it was what the dog was trained from birth to do.

There was only one teammate who'd seemed to connect with his own canine on the same level as Raid had with his...and they'd both paid a hefty price when those bonds were severed in the worst way possible.

Mentally shaking his head, not wanting to go down that road, Raiden dropped his hand from Khloe's neck. There was no way a woman like her would want to be with him. He was too...weird. Too closed off. And they hadn't exactly gotten along since he'd hired her. She'd made her own need for distance perfectly clear.

Taking a step back, Raiden forced himself to look away. He knew he was blushing. With his fair skin, there was no way to hide his embarrassment. He shouldn't have kissed her. He wasn't *sorry* for the kiss, and those few seconds his lips were against hers were already embedded deep in his brain. But he *was* sorry for doing anything that might change things between them.

Hell, who was he kidding. Khloe was an experienced veterinarian who now worked in a library and nearly always kept to herself. It seemed very obvious to Raid that she might've been hiding out in Fallport for some unknown reason. Now that her secret was out, she'd probably be leaving—which would *definitely* change things between them.

With all that in mind, Raid kind've hoped maybe in the chaos of what was happening, she'd forget about his ill-timed kiss.

He leaned over Duke and said, "Hang in there, buddy. I'll see you when you wake up." Then he nodded at Khloe and headed for the door.

* * *

Khloe stared at Raiden's backside as he left the small operating room. She had things to do. A surgery to prep for. But all she could manage to do in that moment was try to control her heart rate and stare at the man she'd been doing her best to ignore for months.

Her life was complicated. Way too complicated to even think about starting any kind of relationship. Fallport had seemed like the perfect place to hide out when Alan Mather's trial was pending. Except the longer she was there, the more she loved the small town...and the people in it.

She'd tried to keep her distance. Tried not to make friends. But that had been impossible around Lilly, Elsie, Bristol, Caryn, Finley, and now Heather. The women she'd met were all amazing in their own rights. Their personalities were so different, and yet when life had thrown them curve balls, they each stepped up to the plate and knocked that ball out of the park. They were strong, much stronger than Khloe.

When her life had gone to shit, she'd run. Hidden out.

Now that Alan's trial was completed, and he was convicted, she could go anywhere. She had a storage facility full of stuff that she could unpack. But instead of getting on with her life, she'd hesitated. Being an assistant librarian at a small-town library wasn't exactly what she'd spent all those years in school for, yet she hadn't made even the smallest step toward getting her old life back.

Until now.

The cat was out of the bag, but Khloe wasn't sorry. There was no way she could've let Duke die from the GDV, not knowing she could save him. But acting would have a high cost. Her friends would know she'd been lying to them all along. It was possible Alan would find out where she was...she knew he was waiting for the moment she started working as a vet again. Not to mention, Raymond Ziegler was going to be pissed that she'd broken into his clinic while he was gone.

Then there was Raiden. She had no idea how her actions would change their relationship. She'd expected him to be upset with her. Mad that she'd so obviously lied about who she was. But instead he seemed...curious. And he'd seemed to accept the fact that she'd been keeping secrets pretty damn easily. She had a feeling if Raid was truly angry with her, she'd have been able to sense it.

That kiss didn't exactly say "I'm pissed at you."

But still, nothing in life was easy. Khloe had learned that the hard way.

She'd have to pay the price for her lies after she saved Duke's life. Raid had said they needed to talk, and she dreaded that prospect with everything in her. But if she had to make this decision again, she'd do the same thing. Duke didn't deserve to die. Not when she could save him. Besides, Fallport needed the hound dog. He'd found more than his fair share of missing people over the years. Yes, Raiden could train a new dog, but in the meantime, how many people would suffer without Duke's nose to find them?

Khloe stared through the small window through the door as Raiden spoke with Simon. She was glad for the police chief's presence. It didn't change the fact that she'd broken the law. Raymond would certainly want to press charges for breaking and entering, along with anything else he could think of, but having Simon there, and essentially getting his approval to do what she'd done, went a long way toward assuring her those charges probably wouldn't stick.

The conversation she was observing seemed serious, if the scowl on Raid's face was anything to go by. He wasn't a classily good-looking man. His red hair and beard made him stand out among his friends, but she secretly liked it. He was taller than any man she'd ever considered dating before. At five-four, she was nearly a foot and a half shorter than Raid. He literally towered over her. She'd overheard one of the other women saying he was six-eight. He stood head and shoulders above everyone he met, but she could tell he didn't like standing out and didn't have much self-confidence...which was ridiculous to her.

Who cared that he was tall? Who cared that his ears stuck out a little bit? He was definitely in shape; tromping around the woods after Duke guaranteed that. She'd actually seen him with his shirt off once, and that glimpse of his perfect six-pack and those V-muscles that pointed down to his crotch were forever emblazoned on her brain.

But more important than his physical looks, Raid was gentle with kids and animals alike, would do anything for his friends...and Khloe melted a little inside when she caught him with his shoes off in his office, petting Duke with his sock-clad feet when he thought he was alone.

The more time Khloe spent around Raid, the more she liked him...and the more she tried to keep him at arm's length.

Yes, she desperately wished she could confide in someone. But she'd never wanted to burden Raid, and all her friends had already been through enough. Alan Mather wouldn't be in jail forever, and she had no doubt that when he got out, he'd come for her. There was no way he was just going to let her go on with her life peacefully.

It was better for everyone—her, her friends, Raiden— if she saved Duke's life, then got the hell out of Fallport.

But that kiss...she had no idea why he'd kissed her or what it meant.

Now wasn't the time to think about it. She had an animal to save.

Khloe turned her back on the door and walked over to the bloodhound. She checked his vitals and, once satisfied that he was stable, headed for the small scrub room off the operating room. Doc Snow and Afton were finishing up when she entered.

As she scrubbed her hands and arms, she went over in her head what the procedure would entail. She cared about all the animals she operated on, but Duke was different. He almost felt like hers, which was crazy since he most definitely wasn't. It would hurt if she couldn't save him. Not to mention, she knew how much it would devastate Raid if Duke passed away.

She hoped there wasn't too much damage to the stom- ach, but she was fairly confident that she'd recognized the signs of bloat early enough that Duke would pull through. She needed to check on the spleen, and watch his heart rate, and if necessary, remove any dead parts of the stom- ach. Then she'd need to do a gastropexy—suture the stomach to the body wall to prevent it from rotating in the future.

Duke would have to be monitored carefully after surgery to watch for heart arrhythmias, stomach motility problems, pain, infection, aspiration pneumonia, and even multiple organ failure. Without vet techs, the monitoring of Duke would fall to her, but Khloe didn't mind.

Taking a deep breath, she held her arms out in front of her as she turned to her assistants. "Ready?" she asked.

Afton came forward to help dry her hands with a sterile towel then put on a gown and gloves. Taking a deep breath, she led them back into the operating room. It was time to save a life.

CHAPTER TWO

Raiden had been pacing for the last hour. He couldn't help it. Every time he sat down and tried to relax, anxiety swam through his veins, making it impossible to sit still. He was stressed about Duke, yes, but he was also going over every conversation he and Khloe had ever had, trying to figure out what signs he'd missed about who she really was.

He shouldn't be surprised she was a veterinarian. He'd known all along that she was overqualified to be a librarian's assistant at a small-town public library. He'd felt it in his bones. Not to mention, she stuck to herself and avoided people as often as possible.

Raid was somewhat ashamed to admit, even to himself, that despite suspecting Khloe had issues...he hadn't wanted to get involved in whatever they might be, attracted to the woman or not. He'd finally settled into a comfortable life. He had friends, his job, his dog...and no one was trying to kill him, lie to him, or evade being captured by him.

Sometimes it felt as if his life in the Coast Guard was

decades ago, and other times it felt as if it was just yesterday that he was hunting down drug dealers and other nefarious criminals. When his mind threatened to turn to the incident that made him finally call it quits on a career he'd once loved, Raid forcefully thought about the woman behind that door in front of him, saving his dog.

Khloe was standoffish. Had been since he'd known her. But he'd also caught glimpses of a completely different person. One who was compassionate, who would do anything for her friends, even as she purposely held back from getting close to Lilly, Finley, and the others. Now that at least one of her secrets was out in the open, Raid wondered what else she was keeping from everyone. Why she'd felt that she had to hide her profession, why she couldn't make friends.

Turning his head, Raid glanced through the opposite door into Doctor Ziegler's lobby. It had quickly become filled to the brim with people who were worried about Duke...and him. Every single member of the Eagle Point Search and Rescue team, along with their women. Heather and Tal had brought their newly adopted daughter, Marissa, and Elsie and Zeke's son, Tony, was currently keeping her entertained by reading her a book.

But it wasn't just his friends who were there. Edna, old man Grogan, Whitney, Karen from the diner, Art, Otto and Silas, and even Davis Woolford, a local homeless man, were all in the waiting room. There were also people Raid only recognized by sight...he didn't know their names. People from Fallport whom he'd met through his job at the library or whom the SAR team—and Duke—had rescued.

Simon was still there. As was Miguel, one of his

deputies. They'd tried to get people to leave, because he and Khloe *had* broken in, after all...but no one was budging. If Khloe was hoping to keep her break-in at the vet clinic on the down-low, she was going to be disappointed. The parking lot was full, which only meant *more* people kept arriving to find out what was going on. That was small-town life for you.

There wasn't a chance in hell of keeping this from Raymond Ziegler. And Raid knew the vet wasn't going to be happy.

But the man's feelings were the least of Raiden's worries at the moment. Thanks to Khloe, Duke's life would be saved. If she hadn't been there, if she wasn't who she was—apparently a librarian's assistant slash secret veterinarian—if she hadn't chosen to break into the vet clinic, Duke's outcome would be questionable.

"How you doin'?" Ethan asked quietly, entering the long hallway.

Raid was still pacing outside the operating room. "I'm good," he said.

"Right. How about you stop the bullshit and tell me how you're *really* doing," Ethan said sternly.

Raid stopped and took a deep breath before turning to look at his friend. "I'm scared to death that I'm going to lose another dog way before it's his time to go. I'm wondering what the hell else Khloe's been hiding from us. Why she moved to Fallport. Why she very suddenly took those two weeks off to go home not so long ago, and wouldn't tell anyone where 'home' was. And I'm overwhelmed by everyone's support."

Ethan stepped toward him and put a hand on his

shoulder. "Duke's tough. And from what I understand, Khloe didn't waste any time getting him here."

"She didn't," Raid told his friend. "If it wasn't for her recognizing the symptoms of bloat, and the fact that she's apparently a skilled veterinarian, his prognosis would be a hell of a lot worse right now."

Ethan nodded and squeezed Raid's shoulder before dropping his hand. "I'm thinking at the moment, you need to just go with it, rather than torturing yourself thinking about stuff you have no control over. Once Khloe's done, Duke's on the road to recovery, and we do damage control with Ziegler, you can work on getting answers to the other questions."

Raid knew Ethan was right, but he couldn't stop thinking about this new version of Khloe. All sorts of worst-case scenarios kept running through his head. What if she was on the run from an abusive ex? What if she was married? What if she was in witness protection? He was having a hard time coming up with good reasons why she'd turn her back on a profession she obviously loved to live in Fallport as a librarian.

Taking a deep breath, Raid did his best to push all the questions to the back of his mind. First things first. As Ethan said, he needed to make sure Duke made it through surgery. Then care for him until he was back on his feet. Deal with Ziegler and the repercussions of Khloe breaking into the clinic.

"How are *you* doing?" Raid asked his friend, needing to turn the conversation to something other than himself. "How's Lilly?"

"We're all right. Won't lie, losing our baby was a blow. For both of us. But we're doing better."

Raid nodded. "Good. If you guys need anything, all you have to do is ask."

"I know, and I appreciate it. What's been helping the most is getting on with our lives. Not dwelling on it. You know? We won't ever forget, but we can't wallow in our sorrow either. Work helps. For both of us. You know what else helps?"

"What?"

"Letting us help *you*. We all love Duke. He's gonna be a handful trying to keep still so he can heal. I'm sure you aren't going to want to leave him alone, at least for a while. So call us. Lilly and I would be happy to come and dog-sit. As would everyone else."

Raid smiled at Ethan. "I will. Thanks." He knew he was lucky. He was able to bring Duke to the library with him when he worked, and even though the dog was definitely partial to his master, his friends would spoil him and treat him like gold when Raid couldn't be with him.

"So...you should know, Rocky's already called one of his contacts to get materials, so he can get the door frame replaced. Not sure if he'll be able to get it fixed before Ziegler gets back from his stupid fake hunting trip, but he's going to do what he can to make that happen."

"I appreciate it."

Ethan brushed off Raiden's gratitude. "Khloe was smart to make sure Simon was here when she broke in."

Raid nodded. She was. Basically, having the police chief present meant she had his approval. So if Ziegler tried to press charges, he wouldn't have much luck. "She's adamant about paying for all the supplies she's using too."

"Whatever," Ethan said with a shrug. "It's not going to

be an issue. Finley's already started an online fundraiser to cover the costs of Duke's surgery."

Raid stared at him. "She has?"

"Yup. And it's already gotten over two thousand dollars in donations."

Raid almost choked. "It's only been like two hours since Duke bloated."

"Yup," Ethan repeated with a smile. "I think we have to face the fact that Duke's the favorite member of the Eagle Point Search and Rescue team." Then he sobered. "You think Ziegler's going to be a problem for Khloe? They don't really get along."

No, they didn't. And her extreme dislike for Fallport's only vet should've been another red flag for Raiden. Khloe had always had a personal stake in the business practices of Raymond Ziegler. She knew more than the average person about how a vet should run his practice.

He shrugged at Ethan. "I'd like to say no...but I think we both know he's gonna be pissed."

"Yeah. Well, even so, keep an eye out for her. The last thing she needs is him all up in her face and making a scene around town. We'll all keep watch too, when you aren't around. You know, just to make sure she knows she has our support."

Raid took a deep breath and closed his eyes as he did his best to harness his emotions. He had the best friends anyone could ask for. When he was active duty, he sometimes felt as if he was an island. That he and his dog were on their own. But in Fallport, he'd found what he'd always wanted...a family. A group of friends who would drop everything to help in any way they could. "Thanks," he said belatedly as he opened his eyes.

"Look, I haven't said anything for the entire time I've known you. I don't know what you do with your free time...but I *do* know that most days, you go home from the library and you don't emerge until the next morning. You're one of us, Raid. We have your back, just as you have ours. We'd all love to see you around a little more."

Raid swallowed hard. He'd always been the odd kid. He didn't get invited to sleepovers as a boy, didn't have any friends in high school. His friends had always been online. He loved the camaraderie with his teammates on the job, and he *did* accept the occasional invite for one event or another. But he'd gotten so used to doing his own thing that it never even occurred to him they'd want to hang out more often.

"I'd like that," he said softly.

Ethan grinned. "Although, you're gonna have to get used to crazy. Our women certainly liven things up when we get together now. Not to mention Tony, Marissa, and the kids that are on the way."

Little did his friend know, Raid wouldn't enjoy anything more. Being in the middle of a rowdy group of people who genuinely cared about each other? Yeah. After a lifetime of loneliness, that sounded awesome.

"Raid?"

Hearing Khloe's voice had him spinning around so fast, it would've looked comical if it had been anyone else. "How is he? Is he all right?"

"He's fine. Made it through surgery with no complications. Afton is suturing him up."

"Is that okay? I mean, shouldn't you be doing that?"

Khloe smiled, but Raid could tell she was tired. "She's good. Really good. I have a feeling she probably does a lot more around here than most vet techs would because of Ziegler's laziness. Anyway, I'm going back in to make sure everything's all set, but wanted to let you know as soon as I could that things went well. He's going to be just fine, Raiden."

Raid felt as if a huge weight had been lifted off his shoulders. He hadn't been able to save his last dog, but he hadn't lost Duke. He stared at Khloe and did his best to make sure she heard the gratitude and relief in his voice as he said, "Thank you."

"You're welcome."

"When can I see him?"

"As soon as we get him sewed back up and moved to recovery."

"Will he be staying here?" Raid asked.

Khloe wrinkled her nose. "It's not ideal. The longer we're here, the more likely it is that Ziegler will find out. But I don't want to move him just yet. Doc Snow said we can use one of the rooms in his clinic once Duke's more stable."

"Um, Khloe," Ethan interjected. "I think Ziegler finding out is inevitable. The parking lot's never been as full as it is right now."

Her eyes widened. "It is?"

"Yup. Everyone's here. And by everyone, I mean *everyone*. Not to mention social media's been doing its thing too."

"Crap," she muttered.

"It's fine," Raid reassured her.

"He's gonna be outraged," she said.

"Yup. Do you care?" he asked.

Khloe thought about his question for a long moment.

It was one of the things he liked most about her. She didn't rush to speak. She thought carefully about what she wanted to say and how to answer questions. Even if those questions came from a five-year-old, she treated them just as important as if someone had asked her to explain the meaning of life.

"No," she said. "Although dealing with him could disturb Duke, and I don't want that. Not to mention, he could take out his anger on the animals that are brought in. He might also be a dick to his staff...especially Afton, since she helped me."

"We'll deal with him when we have to," Raid said. "There's no sense worrying about him right now."

"You're right. Anyway, Duke's okay. I'll come get you in a bit."

"Sounds good. Khloe?"

She paused in her retreat. "Yeah?"

"For the record...I don't care that you didn't tell anyone you were a vet. I don't care why you're here in Fallport. Right now, I don't care about anything other than making sure Duke's all right and you're safe."

Raid knew this wasn't exactly the time and place for such a dramatic statement, but he couldn't stop himself from saying the words. He and Khloe had a lot to talk about, but he didn't want his reaction to the revelation that she was a vet to weigh on her.

Her hazel eyes widened a bit. Her face was flushed, probably from the heat of the lights in the operating room. Her hair was stuffed up under a surgical cap, but a few tendrils had escaped. She looked tired and stressed, but Raiden didn't think he'd ever seen a more beautiful woman in his life.

He suddenly realized that he wasn't upset that she'd kept some pretty big secrets from him. She had her reasons. He knew that without question. There had been times in the past when she'd seemed wary. Even scared. He wanted to know her story, but he wanted her to be comfortable with him even more.

All the times he'd sniped at her, had been curt or rude, had argued with her over stupid things, made a little more sense now. He *liked* her. Admired her. And he'd had no idea how to get under her skin like she'd clearly gotten under his.

Which obviously irritated him. Made him feel even more unsure about himself. As a result, he'd done what he could to hold her at arm's length.

But no more. He was done with that. This obviously highly educated woman had more layers than he'd realized. He didn't value her any less when he'd thought she was a simple librarian's assistant. But he definitely yearned to know what made Khloe the veterinarian tick.

Khloe didn't respond verbally to his statement, just nodded at him and closed the door behind her as she went back to check on Duke.

"You need to go easy," Ethan warned quietly.

Raid turned to him as he continued to speak.

"A person doesn't come to a town like Fallport, keep to herself, and do what she can to *not* make connections if she doesn't have baggage."

"Don't we all?" Raid countered.

"All I'm saying is...be careful. I think we've all learned our lessons with everything that's happened with Lilly, Caryn, Elsie, Finley, Bristol, and Heather."

"So you think...what? I should fire her? Turn my back

on her because she might be in danger or running from something?" Raiden asked, his voice showing his irritation at his friend's warning.

"No," Ethan said, sounding genuinely shocked. "I'm saying for you to be careful," he repeated. "Things have a way of getting out of control and becoming scary real quick, at least they have for the rest of us. The last thing I want is for something in Khloe's past to get out of control or scary for *her*."

They stared at each other for a long moment before Raid looked away. "Noted," he told his friend. But there was no way he was going to turn his back on the woman. He owed Khloe. Big time. She'd saved his best friend. Anything she needed, she'd get...whether she asked for it or not.

But if he was honest with himself, he didn't want to get to the bottom of what was going on with Khloe simply out of gratitude. From the first moment he'd met the woman, he'd been drawn to her. He'd just been too chicken to do anything about it. He'd let her prickliness convince him whatever was going on wasn't his problem. But now that he knew for a fact that she *was* hiding something, and clearly something big, he was done with that.

"Right. On that note, I'm going to go out and let everyone know Duke made it through surgery and see if I can't get people headed out of here. You need anything, call. I'll be pissed if you don't."

"I will," Raid reassured him.

"Let me know how Duke's doing and I'll pass it along to everyone, so you don't have to worry about anything but spoiling that hound."

"Appreciate it."

"Head's up, the women were discussing a welcome home party for Duke when I left them...so you should start thinking about how you want that to go down. At your house, the library, the square, so everyone in town can participate. *Or* if you don't want it to happen at all. Let me know."

"Jeez," Raid said, shaking his head and rolling his eyes.

"You and Duke are way more loved around here than you realize," Ethan said with a smile. "'Bout time you let that sink in."

Ethan clapped him on the back, then headed down the hall toward the door that led into the waiting room. When it opened, Raid could hear all the voices, but he wasn't up to seeing everyone just yet. He appreciated them being there, but it was going to take more than a conversation with Ethan to make him comfortable with being the center of attention.

It was extremely difficult to stay in the hall and not go in to see if Khloe needed help. But she had both Doc Snow and Afton. They'd get Duke settled in the back and she'd come get him as soon as she was able.

He wasn't sure if he was more anxious to see Khloe or his dog.

* * *

Khloe felt buzzed. It had been so long since she'd been in the operating room and it felt like coming home. She hated why she was there, of course. She didn't like for any animal to be in pain. But knowing she had the skills to help Duke survive felt damn good.

She'd thought, after everything that happened, she'd be

fine hanging up her scalpel forever. That she could find another career and be perfectly happy. But she'd been fooling herself. She loved Fallport, and enjoyed spending time in the library and helping people find books that interested them. But she was born to be a veterinarian. Loved everything about it…except maybe abusive owners who brought animals to her to be "fixed" when they were the ones who'd fucked them up in the first place.

It was obvious that no matter how hard she'd tried to tell herself differently, she wasn't ready to give up her life-long dream of being a vet. There was a storage container full of her equipment from her old clinic that contradicted her plans of doing something different with her life. She could've sold it all. Padded her savings account. But instead, she'd carefully packed it all away…just in case.

And now, after saving Duke's life, Khloe was more certain than ever she couldn't give up her veterinarian career.

She had no idea what would happen next. She hadn't actually set out to deceive her new friends, but there hadn't exactly been a good time to bring up the fact that she was actually a renowned vet. That she was living in Fallport because one of her former clients had tried to kill her when she hadn't been able to save the dog he'd brought into her clinic, half dead from a horrific beating.

It was almost a relief that her secrets would soon come to light. It was exhausting trying to be someone she wasn't. Khloe had no idea if she'd stay in Fallport, or even Virginia, but she was done hiding. From her friends. From Alan Mather. From herself.

"You want me to stay?" Afton asked after they'd gotten Duke settled.

It didn't feel right to Khloe to put him in a kennel after everything he'd been through, so she'd made a pallet on the floor with old blankets and towels. Duke's IV was hooked to the wire bars of the kennels behind him. He'd woken up briefly after being settled, and Khloe was satisfied that he wasn't in any pain thanks to the drugs in his veins.

"No, thank you though," Khloe told the vet tech. Doc Snow had gone home a few minutes earlier, after making sure she had everything she needed and reassuring her that he'd be back in the morning to check in with her and Duke.

"Are you sure? I'm used to it. I usually hang around after a serious surgery like this. Since I live so close, it's not a big deal."

"I haven't seen any beds for overnight shifts," Khloe said, as she lowered to the floor to sit next to Duke. It was a question without being phrased as one.

"A bed? There are clinics that have beds for overnight shifts?"

Khloe was pissed at Ziegler for Afton's disbelief. "Yes. The good ones at least."

Afton shrugged. "No. No beds here."

She shouldn't have been surprised, but she still was. "It's okay. I'll stay. I want to monitor him carefully."

"Okay, but if you need me, I'll leave my number. I'm happy to come back and help if you'd like."

"I appreciate it."

"Doctor Ziegler isn't supposed to be back for three more days."

"Right. I'm hoping Duke will be good enough to be

moved to Doc Snow's clinic tomorrow afternoon. And, Afton?"

"Yeah?"

"You don't have to worry about me telling anyone you assisted me in surgery."

The younger woman gave Khloe a small smile. "It's okay. He's gonna find out anyway. I've been trying to work up the courage to turn in my resignation, hoping to find another job first...this'll just give me the push I needed. This is probably presumptuous, but if you ever decide to open up your own clinic, I'd love the opportunity to apply to work with you."

Khloe blinked in surprise. "Oh, um...I haven't thought much about it. This thing with Duke kind of fell into my lap."

"You're a damn good vet, Khloe...er...Doctor Moore. Fallport needs someone like you. Someone who *cares* about the animals they see. All Doctor Ziegler sees is dollar signs. I know I shouldn't be talking about my boss like this, but it's not as if it's a secret. People continue to come here because he's the only option unless they want to drive thirty minutes or more."

"It's Khloe. Not Doctor Moore," she told Afton, not sure what else to say.

"Right. If you don't mind, would it be all right if I came by to check on Duke once he's moved to Doc Snow's clinic?"

"Of course."

"Thanks. Well...I guess I'll see you around."

"You will. And, Afton?"

"Yeah?"

"Don't let Ziegler give you any shit. You're a damn

good assistant. And if I *do* ever open a vet practice again, you'll be on the top of my list of people I want to hire."

The younger woman smiled. Huge. "Awesome. Thanks. I'll tell Raiden you're all set in here and send him in. See ya."

She walked out still beaming. Khloe had barely a few seconds to reflect on their conversation before Raid was there. He must've been waiting at the door for the go-ahead to come in. Not that she could blame him.

"You okay?" he asked softly as he walked toward her.

Khloe nodded, scooting back a little as he knelt on the floor next to Duke. His large hand reached out and smoothed over the bloodhound's head. His gaze ran over his body, from head to his tail, taking in the bandages, the places where Khloe had to shave his fur so she could see what she was doing and to put in the IVs.

Raid then leaned down, kissed his head, and whispered something in the dog's ear.

It was all too much. Things in her life had changed so much, and seeing Raiden's concern for his dog made tears well in her eyes.

She hadn't realized how stressed she'd been until right that moment. She loved Duke. The dog was a ham, drooled nonstop, and was a damn good tracker. He so obviously loved Raiden, was completely devoted to his human, and that devotion was just as obviously recip-rocated.

Khloe was tired, her back hurt, her leg throbbed, and it had been a long time since she'd been in the operating room. She'd used muscles she hadn't used since closing up her practice.

Of course, Raid chose that moment to look up, and he caught her crying.

Her tears didn't even seem to faze him. He turned so his butt was on the floor, his back against the wall, and pulled her into his arms.

Khloe was shocked for a moment. He hadn't asked her permission, hadn't given her a choice. But honestly, this was exactly what she needed. It had been so long since she'd been touched. Since she'd been hugged.

She lay against Raiden's chest, her arms curled in front of her, Raid's arms around her, and watched Duke sleeping. His breaths were even and normal and every now and then, one of his paws would twitch.

"Thank you for saving him," Raiden said softly.

She waited for the questions to start. When he said nothing else, Khloe picked up her head and looked into Raid's green eyes. His red hair and beard were mussed and he had circles under his eyes. His clothes were rumpled and even as she lay in his arms, she heard his stomach growl. He'd been there every minute, same as she had. He might not've been in the operating room, but he'd still been there, refusing to leave. He was the kind of owner she wished every animal had. But she was well aware, unfortunately, how many unkind and downright cruel owners were out there.

"Is that all you're going to say?" she blurted.

Raid nodded. "For now."

That didn't bode well for Khloe, but she was still so relieved, she simply nodded and lowered her head so it rested against his chest once more.

"Can you tell me about the surgery? And what we need to watch for now? I know you talked about some of that before the operation, but I don't remember what you said. Sorry."

"You had other things on your mind," she said with a shrug. It felt good to be with him like this. The time would come when she'd have to answer Raid's questions about her life, but for now, she was going to enjoy the calm.

"He was lucky. There wasn't much damage to the stomach when I opened him up to take a look. When too much time passes between when the belly twists and when the animal has gotten into surgery, there's really nothing I can do. The stomach can't be fixed once it's dead. I checked his spleen and it looked okay. There was a little bit of damage, but I didn't have to remove it. I did a gastropexy...which is tacking the stomach to the body wall so it won't rotate. There's still a ten percent chance that it'll happen again, but that's a hell of a lot better than if we hadn't done it.

"His heart is strong. There were no abnormal arrhythmias during the surgery, but I'll continue to monitor him now to make sure his heart beats the way it's supposed to. He's got a few layers of stitches, in the body wall fibrous layer, the subcutaneous tissues, and then I buried the third layer in the subcuticular layer, mostly so there aren't any stitches or staples to remove later."

"I don't know what any of that means, but...it sounds positive," Raid said.

"Sorry, I'm out of practice talking about what I've done in surgery."

"It's fine. What happens with him now?"

"We'll need to monitor his incision to make sure it doesn't get infected. I want to keep him on the IV and pain meds for at least another two days. That was a serious surgery, and I don't want him to be in any discomfort. He needs antibiotics, but for now I'm administering them through the IV. How is he with pills?"

Raid chuckled and the sound reverberated through her. "If it's smothered in cheese or peanut butter, he's all for it."

Khloe smiled against him. "Yeah, he's definitely a food-motivated hound. Right, so after the IV comes out, he'll need antibiotics for a while. I'd say in about three days, you should be able to take him home and slowly reintroduce soft food in small, frequent meals for a while. While he's here, and at Doc Snow's clinic, he won't get any food or water, and I'll watch for arrhythmias, aspiration pneumonia, and monitor his pain and infection."

Raid nodded above her, and Khloe could feel his beard catch in her strands of hair.

"Will he be okay if you sleep for a while?" Raid asked.

"Yes. He's tough, Raid. I promise. But I'm not tired." Of course, as soon as the words left her mouth, she yawned huge.

Raiden chuckled. "Right, I see that. Close your eyes, Khloe. I'll watch over you both. When you wake up, I'll catch some z's while you keep watch."

She wanted to protest. Tell him that she was fine to stay up and make sure Duke was all right. But being in his arms felt good. Really good. And the surgery had taken more out of her than she wanted to admit. "Okay, but only for an hour or so. Then I need to check on Duke."

"All right."

When she tried to get up, and he made no move to let

go, Khloe picked her head up and looked at him. "Are you going to let go of me so I can lie down?"

"No."

She waited for him to say more. But that was all he said. Just no.

Khloe's lips twitched. "Right." If she wasn't so tired all of a sudden, she would've protested. Insisted he let her move. But truth be told, she was happy right where she was. There was no telling how Raid would react to the talk she knew was coming. If this was going to be her one chance to be near him like this, she wasn't going to let it slip through her grasp.

It was hard to admit how much Raid intrigued her. Always had. From the first interview she'd had with him at the library, she'd felt like a fly being drawn into a spider's web. He was such a dichotomy. Serious and reticent with people. Goofy and unashamed of his affection toward Duke. He was one of the smartest men she knew, but he didn't flaunt his intelligence. He was muscular and handsome, yet he didn't flirt. Khloe wasn't sure he even knew *how* to flirt. He'd always seemed very unsure of his own allure. Which was crazy. Surely the man knew how good-looking he was. Maybe not in the classic sense, but Khloe had never been the sort of woman who was attracted to the guy-next-door type.

"Stop thinking, Khloe. Sleep," Raiden said firmly, but with a hint of humor in his voice.

"Has anyone told you that you're really bossy?" she asked, even as she closed her eyes.

"No."

"Well, you are."

"Only with you, because you never do what I tell you to."

She smiled at that. He wasn't lying. They'd spent many an afternoon butting heads in the library when he found out she hadn't done the tasks he'd assigned her to do that day. It wasn't that she was deliberately trying to disobey him, but most of the time she found other things she deemed more important...or more interesting than what he'd assigned for her.

"Wake me up in an hour," she reminded him.

"I will."

It usually took Khloe forever to fall asleep. Every creak of her apartment, every car driving by, every little noise made her wonder if Alan had somehow managed to follow through on his threat to make her suffer for the rest of her life. But now, snuggled in Raid's arms on the cold, hard tile floor of Raymond Ziegler's vet clinic, she fell into a dreamless sleep almost as soon as her eyes closed.

CHAPTER THREE

Raid held Khloe close as she slept. He kept his eyes on Duke, counting his breaths as his chest moved up and down. Everything that could possibly go wrong kept swirling through his brain. It would be more than cruel for Duke to have lived through surgery, only to have what amounted to a heart attack while in recovery.

But Khloe hadn't seemed overly concerned, so he forced himself to stay calm. That didn't mean that he didn't scoot closer to Duke. It was a miracle he hadn't woken Khloe up as he moved, but what seemed like seconds after he'd reassured her that he'd wake her up in an hour, she was dead weight in his arms.

Feeling better now that he could touch Duke, Raid allowed himself to relax a fraction. With one arm around Khloe, holding her against him, and the other hand on Duke, he closed his eyes and rested his head against the wall behind him.

The next few days were going to be hectic. Raid had no doubt about that. He just hoped they'd be able to get out of the clinic before Ziegler came back. The man was going to lose his mind over everything that happened. He really was an ass. He *should* be happy that Khloe was able to save Duke, but Raid was sure that wouldn't be the case. It would help that Rocky would be replacing the broken door frame, but Raid suspected that wouldn't assuage the veterinarian's anger over what he'd probably perceive as a threat to his role as the only vet in Fallport.

His mind turned to the woman in his arms. There were times over the last year or so when he'd felt as if he was getting to know her fairly well, despite her best efforts, but today had proven that he didn't know her at all. Some men might've been upset that she'd obviously been keeping secrets from everyone, but not him. He hadn't exactly been an open book himself.

He'd been an introvert his entire life. Opening up wasn't easy for Raid. But being on the other side of things —wondering what other secrets Khloe had beyond the fact she was a veterinarian—had him considering his own past. The things he'd never shared with anyone.

He hadn't ever spoken of the events that made him quit the Coast Guard and accept Ethan's offer to come to Fallport. But now he couldn't help thinking about it. Couldn't help thinking about Finn "Tonka" Matlick. Tonka had been his closest friend in the Coast Guard. His only friend, really. Their dogs, Steel and Dagger, had been buddies as well. They all worked extremely well together, and Tonka never cared that Raid didn't talk a lot. Didn't care that he wasn't the type who enjoyed going out with the guys during their time off.

Their last mission had started out so routine. They were patrolling the waters off Virginia for anything suspicious. When they'd spotted the smallish speedboat, they'd decided to board to check for illegal substances.

Raid shivered when he thought about what happened next.

They'd boarded the vessel and were ambushed by Pablo Garcia. Raid had been knocked in the head and shot, and he was damn lucky not to have bled out on that ship. But it was Tonka and their working dogs who'd suffered the most that day. Raid was blessed to have been unconscious during the events that followed. Tonka hadn't been as lucky. He'd witnessed every depraved thing Garcia had done. And as a result, now suffered from severe PTSD.

Raid hated that for his friend. Hated a lot of things about that last mission. He hadn't been able to say goodbye to Dagger. Hadn't been able to comfort him in his final moments. Hated that for years, Tonka'd had to relive what he'd seen. And he definitely hated Pablo Garcia. His only consolation was that the man was rotting away in jail.

Thinking about his own secrets made him look down at Khloe. She was so tiny compared to him. All his life, he'd been called a giant. Strangers would stop him on the street to ask how tall he was. He'd heard all the jokes and hated every last one.

But Khloe hadn't once made a crack about his size. Or his ears. Or his red hair. That didn't mean they didn't snipe at each other about other things. She'd never been afraid to stand up to him...which Raiden actually liked. He found he enjoyed their banter.

But he liked this even more.

Holding her.

Keeping her safe while she was vulnerable.

She'd saved Duke. He knew that as well as he knew his name. Without her, he would've lost another best friend too soon.

His arm tightened involuntarily, and Khloe stirred. Raid forced himself to relax and, to his relief, Khloe's eyes didn't open.

He sighed heavily. His feelings for this woman were complex. He was her boss. He wasn't convinced she even liked him all that much. And now that her secret about being a vet was out, he wondered if she'd leave Fallport.

Things between them were complicated at best.

Raid was no closer to figuring out what to say to Khloe when she woke up of her own accord a bit over an hour later. She shifted against him and slowly sat up, blinking sleepily.

Her hair was mussed from the hectic day and she had a crease on her cheek from lying against his shirt. Raid realized he'd never been as attracted to Khloe more than he was right that moment. Rumpled. Sleepy. With her guard down.

"Hey," he said, realizing it sounded lame after the word was out.

But Khloe didn't seem to notice his awkwardness. "Hey," she returned. "How long was I out?"

"Not too long. Maybe an hour and a half."

She groaned and stretched, and it was all Raid could do not to stare at her chest as she did so. Khloe had a strong, lithe body...with tits that were a little larger than was proportionate to her tiny size. He'd definitely noticed—and appreciated—her womanly assets, but hadn't let himself dwell on them in the past. After having her plastered against his chest for the last hour and a half, and now that she was stretching right in front of his eyes? He couldn't help but appreciate her even more.

"I'd kill for a cup of coffee from Grinders," she mumbled, then turned to Duke. "How's he doing?"

"As far as I can tell, fine. He hasn't woken up. His aspirations are around sixteen per minute."

"Good, that's normal." Khloe shuffled closer to Duke and checked his heart rate and peeked under the bandage over his belly. She checked his IV and she was apparently satisfied, because she nodded and sat on her butt next to the dog as she looked up at Raid. "I'm sure you want to talk."

Raid shrugged.

"You don't?" she asked as one brow rose skeptically.

"It's getting late. I'm tired. My dog's on the mend. Honestly? All I want right now is to sit here and enjoy the calm before the storm."

"Calm before the storm?" Khloe asked with a tilt of her head.

"Yeah. Moving Duke. Having all our friends visit. Dealing with Ziegler. Answering questions from the citizens of Fallport every time I stick my head out of my house. Managing Duke's desire for food against what's best for him. Trying to keep him calm while he heals. Work. Figuring out how to best help you with whatever's troubling you...

"Sitting here right now, in the relative silence, will probably be the least stressful time I'll have for quite a while."

"Nothing's troubling me," Khloe said stubbornly, homing right in on those words.

Raid couldn't help it when his lips curled upward. He

closed his eyes and leaned his head on the wall behind him. "Right," he said.

"I'm fine. Good. Great."

His smile grew. "Yup. And that's why you're living here in Fallport, working at the library, when it was obvious from the start that it had been years since you'd stepped inside one. Why you lied about your experience and your profession. Is Khloe even your name?"

"Yes!" she said defensively.

Raid opened his eyes and looked at her. She was sitting ramrod straight, her legs crossed, one hand resting on Duke's large paw closest to her. She was cute all ruffled and defensive. It struck him again why he always said things to irritate her. Because she got under his skin. And because he liked her like this. Emotion swimming in her eyes, ire aimed at him. He preferred that to the worry he often saw in her gaze. Unconsciously, maybe he'd done his best to help her forget her troubles.

The longer he stared at her, the more she squirmed, and finally she sighed and looked down at her lap. "Fine. Khloe really is my name. But my last name isn't Moore."

Even that little scrap of info was enough to make Raid feel good. She was letting him in without him forcing the issue. At least a little bit. When he didn't react verbally, she looked up at him.

"Aren't you going to ask what it is?"

"Nope," Raid said lazily. "I know what it's like to have secrets. Things you don't want others to know. For their good *and* your own. I want you to tell me when you feel you can trust me. And you *can* trust me, Khloe."

Several seconds went by before she said, "I know."

"Good. How's your leg holding up?"

Khloe blinked. "Fine."

"I'm just asking because you stood for longer than you usually do today. I saw a fridge in a break room down the hall. I can get you some ice or something if you need it."

"I'm okay. I admit it's a little sore, but it's not too bad. Changes in the barometric pressure irritate it more than standing next to an operating table."

"Okay, but if you need something for it, just let me know."

She stared at him for a long time.

"What?" he asked.

"I just...you're being...weird."

"Weird how?"

"I don't know. I'm used to you snapping at me. Pointing out all the things I'm doing wrong. Ordering me around. This...*nice* Raid, I can't get used to."

"Come on, I'm not that bad," he said.

Khloe raised her brow at him again, and Raid couldn't help but chuckle.

"Right. I may or may not be a perfectionist when it comes to work."

"Understatement," she mumbled.

"And you're not?" he countered. "If the roles were reversed and I was a vet tech in your practice, would you not expect me to do things perfectly?"

A small grin formed on her lips. "I may or may not have had a reputation for being a hard-ass in my past life."

Raid returned the grin. "I can totally see that. But I bet your employees loved you."

The smile slowly faded and she shrugged.

Raid mentally kicked himself for bringing up what were obviously bittersweet memories for her. He changed the subject. "So...when do you think it'll be safe to move Duke over to Doc Snow's?"

It was the right thing to ask, as she went into a long explanation of what she'd be looking for in the dog's recovery, and how they'd transport him, and what to expect when the bloodhound woke up.

After a while, Raid got up and scrounged some more blankets and towels for them to use as pillows and for the rest of the night, they took turns taking cat naps as they watched over their patient. As the sun began to rise outside, Raid realized that while it hadn't been the best night's sleep he'd ever gotten, he felt surprisingly good.

Duke had woken up a few times and, while groggy, seemed happy to see his two favorite humans.

"I would kill for a shower, a coffee, and a change of clothes," Khloe said.

"Tell me what you need, and I'll have Caryn and Drew go and grab it for you," Raid told her.

"Huh?"

"Give me your coffee order and let me know what you want from your apartment, and I'll have Caryn and Drew bring it by."

"I heard you, but I don't understand why you'd ask them to get me something."

"Because they're here. They've been outside most of the night."

"*What*? Why?"

"Because we're *inside*, and they were concerned about us and Duke. Not to mention I asked Drew if he wouldn't mind staying and keeping an eye out for Ziegler, just in case."

"He's not supposed to be back for a few days."

"Right, but I'm sure by now he's heard all about how we broke into his clinic, and he's not going to be happy. If it was me, I'd want to get back here to find out what's going on. I'm guessing it's too much to ask that he's just relieved an animal was saved. He's going to be pissed that we broke in."

"*We* didn't break in. *I* did," Khloe said firmly.

"Semantics," Raid said with a shrug.

"They've really been out there all night?" she asked with a furrow of her brow.

"Yup. And Rocky and Bristol are going to relieve them in a bit. I'm sure the others will also return sooner or later. They'll give us a break to go shower if we want, and they want to see Duke for themselves."

"I don't...that's...Raid, that's crazy."

"Why?"

She stared at him as if confused by his question. "Because!"

"You've never seen owners desperate to make sure their animals are all right? Who showed up as soon as you opened so they could visit with their fur babies? Who begged to be able to sleep next to the kennels of their hurt pets?"

"Of course I have. But..." Her voice trailed off.

"But you haven't had the kind of friends who would do that for *you*," Raid concluded.

"I haven't exactly been super friendly toward them," she admitted in a soft voice. "I tried to keep them at arm's length. I didn't want them involved in my shit."

Raid's stomach tightened at hearing those words. He didn't know what her "shit" was, but with that simple sentence, he knew it was as serious as he'd feared. And his determination to do whatever he could to help her increased. "They know good people when they meet them. And you, Khloe whatever-your-last-name-really-is, are good people."

She took a deep breath and let it out slowly, refusing to meet his gaze.

"Coffee?" he asked gently.

"A large quad nonfat, one-pump, no-whip mocha. Please."

Raid's eyes widened. "Quad? That's four shots of espresso."

"I know. I'm thinking I'm going to need the extra caffeine today after last night, and so I can deal with Ziegler without committing murder if he shows up."

Raid chuckled. "Right. Probably a good idea." He pulled out his phone and his fingers flew across the screen as he texted Drew. "And from your place?"

"Jeans and a T-shirt are fine."

He grinned. "And underwear?" He loved the blush that formed on her cheeks.

"Duh," she said with an eye roll.

He was still smiling as he sent Drew another text.

"I'm assuming they'll need my key to get into my apartment," Khloe said.

"They'll figure it out," Raid told her as he hit send.

"Figure what out? Raid, they need my key to get into my apartment. I think one B&E is enough for one week."

"Khloe, this is Fallport, not the big city. They'll talk to the apartment manager and get her to let them in. Don't worry so much."

But she didn't let it go. "So Diedre is just going to let them in because they ask nicely?"

"Yes," Raid told her. "But don't go thinking that she's a pushover or that she'd let just *anyone* in. I'm sure she, along with most people in this town, know what happened yesterday. They'll have heard about your determination to get help for Duke, and that you were willing to upset Ziegler to do so. They're happy Eagle Point SAR is here and they know Duke is necessary. So the fact you're not only able, but *willing* to help when needed, and the fact that you're you, will have her agreeing to open the apartment for Drew and Caryn so they can grab you a change of clothes. But don't worry. I'm sure she'll stand there while Caryn gets your stuff, just to make sure nothing untoward goes on when they're in your space. They'll be in and out in under a few minutes, and Diedre will make sure your door is locked on their way out."

"You sound like you know her well."

Raid couldn't help feeling pleased at the hint of jealousy in her voice. But he was quick to reassure her, because the last thing he wanted was Khloe thinking he was some sort of player or, God forbid, he had a thing for her apartment manager.

"She's a nice woman whose father got lost while visiting her a few years ago. He was here for Thanksgiving and wanted to go on a short hike before they ate. Four hours later, Duke found him three miles off the trail, cold and confused. To say she's a fan of ours is an understatement. And I'll say it again—this is Fallport. It's hard not to know people well when you've been here long enough."

"Oh," Khloe said.

"Yeah, oh. Now, what do you need me to do to help you with Duke this morning?"

And with that, things between them went back to

being more professional. But Raid wasn't concerned about backsliding. His relationship with Khloe had irrevocably changed in the last fourteen hours. He wasn't a fan of the awkward getting-to-know-you phase of a relationship, whether that be a friendship or something more. But with Khloe, he was finding that it was actually exciting.

He had no idea what the future held for either of them, but for now, he was going to enjoy getting to know this woman better...and maybe, if he was lucky, she'd want to get to know the real Raiden in return.

CHAPTER FOUR

Khloe felt off-kilter. The day had been surreal. She'd gone from feeling as if she was living in the background to standing in the spotlight. Not only that, but she'd apparently never been "in the background" as much as she'd thought.

She'd talked to more people today than she had during her entire time in Fallport. Not only Raid's team members and their women, but random townspeople as well. The bell over the front door to Ziegler's clinic had been ringing all day. People she'd only met once in the library kept stopping by to check on not only Duke, but her and Raid too. Expressing their concerns, wishing Duke well... and asking not-so-subtle questions about whether she was thinking about opening up a vet clinic in Fallport in the future.

Honestly, Khloe hadn't thought much about it. But with each story about how cold or downright unprofessional Doctor Ziegler had been when dealing with an animal in distress—and how often he was closed and unavailable to help in an emergency—had her thinking hard about her future.

But before she could seriously consider staying in Fallport for good, she had to deal with her past. Make sure she wouldn't bring any danger to town.

That was her greatest fear...that Alan Mather would try to hurt those she cared about. It was the reason she'd fled in the first place. But now that he was behind bars, maybe, just maybe, she could reclaim her life.

The coffee Caryn had brought had properly woken her up, and she didn't even mind the shit she got from everyone about how much caffeine was in the sweet drink. Jokes about how hooking herself to an IV filled with straight caffeine would be just as effective made her smile. The clothes Caryn brought by were even better than coffee. Clean clothes always made Khloe feel better.

Duke was doing remarkably well, in part probably because he was so fit before he'd bloated. She had no scientific evidence that proved that, but in her experience, animals who weren't overweight and had regular exercise seemed to bounce back faster after major surgery.

The waiting room was still overflowing with people there to support Raid and Duke, when the scenario she'd been dreading actually happened.

Doctor Ziegler returned early from his vacation to find out what in the hell was going on at his clinic.

She heard him yelling from the back room, where she was getting Duke ready to be transported, and her heart fell. She'd really been hoping to be gone by the time he returned. Duke was doing so well, she'd decided to move him to Doc Snow's office a whole day earlier. But apparently that wasn't early enough.

"Deep breath, Khloe," Raid said from next to her.

Having him there went a long way toward helping her stay calm. It wasn't that she was scared of the man, but after what had happened with Alan, she was much more wary of being around men when they were angry.

"He can't do anything with so many witnesses," he went on.

"I know. But it's later, when everyone isn't around, that I'm worried about," she said without thinking.

It wasn't until she felt Raid's hand on the small of her back and felt his warmth next to her that she realized what she'd said. Raid wasn't stupid. In fact, he was one of the smartest people she knew. He'd be able to read between the lines and know she was referring to an event in her past.

"He's not going to lay a finger on you, and neither is anyone else," he said in a tone that Khloe had never heard from the man before. It was low and threatening... and surprisingly, the underlying anger in his tone didn't scare her. Because his ire was clearly over the idea of someone possibly hurting her, it was actually...comforting.

She'd always been independent. Before he died, her daddy had taught her not to take any shit from anyone, taught her how to protect herself. But even with all that training, Alan had still gotten to her.

Yes, having Raid at her side *was* a comfort.

"I know," she said, trying to sound more confident than she was.

"I mean it," Raid insisted. "Ziegler can be as pissed as he wants. He can yell and bluster, but the second he makes the smallest move toward you, he's done. It'll be made clear not only by me, but by every single person on my team, that you're off-limits. *Period.*"

Khloe nodded, but she knew there was no way Raid and his friends could protect her every minute of every day. If Ziegler was pissed enough, if he really wanted to hurt her, he could do it sooner or later. Just like Alan had.

"You don't believe me," Raid said.

It should've worried Khloe that he seemed to be able to read her mind so well, but at the moment, it didn't. "You can't be with me all the time."

"You're right. I can't. But that doesn't mean we can't make it perfectly clear to him that messing with you will be the worst decision he'll ever make in his life."

"Right. Can we please go and get this over with?" Khloe asked, not wanting to think about anyone trying to hurt her again.

Raid didn't respond verbally, but he leaned over, patted Duke, told him that they'd be right back and not to worry, before walking toward the door. Instead of opening it and waiting for her to precede him, he walked through, leaving her behind.

Khloe was confused, because Raid wasn't one to be impolite. In fact, she couldn't remember a time when he didn't hold the door for her, or for any of the women in their circle of friends. But her confusion was cleared up when he turned around in the hall on their way to the waiting area and said, "Stay behind me."

She normally would've gotten irritated with his demand. With what came across as overbearing high-handedness. But truthfully, at the moment, she was just relieved. She wouldn't exactly mind having Raid's imposing presence between her and Ziegler.

When they finally entered the waiting area, Khloe glanced around at all the faces. She knew people had been coming and going all morning, but there had to be at least fifteen people there. Half of them, she didn't even know.

"You!" Raymond Ziegler yelled, making Khloe jump.

She felt movement close behind her and turned to see Lilly and Heather standing at her back. The fact that Heather was there was surprising. It hadn't been that long ago when the woman was living in the woods, hiding out from the men who'd kidnapped her and abused her for years. Her support and strength, in the face of an obviously very angry man, meant the world to Khloe.

Ethan and Tal flanked Raid as they faced off against a fuming Ziegler.

"What the fuck did you do to my clinic?" he raged.

"I didn't do anything," Khloe told him, pushing her way between Ethan and Raid to stand next to the latter, rather than behind him.

"Bullshit! You broke my door! You used my meds. My supplies. Without my permission. That's against the damn law!"

"I'm going to pay for every cotton ball and every drop of drugs that I used," Khloe informed him.

"You better!" Ziegler barked. "Once I'm able to do a full inventory, I'll send you a bill."

"No, you won't," Khloe said calmly. "You'll overcharge *me*, just like you do all your clients. I'll pay you for what I used to save Duke's life, but not a penny more."

Ziegler's face got even redder, if that was possible. He was wearing fatigues, and it was obvious he'd come straight back from wherever he'd been hunting to confront her. He had a thin five o'clock shadow from not shaving for a few days, and his face and hands were filthy. He was in his fifties and overweight, but at around six feet tall, he was still a bit daunting.

As she watched, his hands clenched into fists, and it was all Khloe could do not to take a step backward at the visible sign of his anger.

"I'm going to sue your ass!" Ziegler fumed.

"For what?" Ethan asked, joining the conversation.

"For breaking and entering. For using my equipment without permission. For threatening my livelihood."

"First of all, the police chief was here, and *he* was the one who broke in and informed your alarm company what was going on," Tal explained. "Second of all, Khloe only used what she needed in order to save Duke's life. And third, how in the bloody hell can you think what she did in any way reflects on you? Threatens your business in any way?"

"Because!"

Khloe wanted to laugh. She hadn't done a damn thing to hurt his business. At least, not any more than the man himself. He was just butt hurt and hated that someone other than him was able to swoop in and save the day. He loved being the only vet in town and took advantage of that fact in cruel ways. He refused to come in after-hours when someone had a pet emergency. He closed exactly at five o'clock, didn't work weekends, and didn't have an emergency answering service. Clients had to wait until he opened in the morning, or on Monday, or drive to the nearest emergency vet.

The fact that she was willing to go to such lengths to save Duke's life hadn't gone unnoticed in Fallport, especially if the number of people begging her to open her own clinic was any indication.

With that thought, Khloe decided that maybe Ziegler had a point. Her going above and beyond with the bloodhound probably *had* hurt his business.

"I saw the picture you posted on your social media account yesterday," a man in the waiting area said to Ziegler.

Khloe thought his name was Jim. She didn't know him, had no idea what he did, what his connection to the Eagle Point Search and Rescue team was, or even if he had any animals. But by the tone of his voice, it was obvious his comment wasn't exactly complimentary.

"Yeah? So?" Ziegler said.

"Those antlers had to be...what? About six feet wide or so? Which would make that bull moose around ten years old, right?"

"I guess."

"Not too many moose around here. Where'd you go to hunt? Had to be fairly close, since you were out hunting yesterday and are standing here right now."

Raymond didn't respond, simply glared at Jim.

Then someone else spoke up. A woman this time. "I saw that pic too. And I looked up the company that was on the logo of the truck in the background. They bring animals to their farm for people to hunt...and I use that term loosely. Hunters like you *buy* an animal, and it's released into their fenced property so you can go in and shoot it nice and easy, since there's nowhere for animals to go. It's unsportsmanlike and *disgusting*," she finished, venom dripping from her tone.

"Molly's right. They bring in grizzlies, moose, deer,

pigs...sometimes even kangaroos. It's awful," another woman said. Claire something-or-other. Khloe recognized her from the library.

"It's not like that," Raymond protested, getting even angrier.

"Really? How much did you pay for that moose?" Jim asked, his arms crossing over his chest. "And what happened to the animal after you shot it and took your stupid posed pictures?"

"I'm sure the meat went to good use," Raymond muttered, his face flaming now.

Most of the people in the room rolled their eyes.

"Besides, what I do in my free time is no one's goddamn business," Raymond seethed. "All that should matter is that I take care of Rover and Frisky and all the other animals people entrust to me."

"That's true to a point," another man said. "But when the money we pay you to take care of the furry members of our families goes to the illegal and immoral hunting of an animal that's been brought in for a canned hunt, *that's* when it becomes our business."

"Exactly!" Molly said. "And Miss Khloe here stepped in without hesitation to help Duke. She didn't care that it was after-hours, or insist the surgery was paid for *before* she started. She did what needed to be done. And from what I hear, she hasn't even mentioned charging a fee. Her only concern was saving the dog's life. When's the last time you performed a surgery without it being paid for up front?"

Raymond's face was so red, Khloe was honestly concerned he was going to have a heart attack right then and there.

Throughout the entire unpleasant conversation, Raid

hadn't said a word. Hadn't moved from her side. He'd just stood there with his arms crossed and a frown on his face. He was intimidating even to Khloe, and he was on her side.

But when Raymond took a step in her direction, that changed. Fast.

Pushing Khloe behind him with one arm, he slammed the heel of his other hand against Ziegler's sternum when he got too close. "Step back," he growled.

"You hit me!" Raymond exclaimed. "Everyone here is my witness! This man struck me. I'm suing your ass too!"

"He didn't hit you," the second man who'd spoken said as he rolled his eyes.

"He did! He put his damn hand on me!" Raymond insisted.

"Because you threatened Khloe," Jim said.

"I did not!" Raymond shouted.

"Stepping toward her with your fists clenched is a sure sign of a threat where I come from," Ethan informed him.

Khloe shivered at the look of hatred the vet aimed at her. "You're going to pay for this. I'm going to make sure of it."

"Now *that* was a definite threat," Jim said. Then he smirked. "Everyone here is a witness."

"And I'm thinking if anything happens to her, it won't be hard to figure out who did it," Molly said. "It's definitely time for me to find a new veterinarian," she added, disdain dripping from her tone.

"Good luck. There aren't any other vets around here," Raymond said. "And Muffy is spoiled rotten anyway."

"Her name is *Fluffy*, and who cares if she's spoiled? I'd

rather drive an hour to another vet than have you put your hands on her ever again," Molly told him.

"Like I need your money," Raymond unwisely muttered.

"You're right. You don't. And you won't need mine, either," Claire chimed in.

One by one, the people in the waiting room agreed.

"Not smart," Tal said with a smirk as he shook his head.

"I want all of you out of here! *Now*," Raymond ordered between clenched teeth.

Khloe was never so glad that her patient was doing as well as he was. "We were on our way out when you arrived," she informed him.

"And don't think you're taking any of my supplies with you," Raymond sneered.

"Wouldn't dream of it," she said.

"Come on, let's go get Duke ready," Lilly said, putting her hand on Khloe's arm.

There was nothing more Khloe wanted to do than get out of Raymond's presence, but she kind of felt bad for the man. Even though he was an ass, it had to suck to be on vacation and hear about your clinic being broken into. Even if it was by another veterinarian.

"For what it's worth...I'm sorry," Khloe told him, trying to take the higher road. "I *am* going to pay you for the supplies I used."

"You'd better not dare undercut me," Raymond said.

Her resolve to be fair wavered, but Khloe nodded. "I won't. I'm perfectly aware of the cost of everything I used."

"The door will be fixed by tonight," Ethan told Ziegler. "Rocky's coming over in a while to fix the frame."

"Good," Raymond said, not willing to say thank you.

"What an ass," Claire said, not exactly under her breath.

"I told you—everyone out! The clinic is closed. This isn't a social gathering place," Raymond barked.

One by one, the people who'd witnessed the entire unpleasant encounter filed out, leaving only Ethan, Lilly, Tal, Heather, Raid, and Khloe. And Raymond, of course.

"You people think you're untouchable," he told them, hatred in his tone. "News flash, you aren't. You might have everyone in this goddamn town wrapped around your fingers, thinking you can do no wrong, but they'll see through your goody-two-shoes façade. Mark my words."

Khloe could only shake her head. The man was delusional. The three men standing there were some of the best people she'd met in her life. They were good to their cores. There was nothing Raymond could say or do that would change that. Ethan and the rest of the Eagle Point SAR team had helped too many people—tourists and locals alike—for Ziegler to change anyone's mind. She had a feeling the more he tried to disparage their reputations, the more it would blow back in his face.

"You have ten minutes to be gone," he threatened.

Khloe wanted to ask "or what?" but she refrained. He could call the police, but since Simon was firmly on their side, as were all his deputies, she didn't think they'd actually do anything. But because she was more than uncomfortable in Raymond's presence, she turned and headed for the door to the back rooms without another word.

Heather and Lilly stayed by her side, and once they

were in the room where Duke was still resting comfortably, they all let out a long breath.

"That man is horrible," Heather said. She hadn't said anything while they were in the waiting room, but those four words summed up all their feelings completely.

"Totally," Lilly agreed. "But did you see the way Raid immediately moved when Ziegler stepped toward you?" she asked Khloe.

She nodded.

"He's protective," Heather said quietly. "He likes you."

"Yup," Lilly said with a smile. "It's about time."

"Wait, wait, wait. It's not what you think," Khloe protested.

"Uh-huh," Lilly said, the smile on her face growing.

"Seriously. He's protective of *all* women. I've seen it in the library. And when he's on the scent with Duke."

"It's different," Heather told her. "It's the look in his eyes."

Khloe glanced at the shy woman next to her.

She shrugged. "I know I'm not the most worldly person, and I'm the last person who should be commenting on someone else's relationship. But I recognize it because it's the same look I see in Tal's eyes whenever he looks at *me*. From the first day I woke up in that cave and he was sitting outside, staring at me, I saw the same emotion in his eyes that was in Raid's just now."

Khloe wanted to continue to protest. But more than that, she didn't want to tell Heather she was wrong. The woman was still coming into her own and acclimating after her awful experience.

Besides...she'd seen the look in Raid's eyes just now. She'd dismissed it, but she couldn't deny the relief she'd felt when he'd stepped in front of her to keep Raymond from getting too close.

"Right. Whatever. Doesn't matter. I've got eight minutes now to get Duke prepped and out of here," Khloe said matter-of-factly.

She started to kneel next to Duke when Lilly stopped her with a hand on her arm. "You can talk to us," she said softly. "We aren't going to judge you. You've got friends here, Khloe. Me and Heather, Elsie, Bristol, Caryn, and Finley. You need to talk...we're here."

Khloe swallowed hard to keep the emotion welling up inside her contained. "I know," she managed after a moment.

"Good. Because we're gonna want to hear all about you being a vet and how you ended up here in Fallport," Lilly said with a compassionate smile.

"It's not very interesting," Khloe hedged.

Lilly snorted. An honest-to-God snort. "Right. Sure."

"Just like the story of how I ended up living in the forest isn't interesting," Heather joked.

It took everything in Khloe not to laugh out loud at that. Out of everyone in their group, Heather's story was probably the most traumatic and heart-wrenching. "Okay, it's sorta interesting, but I really need to get Duke out of here before Ziegler comes in to drag him out."

"Over my dead body," Lilly muttered.

"What can we do to help?" Heather asked.

Khloe was glad it seemed the interrogation was over... for now. She knew the time would come when she'd need to talk to her friends. But surprisingly, now that the cat was out of the bag, pun intended, about her being a vet, it didn't seem *quite* as daunting or scary to consider telling everyone what she'd gone through.

Turning her mind to the task at hand, Khloe decided not to worry about the future. What happened would happen. She'd learned that the hard way. But it also felt a little easier to put aside her worries because she had such good friends around her.

It took longer than the ten minutes Ziegler had given them to get Duke ready to be moved. Brock brought his Ford Ranger over so they could put Duke in the bed of the truck. He'd even put a blow-up mattress in the back for the dog to lie on. Khloe and Raiden rode in the back with the dog, while Simon led the way to the square with his lights on. They were only driving around five miles an hour, so the cold didn't bother either Duke or the humans who were sitting with him in the open air.

There was quite the procession as they headed to Doc Snow's clinic. It almost felt like a mini-parade as they wound their way around the square to the back of the clinic. With all the people there to help, it was a matter of minutes before Duke was safely ensconced inside a treatment room in the small medical center.

Khloe was surprised when Afton arrived, saying she was there to watch over Duke to give everyone a break. If it had been anyone but the vet tech who'd told her to go home and get a shower and something to eat, Khloe probably would've refused. But she'd seen the woman's talent firsthand and trusted her implicitly. She hadn't lied when she'd told the young woman that she'd hire her in a heartbeat.

After giving Afton one last spate of directions in regard to Duke, Khloe found herself tucked against Raid as he led her out of the treatment room. He hadn't protested leaving Duke for a while either, telling Khloe that if she trusted Duke's well-being to Afton, he did too.

They were standing in Doc Snow's small waiting room when Finley started laughing.

"What's so funny?" Elsie asked.

"Remember the guy standing in the corner of the room when Ziegler was losing his mind?" Finley asked.

Khloe shook her head. Aside from the people giving Ziegler a piece of their mind, she didn't really take notice of who else was there and who wasn't.

"Wasn't that Rory? The snowplow driver who helped get everyone to Lilly and Ethan's wedding?" Elsie asked.

"That's him. He just posted a video on Fallport's social media site," Finley said. She turned her phone around so everyone in the room could see it. Raymond Ziegler was trying to defend the hunt he'd been on, and the video went on from there. It included him saying he didn't need anyone's money and ended after he'd threatened the SAR team.

"He's done," Elsie said with a small smile.

"No one's gonna want to use his services after seeing that," Zeke agreed as he put an arm around his wife.

Once more the spark of interest to open her own clinic here in Fallport flared to life in Khloe's belly. Elsie was right. Once people saw his disregard and disdain for the residents of Fallport, and after his disparaging remarks about the Eagle Point Search and Rescue team—men who voluntarily went into the forest in all kinds of weather and times of day simply to help others—he was most definitely going to lose customers.

Which opened the door for a new veterinarian to easily recruit new clients.

"As funny as that is, and as much as I think he deserves his words and actions to be well known...he's not going to be pleased with that video," Tal observed.

Khloe frowned. Tal wasn't wrong. She hadn't posted the video. Hadn't had anything to do with it. But just like that, worry crept in once more.

"Just what I need," she muttered. "Someone else who has it in for me."

The room went silent—and when she looked up, Khloe realized everyone was staring at her. Shit. She'd done it again. Opened her mouth and said the wrong thing at the wrong time.

"Khloe—" Brock began, frowning.

"No," Raid said firmly with a shake of his head.

"No?" Brock repeated.

"We aren't doing this now. Khloe's exhausted. She needs a shower, and then food to soak up all the caffeine in her veins from that coffee she drank this morning."

"But if we should be on watch for someone other than Ziegler, we need to know the details," Zeke said in an even tone.

"No one's gonna interrogate Khloe. When she's ready to talk, she'll talk. If she's never ready, than that's how it'll be. In the meantime, we'll keep an eye on Ziegler and make sure he doesn't do something stupid."

Khloe didn't know what she'd done to deserve such loyalty from Raiden. She'd been kind of a bitch since they'd met. She didn't mean to be, but she'd been trying to protect herself from getting in too deep with him or his friends. Clearly it hadn't worked. She couldn't imagine not having him, or the others, in her life now. Especially in a crisis like they'd had in the last twenty-four hours with Duke. Everyone had stepped up to help. They'd proven to be the kind of friends she'd always wanted and never had. And she'd found them when she wasn't even looking or trying.

"Right. We can do that," Zeke said.

"I'll talk to the others," Brock added.

"Operation Shield Khloe starts now," Tal agreed. "She doesn't go anywhere without eyes on her."

"Wait a sec," Khloe started, but Raid spoke over her.

"I'll be in touch," he told his friends.

"I've got a cake I need to bake," Finley told her, "but I can come over afterward to keep you company when you sit with Duke."

"I can bring Tony by too. He'll want to see for himself that Duke's all right," Elsie said.

"I'm not sure that I'll be any help, especially when you've got Afton and everyone else, but I'm happy to do whatever I can to assist with Duke if you need it," Heather volunteered.

"Thank you so much, everyone. But I think we're good. Duke needs to stay calm for now. Maybe once he goes home, you can work with Raid to take turns sitting with him at the library or at his house."

Everyone agreed immediately.

"And I'm thinking we need a girls' night soon," Elsie said firmly.

Khloe wasn't so sure about that, but she could tell Elsie and the others weren't going to budge. And since she had a small reprieve before she needed to figure out how to explain her past to her friends in a way they wouldn't resent her or be pissed that she hadn't already told them what was happening, she nodded.

Everyone hugged her tightly before heading out. After a few more words with Afton and making sure she was good, and thanking Doc Snow again for letting Duke hang out in his clinic for a couple days, Khloe let Raid lead her outside once more.

But instead of heading toward her apartment, he drove away from town toward the small house she knew he owned.

"Raiden? I want to go to my apartment."

"No."

Khloe frowned. Did he really just say that? "You can't kidnap me. I want to go home."

He had the nerve to chuckle. Somehow in the last few hours, she'd forgotten how irritating he could be. "This isn't funny," she said tightly.

"No, you're right, it's not," he said as he sobered. "You're exhausted because you spent the night looking after my dog, who you performed emergency surgery on and saved his life. You slept on the hard floor. Haven't eaten anything worth mentioning. Had to deal with Ziegler being pissed at you, which rattled you more than you're willing to admit. You're also coming to terms with how important you are to our friends, which I *know* is something you've been trying to avoid since the day you took the job at the library. Also, Caryn told me that you didn't have much to eat in your fridge—and yes, I told her to snoop and report back to me.

"So, I'm taking you to my place, where I can make sure you eat something healthy and get some uninterrupted sleep. I'm sure well-meaning but nosy people will be stopping by your apartment to gossip. At my house, you can rest.

"And after that last comment you made at the clinic...if you think I'm letting you out of my sight until I'm sure any threat from Ziegler is mitigated, and I know what *other* threats might be hanging over your head, you're delusional."

Khloe sighed. She liked most of what he said. But that last part...she knew he was protective but hadn't realized exactly how much. "I can take care of myself."

"I know you can," he said without hesitation. "You've been doing it for a damn long time. But you don't need to do it all alone anymore."

"What if I want to?"

He turned then, and his green eyes bored into her own. "Do you?"

It was on the tip of her tongue to say yes. That she didn't want him to get involved. But she couldn't do it. She was tired. Bone-deep tired. It was exhausting wondering when and if someone was waiting around every corner to harass her and maybe try to finish what Alan had attempted in the past.

Raid didn't make her answer. His eyes went back to the road.

Gratitude filled her. He wasn't going to make her acquiescence harder than it already was. Khloe sighed in relief as she shut her eyes. She still felt as if she had the weight of the world on her shoulders, but for now the load was a tiny bit lighter.

She opened her eyes when she felt the vehicle slowing down. Raid was pulling onto the gravel driveway leading to his house. She'd driven by his place in the past and loved it on sight. The house was painted a dark blue and had a porch on the front and along one side. A detached garage sat nearby, but Khloe couldn't take her gaze off the swing on the front porch. She'd always wanted one of those. Could imagine herself sitting there unwinding after a long day.

"I've still got some work to do on it," he told her, "but the important stuff is done."

"And what's the important stuff?" she couldn't help but ask.

"I fenced in three acres in the back so Duke could run around and roam without me worrying about him wandering off. Bloodhounds have a tendency to follow their nose for miles and miles, then look up and wonder where the hell they are."

He wasn't wrong. "It couldn't have been cheap to put in all that fencing," Khloe said.

"It wasn't. But it was important, so I figured out a way to make it happen."

More proof that Raiden was a good guy. "What else?"

"A nice kitchen. A shower where I don't have to bend my knees to get under the spray, and a bedroom large enough for a king-size bed so I don't feel cramped."

It sounded like heaven to Khloe. And of course a tall man like Raid would want to be comfortable in his own home.

"I've got two guest rooms, and two other bathrooms you can pick from to shower, one is an en suite. Take your time, we've got a while before I think you'll want to go back and check on Duke."

"Like you don't want to check on him yourself," Khloe said.

Raid smiled. "Guilty. It's gonna feel weird to be in my house without Duke here. Come on. While you're showering, I'll make us something to eat."

"Don't you want to clean up too?"

"Yeah, but my belly is telling me food is more important at the moment."

"You're such a guy," she semi-complained.

"Yup," he agreed without hesitation as he shut off the engine.

They climbed out and met at the front of his car. He'd parked right in front of the house instead of in the garage, and she followed him up the stairs to the porch.

"Tell me that swing is as comfortable as it looks," she said as he unlocked his front door.

"Don't know. Never sat in it."

"What?" Khloe asked in disbelief. "That's awful!"

"Not my thing. But you can take a turn and let me know how it is," he said as he pushed open the door and gestured for her to enter ahead of him.

That made Khloe remember how he'd walked in front of her into the waiting room at Ziegler's clinic. Putting himself between her and any danger they might be walking into. Raiden had hidden depths, and Khloe was suddenly curious to see what else she could learn about him.

His house was surprisingly tidy. For some reason, she'd expected to see dirty dishes, junk on the coffee table, and general chaos. His office at the library was *total* chaos. Not dirty, but stacks of papers and books everywhere, and his precious, ever-present coffee cup that Khloe didn't think had been properly washed in years. But from the quick glimpse she got as he led her through the main living area, past the kitchen, to a guest room with an attached bathroom, the place was immaculate.

Raid didn't come into the bedroom, but instead stood in the doorway, obviously not wanting to make her uncomfortable. "Take your time in the shower. Chicken marinara all right?"

Khloe blinked. "Seriously?"

"Yeah, why? Are you allergic to chicken?"

"What? No. Is that even a thing?"

Raid shrugged. "Sure. People can be allergic to just about anything these days."

"Not me. But I was expecting something like a sandwich or scrambled eggs or something."

Raid smirked. "Why, because I'm a guy?"

Khloe wrinkled her nose. When he put it that way, she was being sexist. "Yeah?"

He chuckled. "I don't have an unending repertoire of things I'm good at cooking, but my Instant Pot has made things much easier. I'll get our meal started. Again, I've got a kick-ass hot water heater, so take as long as you want. We can both get some sleep after we eat."

With that, Raid gave her a small chin lift, then closed the door as he left her to her shower.

How long Khloe stood there staring at the door after he'd left, she didn't know. She'd gotten used to the Raiden she saw at work. Gruff, standoffish, focused on the tasks at hand...and a man who seemed to find fault in every little thing she did.

This man, the generous, caring, almost flirtatious guy, was hard to get used to.

Eventually, she forced herself out of her stupor and turned toward the bathroom. She found clean towels in the small linen closet, extra toothbrushes and toothpaste in a drawer, soap, shampoo, conditioner, and even a towel warmer. She was under the impression that Raiden was kind of a loner and didn't have a lot of friends outside the SAR team. But maybe she was wrong, if the obvious preparation for guests was any indication.

Half an hour later, Khloe emerged from the guest room. She'd taken her time in the shower and felt a hundred times better. Although the caffeine she'd had earlier had definitely worn off. Yesterday and last night were catching up with her. She was hungry, yes, but the thought of lying down on a comfortable bed and taking a nap was even more appealing.

When she walked into the main room, she stood there for a moment watching Raid without him realizing she was there. The man seemed at home in his kitchen. He'd changed his shirt and now wore a pair of gray sweatpants.

Khloe had never understood why women went so crazy over a man in sweats...until now. The material clung to Raid's legs as if it was a second skin. His thighs were muscular and his bare feet sticking out the bottom made the scene seem even more intimate. But it was the way the sweats highlighted his crotch that made Khloe blush.

It was silly. He was completely and decently covered. But she couldn't look away from the bulge in his pants. It was more than obvious his cock was appropriately sized for someone of his height. Then he turned around, and Khloe's fingernails dug into her palm. Good God, his ass was just as impressive.

How come she'd never noticed that Raiden Walker was built so perfectly until recently?

Probably because when she'd first arrived in Fallport,

she was pretty traumatized and did her best to keep her head down. Also, Raid was her boss, and she needed her job. Needed a place to recoup and hide out.

But as the months passed and her fear began to change to anger at how her life had been upended by an event that wasn't her fault, Khloe had reluctantly—and secretly—acknowledged an attraction to Raid. Which she'd been trying to tamp down ever since.

Now that she was in his house, had been naked in his shower—well, not *his* shower, but close—and he was dressed casually while making her something to eat, all the feelings Khloe had been trying to suppress came roaring to the surface. Making her nervous. And jittery. And self-conscious.

Doing her best not to stare at how well he filled out those sweats, Khloe cleared her throat as she walked toward the large, charming kitchen and tried to pretend nothing had changed between them in the last twenty-four hours.

But she knew she was kidding herself. Everything had changed. And she had a feeling there was no way she and Raid would be able to go back to the way things used to be between them.

CHAPTER FIVE

Raid knew the moment Khloe stepped into the room. He had an innate sense about where she was every time he was near her. In the library, he was aware of when she'd left her office to help clients find a book. Knew when she went to lunch and when she was back. He knew when she left for the day...all without actually seeing her. He had no idea why he was so attuned to the woman, but he wasn't exactly upset about it.

It took everything he had to pretend he didn't know she was there. His spine tingled as he felt her gaze as he finished preparing their meal. Raid had no idea what she was thinking. If she liked what she saw when she looked at him, or if she was wondering why he was being so nice.

It wasn't as if he'd *tried* to be abrasive when he was around her. There was just something about her that made him feel off-kilter. He figured since he'd realized long ago that she was keeping secrets, he wondered if maybe subconsciously, he'd pushed her hard in the hopes she'd lose it and lash out at him, maybe letting something slip.

But he'd never expected to learn one of those secrets the way he had. Raid was still astonished by the fact that Khloe was a veterinarian. And he'd never been so relieved and thankful as he was right now. Duke was alive because of her.

Taking care of her was the only way he knew how to thank her. To apologize for being an ass. For all the times he'd sniped at her. But it was more than that, and Raid knew it. He wanted to get to know her better. She was still keeping secrets, ones that were more significant than just hiding her profession, if her slip from earlier was any indication. It would take time to get under her shields, but Raid very definitely wanted to get there.

But first, he needed to feed her. Make sure she got some sleep. Then he'd see what he could do about chipping away at her tough outer shell. He knew that getting her to open up would mean he'd need to do the same. And for the first time in years, the thought didn't give him horrible anxiety.

When she cleared her throat, Raid turned and gave her a small smile. "Good timing," he told her. "The chicken's just about done."

"Can I help with anything?"

"You want to grab some plates out of that cabinet?" Raid asked, motioning to a door to his right.

Without a word, she headed to where he'd indicated and grabbed two plates. Within five minutes they were sitting at his small table with plates of steaming chicken marinara with polenta in front of them.

They ate in silence for a few minutes before Khloe said, "This is amazing."

"Thanks."

"Seriously, it's *really* great. Thank you."

"You should've seen my first few meals I tried in the Instant Pot. They were disasters."

"Well, you'd never know it tasting this," she said.

Her praise felt good. In fact, sitting at his table with her felt good too. "I think this is the first time I've ever sat here while eating," he blurted.

Khloe stared at him. "What? Why?"

Raid already regretted the impulsive comment. "It's not a big deal. Forget I said anything."

"Seriously, Raid. Why?"

He shrugged as nonchalantly as he could. "I don't usually have people over. It's just easier to eat standing up in the kitchen or sitting on the couch as I watch TV." Or downstairs in the basement, where he spent most of his free time, but he wasn't going to go there. What he did in his spare time definitely wouldn't impress a woman like Khloe.

"What do you mean, you don't have people over?" she asked. "You have a bathroom filled with toiletries for guests. And two bedrooms besides the master."

"I guess that's just something I learned from my mom. She always took home the little bottles from hotel rooms and put them in baskets in the bathrooms in our house, just in case someone visiting needed something."

"I'm sure she loves seeing you carry on her tradition," Khloe said with a smile.

Raid shrugged. "She's never been here."

"Oh. Has she passed?"

"No. She and my father live in Iowa. They're retired and they don't like to travel. I haven't seen them in at least eight years or so."

Khloe's eyes widened. "Really?"

Feeling defensive, Raid's words came out a little harsher than he wanted. "It's not a big deal. I still call every now and then, but they have their life and I have mine. They weren't happy when I quit the Coast Guard, especially my dad. I was such an introvert growing up that he thought being in the service meant I'd finally become a 'manly man'. They were both disappointed in me."

To his surprise, Khloe reached over and put her hand on his forearm.

Raid was so surprised, he froze with his fork in mid-air. The feel of her hand on his skin sent tingles down his spine.

"I'm sorry. I wasn't judging. And they're missing out, Raiden. You're a good man. And not being in the military doesn't make you any more or less manly. You're one of the most masculine men I've ever met in my life."

Raid had no idea what that meant, but her words still made warmth spread through him. "Thanks," he said softly.

Khloe pulled her hand back, and it was all Raid could do not to grab it and put it back on his arm. He had so little skin-on-skin contact in his life that he hadn't realized how much he missed it.

"My mom died when I was in elementary school. It was hard, but my dad was around and he did everything he could to make up for her not being there," Khloe said. She smiled slightly. "When I was a teen, he brought me to a woman who worked in a salon so she could help me with my makeup and teach me how to do my hair. He was the typical dad when it came to meeting my dates, and he was always supportive of anything I wanted to do."

"He sounds great."

"He was."

Was. Shit.

"He died about five years ago. Had a heart attack. We didn't even know he had any heart issues. As far as I knew, he was as healthy as a horse. It sucked."

"I bet," Raid said gently.

"Anyway," Khloe said in a perkier tone. "I'm still surprised you haven't eaten at this table much. What about Ethan and the rest of the guys? Haven't they been over here?"

Raid shrugged. "We usually hang out at one of their places."

"So that's a no. Raid, that's crazy. This house is awesome! You've got that fenced-in yard, and I bet you have a kick-ass deck out there too, don't you?"

She wasn't wrong. Raid shrugged.

Khloe smirked. "Of course you do. Why haven't they been over here?"

He wished she'd drop it. He felt self-conscious now. "They just haven't. It's not that I don't want them here, I'm just not the kind of person to set up a party or arrange get-togethers."

Khloe stared at him for a long minute. Then nodded. "Yeah, I guess I can see that."

Raid wanted to ask what that meant, but he was too chicken.

"I didn't have too many get-togethers in Norfolk either. After work, I was just too tired, and it was easier to come home and make a bowl of cereal or something for dinner and crash than try to further any friendships with the acquaintances I knew."

"Norfolk," Raid said thoughtfully. In all the time he'd known the woman sitting next to him, he'd never known where she came from before she'd landed in Fallport. He'd asked once, and she'd been very evasive in her response, asking if she had to tell him in order to keep her job.

"Yeah," she said quietly, not meeting his eyes. "I know there've been a lot of things I haven't told you about my past, and—"

"It's okay," Raid interrupted, not wanting her to feel obligated to talk to him.

They ate in silence for another minute or so before she said, "I just wanted to say, I get it. I'm an introvert myself. I like spending time alone. Reading. Watching TV. Simply sitting in a quiet room and soaking in the silence. Your friends here like you for who you are, Raiden, not because you invite them over for parties or anything."

"It's a good thing," Raid mumbled.

Khloe giggled, and Raid looked at her in surprise. Had he ever heard her sound so carefree before? He didn't think so.

"Crap. Now I'm getting punchy," she said with a small smile. "When I start giggling over nothing, it's definitely a sign I need sleep."

Raid filed that fact away. He was hungry to know every little nuance about Khloe. Looking at her plate, he was pleased she'd eaten just about everything he'd given her. To him, she was a tiny thing, and he wouldn't mind if she put a little more meat on her bones, but he figured she'd probably disagree and claim that she was overweight. She wasn't. She was curvy in all the right places.

"You want more?" he asked.

She laughed again. "No, I'm stuffed."

"Right, so why don't you head on back to the guest room and lie down. I'll take care of cleaning up."

"I should help," she said.

"Why?"

"Because. You cooked, I should clean. It's only fair."

Raid shook his head. "No. I've got it."

"Okay. Thanks. Do you mind if I lie down on the couch in here instead?"

"Of course not. Can I ask why?"

Khloe shrugged and wouldn't meet his eyes. "I just think the couch looks extremely comfortable."

Raid figured there was more to her reticence to go to the guest room than that, but he didn't pry. "It is. I've fallen asleep there more times than I can count."

She gave him a grateful smile, then stood. He watched as she padded over to the couch and sat. Then her head disappeared as she stretched out on the cushions. He couldn't see her anymore, but he still grinned knowing she was there.

When he was finished putting the dishes from their meal into the dishwasher and cleaning out the Instant Pot, Raid couldn't stop himself from walking into the other room. He could've gone to his bedroom to nap, but there was no way he was going to pass up the opportunity to sleep next to Khloe. Even if "next to" meant in the recliner near the couch.

His first glimpse of Khloe was a shock. Not that she was there, of course, but that she somehow looked like a completely different person when she was asleep. All her shields were down and she looked vulnerable as hell.

She was on her side and her hair was mussed around her head. With her eyes closed and her guard down, Raid's protective side rose even higher. For so many months, he'd forced her to be wary and given her no reason to think he appreciated or even liked her. He was done with that. She'd saved Duke's life, and that meant the world to him. The least he could do was stop being an ass around her.

Raid sat in his recliner and put his feet up, but his gaze didn't move from Khloe asleep on his couch.

He knew what he was and what he wasn't, and he wasn't the kind of man women were drawn to. He'd made peace with that a long time ago. The names he was called in grade school still echoed in his head.

Elf.

Weirdo.

Little Orphan Arnold.

Freak.

He'd heard them all. And the truth of the matter was, his ears *were* pointy. He *was* weird. He had bright red hair and was a longtime nerd. The kids back then hadn't really said anything that wasn't true. He just hadn't realized until he was in high school that being who he was meant girls weren't interested. They wanted the jocks. The blond or dark-haired idiots who looked good but couldn't pass History or Math without cheating.

So Raid had always been withdrawn. Found it was easier to relate to dogs than to people, which carried into adulthood. He'd had the occasional hook-up over the years, but no long-term, serious relationships.

For the first time in his life, Raid wondered what it would be like to come home to someone like Khloe. To have a woman smile at him like she did and ask about his day. He liked cooking for someone other than himself. Liked making sure Khloe was cared for and had her needs met. Though, it was likely he'd already screwed up any chance he might've had with her by picking fights and forcing her to stay on her toes around him all the time.

He'd do what he could to mend their relationship. Maybe they could be friends, at least.

Raid closed his eyes and sighed. It figured that the one woman in a very long time he was interested in happened to not only be his employee, but was also the woman he'd done his best to annoy and antagonize for months.

Just before sleep claimed him, Raid had the thought that he was still a very lucky man. If he hadn't hired Khloe all those months ago, it was likely he would've lost his best friend. He had a roof over his head, lived in a town that had accepted him for who he was, even if they didn't really know him that well. He had friends who would bend over backward to help him, and he'd made it out of some pretty dangerous situations while he'd been in the Coast Guard.

Life was never guaranteed. It was a crapshoot what kind of hand you were dealt when you were born. You couldn't choose your parents, or the country you were born in, but you could choose how to deal with the shit life threw at you. And he'd done his best to take that shit and run with it. To turn his seemingly bad fortunes around to something good.

The last thing he heard before he fell asleep was a soft snore from Khloe. Knowing she was there, that he wasn't alone, felt damn good.

* * *

Alan Mather sat with his two brothers in the visiting area at the state prison near Norfolk. He much preferred the county jail he'd been in while awaiting trial. It had fewer people, the food was better, and he had a bit more freedom. Not to mention the other men he was incarcerated with here were way meaner than in county lockup.

Being here sucked.

And it was all that bitch's fault.

She'd killed his dog, then blamed *him* for the condition she'd been in.

Khloe Watts had to die.

It was a shame he'd fucked up when he'd run her over. He'd intended to crush her skull, but instead had only hurt her leg.

He might be in prison, but he wasn't cut off from the world. He'd been searching for her ever since she'd gotten out of the nursing home where she'd been recovering after the "accident." The bitch had run. Was hiding from him. She'd come back for his trial, and seeing her on the stand, hearing her talk shit about him, made Alan even more determined to make her pay for ruining his life.

His brothers were the key to making that happen.

Scott and Jason were younger than him and would do anything he asked. They'd been scouring the internet for any mention of the fucking veterinarian and where she might be hiding out since he'd been arrested.

And today they'd shown him a viral video they'd seen totally by chance on social media. Apparently, she'd pissed off someone else...no surprise there. A Doctor Ziegler was ranting in the video about Khloe breaking into his clinic and performing surgery on a dog without his permission.

Alan didn't give a shit about the doctor or what the bitch had done to him. All he cared about was her location.

Scott had looked up the vet's office online and found that she'd been hiding out in some hick town called Fallport. It was on the other side of the state in the foothills of the Appalachian Mountains.

"What's the plan?" Jason asked quietly so the other prisoners or the guards lurking nearby couldn't hear him.

"How do you two feel about takin' a trip?" Alan asked.

"Where?" Scott asked.

He resisted the urge to roll his eyes. His youngest brother wasn't the sharpest tool in the shed. He was twenty-six, a high school dropout, and he relied on Jason to support him and keep a roof over his head.

Jason was thirty and not too much smarter than his brother. But at least he had a high school diploma. He'd knocked up his girlfriend when they were twenty and now they had four kids. He worked at various jobs, all of which paid him under the table so he didn't have to pay taxes. His wife brought home the bulk of their income, and if it wasn't for that, he would've dumped her a long time ago. But Jason was smart enough to know if he broke up with her, he'd have to work a lot harder than he did now.

Jason and Scott spent their days smoking dope and hanging around the house when they weren't working. They had the flexibility to head to Fallport and do what Alan wasn't able to...at least until he was paroled. Unfortunately, his fucking lawyer hadn't been able to get the attempted murder charge thrown out, and he would be there for several years. And it was all that damn vet's fault for screwing up her job in the first place.

"Where are you going? Dumb ass," Alan sighed. "Fallport."

"Oh!" Scott exclaimed with a laugh. "Right."

"So, again, what's the plan?" Jason asked, repeating his question.

"I want you to make her life a living hell. Show up everywhere she goes. Spread rumors. Leave presents on her doorstep. That kind of thing."

"What kind of presents?" Jason asked.

Alan did his best not to get annoyed. He hated that he had to spell out every little thing. "Dead animals, piles of shit...I don't fucking know. Whatever will freak her out and make her quake in her boots. That bitch isn't allowed to start her life over as if she didn't ruin *mine*. She needs to be aware every second of every day that she's being watched. That she didn't get away scot-free after what she did."

"Right, got it. We can do that," Jason said with a nod.

"Yeah, this is gonna be fun."

"But don't do anything that will get you arrested," Alan warned. "I'm sure the cops in that backwoods town are dumb as shit, but still. I want her to know she's been found. That there's *nowhere* she can hide. We'll harass her for a while, then back off. Let her think we've given up. Then we'll show back up when she least expects it. The bitch ain't never forgetting what she did."

"Then what?" Scott asked. "I mean, we're gonna get to do more than harass her eventually, right?"

"When I get out of here, she's dead," Alan said in a cold, flat tone. "I'll finish what I started. *I'll* finish it. If you two take that away from me, I'll kill you instead."

"No killing her. But everything else is on the table, right?" Jason asked with a sly smile.

Alan tilted his head as he studied his brother. He'd heard stories about his sexual tastes. How he liked to choke women when he fucked them. How he expected complete obedience. He smiled. "Sure. Again, just don't get caught. The last thing we need is the two of you being thrown in here with me. Who would carry out my revenge then?"

"We aren't gonna get caught," Jason told him. "People who live in those kinds of towns are stupid. We're gonna blend right in and no one will suspect a thing. Besides, from that clip we watched, it sounds as if people hate the bitch anyway. They'll be glad when she's gone."

"Keep an eye on her. If she runs, we need to know where she goes."

"Time's up!" one of the guard's announced.

Alan scowled. He *hated* this fucking place. Hated being told when to pee. When to eat. When to sleep. He should've backed over the bitch after he hit her. Smushed her brains all over the damn parking lot. Instead, he'd left her alive as a witness to testify against him. When he got out, he wouldn't make that mistake again.

Doctor Khloe Watts was a dead woman walking. She just didn't know it.

CHAPTER SIX

Khloe sat in her library office four days later and shook her head as she watched Duke sleep on a pillow in the corner. The dog was doing well. *Really* well. Spoiled rotten not only by Raiden, but by all the citizens of Fallport. He'd had dozens of visitors, people wanting to make sure he was all right. He had more treats and toys than any dog would ever need.

Her friends had wanted to throw a huge party now that Duke was recovering, but Raid managed to talk them out of it. That didn't mean everyone still didn't want to let Raid, Duke, and Khloe know they were relieved the bloodhound was all right.

Duke was definitely a local celebrity, and Khloe had found that she was almost as popular as the dog. She was used to fading into the background. People had been friendly to her in the past, but not like they were now. Everyone seemed to know her name and what she'd done. And more people than she could count begged her to open her own veterinarian practice here in Fallport.

But her newfound fame wasn't the weirdest thing to happen to her in the last three days. She'd only been back to her apartment once, and that was to pack a suitcase. She'd been staying at Raid's house. If someone had asked her a year ago, a month ago, hell, a *week* ago if she ever thought she'd spend even one night under his roof, she would've said there was no way. But here she was.

They'd been able to bring Duke home from Doc Snow's clinic the day after he'd arrived. Khloe had taken the IV out and the dog was still groggy and in a bit of pain, but she told Raid that could be managed with pills. Raid begged her to stay the night at his house, to watch over Duke and make sure nothing bad happened.

One night turned into two, which turned into three.

The truth was, Raid hadn't had to beg too hard. Khloe actually liked being around him, now that he wasn't constantly trying to get a rise out of her. Duke's emergency had definitely brought them closer together.

It was weird to know a person, but not really feel as if you *know* them. Khloe had been around Raid for almost a year, but in the last three days she'd learned that if he didn't have a cup of coffee in the morning (and he drank it black...blech), he was almost completely non-functional.

Watching him with Duke made her heart melt. When he let the dog out in the mornings, Raid walked right by his side no matter how long the bloodhound wanted to remain outdoors. One morning he was gone for forty-five minutes, patiently walking by Duke's side as he sniffed what seemed like every blade of grass in the entire fenced-in three acres. He also sat on the floor by Duke's side as he spoon-fed the dog his mushy wet breakfast.

Raid never lost patience. Never seemed to care about putting Duke's needs ahead of his own. It was a refreshing change from many pet owners Khloe had met over the years. Of course, she'd seen plenty of owners who would do anything for their animals. But she'd also seen way too many who, after hearing how much a surgery would cost, decided to have their pet put down. Or they simply abandoned them. Or they took them home and let them suffer, instead of allowing Khloe to do the surgery needed to save their lives.

Every time Khloe brought up going back to her apartment, Raid nearly panicked. She'd seen it in his eyes. He was scared to death that Duke would have a relapse or that he'd do something to hurt his faithful companion. Khloe didn't have the heart to leave.

So, she'd stayed. She and Raid had eaten together, driven to work together, and stayed up every night talking way past the time she usually went to bed.

But today was the day she was putting her foot down. Duke was fine. Well, not fine, but definitely on the mend. Neither he nor Raiden needed her around anymore.

After work today, she was going back to her apartment. She needed space. Needed to think about what her next steps were going to be. Alan was behind bars, and she should be free to go back to Norfolk. Or she could stay in Fallport. She could be Khloe Watts, DVM, once again. She could open her vet practice and do what she loved.

But a part of her still hesitated. The venom in Alan's voice when he'd told her that she'd pay for ruining his life reverberated in her brain. Just because he was behind bars didn't mean he couldn't still make her life hell. That was why she'd used a false last name and fled to Fallport, which was as far from Norfolk as she could get while staying in Virginia.

Thinking about leaving hurt Khloe's heart. She liked this town. Loved her new friends...even if she hadn't gone out of her way to let them know. She wanted to be there when Finley and Elsie had their babies. Wanted to celebrate with the others when Lilly got pregnant again, and Khloe had no doubt she would. She and Ethan would have the family they craved, she was sure of it.

She wanted to see Heather continue to blossom after a lifetime of hell. And she enjoyed watching Caryn kick butt and take names as she worked with the high school kids.

All-in-all, Khloe loved having a life that was more than going to work every day. As much as she loved being a vet, it had taken over her life in Norfolk. She hadn't taken enough time for herself.

Could she have friends and a life here in Fallport *and* be a veterinarian? She wasn't sure. But she had a feeling if there was anywhere she could do it, it was here.

But what happened when Alan was released? It was inevitable. Would he leave her alone? Would his time in prison knock some sense into him? Would he eventually come to realize that she'd done everything in her power to save his dog?

Somehow, Khloe doubted it. He wouldn't want her to be happy. He'd do whatever it took to make her life miserable—and that included going after those closest to her.

Wasn't that why she'd left Norfolk in the first place? Because of the rumors he'd started about her and the few friends she had? She didn't want to be the reason that kind of ugliness came to Fallport. She couldn't imagine Heather dealing with the nasty things she was sure Alan would spread about her. Or the things he could say or do to the other women who'd befriended Khloe.

And she absolutely couldn't stand the thought of him trying to slander Raid and his friends. She had no doubt they wouldn't care, would ignore whatever was said about them, but she hated the thought of being the one to bring such chaos to their lives.

And that was why she was still hesitating in being completely open with everyone. Telling them everything about herself. Khloe had no doubt they'd support her. Tell her they didn't care what Alan did or said. But *Khloe* cared. Words hurt, no matter how old you were. And her friends had been through enough. They didn't need to deal with whatever bullshit Alan would bring with him on top of everything else they'd survived.

"Khloe?"

She jumped and turned toward the doorway.

"Sorry," Raid said gently. "I didn't mean to startle you."

"It's okay. I was daydreaming. What's up?"

Raid stared at her for a beat, and Khloe had a feeling he knew she was lying. That she wasn't daydreaming, but stressing out about something.

"Instead of sitting on your butt doing nothing, how about you start reshelving the returned books."

It was the kind of thing Khloe was used to Raid saying to her...but the snark was missing. He had a slight smile on his face and his words sounded more teasing than anything else. And instead of responding defensively like she might've just a week ago, she simply nodded and stood.

She went to walk by Raid but he stopped her with a hand on her arm. "Khloe?"

"Yeah?"

"Thank you."

She frowned. "For what? Sitting in here instead of doing my job?" she joked.

But Raid didn't even crack a smile. "No, for staying with us. It's really taken a load off my mind that you've been there, just in case something went wrong with Duke's recovery. But on top of that, I've enjoyed having you around...and I know Duke has too."

Khloe stared at him for a beat before giving him a small smile. "You're welcome." There was so much more she could've said. That she'd enjoyed it too. That he was easy to be around. That she was confused about her feelings toward him.

She could feel his eyes on her after he dropped his hand and she walked down the hall toward the returned books bin. She knew from the past few days that he'd stay in her office with Duke while she was out on the library floor. They'd taken turns, one of them always being in the same room with the still-healing bloodhound.

Khloe's resolve to go back to her apartment after work weakened. If he asked her to stay at his place again, she had a feeling she'd cave without a second thought. After he'd been gracious enough to thank her, and go so far to admit that he enjoyed her company...how could she not?

But there was still a chance that he'd be ready to go back to his normal life. Duke was definitely on the mend. He would be starting back on his regular diet, albeit half the amount, tomorrow. He'd tolerated the soft food he'd been eating without a problem and Khloe had no reason to think he wouldn't do the same with his normal food.

The bottom line was that she *liked* staying with Raid. He was a good man. Quiet and introverted, sure, but he also made her feel comfortable. She could relax around him. And he was someone who could be counted on. Whether that involved the search and rescue team, or his job as a librarian.

Her mind swirling with her thoughts, Khloe did her best to concentrate on the task at hand...namely, putting books back on the shelves in the correct spots. Raid had already logged them all back in, all she had to do was walk around the aisles and return them so someone else could check them out.

There weren't a ton of people in the library at the moment, as it was in the middle of the day. Kids were still in school and many people were at work. But there were some regulars who Khloe made sure to say hello to. The greetings led to questions about how Duke was doing and more thanks to her for saving him.

She was in the history section when Khloe felt someone close behind her. Ever since the incident with Alan, she'd been much more aware of her surroundings. And when the hair on the back of her neck stood up, telling her that someone was near, Khloe turned.

She froze when she saw who was standing there.

She didn't recall the man's name, just that he and another similar-looking man had been in the courthouse every day during Alan's trial. The glares and sneers they constantly shot in her direction had been enough for Khloe to realize that their thoughts about her mirrored their brother's.

"Well, well, well, look who it is," the man said softly.

Khloe's heart began to beat faster and she felt the adrenaline coursing through her veins. He wouldn't do anything to hurt her here, in the middle of the day in a public building...would he? She wasn't sure.

"Remember me? I'm Jason. One of Alan's brothers."

Taking a step back, she lifted her chin and asked, "What are you doing here?"

"Me? I'm looking for a book," the man said.

"You aren't a resident, you can't check anything out," she told him.

"Oh...darn."

They stared at each other for a long ten seconds or so before he said, "Looks like you're doing pretty well for yourself. Unlike my brother, who's currently rotting away in a cell because of you."

"He tried to kill me," Khloe said. She took another step backward, but Jason stepped toward her, not allowing her to put any distance between them. She wanted to run.

Wanted to get to Raid.

It should've been a startling idea, that she thought of Raiden as safety. But she didn't have time to think about it.

"You murdered his dog," Jason sneered.

"I did everything I could. She was too injured," Khloe protested for what seemed like the millionth time. Jason was at the trial. He'd heard everything she'd said about the condition of the hound dog. How desperately she'd tried to stop the internal bleeding, without success.

"Saw a video about you breaking into the vet's place and saving a dog," Jason said in a low, threatening tone. "You think playing hero will endear you to the people around here? It might...in the short term. But wait until they hear all about who you really are, Dr. *Watts*. They'll change their tune fast enough."

Her breathing sped up. This was literally her worst nightmare coming true. She had no idea what Jason was doing here. What his end game was. But he'd obviously found her because of the video of Doctor Ziegler, ranting about her breaking into his clinic.

She braced for Jason to do something. Charge her. Pull out a gun. Hit her.

Instead, all he did was smile and say, "See you around." Then he turned and left her standing there.

It took a full minute for Khloe to be able to move. Just like that awful day, instead of her body going into flight mode when faced with danger, she'd frozen in place instead. Jumping out of the way at the last minute, but not fast enough to avoid getting hit.

Khloe was still standing there, freaking the hell out, when surprisingly, Duke appeared at the end of the aisle and walked toward her. Following close behind him was Raid.

The second her former nemesis saw her, he frowned. Duke's nose nudged her hand and the touch made Khloe's body unfreeze. She fell to her knees and gently wrapped her arms around the bloodhound's neck. She buried her face in his fur and did her best to get control over her emotions and her shaking body.

"Khloe? What the hell's wrong?"

She couldn't speak. Didn't want to admit that her past had caught up to her. If Jason was here, she was fairly certain Alan's other brother was too. They were always together at the trial.

Khloe felt Raid's hand at her elbow. "Come on, stand up, Khloe. I've got you. That's it...hold on to me."

Somehow, Khloe found herself hiding her face in Raid's chest as he led her away from the shelves. She heard him telling people as they passed that she was fine, just felt a little dizzy, and she loved that he was doing his best not to embarrass her as she had her breakdown. He didn't know what was wrong or what happened, and yet he was still doing all he could to take care of her.

It was overwhelming. She hadn't had this kind of support since her dad died.

"Sit," Raid ordered after leading her into his office.

She sat but kept her eyes closed as emotions threatened to overwhelm her. Panic. Embarrassment. Worry. Even her damn leg throbbed. It was as if just seeing someone connected to Alan made her nerves fire up, remembering all the months of rehab she'd had to go through in order to walk again.

Raid didn't speak. Didn't demand she talk to him. Didn't order her to open her eyes. He was simply there. A steady presence. One of his large hands rested on her knee as he crouched in front of her. It wasn't until she heard Duke whine that Khloe managed to open her eyes.

"It's okay, buddy. She's okay. Just getting her bearings," Raid told his dog.

Duke was sitting next to his owner and when he saw her eyes open, he leaned down and nudged her hand insistently.

Obediently, Khloe ran her hand over his head, giving him scratches.

"He led me to you," Raid said quietly. "We were sitting in your office, and all of a sudden his head came up and he got to his feet. He made a beeline for the stacks, which is unusual, since if he needs to pee, he always goes to the back door."

Khloe leaned down and kissed the bloodhound's head. "I'm okay," she whispered. "Thanks for coming to find me."

As if he understood her, Duke licked her cheek, then turned to head back to his dog bed in the corner of the room.

Using her shoulder to wipe the dog slobber off her face, Khloe took a deep breath then looked at Raid. "Sorry about that," she said.

But Raid shook his head and said, "No."

Khloe frowned. "No?"

"Don't do that. You don't want to talk about what happened, fine. Tell me that. But don't pretend that nothing's wrong. Something went down out there. Your heart rate still isn't back to normal and you're breathing way too fast. Your color is off too. I don't know what you saw or who said something to you, but it very definitely freaked you out."

Khloe had always known Raid was observant, but she hadn't realized *how* observant until this moment.

"I...It's a long story," she finally said. And it was. And as she sat there with Raid in front of her, giving her his support, she knew he deserved to know the entire sordid tale. He'd given her a job when she wasn't exactly qualified. He'd let her take two weeks off when she didn't have the leave time saved up, and hadn't asked any questions about why she needed it or where she was going. Even when he was obviously frustrated and irritated with her, he'd never fired her or raised his voice.

These last few days had shown her that he had way more depth than she'd given him credit for. Khloe found that she wanted to tell him everything. Needed to get it off her chest. And with Alan's brother in town, she could no longer put it off.

"Right," he said, looking at his watch. "Can you hang on for another hour? I'll call Cherise and see if she can come in until closing."

Cherise was a part-time library employee who came in when Raid was on search and rescue jobs and when they needed an extra hand. Khloe nodded.

"Okay. Stay here with Duke. I'm going to grab you a Sprite. You don't need any more caffeine in your system to make you any jumpier but the sugar will do you good. I'll get things settled here and we'll head home. I'll make some green chile stew and we can talk. Okay?"

Khloe wanted to protest. Tell him that she needed to go to her own apartment. Hadn't she just made the decision to do that? But the arrival of Alan's brother changed things. What if he was waiting outside to follow her home? What if he tried to run her over when she went out into the parking lot?

Feeling off-kilter, Khloe merely nodded at Raid.

He stared at her for a long moment before saying, "Whatever's going on...you're going to be okay. I'm gonna make sure of it." He stood without giving her a chance to respond.

Then he shocked the shit out of her by leaning over and kissing the top of her head, before turning and striding toward the door.

It wasn't until it shut behind him that Khloe let out the breath she'd been holding.

She hadn't forgotten the kiss he'd given her in the vet clinic, but she'd kind of chalked it up to the emotion of the moment. Figured he'd acted impulsively. But here he was, kissing her again. Even if it was just the top of her head...it was still a very intimate gesture and not something he'd ever done before the other day.

Her world had turned on a dime so quickly. Just last week she was living a fairly boring but safe life. Now she was no longer the assistant librarian who no one knew very well.

There was no way she was going to be able to do any work, and she didn't think Raid expected her to. So she stood, walked over to where Duke was sleeping, and sat next to his head. Being around animals always made her feel better, and hearing his little groan as she began to stroke his head made her relax a fraction. Animals were easy. Their emotions were easy to read and as long as they had affection, they were completely loyal.

She didn't know what Raid's reaction would be to her story, but it was time to tell it. Khloe was tired of hiding. Tired of not being who she was. She was also terrified. Alan had been adamant that she would pay for ruining his life, when in fact she hadn't done anything. It was his own actions that had put him behind bars, but he was too conceited, narcissistic, and too much of a bully to admit it.

Jason being in Fallport didn't bode well. She knew it down to her bones. She needed Raid's help. It wasn't something she liked admitting, but there it was. She'd seen how his teammates and their women had rallied around each other when necessary. Maybe, just maybe, they'd be willing to help her out too. Even though she'd lied to them. Even though she hadn't been there for *them* when she should've been.

Fallport was supposed to be a new start. She wanted to be herself once more. And the only way to do that was to come clean. About everything. She just had to hope Raiden would forgive her for all the things she'd lied about.

CHAPTER SEVEN

Raid was worried.

Khloe wasn't acting like herself. She was usually confident and not afraid to get up in his face and tell him off when he egged her on. But when he'd seen her in the aisle in the library, she'd seemed terrified. Not like the Khloe he'd gotten to know.

Duke had sensed something was wrong and led him straight to her. He had a flash of relief that his dog seemed to be back to his old self, if a little slower than usual, due to his still-healing belly. He didn't even care that his beloved companion was just as enamored with Khloe as the dog was with him—if not more so.

He hated knowing something had freaked her out so badly she was nearly comatose. But he was relieved she seemed willing to talk to him. Finally.

Raid wasn't an idiot. He'd known soon after hiring her that his new assistant was hiding something. He hadn't thought it would take this long for her to talk to him, but his patience was finally paying off.

When he'd gone in to collect her to bring her home, she'd been sitting on the floor next to Duke, absently petting him. She'd gone with him without a word, but he hadn't missed how she'd looked around fearfully as he walked her to his Expedition.

Raid hated that. *Loathed* it. Khloe wasn't the kind of woman who showed fear. At least that he'd seen. He was more and more sure whatever had happened today involved another person. She could've gotten a bad phone call or message, but he didn't think so. She was super jumpy and on alert even as they drove toward his house.

He didn't waste any time getting her inside and made sure to lock the door behind them after they entered. Fallport was as safe a town as he'd ever lived in, but he also knew better than to *not* secure his house. He'd watched too many crime shows where the people being interviewed started out by saying, "So-and-so town was safe, no one locked their doors," and then proceeded to talk about the quadruple murder that happened.

Not only that, but Raid had seen evil up close and personal in the past. No, locking his doors was second nature. And he had a feeling Khloe was about to give him another reason to be security conscious.

"I'll take Duke out before starting dinner," he said after they were inside. He was going to suggest she take the dog out, but didn't think that was a good idea with how nervous she was.

"All right. I think I'll take a shower. Is that okay?"

Raid frowned. Since when had Khloe asked permission to do anything? "Of course."

She nodded and headed for the room she'd been sleeping in.

Raid clenched his teeth. He wanted to go to her. Tell her that whatever was wrong, he'd fix it. But he hadn't earned that right yet.

Somehow over the last few days, Raid realized just how much this woman meant to him. He'd spent just about every day since her first day of work with her, but having her under his roof made his confused feelings about her come into sharp focus.

He liked her snarkiness. Liked her sense of humor. She wasn't afraid to speak her mind. She could tease him just as he teased her back. Not only that, she was smart and obviously a damn good vet. She had compassion toward animals, and just like him, seemed to get along better with pets than people.

It was safe to say Raid felt as if he'd finally found a woman who could take him as he was. Nerdiness and all. But they weren't nearly at a stage in their relationship where he felt comfortable letting her know that he felt more than friendship for her. And now she needed to get whatever she wanted to tell him off her shoulders. He'd listen, offer his support, and they'd go from there.

Thankfully, Duke didn't spend his usual hour outside wandering the property. It was as if the dog understood Khloe needed them, and he did his business quickly before heading back toward the house.

He got settled in his cushy, expensive dog bed in the corner and kept watch on the hallway where Khloe would appear after she was done with her shower. Raid got to work making the green chile stew. It tasted better if it was allowed to simmer for a few hours, but it would still be good even if they ate it right away.

Khloe returned just as the stew finished heating through.

"Can I help?" she asked quietly. She somehow looked more vulnerable with wet hair, wearing a pair of sweats and the long-sleeve T-shirt that was too big for her tiny frame, and her feet in socks.

"I'm about done. Go ahead and sit. What can I get you to drink?"

"Water's fine."

Raid didn't like this subdued Khloe.

Quickly getting their dinner together, Raid made a couple trips to his small table. He sat down across from Khloe and watched as she refused to meet his eyes and focused on the bowl of food.

"It looks good."

"If it's too spicy, I can add some water," Raid told her.

"I'm sure it's fine."

"Khloe."

"Yeah?" But she still didn't look up. Kept her eyes glued to the bowl in front of her as if it held the meaning of life.

"Will you please look at me?"

He watched her take a deep breath, then finally raise her gaze to his.

"Whatever happened today...it's not going to change anything."

"It's going to change *everything*," Khloe returned.

"Okay. Then it's not going to change how I feel about you. It's not going to change how your friends feel either."

She didn't respond, merely sighed.

"Right. Food, then we'll get comfortable, then we'll

talk. Can you tell me one thing? Are you in danger?" Raid asked.

Khloe merely stared at him, the sadness in her eyes nearly his undoing. Raid couldn't stop himself from reaching out. He took her hand in his and squeezed it. "We'll figure it out, okay?"

Khloe pressed her lips together, but she nodded.

Raid wasn't sure he could get anything past the lump in his throat. He didn't like the thought that this woman could be in danger. It pissed him off more than he could've thought possible. He wasn't upset about what she might tell him; he was angry that she was in a position where she had to lie about being a veterinarian and that she was clearly afraid of someone.

It was an odd feeling. Not being angry, but having this kind of visceral reaction over a woman. He was an even-keeled man. Was able to keep his emotions under control in almost any situation. That was part of what made him so good at his job in the Coast Guard.

But the thought of Khloe being in danger made him want to go out and find whoever was responsible and burn them to the ground.

They ate the stew in silence. It wasn't the best batch he'd ever made, but tomorrow, after it had a chance to sit in the fridge overnight, it would be better. Khloe didn't complain. Merely ate without a word.

She helped him carry their dishes to the kitchen when they were done.

"Want to feed Duke for me?"

She nodded, and Raid saw the first glimmer of emotion other than fear and dread on her face. He filled the dishwasher as he watched Khloe feed his dog. The bond between the two was obvious. In any other circumstance, Raid would be jealous. Duke hadn't shown much interest in anyone since he'd brought him home after rescuing him from the side of the road all those years ago.

He went into the living area and sat on the couch, watching Khloe with Duke for a moment before saying softly, "Come here, Khloe."

At first, he didn't think she'd heard him. Or she was ignoring him. But eventually she sighed and stood up from where she was sitting on the floor next to his dog. She looked at him, then at the recliner next to the couch, then back to him.

"Here," he said, patting the cushion next to him.

To his relief, she didn't protest. If she'd needed some space while she told him what had happened in the library, he would've given it to her. But it made him feel good that she chose to sit next to him instead.

She sat, then immediately pulled her legs up so she could hug her knees. It was an extremely defensive position, and Raid hated it. He wanted to pull her into his arms, but he refrained.

"Did someone scare you today?" he asked quietly. "Did they say something offensive to you?"

"I told you earlier that it was a long story, and in order to explain today, I have to go back a few years," Khloe said, staring off into space.

"Okay," Raid agreed immediately.

"As you now know, I'm a veterinarian. It was all I ever wanted to do from the time I was a little girl. I always loved animals, all animals. I drove my dad crazy bringing home stray and hurt critters. I hated zoos growing up, but I loved rehabilitation centers. My idea of a perfect weekend was spending it at the nearest center, helping patch up birds, squirrels, possums, and other wild animals. The staff at the closest place got really used to me being there. Anyway, after high school, I went to college with the goal of becoming a vet."

"And you did it," Raid said when she paused.

"Yeah. I did. Dad was so proud, and I loved what I did. I was a partner in a multi-vet clinic and while I didn't love not being able to make decisions on my own, I did enjoy the camaraderie I had with the others I worked with. Anyway, to move this story along, one day a man came in with his dog. He claimed she got in a fight with another one of his dogs, but it was obvious that wasn't the case.

"She had huge mammary glands, proving that she'd had many litters. She was even still producing milk, which told me she'd given birth not too long ago. The hound looked like a lot of the puppy mill dogs I'd seen. Norfolk isn't exactly puppy mill central, but I had no doubt the man was using the dog to birth as many puppies as possible and was probably selling the dogs to coon hunters around the state and region for top dollar.

"Anyway, this wasn't the first abused dog I'd seen, and I knew it wouldn't be the last. All I could do was my best to help her. But when I examined her closer, I realized that she was in much worse shape than I'd first thought. She was bleeding internally. I didn't say much to her owner before bringing her to the back and prepping her for surgery.

"As far as I can tell, she'd been kicked repeatedly. She had broken rib bones and was bleeding from the head as well. But it was the tear in her spleen that was my main worry at that time. When I opened her up, I knew it was too late. She'd lost too much blood. Not only that, but she had four mammary gland tumors and her uterus was a cancerous mess. The dog had been overbred and neglected in the process. I did the humane thing and ended her pain."

Raid hated hearing the sorrow in Khloe's voice. He reached out and gently pulled her against his side. She let go of her knees and turned into him.

"Death is a part of being a veterinarian. Of course we want to save every animal we see, but that just isn't possible. But having to put down that hound without her ever having known a gentle hand—because I just *knew* she'd suffered every moment of her life—hurt more than usual. After I had control over my emotions, I went out to speak to her owner, who'd refused to leave during the surgery. He was in the waiting room, and when I told him that I hadn't been able to save his dog, he lost it.

"He started screaming at me, telling me I killed his prize bitch and that he'd sue for malpractice. I knew I'd done all I could for the poor baby, and I tried to calm him down. It didn't work. He left absolutely furious and vowing to make me pay.

"I didn't think too much about it, as we always had customers who were upset when their pet died. But he didn't calm down. He called every day and left hateful messages on the clinic's answering service. He sent letters. He posted on social media. In short, he did everything in his power to spread a nasty smear campaign against me.

"I wanted to quit, because I knew the practice was hurting because of everything the man was doing. But my partners were actually very cool and they refused to let me.

Said things would calm down and everyone knew I'd done all I could for the dog."

She stopped speaking again, and Raid dreaded hearing what happened next.

Khloe took a deep breath. "It was about a month or so that he harassed me. He hadn't let up, not even a little, and it was really starting to get to me. I wasn't sleeping well and walking into the clinic every morning almost gave me panic attacks. One night, I was one of the last people to leave because I'd had a surgery that had gone long due to complications. The cat lived, but it had been touch and go for a while. Anyway...I was walking through the parking lot, and the next thing I knew, a huge truck was barreling down on me.

"I threw myself to the side, but I wasn't fast enough. I was struck. The truck ran over my leg. Broke my femur in four places. It took a long time, and a lot of pins, to put it back together. I was in traction for a while and spent a couple of months in a rehab facility learning to walk again."

"Your limp," Raid said as evenly as he could. He was furious on her behalf.

"Yeah. For the most part, I can forget about it, but if I stand for long periods of time it aches. And now I can tell when big storms are coming," she said with a shrug.

Khloe was trying to minimize her injury, but Raid knew it affected her more than she was letting on. "It was him, wasn't it?" he asked.

"Yeah. He'd been waiting for me. He very obviously tried to kill me, was racing toward me head-on, and he probably would've run over me again if one of the vet techs hadn't come out just as he hit me and started screaming. He gunned it and took off, but we both saw who it was."

"What was his name?" Raid asked between clenched teeth.

"Alan Mather."

Raid committed the name to memory. He wasn't a vengeful man...though Lord knew he had reason to be. But even with the incident that was the impetus for him getting out of the Coast Guard, he hadn't felt the need to track someone down and hurt them like he did right now.

"What happened to him?"

"Remember a couple of months ago when I asked for that time off?"

"Yeah. Just before Bristol and Rocky got married, right?"

She nodded. "I had to go to his trial."

"Tell me he was found guilty."

"He was."

Raid sighed in relief, but it was short-lived when she kept talking.

"He's in prison, but he wasn't given a long sentence. And he vowed to make my life as miserable as I'd made his. He has two brothers..."

"Shit," Raid said.

"My last name isn't Moore, it's Watts. I changed it when he was awaiting trial because I was scared of what he might do, since I was obviously the best witness against him. I thought maybe now that he was in jail, I'd be free. I'd even started thinking about opening my own vet clinic again. After what happened to Duke, I thought an emergency clinic in Fallport would be a welcome thing. That way, I wouldn't interfere with Raymond's practice but could fill a needed niche. But after today, I'm thinking that's not a good idea."

"What happened today?" Raid asked. He was thrilled beyond belief that Khloe was thinking about staying, even as he hated what that bastard Alan had done to her.

"You don't care that I lied to you about my name?" she asked, lifting her head to look at him.

"No. You were doing it to protect yourself. Besides, a name doesn't mean shit. It's who a person is inside that matters. And you, Khloe, are a good person down to your little toes."

"I keep thinking about what I could've done differently that might've saved that precious hound," she said.

"No. Don't do that to yourself. Don't let that asshole's words make you doubt your skills. She was too far gone. And you did the kindest thing you could for her...you put her out of her misery. You said she had internal bleeding from her spleen. The asshole obviously kicked her. I'm thinking even if she'd lived, there was no way you would've been able to give her back to him. Which would've made him just as pissed, if not more so."

"Yeah," Khloe agreed.

"So...today?" Raid probed.

She sighed. "Today proved that Alan's not going to give up. His brother Jason came into the library. They found me. Because of that video that went up on social media of Raymond, ranting and raving about me breaking into his clinic."

"What'd he say?"

"Nothing much. He insinuated that when people around here find out who I really am and what happened, they'd turn on me."

Raid couldn't help it. He laughed.

Khloe gave him a hurt look. She tried to stand, but Raid took hold of her arm and pulled her closer.

"Sorry," he said quickly, "but if that asshole thinks he can come to Fallport, spread a few rumors and make everyone turn against you, he's wrong."

"Raid, you don't understand," she said.

"I do," he retorted seriously. And he did. Basically, the abusive asshole who'd tried to kill her was pissed his own actions had put him behind bars and was trying to blame Khloe. He thought he could send his brother to Fallport and ruin her life. He was wrong. "Look, I haven't been here in Fallport all that long myself, only around five years, but I know the townspeople. You saved Duke. You're a hero in his town, Khloe. No one's gonna tolerate some stranger coming in and talking smack about you."

"It's not just him. I'm sure his other brother is here too. The two of them are going to make my life hell."

"Let them try," Raid said stubbornly.

"Raid! Everyone's gonna know what happened! That I lied about my name. They're going to wonder what else I lied about. Like whether I really *did* kill Alan's dog. I need to leave. This time I'll go out of state. Maybe to Seattle. Or LA. I can hide out there. I'll—"

Raid moved without thinking. He lunged toward Khloe until she was flat on her back on the cushions, using his arms to hover over her. He was so much bigger and taller than she was, she stood no chance of fending him off. She stared up at him in shock.

"You aren't going anywhere," he practically growled.

"But—"

"No. Your veterinarian license is in Virginia, right?"

She nodded.

"You aren't leaving. It's a great idea to open up an emergency vet clinic here in Fallport. I admire you for not wanting to disturb Ziegler's practice, but he's an ass. It would do him good to have some competition. Opening an after-hours practice is at least a good start. Fallport's not going to believe some stranger, or two strangers, coming into town and saying bad things about you. They *know* you, Khloe. This isn't Norfolk. It's not the big city. You'll see."

She stared up at him with such cautious hope and fear in her eyes, it was all Raid could do not to get up and go hunt down the asshole who'd threatened her today in what should've been her safe space...her place of employment. *His* library.

"Here's the deal. Full disclosure...I have a stake in wanting you to stay," he said.

"Duke," Khloe said matter-of-factly.

"No. Because I like you." Raid felt stupid saying the words, like some kid with a crush, but he could no longer afford to tiptoe around his feelings. Not when she was talking about leaving. She might not return his interest, but he wasn't getting any younger. All of his friends had found the women meant for them, and he wanted what they had—with Khloe.

Her brows furrowed.

"I haven't done a good job of showing you how much I admire and appreciate you, but I do. I look forward to coming to work every day just because I know *you're* there."

"But...we don't even get along. We snipe at each other all the time."

Raid winced. "Yeah, because I'm an idiot. I liked seeing you get riled up. It made me smile."

Khloe's lips twitched. "So you're saying you were acting like a fifth grader? Pulling my hair and putting a frog down my shirt because you *liked* me?"

Put that way, it sounded completely ridiculous, so Raid simply shrugged.

Khloe's smile faded. "Raid, I can't put you, or Duke, or anyone else in danger. Alan tried to *run me over*. What if his brothers go after our friends to get to me? I don't want to see Lilly hurt. If they go after Heather, it'll be devastating after what she just went through. Or Bristol? She's so tiny, she'd stand no chance against them. And with Finley and Elsie both pregnant, they'd be especially vulnerable. I know Alan; he'll have his brothers dig up dirt on you and the other guys. I couldn't bear to be responsible for everyone else hurting because of me."

"I think you're underestimating our friends. You think Ethan, Zeke, or any of the others will let anything happen to their women? No way in hell. And after all they've been through, the women won't put up with anyone's shit. And Heather's really coming into her own. Tal's given her the strength to stand up for herself. She's already proven she'll do whatever it takes to protect Marissa."

"I can't take the chance," Khloe whispered.

Raid studied her for a long moment before saying, "They'll be able to take care of themselves better if they know what to be on the lookout for. *Who* to look out for."

Khloe closed her eyes and her lip trembled. Raid hated upsetting her, but he *knew* she was strong enough to deal with this. Hell, she'd already survived an attempted murder, had learned to walk again, moved across the state on her own without a support network, kept her veterinarian license up to date, and had saved Duke. She could do anything.

"I know," she whispered finally. "I need to talk to them before they hear any rumors Jason and his brother might spread about me."

Raid nodded.

"They're going to be mad I didn't tell them sooner," she said.

"No, they aren't," Raid said with conviction. "They're going to be worried. And pissed on your behalf...which is way different than being mad at you."

"Raid?"

"Yeah?"

"I like you too," she whispered.

Satisfaction swam through his veins.

"I stayed in Fallport so long because I *also* liked seeing you every day. At first you irritated me, but the more I got to know you and worked with you, I realized that you didn't argue with anyone but me. You kept to yourself and were quiet most of the time. Except with me. I kind've...I liked knowing I could get a rise out of you, as well."

Raid refused to let his mind go to the gutter with that last statement. "So you're staying?"

"For now. But no promises. If Jason and his brother—I can't remember his name for the life of me—make things awful for you or the others, I'm probably going to leave."

"They can try, but we're stronger than you think. I'm going to need to talk to the guys," he warned.

Khloe flinched, but she gave him a small nod.

"And you need to arrange for a girls' night and tell the

others," he continued, pushing his luck. "You can have it here, if you want."

She stared up at him. "Here?"

"Yeah."

"But you never have people here."

Raid shrugged. She was right. He didn't exactly like people in his space. He was an introvert and liked his privacy. "I want you to feel as comfortable as possible. And my place is bigger than your apartment, and Duke is here. Not to mention, it's probably best for you not to be at your place when those asshole brothers are around."

She stared at him for a long moment before giving him a small nod. "Okay."

"Okay," he echoed with satisfaction. "You feel better now that you've gotten that off your chest?" he asked.

Khloe sighed. "Yes. Although it doesn't erase what happened."

"No, it doesn't," Raid agreed. "What happened, happened. You can't change it. All you can do is move forward."

"You sound as if you know what you're talking about," she said.

"I do. And no, tonight isn't the time to talk about it. You've had a long, stressful day. And I know you've still got a lot on your mind. There's a particular incident in my past that I've never talked about with anyone but the person who went through it with me...but if you stick around, I'll tell you."

His words weren't meant to be a bribe in any way, shape, or form. He hoped she didn't take them that way. But he shouldn't have worried. Khloe nodded.

"Raid?"

"Yeah?"

"Are you gonna keep me trapped here all night?"

For a wild moment, he thought about doing just that before sighing and shaking his head. He sat back and moved away so she could swing her legs back over the edge of the couch.

Then Khloe shocked the shit out of him by palming his cheek and leaning into him.

He held his breath, afraid to move, to do anything that would make her move away from him. The feel of her warm palm against his skin felt so foreign. It had been years since he'd been touched in any intimate way.

"Thank you," she whispered. "You don't know how much your support means to me. I hope you don't regret it."

"Never," he vowed. Then put his own hand over hers as he turned his head to kiss her palm. He squeezed her hand and said in a somewhat shaky tone as he tried to gather his composure, "You want to watch that baking competition show?"

She gave him a small smile. "Sure."

Every night she'd been here, they'd watched the show together. Raid loved hearing Khloe's commentary on the ingredients they were given, what the contestants decided to make, and how snarky the judges' comments were.

As they watched the show, Raid memorized the feel of Khloe sitting next to him. She wasn't against his side as he would've liked her to be, but she hadn't moved to the opposite end of the couch or the recliner. He'd also never forget her shy admission that she liked him back. Maybe he wouldn't screw this up and they might have a chance at something together. The chance to be a couple.

No matter what happened, he'd make sure she was free of Alan Mather and his brothers. He was already making plans to search for the court transcripts of the trial and learn as much information as he could about what happened when she was almost killed.

He also intended to find as much dirt as possible on the Mather family—and figure out a way to make Alan understand that Khloe was off-limits. Period.

But for tonight, he was relieved that Khloe was by his side and she'd opened up to him. He hated that she'd gone through so much alone...her rehab, the trial, the stress of fleeing her life in Norfolk. But she was no longer alone. She had him. And their friends. Raid had no doubt when the others found out what Khloe was going through, they'd circle the wagons, so to speak, to protect her. As would the entire town of Fallport.

There had been too much tragedy recently. No one wanted to see anyone else get hurt. Especially by outsiders. Yes, Fallport would step up and protect one of their own, he had no doubt.

CHAPTER EIGHT

It was hard to believe how fast things were happening. A week ago, Khloe could walk around Fallport relatively unnoticed. People were friendly, sure, but they didn't go out of their way to talk to her. Now, she couldn't step into any establishment or walk down the sidewalk without someone wanting to stop and chat. Thank her for saving Duke. Ask her if she was going to open her own vet clinic. It was crazy.

And she couldn't believe she'd finally told Raiden everything about her former life. About what had happened to her. The one thing she couldn't stand was pity. She'd seen the looks all the time when she was in rehab. Everyone in the facility seemed to know what happened to her, that she'd been run over.

But Raid didn't seem to pity her. He was *angry*. Not at her, but at Alan. That reaction was...nice. Which might not make her a decent human being, but she didn't care. It felt good that someone felt the same way she did about everything that had happened. It was crazy that Alan had blamed her for his dog dying. He'd abused her for months, years, and then when she died as a result of his actions, he did his best to shift the blame to Khloe. Even going so far as to try to *kill* her. It was insane.

Khloe would've felt better about finally getting her story off her chest and not having to hide who she was anymore...except she knew Jason and his brother were out there waiting and watching. She had no idea what they had planned, just that it wouldn't be good. It was as if she was constantly waiting for the second shoe to fall. It was stressful, and she hated it.

Today was the day she was getting together with her friends and telling them her story. She didn't want to. Wasn't looking forward to it. But they needed to know. If the Mathers were going to target them in order to get to her, they had a right to understand why.

No matter what Raid said, Khloe wasn't sure telling them they could expect to be harassed as they were walking down the street, that Jason might convince customers to stop patronizing their businesses, that they could very well be in physical danger, wouldn't change how they felt about her.

Of course, things between her and Raid hadn't changed, and she'd warned him that he could be drawn into whatever plans the Mathers had for her. He'd simply shrugged and said he hoped they *did* target him.

But in other ways, things *had* changed. Their relationship was...deeper. It had started when she'd saved Duke. It wasn't as if Khloe thought she'd overly impressed him, it was more that a door had been opened between them. It was hard to believe he wasn't upset in the least that she'd lied. He seemed almost glad she wasn't simply a librarian's assistant.

He'd tried to explain his feelings by saying he'd always thought she was hiding something, and finding out what it was, that she wasn't on the run from the police and wasn't hiding a husband or fourteen children somewhere, was a relief.

Khloe wasn't sure she completely bought his reasoning, but she could admit that she liked how she and Raid were now. A lot. Though, a part of her continued to be reticent around him. Yes, she liked him. But he was still a mystery to her. She might've told him everything about herself, but he hadn't reciprocated yet.

Khloe knew the basics, that he'd been in the Coast Guard as a dog handler, that he'd quit after his dog died, and that he wasn't close with his parents, but that was about it.

No, that wasn't true. She knew he was an introvert who didn't go out of his way to hang out with his friends, yet he was as loyal as anyone she'd ever met, and protective as well.

She knew Raid's house was full of books...science fiction.

He didn't stay up late at night, he didn't have a lot of photographs around, he hovered over Duke—part of his overprotectiveness—and if one of his friends called for help, he'd drop everything to assist.

Okay, maybe she knew more about Raid than she'd first assumed. But his past was still a huge mystery. Much as hers had been up until a week ago, so she'd cut him some slack. But he'd dropped enough hints about whatever happened when he was in the Coast Guard for Khloe to know it wasn't good. That it had messed him up more than he was letting on. That his partner had dealt with whatever happened worse than Raid had.

As much as Khloe wanted to know what happened, she didn't ask. It had only been a week since their relationship had morphed into what it was now and the last thing she wanted to do was push him to remember hurtful things from his past. Also, Raiden had shown all the patience in the world with her; she could do the same for him now.

"You ready?" Raid asked.

Khloe jerked in surprise. Shit. She'd been lost in her head, and now Raid probably thought she was having second thoughts about the evening because she was staring into space. She wasn't. Not telling the other women about the danger they could be in simply by being around her was irresponsible and could get them hurt. No matter how much she hated to have to share what happened, she wouldn't keep it to herself any longer. She couldn't.

"Yes," she told Raid.

They were standing in the kitchen, looking over the piles of groceries on the counter.

"Good. There are plenty of drinks. And snacks. If you guys need anything, all you have to do is give me a yell. I'll be at Rocky and Bristol's place with the guys, Tony, and Marissa."

"I know." And she did. She'd been with Raid when he'd gone overboard at the grocery store. He'd bought more food than she and the other women could eat in a month. There was also enough alcohol to make sure everyone was well and truly hammered.

"You sure you're okay with Duke staying here?" Raid asked.

"He'll be fine," Khloe said. The truth was, she wanted the still-recovering bloodhound at the house as a distraction. If she needed a break, she could always claim she needed to take him outside, or look at his belly, or make up some other excuse to have a moment to herself.

As if Raid knew exactly what she was thinking, his lips twitched.

"What?" she asked a little harsher than she meant to.

"You want to arrange for me to call at a certain time so you can bail?" he quipped.

Khloe's eyes narrowed. "You think you're funny?" she asked, the familiar back-and-forth between them feeling surprisingly good.

His grin widened. "I *am* funny," he said with a shrug.

"Whatever." It was a lame comeback, but Khloe was too happy to be back in a familiar place with Raid to care.

Then he stepped toward her and nudged her with his shoulder.

Khloe pretended his small push sent her flying. She staggered sideways and "caught" herself with a hand on the counter.

Looking up, she expected to see Raid laughing at her—but instead he was reaching for her with a concerned look on his face.

"Shit, Khloe! I didn't mean to hit you so hard. Are you all right? How's your leg? Did you hit the counter with your hip?"

For a moment, Khloe was overwhelmed with his concern. She'd expected him to laugh, to tell her she was a lightweight. To make fun of her size like he'd done in the past. She couldn't deny that his concern felt good. But to hide her feelings, she forced a chuckle past her lips. "Jeez,

Raid, you really think you're that strong? Give me a break."

It took a moment, but the frown on his face slowly morphed into a calculated look.

Khloe didn't have time to brace before he was on her, his fingers digging into her sides. "Ah, she's full of jokes tonight, huh?" he asked as he mercilessly found all her ticklish spots.

"Oh my God! Raid, Stop!" Khloe squealed as she did her best to twist out of his grasp, with no luck. "I'm too ticklish!"

She couldn't stop laughing as he continued to tease her.

When his fingers finally stilled, he didn't let go of her. Khloe looked up to find that he'd backed her into a corner of the kitchen. Raid towered over her, staring with something that looked a lot like awe. And tenderness.

Her heart was beating fast and her own fingers were clutching the short sleeves of the shirt he was wearing. She had to crane her neck to look at him. Khloe had never dated anyone as tall as Raid. When she first met him, she'd thought he was freakishly tall, but now, caged in by him, his large palms on her sides, her head barely reaching his upper chest, she felt...feminine. More feminine than she had in a very long time.

"Raid?" she whispered when he didn't move away from her.

She thought he was going to lean down and kiss her, then he seemed to get control over himself, and he very slowly dropped his hands and stepped back.

"Sorry," he mumbled.

Khloe opened her mouth to ask what he was sorry about, to tell him that even though she wasn't a huge fan of being tickled, she loved his hands on her, when the doorbell rang.

Relief settled over Raiden's face as he turned and headed out of the kitchen.

Understanding hit Khloe then. Raid was smart, snarky, protective, loyal...and shy. Which she knew, of course. Or at least, she'd known he was extremely introverted. But he'd been so open over the last week, she actually forgot.

In all the time she'd known him, she'd never seen him express interest in a woman. He never touched any of his friends' women without their permission. Earlier, when they were shopping, he didn't often meet people's eyes.

And yet with her, he didn't seem to hold back when he had something he wanted to say. He ordered her around at work, had no problem telling her when he thought she was doing something stupid, had been downright chatty since she'd been in his home.

But he rarely ever touched her. Well...rarely before the last week. He'd held her without a second thought after Duke's surgery. He'd let her sit close enough to touch on the couch, while telling her story. He'd reached across the table and touched her hand a time or two. But when a moment turned too intimate, he backed off, looking uncertain.

Khloe knew that if he'd leaned down and kissed her, she would've returned the kiss without hesitation. The longer she spent around the man, the more she was attracted to him. The attraction had been simmering under the surface for months...hidden behind quips and verbal sparring and her attempts to keep her distance from everyone.

But it was slowly dawning on her that if she wanted

anything to happen between her and Raid, she was going to have to be the one to make the first move. The fact that a man as huge and handsome as Raiden could be shy had never occurred to her. But women weren't the only ones who struggled with self-worth. With feeling that they weren't good enough or pretty enough to attract a partner.

Her resolve strengthened. She had no idea what was in her future, but she was more determined than ever to make sure Raid knew what an amazing man he was. How glad she was to have his support for the last week.

Hearing voices, Khloe took a deep breath. Things with Raid would have to wait. She had to get through the evening with her friends first.

She'd just entered the living room when Lilly and Elsie appeared.

Both of them gave her a long, hard hug before letting go and turning to Raid.

"Okay, out. This is now officially a women-only zone," Lilly told him.

Raid smiled. "Right. If I come home to find my walls painted pink and covered in flowers, I'm not gonna be happy."

Khloe chuckled along with the other two women.

"Not happening. But I can't promise our talk about babies, men, and all things female might not seep into the walls and bring some much-needed estrogen to the place," Lilly retorted.

"If you gals need anything, don't hesitate to call," Raid told them.

Elsie rolled her eyes. "As if I haven't heard that a million times already from Zeke," she said.

"Right?" Lilly said with a grin.

"Okay, on that note, I'm leaving," Raid said. But instead of walking toward the front door, he wandered into the living room and crouched down next to Duke's dog bed. The bloodhound hadn't bothered to get up when Elsie and Lilly entered. Khloe knew the dog liked the two women, but apparently his comfy bed was more important at the moment than saying hello to the newcomers.

Raid said something to Duke, scratched his ear for a moment, then stood.

Once again, it struck Khloe how tall the man was. She'd probably always be in awe of his sheer size. He towered over all three of them, and when Bristol was around it was even more comical. But the longer she was around him, the more comfortable she was with his height...and the more irritated she got when people commented on it.

"I'm off," he told them again. "Khloe, can I have a word in private real quick?"

The other two women took the hint and headed for the kitchen. Khloe could hear them oohing and aahing over all the food and drinks that were laid out on the counter.

"What's wrong?" Khloe asked.

"Nothing. I just wanted to let you know I was serious earlier, when I offered to call and give you a reason to bail if you need it. The women are great, and I'd do anything for them, but they can also be overwhelming. You're going to be sharing some pretty personal and emotional history. I know what it's like to need some space. You need me to come up with a reason to get you out of here...let me know."

Lord, this man. He was amazing.

"Thanks. Although I'm not sure how you'll do that when they're all in *your* house."

"I'll think of something," Raid said with a shrug.

"I'll let you know," Khloe told him.

"All right," he sighed. "I know I should go. I'm sure Ethan's getting impatient out there. He's probably got something extra-manly planned. You know, like an obstacle course in the yard or a mock bad-guy house we have to clear. You can take the man out of the SEALs but you can't take the SEAL out of the man."

Khloe giggled at his ridiculousness. "Have fun," she told him.

"Not my idea of fun," Raid said with a shrug.

He definitely wasn't all fired up to go hang out with his friends, and suddenly she felt bad about kicking him out of his own house. It wasn't that he didn't like the other men; he clearly did. He was just wired differently. But he was going anyway...to give her the time and space to do what she needed to do.

"You're gonna talk to the guys tonight, right? About my situation?"

"Yes."

"Are they gonna be upset about me possibly putting their wives in danger? Or girlfriend, in Drew's case?"

"Upset? No. Concerned? Yes. Pissed way the hell off that anyone would dare hurt you, would come into *our* town and try to insult your good name? Hell yes. You have nothing to worry about, Khloe. Promise."

"Okay," she whispered, feeling overwhelmed.

They stared at each other for a moment and just when Khloe was about to take a step forward to give him a hug

—a hug she desperately needed—there was another knock on the door.

"That'll be the rest of the girls," Raid said reluctantly. "Don't hesitate to text me," he ordered, before turning to the door.

Bristol, Caryn, Finley, and Heather were at the door, as he'd guessed. They all entered in a whirlwind, greeting her and Raid as they passed.

"It'll be fine, Khloe. You've got this," Raid said before lifting his chin at her and heading out the door. He was getting a ride to Rocky's house with Ethan, since he'd dropped Lilly off and would be coming back for her later. In fact, most of the men had dropped their women off, and Khloe watched as the caravan of vehicles pulled away from the house and headed down the driveway. The only one she didn't see was Rocky, so Bristol had obviously gotten a ride from one of the others.

She closed the door slowly and took a deep breath before heading back toward the kitchen. Like Raid, she wasn't exactly looking forward to the night, but it would also feel good to finally get everything off her chest with the people she admired most.

CHAPTER NINE

Three hours later, Khloe and the rest of the women were all sitting around Raid's living room. Lilly, Elsie, and Heather were sprawled on the couch. Finley was in the recliner, Khloe was sitting on the floor next to Duke, and Bristol and Caryn were on the floor in front of the couch, sitting on pillows they'd pilfered from one of the guest rooms.

Surprisingly, no one was drinking any of the alcohol Raid had picked up. Elsie and Finley were pregnant, Heather wasn't much of a drinker at all because she didn't like the taste, Khloe was too nervous and knew it wasn't a good idea to get hammered before telling her story, Caryn had to get up early the next morning to work out with the high school kids in the firefighter program she'd started. Lilly claimed she wasn't in the mood, and Bristol said she was hoping to finish a stained-glass project the next day and didn't want to be hungover while she did it.

But they'd eaten a ton of snacks—Raid hadn't over-shopped quite as much as she'd thought—fussed over

Duke, explored the three-acre backyard, taken a tour of Raid's house because everyone was *extremely* curious, since they'd never been there before, eaten *more* snacks, watched an episode of a baking competition show, and everyone had taken a turn talking about what was going on in their lives.

And now it was Khloe's turn.

The other six women all looked at her expectantly. Khloe stared down at Duke, who was snoring in the bed next to her. She'd agreed to do this, but now that it was time, she wasn't sure where to start.

"So...you're a vet. How long?" Lilly asked, breaking the ice with an easy question.

Khloe took a deep breath and reached down deep for the courage to face her friends. "Well, I'm forty-three, and I graduated from vet school when I was around twenty-six. So about fifteen years. Not including the last year and a half or so here, of course."

"Right. When you came to Fallport and became Raid's assistant at the library," Bristol said.

Khloe nodded.

"Why?" Caryn asked.

And there it was. The opening Khloe needed to tell her story. But for some reason, the words were stuck in her throat.

As the pause lengthened, Finley began squirming and wriggling, struggling to get out of the recliner. With her growing baby belly, and the fact that the recliner was laid back, she was having more than a little trouble. "Oh, Lord, I'm stuck in the chair! Someone help me."

Everyone giggled, and Caryn walked over to her on her knees. "Why are you getting up anyway? Things are about to get good!" she exclaimed as she tried to find the lever that would put the leg rest down.

"I want to give Khloe a hug. She's all the way over there, and she looks completely freaked out about this conversation."

Six pairs of eyes swung back around and focused on Khloe.

On one hand, it made her uncomfortable. She never liked being in the spotlight. She much preferred being behind closed doors with animals who couldn't judge her. But these were her friends. Women who'd tried very, very hard to include her in their lives. And the fact Finley wanted to give her physical support made Khloe's reticence fade away.

"Stay there, Fin. I'm okay," Khloe told her. "Seriously, if you get up, I'm just gonna push you back into the chair," she said when her friend didn't stop trying to sit up.

Finley let out a frustrated breath. "Fine. But only because I think this chair is trying to swallow me whole. I don't understand how Raid can sit here."

"Because he's over a foot taller than you and it's obviously made for someone his size," Elsie said dryly.

"True," Finley said.

"I came to Fallport because it was as far from Norfolk as I could get and still stay in Virginia," Khloe blurted. "My last name isn't Moore, it's Watts. I left my vet practice and everything I knew because one of my clients tried to kill me when I couldn't save the dog he brought in after abusing her for years."

Silence met her outburst for a heartbeat—before everyone started talking at once.

"Oh my God, are you all right?"

"What an asshole!"

"I hope he's in jail!"

"He brought you a dog *he* abused and expected you to save it?"

"Who cares about your last name? Are you okay?"

"That's why you limp, isn't it?"

Khloe held up a hand to stop the onslaught. She did her best to answer her friends' questions. "I'm okay...now. And yes, he's in jail, and yes, I think he hoped I wouldn't figure out he'd been the one to kick his dog hard enough to break her ribs and rupture her spleen. And *also* yes—his attempt to run me over with his truck is the reason why I limp."

Six pairs of eyes widened at her answers.

"Right, okay, you need to start from the beginning," Caryn insisted.

Taking a deep breath, Khloe did just that. The more she talked, the easier it got. It helped that her friends weren't staring at her with contempt or anger at her deception.

"The trial took longer than everyone thought, which was why I was gone so long when you were looking after the kittens, Finley. I'm so sorry I put you in the position to get in the middle of that bitch's drug deals."

Finley shrugged. "It's not your fault. I just wish you'd said something. You know we would've been there with you. At your side, giving you support."

"Yeah, I can't believe you testified without having anyone with you," Elsie said.

Her friends continued to support her. Tell her how strong she was. How impressed they were with how she'd handled everything.

"I think it was a miracle you were in the right place at the right time when Duke needed you," Heather said quietly. "I used to wonder why me. Why *I'd* been the one kidnapped. Why I'd had to go through everything that I did. But if I hadn't, if I'd grown up a normal kid in a normal life, I wouldn't have been able to save Marissa. I wouldn't have met Tal. I wouldn't have the life I have now. So, I'm sorry you had to go through all that, but you're here now. We met you as a result. And you saved Duke. And who knows how many other lives you've saved as a result of Duke not dying? He'll recover and be able to go out on many more searches because you were there at just the right time when he got sick."

The room was quiet after Heather's comments.

"She's right," Finley said with a nod.

"She is," Lilly agreed. "So why now?"

"Why now what?" Khloe asked.

"Why are you telling us now? I mean, don't get me wrong, I'm pleased and thankful you're finally opening up to us. We could all tell you were hiding something pretty heavy, but what changed?"

This was it. The moment Khloe could lose these amazing women forever. They could walk out of her life and she wouldn't blame them. They'd each been through their own versions of hell and it wasn't fair for Khloe's past to threaten them once more. But they had a right to know. She had an obligation to tell them.

"The guy who tried to kill me, his name is Alan Mather. He's in jail, hopefully for a long time. But he's not happy, to say the least. He vowed to make my life hell. And it seems he's living up to his word. His brothers are here. Well, I'm assuming they both are, but I've only seen one.

Jason came into the library the other day and took great delight in telling me he was here to basically continue the harassment his brother started back in Norfolk.

"If he sees you guys with me, he'll do what he can to make your lives miserable too. He'll spread rumors about you, about your businesses. Alan and his brothers are masters at smear campaigns. They nearly wrecked my business in Norfolk. They'll tell lies, show up where you least expect them, say vile things, and there won't be anything you can do about it. Believe me, I did what I could to get them to stop back home...but it was no use. They never did anything illegal, so there was nothing the police could do."

"Nothing illegal?" Caryn fumed. "I think intimidating a witness is illegal!"

"Right?" Bristol added, sounding just as mad. "That's bullshit!"

"I'd like to see them try to spread rumors about my bakery," Finley added. "No one is gonna believe anything they say."

"Exactly," Lilly said with a nod. "As if the people of Fallport are going to believe a stranger when he says shit about us."

"And let's not forget what our guys are gonna do if they hear even a whiff of lies about us or our businesses," Finley added.

"Oh, man, this Jason guy is gonna be in a for a rude awakening the first time he dares say something about me," Caryn said with a low chuckle.

"You guys," Khloe said desperately. "You don't understand. You could be in danger. Alan tried to kill me over a dog! He hates me more than anything in the world. And

I'm sure he's passed that anger to his brothers. If they're here, bad things are going to happen. You'll have to constantly be looking over your shoulders, all the time. This is why I didn't want anyone to know who I was. Why I used a fake last name so they couldn't find me. But thanks to that video of Ziegler, they have, and the last thing I want is for any of you to be hurt because of me!"

Khloe was practically panting by the time she finished speaking. Duke whined and scooted closer, resting his heavy head in her lap.

One by one, the six women got up from their seats and came over to where Khloe was sitting against the wall. They crowded closer, standing and kneeling around her. Caryn's hand was on her shoulder, Lilly's on one knee, Bristol's on the other.

It was Heather who spoke first. "All my life, I've wanted friends. Wanted someone I could confide in. Someone I could trust. At first, that was Tal. I wasn't sure I could trust anyone else. But I realized after a while that you guys were nothing like the women I knew growing up in The Community. You had no ulterior motives. You wanted the best for me without strings. I'd never had that, and it was scary at first, but now I can't imagine being anywhere else. I can't lie and say I'll enjoy if this Jason guy or his brother says mean things about me...but I trust Tal, and all of you and your men, to keep me safe. I think you should trust everyone too, Khloe."

In some ways, Heather was like a child. She'd missed out on so much while trapped for years with what was basically a cult, and there were so many things in today's world that were new to her. But other times she was like the wisest old soul Khloe had ever met. She had a unique perspective on the world.

"Those assholes aren't going to succeed in whatever they have planned," Lilly said firmly. "This isn't Norfolk. People around here love you, Khloe."

"Yeah, they liked you before the Duke thing, but now? You're a Fallportian through and through," Elsie said.

"A Fallportian?" Caryn asked with a chuckle. "That sounds like we're aliens or something."

Elsie shrugged. "Whatever. My point is that the second they start talking smack, they're gonna learn that their words have no power here."

"You don't know that," Khloe said softly. "I should probably leave again."

"No!" everyone shouted at once, making Duke lift his head and give a half-heated growl.

"See? Even Duke doesn't want that," Finley said. "Look, we get it. Knowing someone is out there who wants bad things for you isn't fun. We've all been there. But with us at your back, they aren't going to succeed."

All of a sudden, Khloe's eyes filled with tears. She hadn't expected this. She'd lied to these women, kept them at arm's length for months, and yet they were offering their unconditional support. It was overwhelming.

"Okay, guys, give her some space," Lilly ordered. Everyone scooted back and headed back to their chairs except for Lilly. She sat on the floor with her back against the wall and her shoulder touching Khloe's.

"Right, so...we need a plan," she said.

"A plan?" Khloe asked, wiping her cheek with her shoulder as she did her best to get control over her emotions.

"Yup. What does this Jason guy look like?"

Khloe swallowed. "He's around thirty, and his brother is in his mid-twenties. They have brown hair and brown eyes. Jason's hair is cut short and his brother's is longer and kind of shaggy. I've never seen them in anything but jeans and long-sleeve flannel shirts without jackets. Even in court, when they attended the trial every day to glare at me. Jason is tall, probably around six feet, while his brother is a few inches shorter. They're...normal-looking. They don't really stand out in a crowd at all. Which I think is why they were so good at spreading rumors back home."

"I can't find either one on social media," Lilly said, phone in hand.

"Really? But they saw the Ziegler video. And everyone's got *some* sort of account," Finley insisted.

"Apparently not them. Or maybe they deleted them for some reason," Lilly said with a shrug.

"What do they drive?" Caryn asked.

Khloe shook her head. "I don't know."

"It's okay, that's easy enough to find out," Lilly soothed.

"You guys, I don't think we should underestimate them. Again, their brother tried to *kill* me."

"Asshole," Finley muttered.

"We just need to spread the word that they're here and up to no good before they can start with their shit," Elsie said. "And I can start at On the Rocks."

"And I'll talk to my grandfather," Caryn said. "He'll tell Silas and Otto and it'll be all over Fallport in hours as a result."

"No!" Khloe said, feeling panicky over the idea of everyone talking about her.

Lilly put a hand on her knee. "It's okay, Khloe."

"No, it *isn't*. I lied! To everyone! It's bad enough they know I used to be a vet, but if they know the whole story..." Her voice trailed off and she struggled to find the words to explain why she was so freaked out.

"Breathe, Khloe," Lilly told her gently. "You're allowed to change careers. And you didn't lie to anyone. You just didn't tell them what you used to do. Which is cool, because it's no one's business but your own. You think everyone around here has never worked in a different industry? It's fine. *You're* fine."

Khloe took a deep breath and swallowed hard. Her friend was right, but she still felt like she betrayed the whole town somehow.

"Have you talked to Simon?" Heather asked.

Khloe shook her head.

"What about our guys?" Bristol asked.

"Raid's talking to them tonight."

Everyone nodded as if that made sense.

"Look, I know you don't want everyone knowing your business, but this is Fallport. It's only a matter of time anyway. You think people haven't already done internet searches to try to find out more about you? You think they haven't already started to make their own conclusions about why you're here? Information is power. And we need to make sure they hear all about how amazing and strong you are. How you survived someone trying to *run you freaking over*. How you were alone and still persevered through your recovery. How you made a new life in Fallport and how much you love it here," Lilly said.

"And I'm sure it wouldn't hurt if we insinuated that she's thinking about staying, and maybe even opening her own vet practice…but if these brothers make her life too miserable, she might change her mind," Caryn said with a grin.

"Wait, I don't—"

"Oh yeah, I've heard tons of people grumbling about Doctor Ziegler," Finley agreed. "That video did him no favors. If they think the chance for a new vet will fall through if these assholes succeed in spreading their vicious gossip, they'll definitely step up."

"Seriously, you guys, I haven't decided about anything and—"

"No social media," Lilly insisted. "This all needs to be word of mouth."

"I agree," Elsie said. "That way, no one will know where the talk started and there can't be any trail to Khloe or us."

"The brothers will assume Khloe said something," Finley warned.

"So? They can't prove anything," Lilly insisted.

"You need to talk to Simon too," Caryn said. "And maybe even have Nissi get in touch with the prosecuting attorney back in Norfolk. They can have your back, just in case these brothers do anything that crosses a line."

Khloe couldn't speak. She was too overwhelmed.

"Simon's nice," Heather told her, mistaking her silence for fear. "I was scared of him too, but he listened to everything I had to say and didn't judge me. At least I don't think he did."

"He didn't," Elsie reassured her. "He's a great police chief. He really cares about the people in this town."

"And he's not going to be happy if someone starts spreading malicious rumors about any of his constituents," Caryn said.

Khloe let out a huge breath and said simply, "Okay."

The women stared at her in silence for a beat.

"Okay?" Lilly finally confirmed.

Khloe nodded.

Everyone let out a whoop of joy...except for Heather, who merely smiled.

"Okay, operation Kick Assholes' Butts starts tomorrow," Caryn said.

"This is gonna be fun." Elsie grinned.

Khloe could only shake her head in exasperation. How she'd gone from thinking these women were gonna turn their backs on her to them hoisting pitchforks and thumbing their noses at the potential danger of the Mather brothers was beyond her.

"You need to be careful," she warned. "If Jason or his brother...shoot, I *still* can't think of his name...it they get wind of what's happening, they'll be even more pissed than they probably are right now."

"We can handle them. Well, our guys can," Bristol said with a shrug.

"It'll probably be even more fun for *them*," Elsie agreed.

"And don't even think about hiding out and not spending time with us in public," Finley ordered.

"Yeah, there's no escaping us now," Caryn added with a grin.

"As if you guys would let me stay to myself now," Khloe grumbled.

"Damn straight. You're stuck with us," Elsie agreed.

"Now...can we change the subject?" Lilly asked. "Because I want to talk about Raiden and Khloe."

Everyone enthusiastically agreed.

Khloe looked at her watch. "Oh, look at the time. It's getting late."

"Ha, it's never too late to talk about the people we love the most. What's up with you two? The last we knew, you acted like you hated each other," Lilly said with a friendly smile. "You were always picking on each other, and there were times we thought one of you was going to self-combust. But tonight he looked worried, and I thought for a second he wasn't going to leave. What's up, sister?"

Khloe's face was hot with a blush, and she shrugged.

"Come on, we need more than that," Bristol begged, sitting forward on her pillow in front of the couch.

But Khloe wasn't ready to talk about whatever the hell was going on with her and Raiden. Partly because she wasn't sure herself, and everything was way too new to put into words. But also because of how introverted Raiden was. She knew without having to think about it that he wouldn't be comfortable being gossiped about. And while these women would never maliciously do or say anything to hurt him, it would still be awkward if he was aware he was the subject of their curiosity.

"He's very thankful I was there to help Duke," Khloe said diplomatically.

The others rolled their eyes.

"And?" Finley pushed.

"And he's been a good friend this past week," Khloe added, hoping that would be the end of the discussion. But she underestimated her friends' need to know. Need for those they loved to be as happy as they were.

"Raid's a good man," Bristol said.

"Very good," Caryn agreed with a nod.

"He's always willing to help out with a search, no

matter what time it is or what the weather's like," Elsie added.

"And he buys way more than he could ever eat at the bakery, just to support me," Finley threw in.

"He's really tall," Heather said with a small smile.

Khloe couldn't help but laugh at that. "He is," she agreed.

"He's adorable, really," Lilly said quietly. "I've always thought so. He's quiet, and that red hair and beard make me think of a lumberjack."

"And you know what they say...big feet, big...um...you know," Caryn said with a smirk.

And with that, Khloe was done. It was one thing for them to extol Raid's good qualities, but she didn't want anyone thinking about Raid's crotch or talking about how good-looking he was. She was aware that jealousy was rearing its ugly head, but she couldn't help it.

Thankfully, Duke chose that moment to get to his feet with a groan and pad over to the back door.

"Gotta let him out," Khloe murmured as she stood.

The other women began to talk amongst themselves as Khloe opened the door. All but Lilly, who followed her. She stood on the back deck with Khloe as they watched Duke attempt to find the perfect place to use the bathroom.

"You okay?" Lilly asked quietly.

Surprisingly, Khloe found that she was. The night could've gone a lot differently. And while she was still not thrilled with the entire town knowing everything about her, the alternative was that she had to leave and hide out again. She liked Fallport. Liked her friends. Liked Raid. She didn't want to leave. "Yeah, I think I am."

"Good. Because you know if you told us that you really didn't want us to tell anyone about what happened to you, we wouldn't. We'd find some other way to deal with these jerks."

"I appreciate it."

"Of course. It's what friends do."

"How are *you*?" Khloe asked, turning to Lilly. She was more than ready to talk about anything other than herself for a while.

"I'm fine."

"No, Lilly, how *are* you?"

She sighed. "I'm hanging in there. I have days where it's hard to get out of bed and I want nothing more than to sleep the entire day away."

"I think that's normal after a miscarriage," Khloe said.

"I know. But it sucks."

"Yeah."

Lilly straightened. "But Ethan and I aren't giving up. We're going to try to have another baby."

"Of course you are," Khloe told her. "And when you get pregnant, Ethan's going to be overprotective and you'll get pissed at him for not letting you take a step outside the house without him hovering. You'll get sick of him fixing you healthy meals and treating you as if you're made of glass. You'll bitch to us about it, and we'll remind you how much he loves and worries about you. Then you'll have your child and he'll knock you up again. Then again and again, until you have fourteen kids and you can't remember a time when it was only the two of you. You'll both rope all of us into babysitting, and we'll bitch and moan about toddlers and pre-teens and teenagers and you'll live happily ever after."

Lilly stared at her incredulously for a beat before bursting out laughing. "Oh my God, fourteen kids? No way!"

Khloe smiled at her and put a hand on her shoulder. "But you'll never forget the baby you lost. She or he was special and deserves to be celebrated and remembered year after year."

"Yeah. Thanks," Lilly said. Then she turned and hugged Khloe hard. "I'm glad you're here, Khloe Watts."

Hearing her real name on her friend's lips made Khloe feel warm and fuzzy inside. "Thanks. I'm glad I'm here too."

Duke wandered back up on the deck, apparently having finished doing his business, and they all went inside together.

The other women had dived back into the snacks yet again, and someone had turned the TV on and another episode of the baking competition was playing. Khloe settled back down on the floor, this time on a pillow in front of the couch next to the others.

Happiness and contentment filled her, and she realized it was the first time in ages that she wasn't worried about the future. Wasn't worried about a trial, her leg, or what others thought about her. She felt as if she was in a cocoon, safe and protected in Raid's house. She had no idea what the future would bring, but she couldn't help but hope it involved her with her own practice once again... and maybe it would also include Raiden in some way.

CHAPTER TEN

A week had passed since Khloe had her girls' night, and since Raiden had told his friends all about what was going on with her. They weren't happy—which was an understatement. And they'd vowed to do whatever it took to keep Khloe safe.

It shouldn't have surprised Raid that his friends had immediately asked a million questions about Khloe's safety instead of concentrating on the possible threat to their own women. Talk had definitely turned to that, but first, they wanted to discuss how to help Khloe.

It was no wonder Raid enjoyed being in Fallport and working with these men. They reminded him of Finn Matlick, a man he'd worked with in the Coast Guard. Raid and Tonka, as he went by, had partnered together more often than not. Their dogs were just as close. They worked like a well-oiled machine...until that awful day.

Forcing himself to think about something other than his old friend, Raid watched Khloe from behind the circulation counter at the library. She was helping a woman find appropriate books for her teenage daughter.

He could tell she'd been on edge and worried since the day of Jason Mather's visit. The waiting was almost worse than just dealing with whatever the Mather brothers might have planned. And after some research of his own, Raid had no doubt they weren't going to leave Khloe alone without some encouragement. That was where he came in.

Raid had already contacted a few people he knew from his time in the military who might be able to help. Not only that, but Ethan said he knew a man named Tex, a fellow former SEAL, who was an expert at all things electronic. He could apparently destroy the brothers with a few strokes of his keyboard. There was also a guy out in Colorado who was happy to help, as well. His specialty was sex trafficking, but he knew an awful lot of people, pretty much everywhere.

Raid wanted to make sure Alan Mather got the message that he should forget Khloe, do his time, and move on with his life. If he didn't? Well, that would be his biggest mistake.

But the more immediate concern was Jason and Scott... that was the youngest brother's name. He was definitely here in Fallport, as well. Drew had reported seeing the man the other day. He'd been casing the square and watching the comings and goings.

The ladies had come away from their girls' night with Khloe all fired up and ready to do what they could to make sure the people of Fallport knew what was going on. And so far, their plan to spread information around town about Khloe and her situation had worked like a charm. Almost everyone who came into the library made a beeline for

Khloe and commiserated with her about what she'd been through. They'd made it more than clear that anyone who caused trouble for one of their own would rue the day.

It would've been funny if the situation hadn't been about Khloe. Raid could see the toll the situation was taking on her. She hated being talked about. Hated being the center of attention. She didn't like people pitying her about her leg and wanting details about what happened.

Raid had no pity for Khloe. How could he? She was one of the strongest women he'd ever met. He'd read the court documents word for word. Could envision how hard she'd fought to learn to walk again, and how hard the entire ordeal had been for her. He didn't have audio of the trial, but from the transcripts, he knew the judge had been concerned when Khloe talked about walking away from her vet clinic and everything she'd worked so hard to accomplish.

The more Raid learned about Khloe, the more he liked her. But he had no idea how to move their relationship forward. He'd been her boss for so long, and had acted more like an annoying big brother than a man who might have romantic feelings, that he was clueless about how to make her see him in a different light.

She'd insisted on going back to her apartment, which did *not* make Raid happy. He couldn't help but worry about Jason or Scott cornering her there. About what they might do when she was alone. So he insisted on picking her up in the mornings and taking her home at the end of the day.

It also made him feel just a little better that their friends were taking turns spending the evenings with her.

One night, Lilly and Ethan had brought pizza and stayed until past eleven. Another evening, Finley and

Brock had arrived with the ingredients to make cookies. Heather and Tal had shown up the next night to visit. And so it went.

Raid didn't resent his friends for getting one-on-one time with Khloe...but he *was* jealous. Yes, he had the entire day to be around her, but it wasn't the same as it had been when they were alone in his house.

And that was another thing. Now his house, which used to be his sanctuary, felt too empty. Raiden had a feeling Duke felt the same way. The bloodhound was restless, and more often than not preferred to sleep in the guest room on the bed Khloe had used.

Raid missed her. And as someone who enjoyed his own company and had no problem entertaining himself, that was saying something.

Today was Friday, and Raid knew Caryn and Drew were going to go to Khloe's apartment and bring a movie. He would've asked if she wanted to come hang out with him and Duke, but he had plans for that evening. Every Friday night he did the same thing...as long as he wasn't on a search.

But first thing Saturday, he was going to get up the nerve to see if Khloe wanted to hang out. Maybe she'd want to go with him and Duke as they took a walk in the woods. Duke had healed enough to start some short hikes. He needed to start his scent-tracking training once more.

"Raid?"

Her voice startled Raid enough that he jerked. He'd been lost in his head, and obviously Khloe was finished with helping the woman.

"Sorry, yeah?"

"Are you okay?"

147

He wanted to snort. He should be asking *her* that.

"Of course. Are you?"

"Yeah. I just...I hate the waiting thing. I saw Jason out in The Circle this morning. He was just sitting in the gazebo. He wanted me to know he was there. I wish they'd just do whatever it is they're going to do already."

"Yeah. But their waiting and watching works in our favor. By now, most of the townspeople know about them *and* their intentions. When they do decide to strike, they're going to be in for a rude awakening."

Khloe nodded, but Raid could tell she wasn't so sure about that. She'd see. Raid had no doubt Fallport would come through for her in typical small-town style.

"I wanted to ask you something," Khloe said then. She was leaning against the desk, and he thought she looked especially good. Instead of being pulled back, her silky light brown hair was loose around her shoulders. She wore an entirely appropriate blue blouse that buttoned up the front and a pair of tan slacks. But the shirt framed her chest just right, making Raid's mouth water, and the pants hugged her gorgeous ass. He swore every time he saw her, she got prettier.

When she raised a brow in question, Raid mentally smacked himself upside the head. "Yeah? Shoot," he said belatedly.

Then she shocked the shit out of him by saying, "I was wondering if you'd want to come up when you took me home today. I know Caryn and Drew were going to come over with a movie, but I'm not sure I'm up to entertaining anyone tonight. So I thought maybe the two of us—well, three, including Duke—could hang out and watch some more of those baking shows we started when I stayed with you."

Raid stared at her for a long moment. Shit, was she asking him out? He wanted to say yes. So damn bad. But he couldn't miss his Friday night thing for a second week in a row.

He was also shocked and thrilled she'd had the nerve to ask him for a date. She was much braver than he was. Hell, *everyone* was braver than him when it came to relationship stuff.

He was obviously quiet too long, because her gaze dropped and she looked at the floor while saying, "Sorry, it was a stupid idea. I'm sure you're busy. Not a big deal."

But it *was* a big deal, and the last thing Raid wanted was for Khloe to feel awkward or stupid about asking him out. He stood up so fast his chair almost crashed to the floor behind him. He strode around the desk and stood in front of her. He didn't know what to do with his hands. If he should touch her or what. He was also well aware they were at work and there were people milling around in the library.

He settled for reaching for her hand. He held it tightly as he willed her to look up at him. "It's not that I don't want to spend the evening with you," he told her. "I *do.* Shit, I've missed not having you in my house this past week. It's just...I have something I have to do tonight."

"It's okay. I understand."

"I doubt it. But can I have a rain check? I was going to ask if you wanted to come with me and Duke to walk the Fallport Creek Trail tomorrow. I know it's super easy, only a mile, but you said it would be okay to start Duke training again, so I thought since it's supposed to be nice out, not too cold, it would be good to get outside. Then maybe after we can go grab something to eat at the diner, and go see Finley, and if you wanted, you could come back to my place and we could hang out and watch some of those shows."

He was babbling, but Raid couldn't help it. He'd never been good at this kind of thing, asking women out.

"That sounds good. Duke's healing really well and it'll do him good to get out. He's been a bit restless lately."

Raid let out the breath he'd been holding.

"You have a hot date tonight?" she asked, and the tension Raid had just released returned.

"What? No!" he said a little too loudly. He definitely didn't want her to think he was dating someone other than her.

She chuckled. "I was kidding," she told him with a small smile. "But now I'm curious."

Shit, he wasn't ready for Khloe to know what he did on Friday nights. Not this early in their relationship. Eventually, yes, but not yet. He tried to think of something to say that would assuage her curiosity, but didn't want to lie to her either.

She let him off the hook by saying, "I'm gonna go and see if I can get the books that were returned this morning logged in and back on the shelves before it's time to leave. Anything else you need me to do?"

"No, I don't think so."

"Okay. Raid?"

"Yeah?"

"You need to let go of my hand so I can do that."

Jeez, Raid hadn't even realized he was still holding onto her. It felt so good and natural to have her hand in his. He quickly loosened his fingers, and she squeezed him once more before she dropped her hand and turned to go.

He stared after her for a long moment.

He was an idiot. It was no wonder he was still single. He was so awkward around women he liked. Always had been. He *was* like the fifth-grade boy Khloe had accused him of being, picking on the girl because he knew no other way to let her know he liked her.

Shaking his head at himself, Raid went back behind the circulation desk and sat. He couldn't see Khloe. She'd opted to pull the return cart to one of the library computer stations behind him. But he could feel her nonetheless.

Seeing movement from the corner of his eye, Raid looked up and saw none other than Jason Mather strolling through the library. He didn't try to get his or Khloe's attention, but it was obvious he was proud of himself just for being there. He had a smirk on his face as he walked the aisles. Raid saw him wave, so he knew Khloe had looked up and seen him.

Raid stood but Jason didn't stop, he kept on walking and headed toward the door that faced the square.

"Cocky son-of-a-bitch," Raid muttered. He had a feeling the two brothers were done skulking around and were about to put their plan in motion...whatever that was. He didn't think they were here to physically hurt Khloe. But then again, he wouldn't have thought anyone would've been crazy enough to try to run Khloe down in a parking lot either, and look what Alan had done.

He gave it a minute, and when Khloe didn't come back to the circulation desk completely freaked out, he took a deep breath. His Khloe was stronger than Jason thought.

Raid himself didn't freak out about the *his* thing. He'd waited long enough. Starting tomorrow, he was going to do whatever he could to make sure Khloe knew he was interested in her as more than a friend. More than an employee.

* * *

Khloe waved at Raiden from her front door and watched as he gave her a chin lift in return and pulled out of the parking lot at her apartment. She slowly closed and locked her door, then walked the few steps required to drop onto her couch with a sigh. She'd gone from thinking about him as her annoying boss, to the man she wanted more than she wanted her next breath, and she didn't even know how it was possible to change so quickly.

She supposed it was the way he supported her unconditionally. How he'd glare at anyone who stared at her a beat too long. How he couldn't seem to take his eyes off her.

In the past, if a man had done those last two things, she would've been more than irritated. She would've accused him of being overprotective and told him to knock it off. She was more than capable of taking care of herself. And she'd never appreciated a man focusing solely on her ass and boobs.

But Raid looked at her with longing instead of lust. As if he was admiring from afar something he knew he'd never have. His looks were appreciative and oddly respectful...if someone staring at her chest could be considered respectful.

She'd decided today to take the bull by the horns, so to speak, and ask him out since it was obvious he wasn't going to make the first move. It was mortifying when he'd turned her down. For a second, she thought she'd misread everything. That he wasn't into her and he really *had* been helping her out in a friendship capacity.

But then he'd practically knocked his chair over to get to her, held her hand, and babbled nonstop. It was cute. Knowing she'd reduced a man like Raiden to blurting out everything he was thinking without pause was heady. She was thrilled that they'd get to hang out tomorrow. Of course, most women wouldn't be happy with a date of walking in the woods, but she wasn't most women. She couldn't think of anything she'd like more than hanging out with Raid and Duke as they got reacquainted with the forest. Maybe she'd even suggest she hide so Duke could find her.

Well...actually, she could think of one thing she'd like more than that. Sitting on Raid's couch, snuggled up next to him. Maybe she'd continue to make the first move and straddle his lap. She giggled just thinking about how wide his eyes would get, what he might do.

Khloe had dated her fair share of men in the past. And it always seemed like the quieter ones were the better lovers. She let her mind wonder what Raid would be like in bed. Their height difference would make things...interesting. She squirmed a bit, thinking about Raid's intensity focused on giving her pleasure.

No matter if Raid was an expert when it came to sex, or if she'd need to give him hints about what she liked and where to touch, Khloe had no doubt that he'd do whatever he could to make sure it was good for her. That was just who he was. He was constantly watching out for others. His friends, their wives, the library patrons...

After a few more minutes of daydreaming about Raid, Khloe wandered into her small kitchen and sighed as she inspected her fridge, then her cupboards. She needed to make something to eat before Caryn and Drew came by, but she wasn't in the mood for cooking at all. She headed into her bedroom instead and changed into a pair of jeans and a T-shirt. She would've preferred to throw on sweats, but since her friends were coming over, she thought it might be more appropriate to at least make an effort to not look like a total slob.

She took a page from Raid's book and ate a bowl of cereal for dinner while standing in the kitchen, then padded into her tiny living room and flopped down once more on her second-hand couch. It had been an hour since Raid had dropped her off, already dark out, and she couldn't stop herself from wondering what plans he had on a Friday night. If he wasn't with a woman, what could he be doing? As far as she knew, none of the others in their friend group had plans to hang out with him. And Raid wasn't the kind of man who liked to just "hang out" anyway.

He was an introvert. He didn't go out. Hardly went *anywhere*, really, other than the woods. So what in the world could he have planned for tonight that was more important than a date with her?

Okay, that sounded completely snobby, but Khloe could tell he was upset about declining her offer to come over. If that was the case, if he was *truly* upset, why couldn't cancel or reschedule his plans?

Once her mind got stuck on the question, it wouldn't stop spinning. She couldn't stop herself from thinking up all sorts of scenarios.

He was going to hunt down Jason and Scott and confront them.

He was working as a spy and had to research some nefarious local activities.

He was secretly a stripper and drove to Roanoke on Friday nights to strip at some club.

Khloe giggled. Right. No way in hell.

Raid didn't seem to like confrontation, and being a secret spy was difficult when you were as tall as a tree. It was more likely he had a new book he really, really, *really* wanted to read.

Or maybe he wasn't all that into her after all, and was just putting on a good show at the library because he didn't want to hurt her feelings...

Biting her lip, Khloe frowned. The more she tried to think of what he might be doing, the more she fretted.

When another twenty minutes went by and she couldn't seem to stop wondering—okay, agonizing over— why Raid couldn't hang out with her, she made a decision.

She stood and grabbed her phone off the kitchen counter where she'd left it when she'd arrived home. She sent a quick text to Caryn, apologizing and saying she just wasn't up for company tonight, asking if they could do the movie thing another night. She felt awful about blowing Caryn off, but knew she wouldn't be able to quiet her mind if she didn't satisfy her curiosity and find out what Raid was doing tonight.

It was irrational. It was crazy. It was desperate and a little stalkerish. But Khloe didn't let any of that stop her. At this point, almost two hours had gone by since Raid had dropped her off. She'd just run by his place, tell him...

Shit, she had no idea what excuse she was going to use for being at his house.

Shrugging, Khloe figured she'd think of something by the time she got there.

Feeling a touch of excitement about the adventure she was going to go on, despite her crazy thoughts, Khloe quickly headed back into her bedroom to grab a pair of sneakers. A sense of anticipation swam through her veins. It had been a long time since she'd done something this impulsive. She didn't think Raid would be upset to see her, but there was always the chance. If he *was* pissed, she'd rather know now before she fell too hard for the man.

Her excitement lasted until she walked out of her apartment and headed for her little VW Bug. She loved her car. It wasn't practical, but she didn't care. She was about to climb in when she happened to look to her left.

Khloe froze as she met Jason's gaze. She had no idea how long he'd been watching her apartment, but suddenly she was very grateful for all her friends coming over each night. She also didn't know what he wanted or why he was there, but she wasn't going to stick around and ask. She slammed her door shut and immediately locked the doors. Her hands were shaking, but she managed to get the key in the ignition and throw the car into drive.

Her bug was no match for Jason's pickup truck, but she didn't plan on letting him get anywhere near her. She drove way too fast through the back streets of Fallport. She assumed he knew where Raid lived, but if there was even a slim chance he didn't, she wasn't going to lead him there.

It took way too long to get to Raid's house, but Khloe was satisfied that Jason hadn't managed to follow. She felt shaky inside and out, was still trembling when she pulled around the garage. She would've parked out front, but she didn't want to risk Jason or Scott driving by and seeing her car. It wasn't exactly common in Fallport.

Just being at Raid's house gave her a sense of safety. It was kind of crazy, considering there were two Mather brothers and Raid was only one person, but there it was.

Khloe went up to the front door and knocked. She frowned when several minutes went by with no answer. She knocked again, and again, Raid didn't appear. She'd seen his vehicle through the windows in the garage as she walked by, so he should be home. Frowning now, and feeling a little worried, Khloe walked around the house to the back door.

She looked in through the window and the house was dark. Duke wasn't sleeping in his bed and there was no sign of Raid.

Khloe's shoulders slumped. He wasn't home. Whatever was so important tonight was obviously taking place somewhere else. Someone had picked him up and he could literally be anywhere.

She turned to head back to her car, but then remembered Jason. He was probably casing the streets looking for her, along with his brother. Who knew what they'd do if they found her? Shivering, Khloe sighed.

She had no idea what made her do it, but she reached for the knob on the back door.

To her surprise and relief, it actually opened. It was shocking and ridiculous that Raid hadn't locked the door. She supposed that maybe the last time he'd let Duke out, he'd been in a hurry or something and hadn't locked it when he let him in. It was shortsighted and dangerous, especially considering everything that had happened to their friends, and with the Mather brothers in town, ready and willing to cause havoc.

But Khloe had never been so relieved and grateful in all her life that Raid was a little scatterbrained tonight. She'd simply wait inside for him to get back. She felt much safer here than in her little apartment. Yes, she could go to any of her friends' houses and they'd watch over her, but all Khloe could think of was snuggling down on Raid's couch.

Making sure to lock the deadbolt of the back door, Khloe smiled as she wandered toward the couch. The house was warm, smelled like whatever Raid had made for dinner, mixed with his own piney scent. Whatever soap he used smelled like the forest he and Duke loved to walk so often.

Just as she was about to sit, Khloe heard something.

She froze and cocked her head to try to figure out where the sound was coming from. It was...Raiden's voice! But where was he?

Khloe tiptoed through the living room toward the hallway where the bedrooms were located. She stopped when she saw a door cracked open. She'd always assumed it was a linen closet, but apparently it was a door to a basement. She'd had no idea Raid's house even *had* a basement. He'd never offered to show it to her, and she'd just assumed the house was all one level.

Trying to be as quiet as possible, she eased the door open. A light was on down there, and now she could definitely hear Raid's low voice. The possibilities of what he could be doing in the basement swam through her head. Maybe he really *was* a spy, and the basement was where he kept all his computers and modems and things to hack into giant corporations and foreign countries.

Feeling silly, Khloe quietly walked down the steps. She made it about halfway before she stopped once more. She could hear Raid clearly now, but what he was saying didn't make any sense. It took her several minutes to work it out.

The bottom of the stairs faced a cinderblock wall. The rest of the basement was to the right of the stairs. Cautiously, Khloe crouched and leaned forward until she could peek into the room.

She saw Duke lying on his back with his feet in the air on another extremely comfy-looking dog bed. Raid sat at a table with a computer in front of him. The glow from the screen made his red hair look even brighter than normal. There was a small desk lamp shining next to him, but no other lights on in the room.

He had a box next to him with what looked like a castle turret at the top.

As she watched, he lifted a hand and dropped something into the top of the turret, and Khloe assumed it was dice when they rattled in the box. He read off the numbers, and she realized he was video chatting with someone, or a few someones. A pad of paper was in front of him, and he flipped a page and scanned it as someone spoke through the speakers.

Khloe slowly and quietly eased to her butt on the stairs where she could hear what was being said through the computer speakers. She knew she should let him know she was there, but she couldn't resist the urge to listen for a while first.

CHAPTER ELEVEN

Raid concentrated on the scenario his friend and Dungeon Master was reciting. He hadn't been paying as much attention as he should to his Dungeons and Dragons game tonight. He and his friends played every Friday. Not everyone could make it each week, but they did the best they could.

Raiden knew this certified him as a nerd through and through, and he didn't care. He loved the fantasy game, had a whole bio for his character, Bjorn Silverhammer, a dwarven life cleric. Although Bjorn was tall for a dwarf, being four foot eleven was so different from his real-life six foot eight that it always made Raid chuckle.

He also loved creating new characters when he got bored. His latest creation was a druid who could shapeshift into any kind of animal to help fight at Bjorn's side. He'd named her Anise, and she was super powerful. It was ironic that the new character was as in tune with animals as she was...and that she looked an awful lot like Khloe.

He'd swear that he hadn't planned that when he'd first dreamed up the druid, and it was a coincidence that she had such an affinity with animals and the real Khloe turned out to be a veterinarian.

Usually Raid could lose himself in the world of magic and fantasy. It was a way to forget what happened to him in the past and to be a powerful creature in his own right for a while. There were seven or so guys he played with each week. Sometimes as few as four of them were able to get together, but they always made it work. Raid preferred not to be the DM, but he had many scenarios written for when it was his turn.

At the moment, he and his friends had just finished a long and involved campaign, and instead of diving into another one right away, they were running a series of one-shots to give the DM time to prepare a new quest. One of his friends was explaining a situation and he needed to pay attention so he wouldn't get killed. It would suck to have spent so much time and energy building his Bjorn character, only for him to get killed because he couldn't stop wishing he was sitting in Khloe's small apartment watching a cooking show.

"You're in the grasslands and they go on and on for miles with knee-high seas of grass everywhere you look... except for you, Bjorn, the grass is up to your chest, since you're so short. The land is partially civilized, with small farms and ranches here and there. Gnolls are encroaching on the farms though, and the civilians are worried. Your party comes across a battle. Dead humans and gnolls litter the area. Ravens can be heard overhead and hyenas are feasting on the carcasses. You come across a recent battle and the sounds of other carrion creatures can be heard over the moans of the dying, animals and humanoid alike. Everyone, roll."

Raid rolled his dice and everyone read off their numbers. What happened next depended on what everyone rolled.

"There is a dying human gesturing to you," the DM said. "What do you do?"

That was easy for Raiden. His character, Bjorn, was a life cleric, meaning he could easily cast a spell to heal the injured soldier. He did so, and the man explained that he was in charge of the army currently lying decimated around them. The man went on to say the gnolls attacked with no provocation, and all the hyenas turn into gnolls after feasting on the dead. He wanted help with the entire situation.

Raid smiled. The one thing he loved about D&D was the cause and effect of it all. It took critical thinking. It wasn't just a "get to point A and go from there" kind of thing. A good DM had a thousand different scenarios and could even think of plots on the fly to keep the game interesting and ongoing.

For example, his group could help the man on the ground, but that could agitate the hyenas if they overheard. The gnolls obviously had an agenda, so figuring out their deal was extremely important. Raid was more than sure there was probably a huge camp of the gnolls nearby that they'd have to infiltrate. The hyenas were probably guarding it as well. This one-shot scenario was going to be a challenge, and it was just what he needed right now...as long as he could concentrate.

Raid listened to his online friends—men whom he'd never met in person but had clicked with while trying to find a new D&D group to join—banter back and forth with the DM as they did their best to convince the human to trust them and tell them his secrets.

But then a noise caught his attention, and Raid glanced behind him...

Straight into Khloe's eyes.

For a moment, he was confused. She wasn't supposed to be here. She should be at her apartment watching movies with Caryn and Drew. Hell, she wasn't even supposed to know about his basement.

But there she was, sitting on his stairs, watching him with a small smile on her face.

Raid jumped up from his seat at the desk and strode toward her, panic welling inside him. "Are you all right? What's wrong?"

"I'm good. Nothing's wrong," she said calmly.

It was the calm that registered in his psyche, and Raid stopped a few feet away from her and frowned. "What are you doing here?"

Khloe shrugged. "I tried to come up with some excuse, but nothing believable came to mind. Honestly, I was just curious about what you were doing tonight. I had all sorts of crazy ideas in my head, but I never would've guessed you were playing D&D."

"How'd you get in?" Raid asked, trying not to combust from embarrassment right then and there. It wasn't that D&D was something to be ashamed of. Hell, he could be out drinking and causing trouble. But he'd been made fun of enough in high school, in college, and even while he was in the Coast Guard that he didn't make a habit of talking about what he liked to do in his spare time.

"The back door was unlocked. Which isn't safe, Raid. You should be more careful about that."

"Shit. You're right. I was running late and Duke insisted he wanted to go out one more time before we came downstairs. I guess I forgot to lock it."

Khloe gave him another small smile. "So you're obviously an expert at D&D, huh?" she asked, gesturing toward his setup.

Raid nodded. His muscles were tense as he waited for a snarky comment.

"Will you teach me how to play?"

He stared at her in confusion for a moment. "What?"

"I mean, if you don't want to, that's okay. I'm sure it's probably annoying to teach someone all the ins and outs when they have no clue what they're doing."

"No!" he exclaimed, slowly relaxing. "I'd be happy to... if you're sure."

"Raid, it's obvious you enjoy the game. And sometimes, I feel like I don't really know you at all. Learning a bit about the game could help me understand *you* a little better."

He chuckled. "I'm not sure about that."

"Should I call you Bjorn, like the guy on the computer?" she teased as she stood.

"Only if I can call you Anise."

She returned his smile. "Anise? I like it. Is that another character in the game?"

Raid nodded as she approached him. "She helps out my character. I created her."

"Is she cool?"

Completely serious, Raid said, "Super cool."

"Awesome."

Feeling as if he was in the twilight zone—he'd never had a woman he was attracted to show even the slightest interest in the fantasy game—Raid grabbed another chair and pulled it up to the desk in front of the computer monitor.

He introduced Khloe to his remote friends and while they continued to play, he muted his microphone and did his best to explain the basics of the game. He showed her the dice box and taught her what the dice were for and how they worked.

When it was his turn again, he could feel Khloe's eyes on him as he rolled the dice that made the choices for his character, and hers, as to what to do next. The DM informed him that there seemed to be eight wild horses in the distance as they walked toward the fort the dying human told them about.

Raid decided to use Anise's powers to try to befriend the horses. He was only partially successful, but one of the horses allowed Anise to mount it.

When it was the next person's turn, Raid muted his microphone once more and turned to Khloe.

"I like this," she said with a grin. "Does the DM have every little decision already mapped out?"

"Kind of. He has the main ideas but the dice and how the characters act both decide how they get places or even if they follow the plot point the DM has set up. Anything that goes off-script, he makes up on the fly."

"It's like problem solving and reading one of those choose-your-own-adventure books at the same time."

Raid grinned. "Yup."

"Okay, cool...now hush so we can hear what's happening."

The next three hours went by amazingly quickly. As time passed, Khloe got progressively better at the game. Her ideas and suggestions were spot on, and most of them were what Raid would have chosen to do if she wasn't there. She seemed thrilled to have her own character and loved that she was able to talk to and control the animals in the game.

Around two in the morning, the game wound down and the guys all decided to call it a night. They'd been very gracious in welcoming Khloe, and they all said they hoped to see her at a game in the future.

As soon as the camera clicked off, Khloe turned to Raid. "So you do this every Friday night?"

He shrugged. "We try to. Sometimes it doesn't work out, as the hardest part of playing is getting everyone online at the same time."

"I think it's cool. And fun," she said, making Raiden fall for her all the more.

He never would've pegged her for a D&D fan. Granted, he'd done his best not to truly get to know her over the last year...and now he was kicking himself. He'd wasted so much time. Of course, a few months ago, she might not have been in the head space to even *want* to be his friend.

Just as he opened his mouth to tell her it was getting late and ask if she wanted to stay the night in the guest room, she yawned huge.

"I'm exhausted," she said...but she wouldn't meet his eyes. "Any chance I can crash here?"

It was exactly what Raid wanted, but she was being a little weird about how she'd asked. She usually didn't hesitate to speak her mind. She always met his gaze head-on, as if daring him to disagree with her about something. But right now, she was playing with one of the dice from the box and looking everywhere but at him.

"Of course you can stay," he told her.

Her shoulders slumped as if in relief. Raid couldn't believe she'd think he'd say no or tell her to go home. Something was obviously on her mind, and he wanted—no, *needed* to know what it was.

"What's wrong?" he asked.

"Nothing's wrong," she said a little too chirpily.

"Look at me, Khloe," Raid said firmly.

She sighed, then turned his way.

"Talk to me," he cajoled. "The Khloe I've gotten to know recently wouldn't ask to stay. She'd *inform* me that because I'd kept her up too late, she was staying. She wouldn't ask trepidatiously."

"I...I just... JasonwaswaitingformewhenIleftmyapartment," she said quickly, running all her words together.

"What?"

She sighed. "Yeah. When I left my apartment, he was in the parking lot. I drove around and finally lost him before I came here, but I'm nervous to go back now in the middle of the night. I can get out of your hair bright and early in the morning though."

Raid didn't think, he simply acted. One of his hands curled around the back of her neck and the other gripped her thigh, holding her in place. "First, I'm pissed that wasn't the *first* thing you told me when you got here. Second, no way in hell would I let you leave right now after hearing that. And third...that asshole isn't going to hurt you, Khloe. I won't allow it."

Instead of getting pissed at him being all grabby, she

seemed to melt into him. She put a hand over his on her thigh. "Allow it?" she teased. "How are you going to stop him?"

"During the day, you'll have someone at your side at all times. If not me, then one of the other guys. In a pinch, one of the other women will work. And no more sleeping by yourself at your apartment. If you don't want to stay here, then I'll come to your place. Eventually they'll get the memo that you're off-limits. If they don't, I'll have to persuade them otherwise."

"Raid, if you get hurt because of me, I'll—"

"I'm not going to get hurt. And nothing they do is your fault. *Nothing*. Hear me?"

He was being overbearing, and Raid knew it. But this was important.

She stared at him for a heartbeat before dipping her chin.

"Where's your car?"

"I parked behind your garage. I didn't want them to see it from the street."

"Good." Raid stood, reluctantly dropping his hands from her. "Come on, let's get you settled. Duke, wake up, you lazy bum...we're going upstairs."

The bloodhound lifted his head, grunted as if to complain about being woken up, then reluctantly got to his feet and padded after them.

Raid put his hand on the small of Khloe's back as they headed up the basement stairs. He shut the door behind them and said, "I'll let Duke out, you go on and get comfortable. You know where everything is. I can bring in a T-shirt for you to sleep in if you want."

"Yes, please," she said softly.

Raid turned and walked toward the back door before he did something crazy, like invite Khloe to sleep in his bed. He wasn't good at this part of relationships. He had no idea how to let Khloe know what he wanted. He wasn't even totally sure she was interested in him the same way he was interested in her. It was frustrating.

By the time Duke was finished finding the perfect place to pee, almost ten minutes had passed. Raid made sure the door was locked this time and headed down the hall. He grabbed a T-shirt from his drawer and headed to the guest room. He knocked on the door and heard Khloe's voice from inside.

She was sitting on the edge of the bed, obviously waiting for him.

"Sorry it took so long, Duke had to sniff a hundred spots before finding the perfect one to pee on. I brought you a shirt."

She reached out for it. "Thanks."

Raid tilted his head as he stared at her. "Are you okay?"

"Yeah. Just tired," she said with a shrug.

Raid didn't believe her. He wanted to tell her that she could trust him, talk to him. But she seemed...remote. Lost in thought. So he smiled and backed toward the door. "You're safe here, Khloe," he said.

"I know. Thanks."

That was about as definitive as could be. Raid left the room and shut the door behind him. He wanted to bang his head on the wall in frustration. Things were going so well when they were playing D&D...at least he'd thought so. Maybe he'd misread the situation, like he usually did when he was with a woman.

Sighing, he trudged to his room, left his door open a

few inches so he could hear Khloe if she needed anything during the rest of the night, and got ready for bed.

* * *

Khloe did her best to get control of her emotions...with no luck. She was frustrated that Raid hadn't even *tried* to make a pass at her. She'd loved his hands on her. He'd been so commanding and bossy...and all her girly parts stood up and paid attention. But then he'd backed off and hadn't done anything remotely suggestive, not even so much as a kiss good night.

Now, alone in the guest room, she couldn't sleep.

She also couldn't help but tense up every time she heard a car pass on the road at the end of the driveway. Raid didn't exactly live on the beaten path, so every single time, she thought maybe it was Jason or Scott coming to cause trouble.

After an hour, she was done. She'd never get to sleep lying here by herself. The only time she felt truly safe was when she was with Raid. Feminists everywhere, dead or alive, would be turning in their graves or shaking their heads at her, but Khloe didn't care. She was an independent woman who was perfectly able to mow the grass, pay her bills, and feed and clothe herself. But she was no match for the Mathers—or her imagination, it seemed.

Throwing back the comforter, Khloe made a beeline for the door. She didn't think about what she was about to do, she just did it.

She tiptoed down the hallway to Raid's room and pushed open the door. The hinges creaked obscenely loudly in the quiet of the night, and she winced.

"Khloe? Is that you?" Raid asked.

"I didn't mean to wake you up," she apologized.

"You didn't. I'm awake. What's wrong?"

Khloe shivered at the commanding tone in his voice again. Man, she was a sucker for Raiden when he went all alpha on her. Without answering, she shut the door behind her and walked to his king-size bed. She lifted the covers and crawled under the sheet.

Then held her breath, praying he wasn't going to kick her out.

"Khloe?" he said again, this time in a softer, slightly confused tone.

"I can't sleep. I keep seeing the grill of Alan's truck coming right at me, making my leg throb. And every time I hear a car drive by, I wonder if it's his brother. Can I sleep in here?"

Raid's response was everything Khloe ever wanted and more. He reached over and pulled her across the bed. He turned her onto her side, then cuddled up behind her. Khloe was completely surrounded by Raid's large, hard, warm body.

She immediately shuffled backward, getting comfortable in the cradle of his body. "I take it this means I can stay," she said dryly.

"You can stay," Raid said in a deep, gruff voice.

One of his arms went around her waist and the other shoved under her head, so she was using his biceps as a pillow. She was engulfed in his masculine scent, and she could feel the hair of his legs against her own bare skin. He wore a T-shirt, just as she did, yet lying here with him still felt extremely intimate.

"I told you before and I'll tell you again, nothing's

gonna touch you as long as I'm around. And until those asscracks leave, I'm definitely gonna be around," he vowed.

"Okay," she whispered.

She felt more than heard his chuckle rumble through his chest. "You aren't going to fight me? Tell me that you're perfectly capable of taking care of yourself?"

But Khloe didn't laugh. "That's obviously not true, considering what happened before."

"That happened because he's a fucking coward," Raid said. "No one with a shred of decency would do what that asshole did. If you'd had any idea that he was a psychopath, you would've done things a lot differently. Don't beat yourself up for being taken by surprise. You won't be so easily duped in the future."

He wasn't wrong about that.

"Raid?"

"Yeah?"

"Thanks for not being upset I crashed your D&D night. And thanks for sharing something you obviously love to do with me."

He was quiet for so long, Khloe was afraid he wasn't going to respond at all. When he did, he blew her mind.

"You're the first person who hasn't treated me like I'm a freak for enjoying what I do. I got so used to keeping that part of me a secret, it didn't even occur to me to just come out and tell you what my plans were."

"It's okay. And you aren't a freak," Khloe said firmly. "I had fun, and if anyone in the future makes fun of you for liking D&D, let me know and I'll set them straight."

"Right...I'll do that," he said with another chuckle.

"Raid?"

"I thought you came in here to sleep," he teased. "If

you're gonna talk all night, we're gonna be too tired to hike tomorrow."

"I did, but I'm a night person...and if I'm gonna open that emergency clinic, I need to get used to being up all night anyway. But I just want to say this one thing. I don't know what kind of women you've been with in the past, but I like you just the way you are. Quiet and introverted most of the time, occasionally nerdy, but bossy and alpha when you need to be."

His arm tightened around her, and she went on before she chickened out.

"I know things have changed really fast lately, but...I wouldn't be here, in your bed, in your arms, if I didn't want us to be more than just friends."

Her heart was beating out of her chest, and Khloe had no idea what Raid was thinking. Was he freaking out that she'd read the situation wrong? Trying to figure out how to tell her that he wanted nothing beyond keeping her safe? That friendship was all he could offer?

"I wouldn't be in this bed, sleeping so close to you, touching you, if *I* didn't want us to be more than friends," he said after a long, agonizing minute had passed.

That was all Khloe needed to hear.

She sighed and brought the hand resting on her waist up to her lips, kissing the palm, before finally closing her eyes.

CHAPTER TWELVE

Raid felt the moment Khloe's body went limp and she fell into a deep sleep. He wasn't tired, not anymore. How could he be after Khloe's pronouncement?

He felt as if she was a miracle. His miracle. He'd been through hell and yet here she was. She didn't mind that he was a nerd and she wanted to be more than friends. He could count on one hand the number of women he'd been with intimately, and none of those encounters compared to simply holding Khloe in his arms.

They'd been building to this for months. He'd felt the undercurrent of attraction between them for quite a while now, but hadn't done anything about it. He hated that it took her being in danger, and Duke's near-death experience, to finally get his head out of his butt. He was going to do everything in his power to be a good man for Khloe.

It was a good thing she liked his nerdiness and his bossiness, because he didn't know any other way to be. He didn't think about going all alpha on her, he just did what felt right.

When he finally managed to fall asleep, Raid didn't sleep well. For one, he wasn't used to having anyone else in bed with him. And two, he was in a constant state of arousal. Her words kept echoing in his head, even in his dreams.

She liked him.

Wanted to be more than friends.

She felt safe with him.

The second Duke stirred the next morning, Raid was already awake.

He slipped out of bed reluctantly and led Duke to the back door so he could do his business. Feeling lazy, and knowing they had no plans other than to go for a hike, Raid headed for the guest bathroom so as not to wake Khloe, did his thing, then brushed his teeth. The last thing he wanted was for Khloe to be repulsed by his morning breath.

By the time he walked back into his room, Khloe was sitting up in the bed with a smile on her face.

"I didn't mean to wake you," he told her quietly.

"It's okay, I'm a light sleeper," she said.

Raid wanted to roll his eyes. She wasn't a light sleeper that *he'd* observed. She slept like a log, barely moving throughout the night. He'd had plans to slip back under the covers and hold her for a little longer before they got started on their day, but now that she was awake, he felt awkward and unsure about what to do.

He stood in the middle of his room in his boxers and a T-shirt and desperately tried to think of something to say.

"Come here, Raiden," Khloe said, patting the mattress next to her.

He moved without thought. Sitting on the bed, he

scooted toward her and leaned against the headboard. To his surprise, she turned and threw one leg over his thighs and straddled him.

His hands instinctively went to her waist to steady her. "Khloe?"

"Were you serious last night? Or were you just telling me what you thought I wanted to hear?" she asked, looking him in the eyes.

"Um...which part?" he asked.

"The part about liking me and wanting to be more than friends," she said calmly.

"I was dead serious," he said.

Then Khloe shocked the shit out of him by smiling—and reaching for the hem of her shirt. Before he could say or do anything, she had it over her head, and he was staring at the most perfect pair of tits he'd ever seen in his life.

Raid was literally speechless. He couldn't think. Couldn't talk. All he could do was hold onto her waist and try not to come there and then.

"Good. Because I was serious too," Khloe said with a grin. "And I'm thinking if I don't make the first move, we might be dancing around each other for a long time. I hope this is okay."

She wasn't wrong. Raid probably would've taken a *very* long time to work up the nerve just to kiss her again. This? It was a dream come true.

Without speaking, he placed one hand between her shoulder blades and the other reached for one of her plump tits. He held it still, then leaned forward and wrapped his lips around the hard nipple practically begging for his touch.

Khloe moaned and her head tilted back as he feasted on her. He felt her fingers spear into his short hair as she held him against her breast.

She squirmed on his lap, but Raid tightened his hold, keeping her still as he fulfilled one of his fantasies. He moved to the other tit and gave that nipple the same attention. Several minutes passed before he found the willpower to pull back and look at his handiwork. Her nipples were hard little spikes on her chest and she was breathing hard. Her upper chest was red and blotchy with lust, and it was all he could do not to throw her back on the bed and rip her underwear off.

He looked into her eyes for the first time and nearly melted at what he saw there. Delight. Lust. Humor. And need.

"I'm guessing this was okay," she quipped.

Raid smiled. He'd never laughed during sex before. It felt good. Really damn good.

"Anytime you want to strip in front of me, feel free," he told her.

"I think one of us is overdressed," she said, running her hands up under his T-shirt and running her fingernails over his chest and catching his nipples in the process.

Raid was two seconds away from exploding with just the feel of her fingers on him. Knowing he needed to take control of this situation before he embarrassed himself, Raid moved.

He lifted Khloe off his lap as if she weighed nothing and dropped her back to the mattress, her head facing the bottom of the bed. Then he straddled her hips, keeping her where he wanted her as he took off his own shirt.

Her hands ran up and down his thighs when he was

otherwise occupied, and he drew in a sharp breath when she didn't hesitate to cup his dick through his boxers.

"Holy shit, Raid...you're huge."

Brushing her hand away—not because he didn't like her touch, but because at the moment it was too much—Raid leaned over her and smiled.

"Rumor says that the bigger a man's feet, the bigger his cock," she teased.

He shrugged. "I don't go around comparing a man's dick to his feet, but *I've* heard that a man's cock is about as big around as his wrist." He held up his arm in front of Khloe.

Her eyes widened comically as she lifted a hand and wrapped her fingers around his wrist. Or tried to. The fingers wouldn't touch, and she breathed, "Holy crap."

"I won't hurt you," Raid said, his smile dying.

"I know you won't," Khloe answered without hesitation. Then she arched her back under him. "You haven't kissed me," she said with a pout.

"I did," Raid countered, then flicked one of her hard nipples. "And you liked it."

"Kiss me, Raiden," Khloe ordered, lifting a hand and doing her best to force his head down to hers.

Since he couldn't think of anything he wanted to do more, Raid obeyed. He brushed his lips against hers softly. Once. Twice. When she whined deep in her throat, Raid was done teasing.

He slammed his lips to hers and she immediately opened for him. The kiss was long, deep, and the most sensual kiss he'd ever experienced. Khloe gave him everything she had, kissing him right back. By the time he pulled away, they were both breathing hard.

Then without hesitation, Raid moved. He licked his way down her body, spending quite a bit of time on the breasts he'd already gotten to know.

He learned she liked a harder touch on her nipples. When he sucked hard while pinching the other, she squirmed and moaned under him. How long he feasted on her tits, Raid didn't know. It wasn't until he realized Khloe was begging him and trying to push him lower that he complied.

Wanting to imprint this moment on his memory forever, Raid kissed the front of her cotton underwear. He could smell her desire, see a wet spot on the material. Raid was breathing hard and he licked his lips in anticipation.

Khloe lifted her hips to assist him as his fingers slipped under the material and began to draw it down her legs. There was an awkward moment when she kneed him in the chin, but Raid didn't even feel the pain. Her giggle reminded him of how different this was than any other time he'd been in bed with a woman.

In the past, he was nervous and constantly worried about what he was doing. Where he should put his hands. If she wanted him to keep going or stop. But with Khloe, everything seemed natural.

When he was finally face-to-face with her pussy, Raid stared. She was perfect. Her pubic hair was trimmed, which was sexy as hell. He ran a finger over her mons, loving how her hips lifted in encouragement.

Raid lowered his head and kissed her inner thigh, making sure to brush his beard against the sensitive skin there. In response, Khloe moaned.

"Please, Raid."

"Please what?" he asked.

"Suck my clit," she said without hesitation.

Khloe's ability to ask for what she needed was a huge turn-on. Raid dropped his head and did as she asked. His lips closed around her clit and he sucked. Hard.

"Holy crap!" Khloe exclaimed as her hips slammed upward.

Chuckling, Raid brought a hand up and rested it on her belly. His hand seemed huge against her. He held her down as he found her clit once more, this time using his tongue to stimulate the little bud.

He'd learned—through reading a lot of books, and even watching some videos on the internet—that while licking a woman's entire pussy could feel good, the nerve center was where her pleasure lie. He brought his other hand up to play with her inner lips, to spread the wetness that was being produced by his ministrations.

Her delicious musky scent increased as he continued to play with her clit. He alternated sucking with licking, and even nibbling now and then.

Raid had never seen Khloe out of control. She had more control over herself than anyone he knew. So he felt even more powerful to have her writhing under him. Her hands were in his hair, trying to pull him closer, and her hips constantly bucked under his hold. Her head moved forward and back, digging into the mattress, and he could feel her thighs shaking as her orgasm approached.

"Raid, yes...there...harder! Oh, shit!"

The joy and pride Raid felt as she flew over the edge rivaled how he'd felt when he was accepted into the Coast Guard's dog handler ranks. *He'd* done this to her. Made her feel good.

Just when it seemed she was coming down from her

orgasm, Raid eased a finger inside her soaking-wet body and lowered his head once more. It didn't take long for her second orgasm to explode through her body.

He'd never seen or felt anything more beautiful. Seeing Khloe let herself experience pleasure was the most exciting thing he'd witnessed in his entire life. Her hair was mussed now, and she had a sheen of sweat all over her body. She practically glowed.

Picking up her head, she stared down at him when he didn't move from between her legs. "Raid?"

"Yeah, sweetheart?"

"It's your turn now."

"Nope," he said evenly.

She frowned. "What do you mean, no?"

"I want to see that again."

Her head flopped back onto the mattress as she let out a breath with a huff. "I can't," she informed him.

Raid only grinned. "You do know that's like waving a red flag in front of a bull, right?"

"I want you to enjoy this too," she said, picking her head back up.

Raid loved that she wasn't trying to hide her body from him. She seemed perfectly content to lie naked in his arms.

"You think I'm not enjoying this?" Raid asked. "Khloe, your scent is all over my face, in my beard. I've never tasted anything as delicious in my life, and I'm contemplating not washing my face before we head out later so I can smell you all day. My cock has never been so hard, and that's without me even touching it. I'm leaking precome constantly and I have a feeling the second you look at my dick, it's gonna go off. I'm enjoying this more than you'll ever know."

"Okay," she whispered. "Do your worst."

Raid grinned. "How about I do my best instead?" And with that, he decided to try something he'd seen on the internet. It was his favorite video...and it wasn't even porn. It was more of a tutorial. A woman lay on a massage table and the man with her was fully dressed. He slowly and instructively showed his viewers how and where to touch a woman to give her a G-spot orgasm. Raid had watched the video countless times, and there was nothing more he wanted than to see if he could give Khloe the ultimate pleasure.

"Have you ever had a G-spot orgasm?" he asked as he rose to his knees between her legs.

"Oh, shit," was her response.

He took that to mean the answer was no. He used the thumb of the hand on her belly to lightly manipulate her clit as he reached over to the table next to his bed with the other. He pulled a bottle of lube out of the drawer and smiled down at her.

Shrugging at her grin when she saw the bottle, he said, "I'm a guy...what can I say?"

"I wasn't going to comment," Khloe told him. "If you have lube in your drawer, that's your business. Just as the vibrator in mine is *my* business."

"You have a vibrator?" he asked, feeling his cock twitch.

"Of course."

"Damn, that's sexy." Raid squirted a healthy dollop of lube onto his fingers and eased two inside her body.

Khloe shifted under him. "It's cold!"

"Won't be for long," Raid soothed as he began to gently thrust in and out of her pussy. Within a minute, she was once more moaning deep in her throat and lifting her hips with each thrust of his hand.

Thinking about the video he'd seen, Raid began to rub her clit harder, even as he increased the speed of his fingers in and out of her body, making sure to press against the spongy spot inside that would send her flying.

The sound his fingers made was sexy as fuck, and that, along with the noises coming from her mouth, made Raid's lips curl into a smile. He loved that she was trusting him to do this. To touch her like this.

It took a while—and a surprisingly amount of strength on his part to hold Khloe where he wanted her—but soon he could tell she was on the edge of another intense orgasm.

"It's too much! I can't..." she wailed.

"You can. Let go, Khloe."

With another few cries, she did. Liquid squirted out of her pussy, all over his fingers, as she bucked and shook in his arms.

Raid couldn't wait another second. He needed to be inside her. *Now.*

Pulling his fingers out of her body, Raid reached for the condom he'd grabbed at the same time as the lube. He shook as he pushed the elastic of his underwear down and rolled the rubber over his throbbing cock. Not taking the time to remove his boxers, Raid pressed Khloe's still shaking legs apart and pushed inside her in one long thrust.

He immediately felt her spasm around him once more. Just entering her had triggered another orgasm. Khloe was practically crying now, but her hands gripped his butt, and she tried to pull him even closer, letting him know that she was still with him and wanted this. Him.

It was all Raid could do not to blow right that second. He reached down and grabbed the base of his cock and squeezed tightly. He wanted this to last. This was his first time with Khloe; he didn't want it to end in seconds.

* * *

Khloe could barely think. She was on pleasure overload. She'd never felt anything as amazing as Raid's hands and tongue on her. She'd come more than she ever had in one sexual encounter before. And that last orgasm had almost killed her.

Raid had been tender but determined. She had no idea where he'd learned how to do what he'd done, but she wasn't complaining. She'd barely come to her senses when she felt him between her legs once more.

His cock was big. Larger than anything she'd taken before, but as soon as he got inside her, she came again. The orgasm wasn't as intense as the one she'd just had, but with him filling her up, it was almost more pleasurable.

This was what she'd been missing the other times he'd gotten her off. She'd felt so empty. And now she was anything but.

"Holy crap, Raid!" she exclaimed as she gripped his butt and dug her fingernails into the skin through his boxers. "Move!"

"Can't. Need. To. Wait. A second," he panted.

Screw that. Khloe thrust her hips upward and was rewarded with Raiden's surprised grunt as he threw out his hand, which had been wrapped around his cock, to catch himself. He was even deeper inside her now.

"Fuck me, Raid," she ordered.

His eyes came to hers, his pupils dilated.

"There's no going back," he told her, still not moving.

"I don't want to go back," she reassured him.

His nostrils flared and his hips finally moved. He pulled back slowly, then slammed inside her.

Khloe could feel her boobs bounce on her chest, and she smiled. "Yes," she whispered. "More."

And just like that, it was as if the control he'd been holding onto by a thread was broken. Raid fucked her. Hard.

And it was glorious.

Khloe was more than wet enough to comfortably take him, Raid had made sure of that. He shifted, grabbing her hips and holding them up as he rose to his knees. A lot of her weight was resting on her shoulders now, but Khloe didn't care. All she could do was look at the ecstasy on Raid's face as he plunged in and out of her.

"That's it. Take what you need," she gasped.

"Mine!" he exclaimed as he tore his eyes from where his cock entered her to meet her gaze.

"*Mine*," she returned.

"Yes. Yours!" he agreed.

It was somewhat of a submissive thing to say, but Raid was anything but submissive at the moment. He had complete control of her body, and Khloe loved it.

She loved watching him come closer and closer to orgasm. And she saw the moment it overtook him. His eyes never closed, but he shoved his giant cock inside her as far as he could get it, and she actually felt him twitching as he released his load.

But he wasn't done. Somehow, even as the pleasure was still coursing through his body, he lowered her hips until her butt was resting on his thighs and once again began strumming her clit.

"Raid!" she exclaimed as pleasure rose hard and fast inside her. "I'm too sensitive!"

"Good. Then you'll come faster," he told her with an intense look of concentration on his face.

He wasn't wrong.

It took a ridiculously short amount of time for Khloe to feel the familiar rise of an orgasm make its way through her body.

She let out a small cry as her body shook uncontrollably in his arms.

"*Fuck*, that feels so damn good," he growled as his fingers finally fell away from her swollen clit.

"Yes, it does," Khloe agreed.

She kept her eyes glued to Raid as he reached down and held onto the condom as he pulled himself out of her body.

"Holy crap, Raiden. *That* was inside me?" she asked incredulously as she got a good look at his cock for the first time.

"All the way, and you took me as if you were born to be mine," he said.

She supposed he'd earned his cockiness. She was a pile of mush at the moment and couldn't even think about moving.

Raid climbed off the bed and headed into the bathroom. He was back a moment later, sans boxers, and

Khloe couldn't take her gaze from his cock and balls swinging as he strode back to her.

He didn't hesitate in grabbing her and moving her around so her head was back on a pillow and her feet were facing the footboard once more.

"I'm not sure I like you moving me around without breaking a sweat," she grumbled as Raid climbed under the sheet with her.

"Yes, you do," he countered as he pulled her into his arms.

She didn't say anything because he was right.

The feel of his naked body under hers felt amazing. She melted against him, hiking one of her legs up and over one of his thighs.

Several minutes went by with neither of them speaking. Finally, she blurted, "Are you okay with me making the first move?"

"Yes."

She waited for him to elaborate and when he didn't, she came up on an elbow and stared at him. "That's it? Just yes?"

"Uh-huh. If you hadn't, who knows how long it would've taken me to get up the nerve to even attempt to kiss you again. So yeah, I'm all right with you making the first move. And it was an amazing move, by the way."

"You're a boob man," she teased.

"Nope, I'm a Khloe man."

Khloe melted inside and put her head back down on his chest. She loved how safe she felt with Raid. It was his size. His quiet confidence. His entire being. She had no idea what was in her future, but she prayed it would include Raiden.

"You said something last night..." he began, but didn't finish his thought.

"I said a lot of things last night," she prompted.

"Are you truly serious about opening an emergency vet clinic in Fallport?"

She nodded. "Yeah. Why?"

"Because I think it's a great idea."

His support meant the world to Khloe. "It might not work out like I want it to," she warned.

"Of course it will. It's a niche that needs to be filled. You'll see. Anything you need help with, all you have to do is ask."

"Thanks. You might regret that, because unlike a lot of people, I'm not afraid to ask for help."

"Good. Because you'll have a lot of it with me, the guys, and all the women. There's a building not too far from Brock's auto shop that's for rent. It's right on Main Street and would probably be a great location...if it can be configured to work for what you need."

Khloe lifted her head once more. "Really?"

"Uh-huh. What about supplies? Like surgical stuff? I'm assuming there's a lot you'll need. We can go to the bank and see about getting you a loan, and I can help with costs if you need it."

"I appreciate that, but I've got a whole storage unit full of stuff in Norfolk."

"That's great."

It hit Khloe then. "Am I really going to do this?"

"I hope so. As much as I don't want to lose my assistant, being a vet is what you were meant to be. From what I've heard around town, people are already very excited about the possibility of you staying and opening shop."

"Except Raymond."

"Screw that prick," Raid said with a scowl. "He should've been a better person and vet if he wanted to continue to have a monopoly around here."

Khloe couldn't help but laugh. She felt amazingly good. Positive. She'd just had too many orgasms to count, she apparently had a new boyfriend, a man she respected and looked up to, she was going to open up another vet clinic, and apparently she had the support of the entire town.

"You hungry?"

Raid's question triggered her stomach to growl just then, and he chuckled.

"Right. I'm gonna get up and fix us something before we head out on our hike. Pancakes all right?"

"Got any chocolate chips to throw in them?" she asked.

"I might."

"And sausage or bacon?"

He lifted a brow in response.

"What? If we're going to go out and burn some calories, I'll need energy. Especially after all my reserves were used up this morning."

The proud look on Raid's face wasn't something Khloe would forget anytime soon.

"If you want chocolate, bacon *and* sausage, that's what you'll get. Go ahead and jump in the shower while I cook."

"We could shower together," she suggested with a smirk.

"We might never leave the house then. Besides...I don't want to risk getting my beard wet this morning."

Khloe blushed but rolled her eyes. "You know that's kind of gross, right?"

"No way. Smelling you all day is anything but gross."

Then he leaned down and kissed her long and slow. He stared at her for a moment when he pulled back, then said, "Best morning ever."

Khloe watched as he unselfconsciously climbed out of bed and headed for the bathroom butt naked. She had nothing to put on after her shower but the clothes she'd arrived in, and she didn't care. Raid would stop by her apartment and let her change into hiking clothes before they headed to the trail.

Nothing would ruin this day. She'd risked everything with Raid by making the first move, but luckily it turned out perfectly. Khloe was happier than she could remember being in a very long time. Things were finally looking up.

CHAPTER THIRTEEN

Raiden felt as if he was a completely different man than he'd been only twenty-four hours ago. He felt stronger. More confident. Happier.

Breakfast had been fun, and he loved seeing the enjoyment Khloe got out of eating the food he'd prepared for her. Their hike with Duke had gone exceptionally well. The dog seemed happy to be outside on the trails again, and when Khloe had "hidden," he'd sniffed her out in twenty seconds flat.

Raid was thankful for so many things in his life, but none more than the thought of Khloe moving to Fallport permanently. And he loved how laid-back she was becoming as well. He had a feeling it had been a long time since she'd been able to truly relax.

He supposed his happiness was why his guard was down, and why, when he and Khloe stopped by Sunny Side Up for lunch, he was concentrating more on her than on who was coming and going from the diner.

When Khloe whispered, "Oh, shit," Raid looked up—

and every muscle in his body tensed. Jason and Scott had entered and, while waiting to be seated, were having a very loud conversation.

"I can't believe that dog killer is allowed in here."

"Right? If everyone knew how badly she'd fucked up that surgery and killed Alan's dog, they wouldn't be so friendly."

"I wouldn't let her near any pet of mine with a ten-foot pole."

"The state should've revoked her license."

And so it went. They kept haranguing Khloe and her skills in loud, obnoxious voices. Looking across the table at Khloe, Raid saw that her shoulders were tense and he had a feeling if she thought she could get away with it, she would've fled already. He immediately reached over and grabbed her hand. "Look at me, Khloe."

It took a moment, but eventually she lifted her gaze to his.

"Don't listen to them."

She huffed out a breath. "Kinda hard not to," she told him.

"Oh, look, she's actually conned a guy into dating her. I wonder if he knows she's a murderer."

"Yeah, well, he looks like a pansy."

"Maybe an elf...look how pointy his ears are!"

Raid felt more than saw Khloe's mood shift. Her hand tightened in his and she moved as if she was going to stand up. He didn't want her confronting these assholes. He didn't give a shit what they said about him—he'd heard all the insults before—and he didn't want her giving them the satisfaction of knowing they'd gotten under her skin.

As it turned out, he didn't have to do or say anything in

her defense, because Sandra, the owner of the diner, came barreling out of the kitchen and made a beeline for the Mather brothers.

Not only that, Bo, a Fallport police officer, stood up from a back corner of the diner. He was tall and extremely muscular, since he enjoyed weightlifting in his spare time. Raid thought he'd heard through the grapevine that he'd even won a couple of competitions.

"Out!" Sandra hissed, pointing a finger at the door.

"What?" Scott asked, obviously shocked.

"I said, get out!" Sandra repeated. "You aren't allowed in here. Don't come back. *Ever*."

"Wait, you can't do that!" he insisted.

"I can't?" Sandra asked, crossing her arms over her ample bosom. "I just did. I own this place, and I can refuse service to anyone I want. And I'm refusing it to the likes of you. Khloe Watts is one of the nicest people I know, and if you're going to come in here and badmouth not only her, but one of our local heroes, I don't want you back!"

"She's laying it on a bit thick," Khloe murmured for Raid's ears only. "The nicest person she knows? Please."

It was tough to keep from smiling, but Raid managed. Barely.

"She's an animal killer!" Jason barked, taking a step toward Sandra.

Bo put himself between Sandra and an irate Jason and said, "You heard the lady. It's time for you to go."

For a moment, Raid thought Jason was going to refuse to leave, but then he clearly thought better of taking Bo on and instead, turned to his brother. "Come on, Scott. I'm sure the food here sucks. Besides, I don't want to be around that murderer."

"Actually, the food here is awesome!" someone chirped from a table to Raid's right.

"Yeah, it's the best in town. You're missing out for sure!" someone else called out.

Jason and Scott left without another word. And while Raid hoped that was the end of their intimidation tactics, he had a feeling they were just getting started.

He looked over at Khloe and saw that she was back to staring at the table in front of her.

"This is a good thing," he told her.

Her gaze came up to meet his once more. "What? How, by any stretch of the imagination, is them being here and calling me a murderer good?" she huffed.

Raid was glad to see the anger in her gaze. It meant she was still willing to fight. Hopefully she wouldn't get it in her head to run again.

"Because they got a glimpse of how Fallport looks after one of their own."

"Raid, I'm not sure—"

"No," he said with a shake of his head, not letting her finish her thought. "You'll see. This is just the beginning. I was thinking after we finish our lunch, we could head over to see Heather and Marissa."

Khloe stared at him so long, he thought she was going to protest, but finally she nodded.

Forty minutes later, they stood to head out of the diner. As they passed by the tables of the other patrons, Khloe learned firsthand what Raid was trying to tell her. Almost every single person stopped them to tell Khloe how much they appreciated her. How happy they were that she was there. How they couldn't wait to visit her clinic when she got it set up.

Everyone assumed it was a done deal not only that she was staying, but that she'd open her practice soon as well.

They'd almost made it to the door when Sandra approached.

Khloe tensed, and Raid put his hand on the small of her back in support.

Without a word, Sandra pulled Khloe into her arms and almost smothered her with a hug. When she pulled back, she put her hands on Khloe's shoulders and stared into her eyes. "Don't you listen to those assholes," she said firmly. "We all know they're only here to try to get a rise out of you. Don't let them. They're going to find out very quickly that no one around here—well, no one who matters—will do business with them. They won't be able to spread their venom because we won't have it. You can't save every animal you see, everyone knows that. And from what we hear, that poor dog had been abused for years. Keep your chin up, Khloe."

Raid kept his eyes on Khloe, wanting to make sure she wasn't freaking out.

"And," Sandra went on, "don't you worry about your man either. He's caught the prettiest girl in the county. Why would he care what two outsiders say about him? And with the way you were looking at him when you two came in here, he knows you *more* than like the way he looks."

A blush formed on Khloe's cheeks, but she raised her chin and said, "I definitely have no complaints, zero, about how Raid looks."

"Good," Sandra said with satisfaction. "Our Raid deserves someone like you." Her voice lowered, and she leaned in and said only loud enough for Khloe and Raid to hear, "And if the way he can't take his eyes off you is any indication, he doesn't have any complaints either. Hold onto this one, girl. Any man who looks at you the way Raiden is right now is worth his weight in gold."

Khloe turned her head and caught Raid's gaze. He wasn't embarrassed she'd caught him staring at her. "You good?" he asked gently.

For the first time since Jason and Scott entered, a smile formed on her face.

"I think I am, yes."

"Good. Let's go see what Marissa and Heather are up to."

Khloe nodded at him, and Raid turned to Sandra. He gave her a quick hug and whispered a thank you into her ear.

Walking outside with Khloe, Raid kept a wary eye out for Jason or Scott but thankfully didn't see them around. He didn't expect they'd seen the last of them, but for now, maybe they'd gotten the hint that harassing Khloe wasn't going to be as easy as they'd assumed.

The next week went by with several more confrontations with Jason and Scott. One or both of them would show up when Khloe and Raid least expected them. One day they followed them into the bakery, and Liam promptly threw them out...but not before enduring several racist slurs about his Hispanic heritage.

Another time they were walking across the square after getting a coffee at Grinders. The brothers walked close behind, saying all sorts of shit to Khloe. Raid had just spun around to beat the living hell out of them both when Davis appeared out of nowhere, throwing himself between Raid and the brothers.

Raid had never been intimidated by the homeless man, but in that moment, he'd looked positively feral and definitely not like someone to mess with. Jason and Scott apparently agreed. They'd hurled one more insult before retreating back to whatever rock they'd slunk out from under.

They also didn't just appear when Khloe was out and about. She'd received a couple of "gifts" on her apartment doorstep. A dead squirrel one day, and a note that said, "*A murdurur lives here*," another. Khloe had done her best to blow them off, even making fun of the misspelling on the note, but Raid knew the harassment was getting to her.

Finally, there was the day she'd gone back to her place to get some more clothes—and it looked as if someone had tried to break into her apartment. They'd immediately gone to see the manager, and she said she'd keep a closer eye on Khloe's place, but Raid couldn't help but wonder what the brothers would've done if they'd gotten inside.

She'd talked to Simon about getting a restraining order, but since a lot of the things that happened couldn't be proven to be the brothers' handiwork, the chief had told her the courts wouldn't likely grant it. But he promised to have the deputies keep an eye out for the two men.

As much as Raid appreciated Fallport standing up for Khloe, he hated to see the apprehension and fear in her eyes every time they stepped outside his house or the library.

She'd spent every night at his place since the first time they'd made love, and it felt so...right. They'd played another game of D&D in his basement, and it had been just as fun as the first. Khloe honestly seemed to enjoy the game, which made Raid feel good. He never wanted her to do something just to try to please him. For a few hours, she seemed to forget about the Mather brothers. And when, after the camera on his computer was off, she went to her knees under the desk to blow his mind, Raid had forgotten about them too.

But the constant threats of what the brothers might be planning next were taking a toll, and Raid had had enough —but he wasn't sure what to do. He couldn't exactly lay a hand on them because they'd go straight to the cops. And so far they hadn't done anything illegal...there was no proof the attempted break-in at her apartment was them, even though it was highly unlikely it was anyone else.

Most of the businesses on the square had banned the brothers from entering. The post office was one of the few places that couldn't keep them out since it was a government building...but Silas, Otto, and Art were doing a good job of making sure Jason and Scott kept their distance. The three older men might be harmless gossips, but they had sharp tongues when needed.

Today, Raid was taking Khloe and Duke on a longer hike. They all needed the fresh air and the relaxation that came from getting out into nature. The day was sunny and brisk and perfect for hiking. He'd called Cherise to come in and work the second half of the day at the library, and he was heading out the back door with Khloe to the parking lot when they ran into Jason and Scott once more.

The two men had obviously been waiting for Khloe, because as soon as they walked out of the library, Jason was pushing off his truck and walking toward them—but not too close. Raid couldn't help noting the coward stopped several yards away.

"You think you have a pretty good thing going here, don't you?" he called out aggressively.

Khloe took a step back, and Raid hated seeing the fear in her face. "Why don't you give it up already?" he growled. "You've seen for yourself that the people around here don't give a shit what you have to say. Khloe's been accepted as a part of Fallport, and your brother's paying for his crime. Go home and get a life."

"Fuck you!" Jason shouted. "That bitch ruined Alan's life! She's gonna pay for it."

"She didn't ruin anything," Raid retorted, his voice rising. "Alan fucking ran her over! She did nothing but her job to the best of her ability. If your *brother* hadn't abused his dog, kicking her over and over, she wouldn't have been at the clinic in the first place." Even as he said the words, Raid knew he'd never get through to the men in front of them. They had a warped view of what happened, and they'd never stop trying to get retribution for their brother, no matter how misplaced.

Duke growled from behind him, and Raid glanced back to make sure Khloe was all right. His dog had moved so he was standing in front of her and the hackles on his spine were standing straight up. The bloodhound might not look all that scary with his droopy ears and sad countenance, but his teeth were just as sharp as the next dog's, and the hundred pounds he weighed should certainly be enough to make anyone think twice about pissing him off.

"Mark my words, she's gonna kill your dog next!" Scott yelled—from behind his brother, of course. "She's incompetent, and if you were smart, you'd get as far away from her as you can."

"I might not look like much of a threat, but if you touch one hair on Khloe, or my dog, you'll find out just how deadly I can be," Raid retorted, menace dripping from his words as he stepped toward the brothers.

"It's time you boys were on your way," a deep voice said from their right.

Raid looked over his shoulder to see none other than Whip Johansen standing outside the back door of The Cellar, the pool hall he owned.

In all the time Raiden had lived in Fallport, he'd never seen the man go out of his way to help *anyone*. He didn't participate in the parades and festivals the town held in the square, and all the riffraff in the county tended to congregate at his bar. The man was seriously antisocial, and Raid could count on one hand the number of times he'd even spoken to him.

So for him to be there now, looking pissed off as hell, inserting himself into the situation, was a shock.

"We're allowed to be here just as much as anyone else," Jason told him.

"This parking lot is private property," Whip said.

"Is not. This here is library parking. And the library is owned by the county. So you can't make us do shit," Scott retorted.

Whip growled low in his throat, and Raid actually took a step backward closer to Khloe. He wasn't afraid of the bar owner, but he didn't know a lot about him. He was unpredictable, and the last thing he wanted was Khloe getting caught in some sort of crossfire if anyone pulled out a weapon.

But Whip didn't need a gun to make his point. He took a step toward the Mather brothers and pointed to a sign on the side of the building. The library shared a wall with the pool hall, which wasn't ideal, but because the two establishments had opposite schedules in terms of their busiest times, it hadn't actually been an issue. When the pool hall was at its most noisy and rowdy, the library was closed.

The sign on the wall said *The Cellar Parking Only*.

Raid hadn't ever thought twice about it, since when he arrived at work, the lot was always empty.

"Wrong," Whip said. "*I* pay to maintain this lot. Therefore, it belongs to me, and I can decide who's allowed to park here and who isn't. And you definitely aren't. If you don't turn around, get back in your truck and leave, I'll call the cops. And from what I hear, they aren't too happy with the two of you. They've been answering a lot of calls lately from citizens complaining about two outsiders harassing their customers and being a general nuisance. I'm sure it wouldn't take much for them to decide enough is enough and haul you in on a malingering charge."

"They can't do that!" Scott sputtered.

"Sure they can. They're the police," Whip said, crossing his arms over his chest.

"That bitch must have a magic pussy. She's got everyone around here completely snowed," Jason sneered.

Raiden saw red at his comment.

Apparently, it also pushed Whip over the edge. He turned toward the back door to the pool hall and picked up something that was leaning against the wall. Raid was already heading in their direction when Whip caught up, a piece of metal pipe in his hands about three feet long. He smacked one end into his palm and continued marching toward Jason without a word.

Raid didn't have a weapon, but he could hold his own with his fists. This wasn't the bar owner's fight, and he'd be damned if he stood back and let him take on the brothers by himself.

Jason might be an asshole, but he wasn't *completely* stupid. He and his brother ran toward their truck as if the devil himself was at their heels when they saw the two men coming for them.

Raid assumed the threat of a metal pipe was just that... a threat. But even as Jason floored his truck and the tires spun as he did his best to leave, Whip raced forward and swung the metal pipe as hard as he could, smashing the back right taillight of the vehicle. Pieces of plastic went flying everywhere as the truck roared away.

Whip and Raid stood in the parking lot for a long moment, watching the truck speed off, before Whip turned toward him.

Raid tensed as he stared at the bar owner. The entire scene had been surreal. He wasn't sure why Whip had bothered to insert himself into the situation. As far as he knew, the man had never bothered to defend a local in the past. Even when Finley had been threatened because she'd witnessed a drug deal in this very parking lot—between one of Whip's servers and a drug dealer—Raid had heard through the grapevine that Whip decided it wasn't any of his business.

So he remained on edge as he waited to see what the man would do next.

To Raid's surprise, he saw respect in the bar owner's

eyes as the man gave him a chin lift. Then he turned to Khloe. "You okay?"

Khloe nodded. "Thank you."

Whip shook his head. "Don't want your thanks."

"What *do* you want?" she asked.

"I want you to hurry the hell up and open that emergency clinic you've been thinking about opening."

Raid blinked in surprise. That was the last thing he'd expected the man to say. As far as anyone knew, the only business Whip cared about was his own.

"I'm working on it," Khloe told him evenly. "And with those two in town, everything I do is more difficult. I wouldn't put it past them to sabotage any clinic I try to open. Deface the property, talk to the bank to convince them I'm high risk, picket out front to drive my customers away."

"They won't. I'll make sure of it."

Raid wasn't sure he wanted Khloe to be in this man's debt. There would come a time when he'd want her to pay up for his support. "Why?" he asked bluntly.

"Why what?"

"Why would you help Khloe? It's not exactly a secret that you don't even really like Fallport. You don't participate in any of the town's activities, you were the only business on the square that didn't decorate for Christmas, and you scorn everything most of us love about this place. Plus, hate to say it, but...you're kind of an ass to everyone. Why are you going out of your way to get involved when you've never made the slightest effort to do so before?"

"My cat," Whip said without hesitation. "She got in a fight with something. Maybe a bobcat, I don't know. But she was in bad shape and needed care immediately. It was around five o'clock in the afternoon, and I called Ziegler. *Begged* that fucker to wait for me to get to the clinic so he could help her. He said no. Told me he was leaving, that he closed at five. No matter how much I pleaded, he refused. That asshole doesn't give a shit about anything but himself."

"Did she make it?" Khloe asked softly.

"I had to drive to the emergency clinic in Christiansburg. She almost bled out by the time I'd arrived. She lost both eyes and they had to remove one of her legs. But by some miracle, she lived. She's now an inside cat, is scared of her own shadow, and stays hidden under my couch when I'm not there."

"And when you *are* there?" Khloe asked with uncanny insight.

Whip shrugged, looking away. "She likes to perch on my shoulder or curl around my neck when I'm on the couch watching TV...or doing anything, really."

Raid couldn't have been more shocked if someone had told him Whip Johansen was Santa Claus. There was a lot more to the bar owner than he'd—hell, *anyone*—had given him credit for.

"So," Whip continued, clearing his throat, "you setting up a clinic benefits me. I want to see it happen as soon as possible. And getting rid of those two yahoos will make it happen faster. So I'm gonna do what I can to encourage them to go home. To leave you alone so you can hurry the fuck up and set up shop."

"Their brother's dog *did* die on my operating table," Khloe said softly. "I couldn't save her. I might not have been able to do anything for your cat either."

"Bullshit. The vet said if he'd gotten Mittens into

surgery faster, she might not have lost both of her eyes...
and he definitely could've saved her leg. I'm not an idiot, I
know you won't be able to save every animal you treat. But
you being here will give them a hell of a better chance than
if we continue to have to drive half a fucking hour to the
nearest vet who gives a shit."

He wasn't wrong. Raid turned to Khloe. She had tears
in her eyes, and she was looking at Whip as if she'd never
seen him before. He understood; he felt a little off-kilter
himself.

"We'd appreciate your assistance," Raid finally
told him.

Whip's gaze turned to him. "Not doing it for you,
pretty boy," he said. "I don't much like you or your friends.
I'm doing it for myself. And Mittens and others like her."

"Right," Raid said with a nod. He didn't give a shit if
this man liked him or not. He didn't understand his atti-
tude, but in the scope of things, it didn't really matter.

"I'll see what I can do to hurry the process of opening
my clinic," Khloe told him.

"Good. I'll be watching out for those two. If they come
back here, I'll make sure they understand just how unwel-
come they are."

"Thank you."

Whip didn't say anything more, simply turned and
headed for his bar. When the door shut behind him,
Khloe let out a long breath.

"Holy crap."

Raid couldn't help but smile.

"Wait until I tell the others that Whip Johansen has a
cat named Mittens that rides around on his shoulders," she
said with a big grin.

Raid couldn't stop himself from touching her if his life depended on it. He stepped into her space and wrapped a hand behind her neck. He rested his forehead against hers. "That was intense. You okay?"

He felt her hands slip under his long-sleeve T-shirt and her nails dig into the skin of his lower back.

"Do I have the option *not* to be okay?" she asked seriously.

Raid lifted his head but didn't let go of her. "Of course. You're allowed to be pissed. To have a breakdown. We can go to my place and you can change into sweats, have a good cry, sit on my couch with Duke's head in your lap, and drink that complicated coffee you like so much that I'll buy you before we go home."

"Or?" she asked with a tilt of her head.

"We can go on that hike we'd planned. When we get home, you can call Finley and the others and tell them all about Mittens. Then you can talk to Drew about your finances and see about moving your timetable for opening Fallport's first emergency vet clinic sooner rather than later. Then, after I make you a protein-rich dinner so you'll have plenty of energy, you can take me to bed and have your wicked way with me."

She chuckled. "Every time you say I can be in control, I end up on my back with your head between my legs, completely incoherent as you make me orgasm over and over again."

"Are you complaining?" he asked seriously.

"Um...duh. No," she said. "Have you ever seen that eighties movie *Revenge of the Nerds*?"

"Of course," Raid said with a furrow of his brow. "Why?"

"Because there's a part in it where Lewis, the geek and the hero of the movie, says something about how all jocks think about is sports, and all nerds think about is sex. I'm thinking he wasn't wrong."

Raid smirked. Then he sobered. "I've waited a long time for a woman like you."

"Like me?" Khloe asked. "Crippled, moody, and snarky?"

"Beautiful, loyal, funny, able to hold her own when I give her crap, and who sees past my freakish height, bright red hair, and pointy elf ears."

Khloe reached up and ran her fingers over one of his ears. "You're perfect, Raiden. So much so, I have to keep telling myself this isn't a joke. That you really do like me and that you aren't just playing me."

"I tell myself the same thing every night when I'm holding you in my arms," Raid reassured her.

Khloe went up on her tiptoes and Raid lowered his head to meet her halfway. The kiss felt different from others with her in the past. It held a promise. A promise of many more days and nights to come.

When she pulled back, Khloe said, "I think I'll pass on the nervous breakdown and choose door number two. But I'm reserving the right to have said breakdown in the future if things go to hell."

"Deal," Raid told her.

Then Khloe turned her attention to Duke. He was still standing at her side and a large line of drool was dripping from his jowl to the gravel at his feet.

"Who's a good boy?" Khloe singsonged. "You are! Duke's a good boy."

His dog ate up her attention, but Raid couldn't blame

him. Finally, Khloe straightened and said, "So, are we gonna do this hike or what?"

She might not think so, but Khloe was exceptionally strong. Raid didn't like that she'd called herself a cripple. Her limp might slow her down physically, but she had a spine of steel. There weren't many people who could go through what she did and come out as well as she had on the other side.

Raid knew her struggles weren't over. There would be days her leg pained her more than usual, when she'd have to deal with someone bringing up Alan and the trial, and possibly even years of the Mathers doing their best to harass her. But she was a survivor, and he was a lucky son-of-a-bitch to be by her side. He'd never take her for granted. Ever.

CHAPTER FOURTEEN

Khloe's head spun with how fast things were moving when it came to opening the emergency clinic. She honestly hadn't expected to be arranging for the supplies she'd put in storage back in Norfolk to be delivered so soon.

Jason and Scott continued to be a pain in her ass, but in the couple of weeks since Whip and Raid had stood up to them, they'd been a little less confrontational. That didn't mean she wasn't still very aware they were lurking around. She had no idea how they were able to afford to stay in Fallport for so long. If they had jobs or where they were staying, but she refused to use too much of her brain power thinking about them.

Her life was going amazingly well and she didn't want to think about anything messing with that. She wasn't an idiot, she knew there would be bumps in the road, but at the moment, she just wanted to enjoy being with Raid.

She'd never dated a man as devoted and...present...as he was. Maybe it was because they both worked in the library and were together nearly every moment of every day. Whatever the reason, Khloe liked it. A lot. Things would change once she opened her practice, but for now she was soaking in his attention and affection.

Their nights were spent exploring each other, and Khloe enjoying the benefits of Raiden being obsessed with making sure she was always well satisfied and boneless before he took his own pleasure. From the outside, Raid might look like a typical nerd. Dungeons and Dragons, librarian, an introvert who wasn't interested in sports or other so-called "manly" hobbies. But Khloe was finding that she'd take a nerd over any other kind of man, any day. Well, at least she'd take *Raid* over anyone else.

She'd never felt more loved. More worshiped. More seen than when she was with him. He was still snarky and never had a problem telling her when she'd screwed something up at work. That hadn't changed with their new relationship status.

But the man was seriously insatiable and enjoyed taking charge in the bedroom. Khloe secretly loved it. She was independent and had been on her own for a long time, but there was something so freeing about being able to lay back and let Raid do what he wanted with her. Because everything he wanted to do made her feel really damn good.

For instance, the night before, he'd insisted on giving her a full-body massage. From head to toe then back up. But on the second pass, he did everything he could to arouse her. Pinching her nipples, "accidentally" slipping a finger inside her pussy as he rubbed her thighs. By the time he was done, she couldn't say she was actually very relaxed, but after he gave her two monster orgasms in a row, she was a boneless mess.

The other thing Khloe found almost unbelievable was how Raid always seemed surprised when she wanted to reciprocate. Apparently he'd been with selfish women in the past who only wanted to take instead of give. One of her favorite memories so far was the night Khloe got on her hands and knees and told Raid to take what he wanted —*how* he wanted. It was obvious he'd never been given free rein like that in the past, no matter *how* alpha he was in the bedroom. Having him towering behind her, fucking her at a brutal pace, had been just as pleasurable for her as it was for him.

Yes, it was safe to say her sex life with Raid was better than she'd ever had. But there were also nights when they were content to simply hold each other. Khloe didn't know which she liked better.

It was Monday evening, and she and Raiden had finished work and headed to the building she was renting next to Brock's auto shop. Rocky was already there when they arrived, working on putting in walls to create rooms for her to meet with owners and their pets, as well as configuring the space she'd use for surgeries and the recovery room.

When Khloe had called Afton and asked if she'd be willing to apply as a vet tech, the other woman had let out a loud screech and agreed gratefully. She'd also recruited two of her friends from her vet-tech program. One already lived in Fallport and was still living with her parents, and the other would be moving from Richmond to join their team.

It was nerve-racking and almost overwhelming that she really was doing this, but Khloe was happy.

Jason and Scott had shown up at the under-construction clinic once, but someone had apparently alerted Whip—who was now being looked at in a different light by some of the townspeople. The second he'd pulled up, tires screeching, Jason and Scott had left in a hurry.

Khloe was cautiously optimistic that things in her life might work out after all.

She was watching Rocky measure out a space on the floor where she wanted him to erect the drywall for the exam rooms when Raid's phone rang. She heard him answer the call.

"Tonka! Long time no hear. What's up?"

Khloe glanced over at him. She couldn't hear the other side of the conversation, but the longer Raid listened to him, the more he frowned and the harder his body got.

"How the fuck did that happen?" he suddenly barked.

Khloe jumped. She'd never heard the kind of hatred in his tone as she did in that moment. Feeling a hand on her elbow, she looked up to see Rocky at her side, frowning at Raid.

"That's bullshit! Don't they know what he's capable of?"

Khloe felt sick inside. She had no idea what was happening, but it wasn't good, she knew that much.

"What are the odds he'll stay put?" Raid asked the mysterious Tonka. "Yeah. I will. You too. If you find out anything more, let me know. Yeah, same. I hear you're married now. You need to stay safe. If need be, I'll take care of this. I know, and Khloe means the world to me, but *no one* is safe with him on the outside. Right. Yeah. Thanks for the heads-up. I'll be in touch."

Raid clicked off the phone but didn't move. He simply stared off into space.

"Raid?" Khloe asked softly.

He jerked, as if he'd forgotten where he was and that she was even there. Then he turned without a word and left the building.

"What the heck?" Khloe muttered.

"Stay here, I'll go talk to him," Rocky told her.

"No. I'll go."

"I'm not sure that's the best idea. Something's wrong, and he might take it out on you," Rocky said.

Khloe turned to him with her hands on her hips. "I can take his bad mood," she told him. "I'm not some fragile flower who'll wilt if he raises his voice. I handled him for a year before we started going out, I can handle him now."

"All right, but if he says anything hurtful, don't take it personally."

"Who's Tonka? Do you know?" she asked Rocky. She wanted to tell him there was no way Raid would hurt her, but she settled for asking him who was on the other end of that call.

"He was his partner in the Coast Guard before he got out. He's never talked about what happened to make him want to leave, but I got the impression it was bad."

Khloe swallowed hard and nodded.

"He needs you," Rocky said as Khloe turned to follow Raid. "He's got a lot bottled up inside. He hides it well, but he hasn't had an easy life. He actually believes the stereotypes people have forced on him. That he's some geeky weirdo, not as worthy as others."

"Which is all bullshit. I love everything about him."

"Good. Go. I'll lock up here when I'm done. Take him home, get him to talk to you. See if you can pull him out of whatever pit his old friend's call dropped him into."

Khloe nodded and determination rose within her. Raid had done so much for her. Had supported her unconditionally. Hadn't even blinked when he'd learned just how much she'd been hiding from him and all their other friends. He'd accepted her exactly how she was. It was her turn to be there for him. To be his rock just as he'd been hers.

It wouldn't be easy. He'd spent a lifetime holding back his emotions. Showing the world only what he thought they wanted to see. And whatever had happened between him and Tonka, whatever his old friend had told him, had probably brought back bad memories.

Taking a deep breath, she headed out the door to see what she could do for the man who meant the world to her. Meant more than her career. More than her secrets.

"Get in."

Raid turned to see Khloe gesturing to his Expedition with her head as she walked toward the driver's side.

"I don't think—" he started, but she didn't let him finish.

"Good. Don't think. Just get in. We're going home."

Raid's head was swimming with the news Tonka had just told him. It was literally his worst nightmare come true.

He knew this day would come, but he expected it to be years in the future.

It was too soon. Way too soon. He and Khloe had barely begun...

And now he needed to break up with her. For her own

good. Putting space between him and the people he loved was the only possible choice. They were *all* in danger. He knew it down to the marrow of his bones.

And not from the kind of petty bullshit the Mathers were indulging in.

Moving as if through thick molasses, Raid walked toward the passenger side of his car. Normally seeing Khloe pull the seat all the way forward so she could reach the pedals would make him chuckle, but he couldn't feel anything right now. He felt numb.

Duke had jumped into the back seat after Khloe opened the door for him, and he could hear his dog still getting settled as Khloe pulled out of the parking lot. It didn't take long for them to arrive back at his house. Woodenly, he got out and grabbed Duke's leash and headed for the front door.

As soon as the door shut behind them, Raid turned to tell her that she should get her stuff and go, but Khloe spoke first.

"Take Duke outside. Let him do his business. Then come back inside and change. I'll start something for dinner. We'll eat, then sit on the couch, and you'll talk to me."

He blinked in surprise. Had he ever heard her be quite so bossy before? Well, yes. Of course he had. "I think you should go, Khloe."

"Well, yay for you for thinking that, but it's not happening. Duke needs to shit, Raid. You know he only likes to poop in his own yard. Go let him out."

Surprised at her resistance, and her nonreaction to his declaration that she should leave, Raid turned and headed for the back door with Duke.

Twenty minutes later, after the damn dog had managed to sniff every inch of the yard and find the perfect bush to squat over, Raid had regained a little of his senses. But with that came the pain he'd experienced all those years ago. Memories assailed him as he remembered the last time he'd seen Tonka.

He was even more determined to get Khloe to leave than before. Jason and Scott were nothing compared to the danger being with him could now bring to her doorstep.

"Go change," Khloe ordered as he entered the living room.

Raid hesitated. He wanted to protest, but he needed a shower even more. Maybe that would wash off the cloying fear that seemed to be clinging to him.

When he finished showering, he was clean, but didn't feel any better. He went into the living room and saw Duke lying on his back, paws in the air as he snored on his bed. Turning his attention to the kitchen, he saw Khloe dishing up one of his favorite meals ever. Spaghetti with hot dogs.

It was childish and kind of gross, but it was what his mom always made for him when he came home crying after being bullied at school for his red hair, his height, his ears. He might not be close with his parents these days, but he'd told Khloe that spaghetti and hot dogs was a comfort food that never failed to make him feel good.

And she'd remembered. And somehow knew it was just what he needed right now.

Of course, pasta and hot dogs wasn't going to change what Tonka had told him.

He didn't remember eating, but he obviously had

because the next thing he knew, Khloe was taking his empty plate into the kitchen.

"Khloe...please stop. You really need to go. I'm sorry, but—"

"I heard you the first time, Raid. And I'm still not going anywhere."

"That phone call I got earlier..." He closed his eyes briefly. "Being with me puts you in danger now, and that doesn't work for me. So we're done. Nothing you say will change my mind," he told her stiffly, as she put their dishes in the washer.

Khloe whipped around, and the look she shot him was so full of anger, Raid actually flinched.

"I know you got bad news today, and you're still reeling from whatever you heard, but you're starting to piss me off."

It was weird that Raid was both scared out of his mind for her and proud of her at the same time.

When he didn't respond, she shook her head. "Why don't you go downstairs to your man cave and chill out for a while," she told him in a disappointed voice.

The truth was, Raid *didn't* want Khloe to leave, of course. So he turned and headed for the basement without a word.

The second the door closed behind him, he regretted walking away. He was being an ass. But it was for a good reason.

He didn't know how long he'd been downstairs when he heard footsteps coming down the steps. Raid had been sitting on the couch, staring into space, lost in the past. He turned to see what Khloe wanted.

But it wasn't Khloe, it was Rocky who appeared.

"Hey, buddy. Khloe called me."

Of course she did. But surprisingly, Raid wasn't upset about it. He needed to talk to *someone*, and he wasn't quite ready to share this awful story with Khloe. She loved animals so much, he knew it would hurt her almost as much as it hurt him.

Rocky had been a SEAL. Raid had no doubt his friend had known his fair share of people who'd wanted revenge against him because of his job.

"Hey," he said belatedly.

Rocky sat in the chair in front of his computer and leaned back, looking completely relaxed, as if this was nothing more than a social call. But they both knew differently.

After a long moment, he spoke. "Khloe said that call really affected you. Which I know, since I was there. She also said you're now being a moody bitch, and you need a manly man to talk to about it."

Raid couldn't help but laugh. That sounded exactly like something Khloe would say. But then he sobered. "Being with me could put her in serious danger."

"Why don't you start from the beginning," Rocky suggested.

So he did. Raid told his friend everything. He didn't leave anything out.

When he was done, almost thirty minutes had gone by. Rocky hadn't interrupted, had simply listened. When he didn't immediately comment, Raid said, "So you understand why I need her to go. She's in danger just being around me."

"What I understand is that you and Khloe are so much alike, it's not even funny," Rocky said.

Raid's brow furrowed.

He continued. "She wanted to leave the second she realized the Mather brothers had found her...right?"

"Yeah," Raid said with a shrug.

"So what makes this any different from that? You found out about this *possible* threat—no one has any proof that there even *is* a threat at this point—and you're ready to break up with her, kick her out of your life, and go back to being the hermit you were a couple months ago...just in case."

Raid stared at his friend. He was technically right. There was no way to know a threat was imminent, yet his instinctive reaction was to push Khloe away for her own good. He'd even contemplated giving Duke to one of the guys on the team and leaving Fallport altogether. "It's not exactly the same," he protested. "She's not being hunted by a psycho killer."

"Neither are you. First off, you don't know if he's going to come after you at all," Rocky said. "But putting that aside...Alan Mather tried to *kill* her. Ran her down with a fucking truck, and it was mostly luck that kept him from crushing her skull. If that's not psycho, I don't know what is. And it seems to me she has every reason to think his brothers might attempt to finish what he failed to accomplish."

Raid pressed his lips together. Damn. Rocky was right.

"I need to talk to her," he said after a moment.

"Yup," his friend agreed.

"I wanted to shield her from all of this, Rocky," Raid muttered.

"And I'm sure that's why she kept *her* secrets for so long, as well. She wanted to protect her new friends. You."

Rocky stood. "I'll send her down and lock up on my way out."

"Thanks." Raid had the best friends. He was sure Rocky had better things to do tonight than come over here. And yet, he was equally sure he hadn't hesitated when Khloe called him.

She must've been waiting anxiously upstairs because almost as soon as Raid heard the basement door close after Rocky, he heard Duke's paws on the stairs and Khloe following close behind.

"Is it safe to come down?" she asked as she appeared at the bottom of the stairs.

Duke padded right over to Raid and put his head in his lap for a moment, before going to his dog bed in the corner and lying down with a sigh.

"Thank you for calling Rocky," Raid told her. It was obvious that she was anxious, because instead of sitting next to him on the couch, she took the seat Rocky had recently vacated.

"I understand the need for secrets," Khloe said seriously, not acknowledging his thanks. "I'm the last person who would get mad at anyone for having them. But I thought we were building something together, Raid. I don't need you to be happy and carefree every second of every day. You've been through some shit...shit I know nothing about, and that's okay. But it's a part of who you are. It's made you into the man you are today. The man I'm falling for.

"I even understand you trying to push me away to protect me. Hell, I did the same thing for months to you and everyone else in this town. But you made me see that I'm stronger with people by my side. Having my back.

Does it mean my troubles went away? No. Am I completely safe from Jason, Scott, and Alan? Again, no. But I don't want them to control my life anymore. I want to do what I love—help animals—and I never would've been able to come as far as I have without your support.

"I'm still worried. I still get scared. But I'm not willing to let them control my life anymore. If I run, if I give up everything here, they've won. And I don't want that to happen."

Raid stared at Khloe. She was smart. So damn smart.

She went on. "You had a shock today. I get it. I've been there. The fight-or-flight response kicks in and it's so much easier to run than to stay. But I'm here. As are your friends and teammates. We'll fight by your side if that's what it takes. But what I'm *not* going to do is let you push me away. I'm tougher than you think, Raid. I can handle whatever it is that's got you so freaked out. Let me stay by your side. Let me have *your* back. I might not be a badass SEAL or a Coastie, but I'm pretty scrappy."

"Come here," Raid ordered, holding out his hand. He held his breath as he waited to see what she'd do. She had every right to roll her eyes and tell him no, but to his immense relief, she stood up immediately and walked toward him.

She sat in the circle of his arm and snuggled in, putting one arm around his stomach and forcing the other between his back and the couch. Her cheek rested on his chest and she sighed, as if she'd been worried what her reception would be.

And Raid hated that. She'd done everything right. Had given him space, had ignored him when he'd half-heartedly tried to break up with her, had called Rocky.

"I loved being in the Coast Guard," he said. It wasn't a hard decision to tell her about that last mission. But she needed a little background first. "I worked my ass off to be accepted to the dog handler program. Very few people are and it's extremely rigorous. I wasn't the best candidate because of my height. But I refused to give up. I went through training with a guy named Finn Matlick. His nickname is Tonka, because he's built like a truck. Anyway, we clicked immediately and we became friends.

"His Belgian Malinois was named Steel, and mine was Dagger. They were awesome. Did everything we asked them to without hesitation. They trusted us completely, as we did them. We were a well-oiled machine, and together, the four of us made a ton of drug busts." Raid took a deep breath. He didn't like thinking about that last awful day, but Khloe deserved to know what happened. What the phone call today was about.

She didn't interrupt him. Didn't give meaningless platitudes. Simply squeezed him tighter, letting him know she was listening.

"We were doing a search of a suspicious vessel. It was pretty routine, so instead of waiting for backup—which was so stupid—we were cocky enough to assume we could handle it. It was a fairly small speedboat. We could only see one person onboard when we pulled up next to it. We boarded the boat...and almost immediately, I was knocked unconscious. Someone came up behind me and did their best to crack my skull open. Then they shot me to make sure I wasn't going to wake up and ruin their fun."

"Shit!" Khloe muttered.

"Yeah. I was out like a light. I wasn't aware of anything

that was happening around me. They could've just tossed me overboard."

When he didn't say anything for a full minute, Khloe asked, "What happened?"

Raid swallowed hard. "Hell happened. We didn't know the driver of the boat was Pablo Garcia. One of the most notorious and ruthless drug lords in South America. One of his men had been hiding behind some crates onboard, and he was the one to bash me over the head. Tonka wasn't so lucky. When Pablo threatened to shoot me a second time, he surrendered and was tied up. Then for fun...Pablo started torturing Dagger and Steel."

Khloe inhaled sharply and lifted her head. "What?"

"Yeah. They tied the dogs up, zip-tied their legs together, and proceeded to torture them. I'll spare you the details...but Tonka had to witness every second of it. Had to look into Steel's pleading eyes, unable to do anything to help him. You have to understand, those dogs were our partners in every sense. We would've done anything for them, and they'd do the same in return. Watching them suffer...it broke something inside Tonka.

"When Pablo and his men got sick of their games, they threw both Steel and Dagger overboard, but not until they'd weighed them down with some stuff they'd had onboard."

Khloe gasped. "Alive?"

Raid nodded.

"Oh my God, that's horrible!"

It was. It was more than horrible. And Raid had to live with the fact that he'd been unconscious during Dagger's last moments in this world. That the dog had probably looked to his master for help, not getting even the smallest shred of comfort since Raid had been out cold.

"Apparently Garcia's intentions were to do the same to us. Torture us and throw us overboard while we were still alive, but our backup finally arrived. There was a shootout, and Tonka was hit a few times by stray rounds, but miraculously he wasn't killed."

"Thank God," Khloe breathed.

"He wasn't the same afterward," Raid said sadly. "The man I knew and loved like a brother was gone. Watching his faithful companion suffer like he did..." Raid's words tapered off, and he had to clear his throat before he could talk again. "And my guilt was so intense, I knew I'd never be able to continue in the Coast Guard. We both quit and went our separate ways."

"Is he okay?" Khloe asked.

"Amazingly, yes. Now. He's living in New Mexico. He and some men he met started a resort of sorts for people suffering from PTSD. He lives in the woods surrounded by animals big and small. Cows, goats, dogs, cats, even some chickens, from what I understand. Not only that, but he's married, with a teenage stepdaughter and a baby now too."

"Good," Khloe breathed. "I'm happy for him."

"Me too," Raid said. And he was. The man had been through hell and deserved to finally be happy. Content. And from what he saw from The Refuge's website, his old friend was doing very well for himself.

"So what was the call today about?" Khloe asked.

Raid sighed. "Pablo Garcia was released from prison due to overcrowding and supposed good behavior."

She shot upward, staring at him with wide eyes. "What?"

He nodded. "The call was Tonka letting me know that Garcia was free. He was deported, but we both know that means nothing. Before he was hauled off that boat from hell, he vowed to finish what he'd started. To end us both. I have no doubt somehow, someway, he'll find us eventually."

Instead of looking scared or worried, a determined look crossed Khloe's face. "I'd like to see him try," she spat. "Asshole, dog-killing fucker."

To his surprise, Raid found himself trying not to smile. Not at Khloe, never at her, but she wasn't generally a swearer. And to hear her cussing up a storm was so out of character, and it told him exactly how upset she was on his behalf. But then he sobered. "That's why I think it's better if you and I took a break for a while. At least until Tonka and I can figure out where he is and what he might have planned."

"No."

Raid frowned and waited for her to say more, but she didn't.

"Khloe—" he started, but she shook her head against him.

"No. I'm not afraid of him, and I'm not going to leave you alone to deal with this."

"You *should* be afraid of him," Raid returned.

"Well, I'm not. I don't know why. If he *is* stupid enough to come here to kill you, he'll be totally out of his element. This isn't a boat in the middle of the ocean. He can't just waltz into Fallport and think he can kill you and leave. We can do what we did for me. Let people know what's going on, and to be on the lookout for a stranger who might be more than a little interested in you."

"No way," Raiden said with a firm shake of his head.

Khloe sat up, and he immediately missed her warmth against him. "Why?" she asked.

"Because I don't want people up in my business," he told her.

"So it's okay to have people up in *my* business, but not yours?" she asked, annoyingly reasonable.

"It's not the same," he protested.

"Look, I know you have guilt about what happened, but it wasn't your fault, Raid. You were knocked unconscious. Shot! If you'd been awake, you would've suffered just as badly as your friend. And in a lot of ways, it was *worse* for you because you had no idea what was happening and you didn't get to say goodbye to Dagger. But you didn't do anything wrong. *Nothing.* Who's to say this Garcia guy wouldn't have done worse things to you or Tonka if you were conscious? Maybe he would've started in on your friend instead of the dogs, just to torture you. It sucks, Raid. There's no doubt. But you have nothing to be ashamed of."

He wasn't completely convinced she was right, but she wasn't the first person to tell him that. Hell, the last time they'd talked about that day, Tonka had even flat-out said he was glad he'd been unconscious the entire time. That Raid hadn't seen what he had.

"Besides, we don't have to spread all the details about what happened. Just that someone you busted while in the Coast Guard has it out for you and might come to town to settle a score. You know that will be enough for people to be reporting every single stranger they see to poor Simon and the rest of his deputies. If I've learned *anything* during the last month, it's that the people who live here will do whatever it takes to protect one of their own. There's been enough trauma lately to last a lifetime. Besides...you're a hero here. How many lost people have you and Duke found?"

"I don't know," Raid said with a shrug.

"Well, it's a lot. And once people hear you and Duke might be in danger, they'll step up."

"If you get hurt because of me..." His voice trailed off.

Khloe straddled his waist and took his face in her hands. "Now you know exactly how I feel," she said softly.

Raid's hands went to her waist and he held on tightly as she kept speaking.

"I can't promise nothing will happen to you because of the Mathers, just as you can't promise nothing will happen to *me* because of your troubles. All we can do is stay aware and communicate with each other. We're already being careful, we'll just be *more* careful. But despite the Mathers, I've been happier these last few weeks than I've ever been in years, and that's because of you. Don't let me go, Raiden. Please."

His hands tightened and he pulled her into him, burying his face in her neck. It took him a few moments to gather his composure, but when he did, he pulled back. "You'll do everything I tell you, without argument," he ordered.

Khloe nodded.

"You won't take any chances. You won't confront anyone. You won't do anything that will allow Garcia to get his hands on you if he comes."

"I won't," she agreed. "Just as you won't do anything crazy either. You won't go off the deep end. You won't push me or the rest of your friends away."

Raid couldn't help but smile at that. "I won't," he told her.

"Good. We're a team, Raid. You, me, and Duke."

The bloodhound, hearing his name, groaned and rolled over, coming to his feet. He climbed up onto the couch and pushed his head between Khloe and Raid.

Raid let go of Khloe with one hand to pet the slobbery hound.

"You feel better?" Khloe asked him.

"Yeah."

"Good. Don't ever do that again, Raid," she said in a pissed-off tone.

It was such a change from the loving woman he held in his arms, Raid could only nod, feeling guilty.

"I mean it. If you ever try to break up with me 'for my own good' again...I won't be so nice the next time."

He smiled. "Noted."

And Khloe being Khloe, she nodded and let it go. "Can we go upstairs now? I'm thinking you need another shower."

"I do, huh?" Raid asked.

"Yup. Because I'm sure you need assistance with those hard-to-reach places on your back."

"And you'll help me with those?"

"If I must," she said with an exaggerated sigh. Then she took his face in her hands again and leaned in. "It's going to be fine. Everything's going to work out," she told him.

"I hope so."

"I know so," she said firmly. "I couldn't have just found the man I can see myself growing old with, only to lose him now."

Contentment spread through Raid's veins. "Same," he said gently.

"Right, before we melt into a pile of goo right here on the couch, get your butt upstairs and into the shower, mister."

She let out a screech when Raid scooted forward on the couch with her still in his lap and stood.

"Raiden!" she exclaimed as she threw her arms around his shoulders to hold on. "Don't drop me!"

"Never," he told her with complete confidence. "One good thing about being as big and strong as I am...I can carry you easily." He could feel her relaxing in his arms.

"Yeah? Maybe I should have you carry me everywhere then. My leg and all, you know."

He chuckled. "You're too headstrong and independent for me to carry you all the time," he told her.

"True. You know me well."

"I do," he returned with a small nod. "Just like you knew it was best to give me some time and to call Rocky to come over and talk me off the ledge. And I didn't thank you for the awesome dinner."

She wrinkled her nose and stared at him as he neared the top of the stairs. "For the record...spaghetti and hot dogs is just gross."

He chuckled. "Noted."

"But if it makes you feel better, I'll fix it every day if necessary."

Raid stopped in the hallway at the top of the stairs and stared at her. How he'd gotten so lucky to have Khloe with him now, he had no idea. "I'm not going to screw this up. But if I do something to piss you off in the future, like I did today, please call me on it."

"Oh, I will," she said with a smile. "And the same goes for you. I kind of like when we pick on each other, but if I ever go too far, or say or do anything that crosses a line, please let me know."

"You know me better than anyone," he said. "Before today, I've never talked about that mission and what happened. And now you *and* Rocky know. There's nothing you can say or do that'll make me want to give you up. Unless you truly want to leave and aren't doing so just to be noble."

"Same," she whispered. "I need you, Raid. Please."

And just like that, his cock twitched. "I like when you beg," he teased as he began to walk down the hall once more.

"I know you do," she quipped.

Later, much later, when Raid held an exhausted, sleeping Khloe, he thought back over everything that happened that day.

The fear that he'd felt when he'd learned Garcia had been released, fear not for himself but for Khloe and all his friends, had morphed into something different.

Anger.

Pablo Garcia was a dangerous murderer. And whoever made the decision to let him free had made a huge mistake. But it was done, and the only thing to do now was move forward. Prepare in case the man made good on his promise to make him and Tonka pay for his arrest. The guy wouldn't take him by surprise again. Raid knew what kind of man he was—and he would be ready for him.

Not only that, but the harassment Jason and Scott Mather were heaping on Khloe needed to stop—now.

Raid needed to make those phone calls. Talk to some

of the contacts he'd made over the years that he'd considered calling the second he'd heard about Alan Mather.

He loved Khloe. There was no doubt about it, even if they hadn't shared the words. No one would take her from him. They deserved to live a happy, uneventful life and grow old and gray together.

Raid didn't know what the immediate future held, but he was more determined than ever to fight for what he wanted. And that was Khloe. And Fallport. And his friends.

And for neither him nor Khloe having to look over their shoulders for the rest of their lives. He'd do whatever it took to make that happen.

CHAPTER FIFTEEN

Raid didn't usually do this. Didn't ask for a meeting with his friends. They hung out when the women were doing their thing, and of course they talked after a search and the person was found. But never in all the time he'd been a member of the Eagle Point Search and Rescue team had *he* asked for a meeting with all the guys.

So they were all looking pretty concerned when they gathered in the conference room at the library. Raid wasn't willing to leave Khloe alone, even though he had no proof Garcia was anywhere near Fallport. Until he knew where the man was, Raid wouldn't relax. Not only that, but Jason and Scott Mather were still out there, probably scheming on how next to harass his woman.

Not being one to beat around the bush, Raid didn't attempt any idle chitchat after everyone had arrived. "There's a possibility my past might come back to haunt me," he started. Then proceeded to tell the best friends he'd ever had all about Pablo Garcia and what happened on that boat several years ago.

He expected his friends to be pissed. He expected them to be concerned. He didn't expect to be put in a position where *he* was the one trying to talk *them* down from their extreme anger on his behalf.

Rocky had already heard the story, but the others were beyond shocked. Not that a man like Garcia existed, they'd all seen their own versions of the evil that was inside the drug dealer, but at his utter ruthlessness when it came to the dogs he'd killed.

"I have no proof he's going to come here," Raid said.

"But you have no proof he's not either," Zeke pointed out.

"Exactly. I have no doubt he spent his time behind bars coming up with all sorts of ways to torture you and Tonka," Drew agreed.

"What does your friend say?" Ethan asked.

"He's not happy. He's over in New Mexico, and he has a family. Not to mention a barn full of animals he looks after and a bunch of friends he works with. He's just as concerned as me," Raid informed the group.

"As he should be," Tal said. "Are we hunting this asshole down? Who are we calling?"

Raid couldn't believe he was smiling. His friends' reactions were reassuring. He wasn't overreacting or being paranoid. They were just as concerned as he was.

"I thought Ethan could contact his friend Tex. Maybe he can do some searches and see what he can find out about the man. See if he can figure out if he stayed where the immigration officials left him or if he's in the wind," Raid said.

"Rex, my acquaintance in Colorado, mainly deals with domestic sex traffickers these days, but I'd bet everything

I own he's still got connections who could find out more information for us," Rocky said.

"Don't forget Silverstone," Zeke added. "From what I've heard, they're not really in the business anymore, but men like that don't just go cold turkey. And they have plenty of connections in the FBI and other government sources."

Everyone nodded.

"I'll call the fucking president if I have to in order to get info," Ethan growled. "How the hell someone like *that* could've been let out is beyond me. Someone fucked up big, and I intend to do everything I can to make sure whoever made that decision is fucking fired."

"So what's the plan in the meantime?" Drew asked, a little more calmly than his friends. "What about Khloe?"

"Not to be butting into your business, but you two seem exceptionally close lately," Brock added. "I'm assuming things have progressed beyond boss and employee?"

"Yes," Raid said simply. He'd never been the kind of man to kiss and tell, but he had no problem with his friends knowing how much she meant to him.

"Right, so we need to make sure she's covered at all times," Drew said with a nod.

"Which we already are, because of Tweedledee and Tweedledum being in town," Zeke grumbled.

"Fuck, forgot about those two assholes," Drew said with a shake of his head.

"You know, I kind of miss the days when the only thing we had to worry about was if and when we might get called out on a search," Ethan said wryly.

"You do not," Tal said, throwing a pen across the table at his friend.

"Okay, you're right. I wouldn't change having Lilly in my life for anything. But life sure seemed a lot easier before stalkers, psychos, and exes were in the picture."

"Easier, maybe," Brock conceded. "But not nearly as awesome."

He wasn't wrong.

"Other than covering Khloe, what else are you thinking?" Drew asked.

"Khloe suggested we spread the word about Garcia," Raid said. "Not everything, but enough to make sure the good citizens of Fallport are on watch."

"You okay with that?" Ethan asked with concern. "You haven't exactly been an open book since you've moved here. Hell, we're your best friends, and we're just now hearing about the shit that went down on that mission."

Raid nodded and made the decision to open up to these men even more. It was the least he could do after all their help with Khloe's situation...and because it was time.

"All my life, I've done what I could to fade into the background. When I was in school it was because I'd do anything not to be noticed by the bullies. As I got older, it was because I didn't fit in with the popular crowd. I was a nerd who enjoyed spending time with his video games more than people. When I was in the Coast Guard, I had Dagger to keep me company. I still spend Friday nights playing Dungeons and Dragons with some people I met online. And I prefer my own company. That doesn't mean I don't like you guys, just that...I guess I never really thought you'd want to know the real me. But I also know I didn't give you the chance."

"I played D&D when I was in high school," Drew said. "I might be interested in joining you...if you wouldn't mind."

"There's nothing wrong with being a loner," Zeke added.

"And I wasn't saying it was a bad thing that you've kept to yourself," Ethan told Raid. "We like you exactly how you are. But being the center of gossip around Fallport isn't exactly fun."

Raid leaned forward. "I don't care. I'll do whatever it takes to keep Khloe safe and get Garcia off the streets. He's a menace. There's not a chance in hell he's going to go home and just count himself lucky for getting out of prison early. He's a psychopath. He doesn't care who he hurts."

"That's obvious, after you told us what he did to Dagger and Steel," Brock said in a hard tone.

"I have no doubt he's eventually gonna come for me and Tonka. I can handle him, but I need all the eyes I can get on the lookout, so he doesn't ambush me...or Khloe. Or any of you, for that matter," Raid said.

"You mean, *we* can handle him," Ethan said firmly.

"This isn't your fight. And you've got a wife to worry about. All of you do. Zeke and Brock, your wives are pregnant. And then there's Tony and Marissa," Raid said with a shake of his head.

"You're so fucking wrong," Drew said. "Your fight is *our* fight. We're teammates. Friends. And if you think I'm gonna sit back and let this psychopath hurt someone I love, you're as crazy as him."

Raid swallowed hard. This was what he'd wanted his entire life. Friends like these.

It was just hitting home that he'd done these men a grave injustice. He'd kept them at arm's length because of his own prejudices, his own insecurities. He'd assumed they wouldn't like him as much simply because he chose to read or play a fantasy game, instead of going camping, hunting, or other more physical pursuits.

He'd let his oldest childhood fears follow him into adulthood.

"Don't underestimate him," Raid said quietly. "He's smart. He's not going to simply stroll into town. He'll do reconnaissance. He'll want as much information as possible before he strikes. And he's not afraid to hurt people to get what he wants."

"We've all known men like him," Zeke said. "He's not going to win. No way in hell."

The others all agreed and, once more, Raid was overwhelmed with gratitude for his friends.

"All right, so we're contacting anyone and everyone we can to find out where this asshole might be; we're going to carefully share intel about how someone might come to town wanting information on Raid; we'll make sure Simon and his deputies are informed; and we're gonna do our best to keep our eye on Khloe and our women and kids. *Now* can we talk about Raid and Khloe?" Tal asked with a grin.

"Yeah, I thought you two didn't like each other," Brock said.

"Oh, they liked each other." Ethan laughed. "It was obvious."

"Right? The more they bitched about each other, the more I was sure they were going to get together," Rocky said.

"They're actually perfect for each other...neither love

the company of others and they like animals better than people," Drew noted.

Raid crossed his arms and didn't even try to stop his friends. He knew from experience when they had something to say, they'd say it no matter what anyone else thought.

"That's so true!" Ethan exclaimed. "I mean, Duke likes Lilly, but he *loves* Khloe."

"Wait, does she know about your D&D games?" Rocky asked.

Raid smirked. "Yes. She's even played with me. She's really good."

His friends all beamed.

"Right, so...if everyone is done being Nosey Nellies, I need to get back to work," Raid said with a shake of his head.

"Yeah, we all do," Ethan agreed.

"We've got your back," Brock told him.

"Yeah," Tal agreed. "No matter what, Garcia's not going to win."

"Neither are the Mather brothers. And Khloe's gonna open her vet clinic and put Ziegler out of business in no time," Zeke said with a grin.

Each of his friends clapped Raid on the back as they stood and filed out of the conference room. Raid couldn't say that he felt better about the entire situation, but he was content in the knowledge that he was doing all he could. He had no doubt Tonka's friends at The Refuge, the retreat they all owned together, were doing the same thing.

After he'd said goodbye to everyone, Raid turned and wasn't surprised to see Khloe nearby. He jerked his head toward his office and she eagerly made her way toward it.

The second the door was closed, she wrapped her arms around his waist. "How'd it go? Is Operation Keep That Fucker Away From My Boyfriend underway?"

Raid couldn't help it, he laughed. If someone would've told him yesterday that he could find anything humorous about this situation, he would've told them to fuck off. But Khloe had a way of making things seem not quite so desperate.

"Yeah."

"Good. Now, since you were so stressed and grumpy this morning, I didn't get my morning kiss. Think you can remedy that now, Bjorn?"

Raid was still smiling when he lowered his head. Only his Khloe would use his D&D character's name as a term of endearment. He kissed her long and deep, apologizing for neglecting her. She returned the kiss enthusiastically.

When she pulled back, she stared up at him with a serious expression on her face.

"What?" he asked.

"We're going to be okay," she said firmly. "I don't know what the future holds, but after everything we've been through, there's no way either Alan or Pablo is gonna win."

A shiver shot up Raid's spine, but he ignored it. "Damn straight," he told her.

She beamed up at him. "Now, can I talk you into doing the inventory on the returned books while I work the checkout desk?"

Raid snorted. He knew restocking shelves wasn't Khloe's favorite thing, but he had some calls to make and he couldn't do that if he was out on the library floor.

"Nope," he said. "But I'm thinking I can make it up to you tonight."

She shivered in his arms. "Deal," she whispered. Her hands slid under his shirt and caressed the bare skin of his lower back for a moment, before she took a step back. "Is it hot in here?" she asked with a grin.

"Very," he agreed.

Then she sobered. "Raid?"

"Yeah, Khloe?"

"I wasn't ready for you. I thought I was fine on my own. But being with you these past several weeks has made me see what an idiot I was for keeping you and everyone else at arm's length for so long. No matter what happens...I know I can trust you to make it right."

After dropping that bomb, she turned and left his office and headed to the drop box to gather books.

Raid stood there for a long moment. Her words had left him dumbstruck. She'd said exactly what he felt. He'd waited too damn long to acknowledge his attraction to her and he regretted it with everything he was. And her trust in him meant *everything*. He wasn't going to let her down. No matter what, he'd do whatever it took to make sure they could both lead a very long happily ever after. Together.

And the first step toward that was to call Tonka. Now that they'd both had some time to come to terms with the fact that Garcia was free, they needed to talk. No one knew the bastard like Tonka did. He'd spent a hellacious couple of hours with the man, and if anyone had any idea what he might be planning, it'd be him. It sucked that he was all the way on the other side of the country, but maybe that was best, considering Garcia's vengeful personality.

* * *

That night, as Khloe frantically rode his cock, Raid couldn't take his eyes off her beautiful face. She was his life. She'd gradually slipped under his shields over the last year or so, but recently she'd completely shattered them. He was a different person because of her. The kind of man he'd always wanted to be.

His fingers dug into her hips as she smiled down at him. Her tits bounced on her chest and she was completely uninhibited. As he watched, she arched her back and brought her hands up to tweak her nipples, doing her best to tease him.

Raid's hand moved between her legs to roughly flick her clit, which had to still be sensitive after the two orgasms he'd already given her. He'd let her climb on top of him to give her some semblance of control, but it was a façade. He couldn't help taking over anytime they were together. And he knew she loved it.

The second he touched her, she moaned and stilled above him. Raid mourned the loss of the friction of her sheath stroking his cock, but loved how tightly she clamped around him.

"Raid," she begged as she began to shake over him. Her hands came down on his chest to brace herself when he continued to rub her.

"Come for me," he ordered.

She shook her head, but her body continued to tense.

Raid wondered if there was something wrong with him for loving how much he forced her to orgasm. Nothing made him feel more powerful than watching Khloe fly over the edge at his touch and command.

The second she started to convulse, he sat up, keeping her impaled on his dick, and put her on her back. Then he thrust hard, pushing through her tight muscles as they spasmed through her orgasm.

She groaned and Raid thrust harder. She felt so damn good. He'd never felt anything as wonderful as being deep inside her like this.

Her legs wrapped around him and her heels dug into his ass as his balls drew up closer to his body. He was on the verge of exploding when Khloe reached up and pinched his nipples. And she wasn't tentative about it either.

The shock of the stinging pain and the way her pussy still fluttered around him made him lose any control he might've had. Shoving inside her as far as he could go, Raid came. And came and came and came. He didn't think he'd ever stop spurting. It was all he could do to hold himself and not collapse on top of her and crush her under his much bigger body.

When he couldn't hold himself up anymore, he fell to the side, taking her with him, not willing to leave her pussy just yet. It was several moments before he could speak. "Damn, woman, you about killed me!" he mock-complained.

"Which you do every time we're together," she said with a smile on her face. "You liked that."

Raid couldn't help but chuckle. "Duh. But so we're on the same page, what exactly is the 'that' you're talking about?"

"Me pinching your nipples," she said.

Raid came up on an elbow and stared down at her. "I like everything you do to me."

"Except letting me be in charge," she retorted.

He shrugged. "What can I say? I like having you at my mercy."

She giggled, and Raid felt it on his dick. Which reminded him he needed to take care of the condom. "Don't move," he ordered. "I'll be right back."

He waited until she nodded before pulling out of her and rolling out of the bed. He was back in less than a minute, a grimace on his face.

"Why the frown?" she asked as he turned her around in the bed and got them situated under the covers.

"The condom broke," he said, not beating around the bush.

"Oh."

Raid waited, but she didn't say anything else. "That's all you have to say about it?" he asked.

Khloe shrugged. "I have an IUD. The chances of me getting pregnant are very slim."

"You do?"

She nodded. "I'm sorry I didn't say anything before."

"Why didn't you? I mean, I'm glad you've taken the steps to protect yourself, I'm just curious."

"Are you the kind of man who's going to go crazy if I talk about being with someone else while we're in bed?" she asked.

Raid thought about it for a moment before shaking his head. "No. I'm forty-one years old. I know I haven't had the kind of sexual experience most men...and women, for that matter...have by my age."

"Okay. But for the record...I'm *definitely* the kind of woman who gets possessive and jealous, so I don't want to hear about your other women and how you got to be as good in bed as you are."

"The internet," Raid said without hesitation. He should be embarrassed about this, but with Khloe he couldn't be.

"What?"

"That's how I learned how to please a woman."

"There's no way you learned that thing with your tongue and how to give me a G-spot orgasm through porn," she said skeptically.

"You're right. A lot of porn is gross. And the hardcore stuff is mostly about violence toward women, and I can't stand it. But there are a lot of tutorial type videos out there. Where men stay fully dressed, and it's all about demonstrating how to bring women to orgasm."

Khloe was quiet for a moment. "Really?"

"Really."

"Well...all right then. And to answer your question, I didn't mention the IUD because in the past when I've told men that I have it, they pressed me hard to have sex without a condom. And while I'm not opposed to that after being in a relationship for a while, there's no way I'd let someone I just met inside me without one. I don't know where his dick's been, and I don't want to get the creeping crud because a guy was too much of an ass to suit up with other women."

Raid couldn't help but laugh. "Well, you don't have to worry about me having the creeping crud, because it's been a very long time since my cock's had anything but my fist. And I'm okay with using condoms to protect you for as long as you want."

"Do you want kids?" she asked.

Raid couldn't help but tense at her question. It was too early to be talking about children...wasn't it? Then again, she hadn't asked if he wanted them with her, just if he wanted them.

Raid hadn't ever admitted this to anyone before, but this was Khloe. "Yes," he said softly. "I've always wanted them. But I'm not sure I'd be the best dad. If I had a boy, I wouldn't know anything about throwing a baseball back and forth or fishing or any of that dad stuff. And a girl? Forget about it. I know *nothing* about girls."

"Oh, I'd say you do," Khloe said suggestively. Then she rolled over until she was lying on top of him. "I think you'd make an excellent dad. And who's to say your son would even *want* to throw a ball around the yard? Maybe he'd be more into putting together Lego sets with you. Or you could teach him how to play D&D. And your daughter would have you wrapped around her little finger. She'd be a daddy's girl for sure."

"Do you want kids?" he asked.

Khloe shrugged. "I told myself I didn't. That I was content to take care of the animals in my clinic. I'm also forty-three...it's probably not even an option anymore. But with you? Yeah, I think I'd like that."

They were no longer talking in abstracts, and Raid felt his dick harden between her legs.

Khloe smiled and sat up. She scooted back until his cock was right where she wanted it. He was only half hard, but she rose up and notched the bulbus head between her pussy lips. Then she sank down on him.

The feel of being inside her without a condom was indescribable—and his dick grew even harder.

"Oh, wow! That feels so weird...but wonderful," she said with a groan. "I can feel you getting hard inside me."

"I don't have a condom on," he reminded her.

"I know. I trust you, Raid."

Fuck, she was going to make him blow like a teenager. He wrapped his arms around her and rolled, staying inside her as he did. When they got situated again, he stared down at the woman who'd turned his life upside down. "Hold on," he warned her.

"To what?" she asked.

"To me."

Then Raid proceeded to show Khloe how much she meant to him. How he'd never be the same if she left him. How he'd do whatever it took to keep her safe from anything and everything.

CHAPTER SIXTEEN

A month later, Khloe could hardly believe how much her life had changed. It felt as if everything was moving so quickly, but she was thrilled with the way things had been going.

Rocky devoted all his time to renovations, with help from Ethan, so she was able to open her emergency clinic almost two weeks ago. She'd already had several customers. Being open from eight at night until six in the morning meant she didn't have a steady stream of clients coming through the doors, but those she did have, she knew she was making a difference in the lives of their pets.

She didn't spend every night at the clinic. Afton and the other vet techs she'd hired were responsible for manning the desk. When emergencies came in, they called her if she wasn't already there.

She'd cut back her hours at the library, which made her sad, but it was inevitable. When she worked at the clinic, Raid dropped her off after they ate dinner together, and then came back to pick her up in the morning. He'd take her back to his house, they'd eat breakfast together, and she'd lie down to get some sleep. Sometimes he joined her and they made love before he left for work, and other times he simply hung out in bed next to her reading before he'd leave to start his day.

She got up around noon and headed into the library to work a few hours with Raid—and the new assistant he'd hired—then they'd head out. They frequently spent time with one of their friends, or they'd go on a short hike to get some exercise.

Raid and the rest of the SAR team were still on edge, watching and waiting for Garcia to make his move, but so far they hadn't seen hide nor hair of the man. Khloe knew it was too early to hope he'd crawled back under the rock he'd come from, never to be heard from again, but she did so anyway.

Jason and Scott had disappeared for a while as well, and the few weeks they'd been gone had been some of the best of Khloe's life. She was able to relax for the first time in a very long while and enjoyed all the time she got to spend with Raid.

Duke was back to his pre-surgery self and as tourist season got into full swing, the Eagle Point Search and Rescue team was being called out more frequently to find lost hikers.

Because things had been going so well, Khloe wasn't prepared to literally run right into Jason and Scott Mather when she left the library one day, heading across the square to grab a much-needed cup of coffee from Grinders and a cinnamon roll from Finley's bakery that she'd promised to save for her.

"Well, well, well," Jason said with a sneer as he stared at

her with a mean look in his eye. "If it isn't Fallport's newest veterinarian. Kill anyone's dog lately?"

Taking a deep breath, Khloe did her best to ignore the big bully. She walked past The Cellar, which was currently closed, and crossed Cedar Street, heading past the barber shop.

Art, Silas, and Otto were sitting in front of the post office, as usual, and they looked up as she neared.

"She thinks ignoring us will make us go away," Scott added as he trailed his older brother.

"Well, we aren't. Alan's making plans for you, sweetheart. And so are we. I wouldn't get too comfortable here."

And with that, Khloe was done. D-O-N-E. She hadn't done *anything* to these guys. And she'd done all she could for Alan's dog. *He* was the one who'd kicked her, causing the internal bleeding. *He* was the one who couldn't handle a woman being smarter than him. *He* was the one who'd tried to kill her and fucked that up as well...not that she was upset about that part.

She turned abruptly and poked Jason in the chest. He was that close to her. "Why are you still here?" she snarled.

Startled at how fast she'd turned on him, Jason took a step back and bumped into Scott, who stumbled and fell on his ass right there on the sidewalk.

"Seriously," she said, poking Jason one more time before he stepped over his brother and out of her reach. "Look around, you aren't welcome here. No one likes you and you've been banned from every single business. Hell, even Whip doesn't want you in his pool hall, and that's saying something because everyone knows that's where the troublemakers in this town hang out. Your brother is an *asshole*. Just like you are. He tried to *run me over*. That's not okay in any state or country. He's paying the price for losing his fucking temper. If he'd just gone on with his life, he wouldn't be in prison right now. And you coming after me, a woman who was just doing her job, makes you just as stupid as he is!"

"What did you just say?" Jason said, aggressively taking a step toward her. "You're a little too uppity. We should've done what Alan wanted us to do *way* before now."

Khloe realized she'd probably gone too far and stepped back—and felt someone behind her. Turning her head, she saw old man Grogan. The general store was just down from the post office, and he'd either seen or heard what was happening.

Art, Otto, and Silas had also stood up. Khloe could see Silas had their chessboard in his hand, as if he was ready to use it as some sort of weapon...not that it would be very effective.

From behind Scott and James, Khloe saw Raid coming toward them, moving fast, and Tal was exiting the barber shop where he worked.

The cavalry was coming, and it made Khloe relax a fraction.

"It's time you moved on," Harry Grogan said in a deep growl.

"Oh, yeah? You gonna make me, old man?" Jason asked, his hands clenching into fists.

"He might not, but I will," another voice said from behind them. Davis Woolford.

"Me too," Clyde Thomas said. The older man was famous in Fallport, and around this part of Virginia, for his excellent moonshine. He was also a very good friend of Caryn's.

"You two have made fools of yourselves for long enough," Dorothea Reese said in disgust. The senior was flanked by her three best friends, Cora, Ruth, and Clara... the four ladies were always in the beauty shop next to the post office, and they obviously couldn't resist joining in.

Looking around, Khloe saw more and more people arriving. Neli from the used bookstore; Guy, who worked the counter in the post office; Sandra was coming across the square with Karen, one of the waitresses. Not only that, but Elsie and Zeke were running toward them from On The Rocks, with Hank and Reina—two of Zeke's employees—close behind.

It seemed as if the residents of Fallport were as sick and tired of the Mather brothers as Khloe.

She lowered her voice and did her best to hide any trace of her annoyance. "I'm sorry about what happened," she told Jason and Scott. "If I could've saved Alan's dog, I would've. But she was too far gone before he brought her in."

"You ruined his life!" Scott said. He'd gotten to his feet behind Jason.

"And you've been beaten with a stupid stick," Harry Grogan said, shaking his head. "She's not God. She can't save every animal that's brought to her. And she didn't ruin your brother's life. He did that all by himself."

"Stay out of this, old man," Jason warned.

"You need to leave—*now!*" a loud voice boomed.

Everyone's heads turned to see Simon, the police chief, coming toward them from the grassy square.

"You can't make me," Jason said childishly.

"You're right, I can't. But you can see that you aren't welcome. No one's gonna tolerate your bullying and intimidation anymore. And sleeping in your truck in the hiking trail parking lots is illegal. I'm guessing the number of tickets I can give you will outlast your stubbornness. Your best bet is to go back to Norfolk and live your lives. Forget about Dr. Watts—and urge your brother to do the same."

Khloe hadn't realized the brothers were living in their vehicle, but she supposed she wasn't surprised. Fallport had closed ranks...and it felt really good.

Jason glared at the huge crowd of people around him.

Khloe met Raid's eyes. He'd stopped close to the Mather brothers but stayed silent—and she loved him all the more for it. He was letting her and the citizens of Fallport fight this battle, while still being ready in case he was needed.

It hit her then—she loved him. So much. She smiled just thinking about it.

"What are you smiling about, bitch?" Jason asked. In an obvious fit of anger and frustration, he lunged forward, hand raised.

Before he could make contact with her cheek, Harry Grogan pushed Khloe aside and knocked Jason's hand away. A split-second later, Zeke took him to the ground, while Tal made sure Scott wouldn't join the fray.

Khloe couldn't do more than blink before Raid was at her side, pulling her backward several steps.

Simon sighed dramatically, if insincerely. "*Now* I'm going to have to arrest you for attempted assault."

Jason howled as Zeke wrenched his arm behind his back while hauling him up from the ground.

"This is bullshit!" he yelled. "I've got witnesses. This man assaulted *me*!"

"Yeah, we're witnesses all right!" Sandra yelled. "Of you trying to hit Khloe!"

Everyone was speaking at once, agreeing with Sandra and Simon.

"You'll regret this!" Jason yelled at Khloe. "You better keep an eye on that dog. Wouldn't want him to end up as dead as Alan's!"

Khloe tensed, looking down at Duke who, of course, was at Raid's side. It was one thing for Jason to bully *her*, but to threaten to hurt or kill Duke? No. Just *no*.

She opened her mouth to tell Jason to stay the hell away from Duke when, once again, the townspeople came to her aid.

"You touch one hair on that dog's head, you'll have more to worry about than Simon taking you in for a misdemeanor," Clyde growled.

"Them's fightin' words," Guy said with a shake of his head.

"Duke's royalty around here," Finley added. "It's not in your best interest to be threatening him."

"He'll tear your face off!" Reina shouted.

Khloe heard a few chuckles at that. Duke didn't really have a vicious bone in his body. But then, she remembered the way Duke had growled at the brothers the last time they'd confronted her behind the library, when Whip had come to her aid.

"Come on," Simon said. "A little time in the tank will do you some good. Maybe it'll cool you off a bit."

"Fuck you!" Jason yelled. "And fuck all of you backwater hicks! You've got a killer in your midst and you don't even care!"

"Yeah!" Scott added like an idiot, following his brother

and Simon as they headed toward the police department.

The last thing she heard was Jason still yelling threats against her, Duke, Raid, and everyone else in town.

"You okay?" Raid asked in a low voice as he bent close to her ear.

Khloe thought about it for a second, then nodded. She was. That hadn't been pleasant, not at all, confrontation wasn't her thing, but seeing how everyone in town didn't hesitate to race to her side when she needed them most was amazing and humbling.

She took her time in thanking everyone for coming to help with the situation, even giving out a few hugs. Khloe could tell she surprised people with her demonstrative actions, but she was done being the reclusive, standoffish woman she'd been since arriving. She had nothing to hide anymore. All her secrets were out and everyone seemed to accept her as she was.

Most people had gone back to what they were doing before the commotion, an encounter Khloe knew would be talked about for months to come and probably blown way out of proportion. Knowing how gossip worked, she wouldn't be surprised to hear that Jason had pulled a weapon and she herself had done some sort of ninja move to knock it out of his hand and render him unconscious on the sidewalk.

Finley and Elsie had given her huge hugs and told her how strong she was and how they loved that she'd stood up to Jason. Zeke and Tal weren't quite as effusive, but gave her supportive hugs as well.

Raid stayed by her side as she continued toward the bakery and the coffee shop. "I need that caffeine more than ever now," she joked.

He didn't respond to her attempt at lightening the mood.

"Raid?"

He shook his head. "That could've gone sideways in a heartbeat," he said quietly, not looking at her.

Khloe waited until they'd crossed Main Street and were standing in front of the used bookstore. She stopped walking and, of course, Raid did too. She threw herself at him, and even though she'd surprised him, his arms immediately surrounded her, holding her against him.

Khloe looked up at him and said, "You're right, it could've. But it didn't."

"I don't like that he blatantly threatened you. Hell, he tried to *hit* you."

"And I don't like that he brought Duke into it," she countered, looking down at Duke, who'd sat next to them when they'd stopped. "But you know what?"

"What?"

"It felt really good to stick up for myself. Bullies hate that."

His lips twitched. "They do."

"So we're moving on," she said firmly. "Maybe spending some time behind bars will make them rethink being here."

"Maybe," Raid said skeptically.

"I had an epiphany back there," she told him.

"Yeah?"

"Uh-huh." Khloe was nervous about this, but she didn't want to keep it to herself anymore. In for a penny, in for a pound...or however that saying went. "You didn't rush in and ferry me out of the situation. You let me say what I needed to. But you were nearby, just in case I needed you."

"I wanted to," Raid said. "Get you out of there, that is. But you've made it clear over the last year that you're a grown woman who values her independence."

"I am," Khloe agreed. "And when the situation changed, when he threatened me, you were there. Making sure I was safe."

Raid simply nodded.

"My epiphany was realizing how much I love you," Khloe blurted. This wasn't exactly the most romantic time or place for this conversation, but she couldn't keep her feelings to herself. They were too big. She felt as if she was going to burst if she didn't tell him.

"Took you long enough," Raid retorted, but he had a huge smile on his face. "I've known I've loved you since you found me playing D&D and wanted in on the game."

Khloe let out a small sigh of relief. Then what he said registered. "You love me?" she whispered.

"So much, I don't even remember what my life was like without you in it."

"Probably a lot less hectic and stressful," she quipped.

"Boring," he countered. Then he lifted his hands to her face, tipped it up to him, and kissed her. Hard. Right there on Main Street in plain view of anyone who happened to be walking around or looking out their windows.

At one time in her life, Khloe would've hated to be the center of attention, but when cars honked and people hooted and hollered as they continued to kiss, she didn't care one whit.

When Raid pulled back, he smoothed her hair away from her face. "Not how or where I envisioned this conversation taking place," he said ruefully.

Khloe shrugged. "It's us. We don't do anything the normal way."

"True. Although I'm thinking I could do with a little less excitement than we've had lately."

Khloe chuckled. "Yeah. Fewer stalkers and harassers and drug dealers hell bent on revenge lurking in the shadows."

"Speaking of which, let's get you off the street and grab that coffee and cinnamon roll," Raid said.

Sighing, and wishing she'd kept her mouth shut, Khloe let Raid turn her toward the coffee shop. She fit perfectly under his arm, and she wound her own around his waist. Duke groaned as he got up and followed them.

"Khloe?" Raid said as he reached for the door.

She could smell the scent of coffee even through the door, and her mouth watered. "Yeah?"

"Tonight, I'm gonna show you exactly how much I love you, and how relieved I am that you took the first step yet again and told me how you felt."

Khloe shivered as she looked up at Raid. She didn't see a freakishly tall man. Didn't see his uniquely colored hair and beard. Didn't notice that his ears were pointier and stuck out a bit more than most people's. All she saw was the man she loved. The man who wouldn't hesitate to put himself between her and anything that might hurt her.

"I can't wait," she said with a grin.

And with that, he opened the door and urged her inside.

Yes, it was safe to say, even with everything that had happened to bring her to this spot right this moment, Khloe wouldn't change a thing.

CHAPTER SEVENTEEN

Raid couldn't relax. Things were too good. And when life seemed to be trucking along nicely, there always seemed to be a huge bump in the road coming.

Ever since the confrontation in the square, Jason and Scott Mather had disappeared. Raid was sure they were still out there, plotting and planning and *seriously* pissed off, but for now they were the least of his worries.

There had been no trace of Pablo Garcia. And even though he and his friends had called in as many markers as they could and used all their connections, no one had been able to find hide nor hair of the man. Which didn't exactly make Raid feel all warm and fuzzy.

He was planning something, he knew it without having to think twice. But *what* the drug dealer was planning... that was the question.

And Raid hated not knowing. Hated being on edge. He wanted to be able to relax and enjoy being with Khloe. She was still snarky, and he still loved picking on her, but now that they'd admitted their feelings for each other, their nitpicking had a different tone. More teasing. More play-ful. And he loved it.

Not only that, but he was making an effort to be more social with their friends. He and Khloe ate at On the Rocks regularly, sometimes with the others, sometimes alone. He also took the occasional day off to hang out with Rocky on some of his worksites. Not that Raid was all that much help, but he did what he could, and he enjoyed hanging out with the former SEAL. Ever since Rocky talked him off the ledge, and Raid had confessed about his last Coast Guard mission, they'd gotten a lot closer.

He hung out with the rest of the guys more often too, although their get-togethers usually involved the women, which Raid didn't mind at all. It felt as if he was in a completely different world, watching and listening to the giggling and conversations in a nearby room as he and his friends played poker or simply sat around and talked.

Khloe's vet practice was doing extremely well. More and more clients were begging her to open up for more routine matters for their pets. She wasn't sure she wanted to do that yet, in deference to Ziegler, but Raid had a feeling it was only a matter of time.

He was in his office in the library, and Khloe had just arrived after getting some sleep. She'd been called into the office because a pug was having a hard time giving birth to her puppies. It had taken hours, and eventually Khloe had to cut the puppies out. They'd all made it, and now it was a waiting game to see how they did.

Khloe was sitting with Tony at a table in the kids' area of the library, and they were discussing the book *Watership Down*, which he was currently reading. It was a long book, and while on Tony's reading level grade-wise, typically it was more of interest for older kids. But he'd taken to it right away, and Khloe loved talking to him about the deeper meanings of social allegories, repression, and the dangers of not thinking for yourself and giving in to peer pressure.

Raid was concentrating on the budget spreadsheet in front of him when he heard some sort of commotion in the library. Which was unusual because, well...*library*. It was generally a quiet space. Raised voices were an anomaly.

But with everything going on in recent months, he was on the move before it registered *who* was causing the commotion.

Raymond Ziegler was standing next to the table where Tony and Khloe were sitting, letting Khloe know in no uncertain terms what he thought of her.

"You have no right to come here and steal my clients! It's unprofessional and unethical and I'm going to turn you into the Virginia Board of Veterinary Medicine! I'm sure they'll be very interested to know what you're doing. That a vet who was accused of malpractice has gone back into business."

Raid opened his mouth to tell Ziegler to get the fuck out of the library, but Khloe stood abruptly, her chair hitting the floor behind her. She didn't back down from the furious man, instead actually stepped closer, literally going head-to-head with him.

"I have *every* right to open a business here in Fallport. There's nothing wrong with competition. And go ahead and notify the board, I haven't done anything illegal. *Nothing*. And the key word in your rant was 'accused'. I was *accused*, but through Mather's trial, it was proven that I did nothing wrong. That there was no way to save his dog because of the injuries she'd sustained prior to arriving at the clinic."

Ziegler scowled. "Your reputation is that of a dog killer."

"Wrong," Khloe fired back. "My reputation is that of a vet who does whatever it takes to save all of the animals in her care. No matter what time it is. No matter what my plans are. I drop everything to do what I can to help. Can you say the same?"

If possible, Ziegler's face got even redder.

Raid stepped in. He didn't want to give Raymond a chance to do something he'd regret...or that would physically hurt Khloe. "Step back, Ziegler," he said in as calm a voice as he could manage.

The man acted as if he didn't even hear the warning. "You've been spreading rumors about me, and I won't have it!" Ziegler told Khloe.

"What rumors?" she asked.

"You *know* what. That I'm a crappy vet and I don't care about animals."

Khloe laughed. It probably wasn't the smartest reaction to his accusation, but then again, Khloe was as authentic a person as Raid had ever met. She wasn't one to sugarcoat anything. "I haven't said a word to anyone. If rumors are going around, it's because of your own actions, not anything I've said," she told him.

"Bullshit! I didn't have any issue before you got here," Ziegler said.

"That's because the citizens of Fallport didn't have a choice of vet unless they wanted to drive thirty minutes or more." Khloe took a deep breath. "Look, my intention isn't to run you out of business. Not at all. It's too difficult being the only one in a town who offers a certain service. I'm currently operating as an emergency vet only, open during the hours that you aren't. That way, I can take care of the after-hours stuff and you can continue your daytime hours."

"Don't lie!" Ziegler boomed. "I've heard people talk. You're looking to hire someone else to handle the emergency shit and you're going to be open during the day too!"

Raid couldn't help but be impressed by the way information spread in this small town. Ziegler wasn't wrong. So many people had begged Khloe to treat infections, clean teeth, and give normal checkups that she'd be stupid to not consider expanding her hours and business. But as far as he knew, she hadn't made that decision yet. It looked like the good people of Fallport decided it was as good as done though.

"You're right," Khloe said calmly, taking a step back from the angry man. "I *am* looking into hiring more help. There's enough business for both of us here in Fallport, but I'm thinking if you want to *stay* in business, you'll have to make some changes to how you do things."

Raid reacted a split-second after Ziegler. When the man stepped toward Khloe, Raid was there to block his attempt to put his hands on her.

"Don't even think about it," he growled as he shoved the man backward not too gently. "You've said what you came here to say, it's time for you to go."

"Fuck you, Walker! I'm not done."

"Yes, you are," Raid countered. "This is a library. Look around you, do you see anyone else yelling and carrying on? No. And there are kids present. Get a hold of yourself, Ziegler."

"I don't give a shit who's here. She's stealing my clients!" he roared.

"No, she isn't," a woman said from several tables away. She was sitting with her young daughter, who had a pair of headphones on and was playing some sort of educational game on the tablet in front of her. "She opened her emergency clinic specifically so she *wouldn't* be competing with you. Even though the entire town wants her to open during the day as well, myself included."

She stood, staring down Ziegler. "A couple of months ago, I brought our new kitten to see you. You barely looked at her and said I was overreacting and there was nothing wrong with her. I wanted a second opinion because you didn't even examine her. I had to drive all the way to Christiansburg, and they confirmed she had feline leukemia. You refused to even run the tests to see what might be wrong."

"Right," a man chimed in. "And my dog was running with a stick in his mouth and it got jammed into his jaw. He was in a great deal of pain, there was blood everywhere...but when I called to get help—during business hours, I might add—I was told your schedule was full and I'd have to make an appointment for two days later! You actually expected my dog to wait *two days* to be seen when he had a freaking hole in his cheek from that stick!"

"I called Dr. Watts half an hour after she closed last week, because you weren't open yet and I was desperate," another woman said. "My dog was pregnant, and something was going wrong with the delivery. Dr. Watts not only told me to come in right away even though she was closed, she worked on my Muffy for hours and saved not only her, but the puppies as well. She worked four hours past closing and didn't even charge me extra for it."

"Seems to me you're doing a good job of driving your clients away all by yourself," Raid said. "Khloe's not doing a damn thing other than the job she loves."

"Fuck you," Ziegler spat at Raid. Then he turned to Khloe. "And fuck you too! You aren't the paragon everyone thinks you are. You'd better watch your damn back." Then he turned around and stomped out of the library.

"That's so going on social media," a teenager said from a table nearby.

Glancing over, Raid saw her fiddling on her cell phone and guessed she'd videoed the entire encounter. Ziegler really was an idiot. He wasn't doing himself any favors.

"I really could have gone without someone *else* threatening me," Khloe said with a sigh.

Raid turned, ready to reassure her that Raymond fucking Ziegler wasn't going to touch a hair on her head— but she was grinning.

"This isn't funny," he told her.

She sobered. "I know it's not. It's sad, really. I meant what I said. We could've really worked together. But it's obvious he's gotten too used to being able to do whatever he wants and getting away with it because the people here didn't have any other option. Whatever happens is on him. I haven't badmouthed him to anyone since I opened my clinic."

"Why is he so mean?" Tony asked, looking up from his seat at the table.

"I have no idea," Khloe said, ruffling his hair.

"Well, when we get a dog, I'm telling Mom to bring it to you for stuff. Not him."

"As if I'd let you take it anywhere else," Khloe said, smiling at him.

Raid still wasn't happy. He was sick and tired of people threatening those he loved. He pulled Khloe against him then turned to the patrons who were still watching. "Show's over. Go back to what you were doing...quietly, please. This *is* the library."

Several people chuckled, but to his relief, they turned their attentions away from him and Khloe. He wasn't an idiot, he knew what happened here would spread far and wide, and not only because of the girl who was probably even now posting the video online. Ziegler would find more clients than ever before canceling their appointments because of his latest outburst.

He pulled Khloe a little ways from the table to give them a bit of privacy. "You okay?" he asked quietly.

She turned into him and hugged him hard before nodding. "Yes. Are you?"

"No."

She shook her head. "I'm not surprised he lost it," she told him. "Some of the people I've talked to, or who've begged me to open during the day, have been telling me how grumpy Raymond's been getting. He's jealous and upset that I've disrupted the good thing he had going here. But he's a jerk. And if anyone should be contacting the veterinary board, it's me."

"But you won't," Raid said.

"Nope. He's doing an excellent job of sabotaging his business all by himself. He doesn't need my help."

"If he leaves, you're gonna have more clients than you can handle," Raid warned.

"I know," she said with a shrug. "If it happens, I've got some friends around the state that I've gotten to know from conferences and consultations. I'll put out the word about how awesome Fallport is, and that there's an amazing business opportunity for someone to open up another clinic here. Or maybe I could expand my hours and hire a couple of colleagues to work here with me."

Raid was as proud as he could be of Khloe. She was a smart businesswoman, compassionate, and a hell of a vet to boot. "This goes without saying, but I'm going to say it anyway," he warned. "You need to be careful. Ziegler's pissed as hell and there's no telling what he'll do."

Khloe sighed. "I know. But you and the others are already watching me like a hawk. He's not going to get a chance to get me by myself."

She wasn't wrong. Raid couldn't think of many times she'd been alone in the last couple months. She was either with him, one of their friends, or surrounded by the good people of Fallport. "I'm just saying, he's losing control and desperate people do desperate things."

"I know, Raiden. I'm not happy I'm the recipient of another batshit-crazy person's attention, but it is what it is. What's the alternative? I close up my clinic and let him win?"

"No," Raid said succinctly.

"Exactly. So we'll do what we've been doing. Watching our backs and not letting assholes get to us. Now, can I get back to Hazel and Fiver?"

"Who?" Raid asked.

Khloe grinned. "The rabbits from *Watership Down*."

He chuckled. "Right. Yes. After you kiss me. And not one of your 'I really liked that third orgasm you just gave me' kisses, but an 'I love you and we're in public' kiss."

She snort-laughed at that. "Right," she said before going up on her tiptoes.

Raid still had to lean down so she could reach his lips, and he still had to pinch himself that this was his life. That he, Raiden Walker, had somehow caught the attention of someone like Khloe.

He could feel her smile against his lips and he was relieved the encounter with Ziegler hadn't dimmed her positive outlook.

As if she could read his mind, when the kiss was over, she looked up at him and said, "I'm happy, Raid. And nothing is going to change that. I'm doing not one, but *two* jobs I love, enjoying the friendships I've made, and reveling in being with a man who not only loves me, but lets me be exactly who I am."

"Never change," he told her.

"Same goes for you. Speaking of which...we're playing D&D tomorrow night, right?"

"Yes." She'd joined him and his friends for their weekly D&D nights and the game was even more fun. She'd embraced Anise, the character he'd made with her in mind, and he'd never laughed as much as he had with her by his side on those Friday nights.

"Cool," she said and squeezed his arm. She started back toward the table, but stopped and turned. "By the way... thanks for stepping in with Raymond. I noticed and it was appreciated." Then she smiled and went back to Tony's side.

Raid scanned the library once more to make sure all

was well, and when he was reassured that there wasn't anyone else lurking nearby to jump out and threaten to do him or Khloe harm, he went back to his office.

The next week, Khloe was sitting in Bristol and Rocky's living room with the rest of the girls. Lilly had arranged for a paint-and-sip party. Khloe had never heard of them before, but now that she was here, she had to say she was enjoying it very much.

Lilly had taken family pictures for the high school art teacher and they'd gotten to talking about how these paint-and-sip parties were all the rage, and Lilly asked if the woman had ever hosted any. The conversation had led to her and her friends sitting at Bristol's dining table in front of easels, with a massive plastic sheet under their feet and paintbrushes and jars of paint all around them.

Every other square inch of the table was packed with snacks and drinks...non-alcoholic choices for the pregnant ladies and wine and moonshine for everyone else. Their men, along with Tony and Marissa, were outside playing in the barn and throwing a football, generally doing their best to stay out of the women's hair.

Khloe had been reluctant to do this painting thing, because she didn't have a creative bone in her body. But she'd said yes because she wanted to spend time with her friends. And since she was working more, she'd been kind of slacking in that department. After her secrets came out, she'd made the decision to do what she could to hang out with the women who'd never given up on her and accepted her just as she was...closed off, moody, and kind of grumpy.

She was pleasantly surprised when she arrived to see the art teacher had actually outlined what they were going to be painting—a moose standing by a lake with Christmas lights tangled in his antlers—which would make it much easier not to make a fool of herself by painting something that looked like it came from the imagination of a two-year-old.

Their paintings were three quarters of the way done and Khloe was pleasantly buzzed from the glasses of wine she'd consumed. Their teacher would suggest doing something like using broad strokes to paint the trees, and when they second-guessed themselves, she encouraged them to take a drink. So a few of them had followed her advice to the letter.

Now, Bristol, Caryn, and Khloe were drunk. Heather didn't like the taste of wine, but she'd taken a few shots of the moonshine Caryn had brought. Elsie and Finley were drinking Sprite out of wine glasses.

Khloe stopped mid-dabbing colorful paint for the lights on her moose's antlers when something occurred to her. She looked down the table at Lilly, then exclaimed, "Lilly's drinking Sprite!"

Everyone stopped what they were doing and their heads turned in unison to the end of the table, where Lilly was sitting.

"Lilly...are you..." Elsie whispered.

"No. But it's that time of the month. And I don't want to do anything that might make it harder for me to conceive," she said with a shrug. "And I know there's no correlation between drinking and getting pregnant, hell, a lot of women get knocked up when they're hammered, but I'm paranoid and don't want to take any chances."

Paintings forgotten, everyone leaped out of their seats and crowded around Lilly, arguing over who got to hug her first. They were just as excited as if she'd announced she was already pregnant.

Laughing, she shooed them all away. "You guys are crazy! Go sit down. Jeez."

"You're gonna tell us the second you pee on a stick and it's positive, right?" Caryn asked.

Lilly rolled her eyes. "No."

"What? Why not?" Elsie pouted.

"Because you'll all go overboard. You'll treat me as if I'm made out of glass. You'll be as bad as Ethan," Lilly told them.

"So?" Finley asked. "Would that really bother you?"

"As if you aren't going to treat *yourself* like you're made of glass," Bristol argued.

Lilly gave them a sheepish smile. "True. I just...I don't want to jinx anything."

"Studies show that most women can go on to have babies after a miscarriage," Finley said gently.

"I know. But until I get far enough along, I'm going to be paranoid," Lilly said with a shrug.

"Right, so...I'm thinking we need to get these paintings done so our Lilly can go home and make her husband impregnate her!" Caryn announced, her words slurring a bit.

Khloe couldn't stop grinning. She wasn't sure why, although the alcohol running in her veins probably had something to do with it. But she was just so happy. She had no doubt Lilly would get pregnant again. Elsie and Finley were practically glowing, and it wouldn't be long before their babies were born, Heather was fitting in as if she'd always been a part of their group and hadn't been hidden away in the forest for most of her life, and Khloe felt as if she was truly part of a close-knit family for the first time since losing her dad.

"So...I heard that asshole Ziegler came into the library and lost his shit," Caryn said as they all worked on finishing up their moose paintings.

"I saw the video. He's so done in this town," Elsie said.

"Wait, there's a video?" Lilly asked. "I didn't know that!" She put down her paintbrush and picked up her phone.

"No! You aren't allowed to stop," Caryn ordered, pointing her paintbrush at Lilly. "Put down the phone and paint. You've got a baby to make and that can't happen until that moose is done!"

Everyone giggled.

"I'll find it for you," Heather volunteered as she took her own phone out of her pocket.

"Look on the Fallport Community Page," Elsie said. "That's where I saw it."

Within seconds, Heather stood up and took her phone over to where Lilly was sitting. Everyone was quiet as they listened to Raymond rant and rave at Khloe. When it got to the part where he told Khloe to fuck off, everyone gasped.

Then Caryn said, "He's toast!"

"And *we* should toast!" Finley announced. "To Khloe's expanding business!"

Everyone raised their glasses, even the art teacher, who'd mostly been watching and listening to the chatter.

"To Khloe!" Bristol announced.

"To Ziegler going out of business!" Elsie added.

"To Fallport finally being able to have a vet who gives a shit!" Finley added.

"To friends," Heather said after retaking her seat.

All of a sudden, Khloe felt tears pool in her eyes. She blinked quickly, trying to hold them back, with no luck.

"No crying!" Elsie said frantically. "If you start, with my hormones, I'm going to lose it!"

"Too late!" Finley said with a sniffle.

It felt weird to be laughing and crying at the same time, but somehow Khloe managed it. "Thank *all* of you for not giving up on me. I know I wasn't the nicest person over the last year or so."

"Whatever," Caryn said, waving her hand. "If someone had tried to kill me, I would've been the same way."

"Someone *did* try to kill you," Lilly reminded her.

Caryn shrugged. "Stupid shit tried to burn a firefighter to death. Not smart."

Khloe definitely didn't want to rehash what happened to her friend and didn't want to dwell on what happened to her either. "From this point on...there will be nothing but good things for all of us. Babies, sex, parties, small-town parades, and our businesses prospering!"

"I'll drink to that!" Caryn exclaimed.

"You'll drink to anything," Bristol said with a laugh.

It didn't take them long to finish up their paintings, especially since they wanted Lilly to head home with Ethan to hopefully get knocked up. The party broke up not too long after she left. Everyone said their goodbyes and before she knew it, Khloe was sitting next to Raid in his Expedition.

She rested her head against the back of the seat and stared at him as he drove them to his house.

"Is it weird that I'm living with you?" she blurted.

"No," he said without hesitation.

"Is it just because of the Mathers? And that drug guy? And now Ziegler?"

"No," he repeated.

Khloe frowned. "It's not?" She knew she was tipsy and chattier than usual, but Raid didn't seem to mind.

"Nope," he said with a shrug. "It's because I love you and with you around, I feel like the man I've always wanted to be."

Khloe didn't know how to take that, but Raid being Raid, he went on to explain without her having to ask.

"You let me be me. You accept me as I am."

"I *love* who you are," she told him.

"But that's not the main reason it's not weird that you're living with me," he said with a small smile. He continued before she could ask what he meant. "It's because I can't stand not being with you. When you're not with me, all I can think about is what you're doing. Thinking. I want to be with you all the time. At work, at home, running errands. Even when I'm with Duke in the woods, I'm thinking about you."

Khloe practically melted in her seat. That was the most romantic thing anyone had ever said to her before. "I...me too," she said, knowing her words were lame and didn't express everything she was feeling.

But Raid simply smiled at her, then reached over to take hold of her hand.

They drove like that, holding hands for a few seconds, before Raid said, "I haven't done this in the past."

"This?" Khloe asked, confused.

"Held hands with women. It's nice."

Khloe felt sad for him, even as a feeling of possessiveness surged through her. She was the only woman he'd ever held hands with. He'd never played D&D with any other girlfriends. And she was fairly certain many of the things they'd done in the bedroom had been firsts for him as well. They sure were for *her*.

This man was hers—and she wanted to experience many more firsts with him.

"You ever made love to a drunk woman before?"

He smirked but didn't take his eyes from the road. "Can't say that I have. Is it any different from making love to a woman when she *isn't* drunk?"

"Guess you'll have to find out," Khloe teased.

He looked over at her then. "When we get home, go straight to bed. I'll let Duke out and be in after. I want you naked and waiting for me."

Khloe shivered. "Okay," she told him.

Yes, it was safe to say she was happier than she'd ever been.

"Raid?"

"Yeah?"

"Thanks for being awesome."

A slight flush formed on his cheeks. Her man never took a compliment very well, but it was a part of his charm.

He lifted her hand to his lips and kissed the back gently.

The rest of the short trip to his house was done in silence, but with every pass of his thumb over the back of her hand, Khloe's lust ramped up. She was Raid's. Anything he wanted, she'd bend over backward to do.

Although he wouldn't ask; that wasn't who he was. Which made her want to please him even more.

Their future was uncertain—with Jason and Scott still out there, probably waiting for a chance to strike, Raid's past lurking in the shadows as well, and Khloe having to figure out her new business model—but she was sure of one thing...whatever happened, she and Raid would face it together.

* * *

The man stared through his binoculars at the house in the distance. He'd parked at a hiking area half a mile away or so and walked through the woods to where he was currently lying in the grass. He made certain no one saw him...because that would ruin everything.

He'd been watching the couple for a while now, learning their routine and collecting information. He could be patient, as timing was extremely important. His actions had to be perfect. If he moved too quickly or got too cocky, all of this would be for nothing. The last thing he wanted was to give either Raiden Walker or Khloe Watts a heads-up that they were being watched. He needed them to be blissfully unaware.

A couple of ideas were coming into focus, but whatever he decided, it would need to be executed carefully. Tourists were flooding the area, which helped him blend in. But reconnaissance in a small town was still a pain in his ass. Everyone was nosy as hell and they were prone to calling the police if someone so much as farted in their direction.

But that just made this more of a challenge. Which he liked.

"That's it," he said softly as he watched the silhouettes of his targets pass by a window. "Enjoy your time while you can, because soon you'll learn what happens when you piss off the wrong person."

With a grin, the man lowered the binoculars and got up off the ground. He made the walk back to the parking area without incident. He picked up a burner phone he'd stashed in his vehicle and made a phone call to report what he'd seen, and to discuss one of the plans forming in his mind.

CHAPTER EIGHTEEN

Raid stared out the window, lost in thought.

He'd been speaking with Tonka every few days, and neither had any more clue as to where Garcia was than the day they'd heard he'd been let out of prison and flown back to his country. He could literally be anywhere, and that didn't sit well with either of them.

For his friend, the drug dealer's release brought back horrible memories. Things that Tonka had finally dealt with in his head and through therapy, and he'd done an amazing job of compartmentalizing and moving on. Knowing Garcia could be after them even now had put him in a dark place for a while, but with the help of his wife and daughters, and his friends at The Refuge, he was pulling out of it. More determined than ever to make sure those he loved weren't hurt at Garcia's hands.

Because Raid had been unconscious, his knowledge of what happened that day came from the reports and what others had told him. Many days he felt as if that was just as bad, because his imagination would kick in as he pictured how it all went down.

The thought of Garcia getting his hands on Khloe, or Duke for that matter, kept him up at night. The more time that went by with no information on the man's whereabouts, the more on edge Raid became. The guy could wait years to take his revenge, or he could do it today. Raid was trying not to be paranoid, but with every day that passed, his anxiety ramped up.

Tonka felt the same way. Both men were certain that Garcia would definitely do *something*. They didn't know what, didn't know when, but both were completely sure that he'd make a move at some point.

It was ironic that Pablo Garcia and Alan Mather had something in common. They'd vowed to make their perceived enemies suffer...when in reality, both men had brought their incarceration on themselves.

Thinking about Alan had Raid's lips twitching. At the moment, he and Khloe still needed to be on their toes. But markers had been called in, and soon it would be made very clear to Alan that if he continued his harassment of Khloe Watts, he wouldn't like the consequences.

Raid wasn't exactly proud of using threats against Alan, but men like him didn't understand any other way of communicating. Case in point: the piece of shit was still threatening Khloe from behind bars, using his brothers to do his dirty work.

Therefore, a certain mercenary out in Colorado had volunteered to use his connections to set things in motion. He'd make sure Alan wouldn't be a problem for Khloe in the near future.

Raid jerked as Khloe's arms wrapped around him from

behind. He immediately covered her hand on his belly with his own.

"Whatcha thinkin' about so hard?" she asked quietly.

Raid had no intention of stressing Khloe out by telling her about his worries—or what was about to happen to the man who'd tried to kill her. He turned in her grasp and pulled her closer, resting his chin on top of her head...and lied his ass off. "Just how happy I am."

It wasn't that he *wasn't* happy. He was. But his happiness was tainted by an expectation of evil lurking in the shadows.

"Me too," she told him. "Has Ethan said anything to you guys?"

Raid's lips twitched. Khloe'd told him all about what Lilly had said at their painting party a few weeks ago. Ever since then, she'd periodically asked him if Ethan had let it slip that his wife was pregnant again.

"No. It's not like we sit around and chat about cycles and pregnancy," he said with a small chuckle.

"I know. I just thought maybe when it happens, he'll be so excited, he won't be able to keep it a secret."

"And you think Lilly could?"

"Yes," Khloe said. "She's worried. And scared. She lost one baby, and I'm sure she doesn't want to get her hopes up with another pregnancy until there's an above-average chance the baby will survive. She could be five months into her pregnancy before she feels comfortable sharing."

"And that's bad?" Raid asked, pulling back and looking down at the woman in his arms.

"No! Not at all. She needs to do what she needs to do in order to feel comfortable. But I want to know so I can help keep an eye on her. You know, when she's on her feet too much, I can make her sit. Or I can go see her instead of having her come to the clinic or here. Things like that. I worry about her."

Raid's heart melted. His Khloe was such a good person. "If I hear anything, I'll let you know."

"Thanks," she told him quietly. "I want this for her so much. She was so excited about being a mom. She and Ethan will make such good parents."

Raid had to agree.

"Anything in particular you want for lunch?" she asked.

He smiled. He was used to Khloe changing subjects quickly. He figured it was a result of her being so smart, her mind constantly churning about a dozen things at once. When she decided she was done with a topic, she was *done*.

"Grilled cheese sandwiches?" he asked.

"Sounds good. I'll let Duke out and get started. You can hang out here, staring off into space thinking until I'm done."

Raid chuckled. "I'm done thinking for now. I'll go start heating the pan."

Khloe went up on tiptoes and kissed his chin. "Okay."

Raid forced himself to let go of her and watched with a small smile as she roused Duke and convinced him that he should go outside. Yesterday, he and Duke had gone on their first search since his surgery, and he'd done fantastic. They hadn't found the missing hiker before he'd walked out onto the main road and got himself rescued, but Duke showed no signs of fatigue and seemed very happy to be back on the job.

The sandwiches cooked quickly and after they'd eaten, Raid sat on the couch with Khloe tucked up against him as they watched another cooking show. It was somewhat amusing that these kinds of shows entertained them so much, as neither of them was a great cook.

It wasn't until around three that Raid noticed Duke wasn't in his normal spot in his dog bed in the corner.

"Shit! We forgot Duke!" he exclaimed, feeling incredibly guilty.

"Oh no!" Khloe said as she immediately got up off the couch with him and headed for the back door.

Raid opened the sliding-glass door with a little more urgency than normal. Duke was probably out in the huge yard napping under a tree...in the mud. There were plenty of rabbit, squirrel, and raccoon scents in the three acres to keep him busy and tire him out.

"Duke!" he yelled after looking around and not immediately seeing the bloodhound.

But the dog didn't come loping through the trees toward him at the sound of his voice.

"You go that way," Khloe ordered, pointing to the right. "I'll go this way."

Raid nodded, panicking slightly that his dog hadn't immediately come when called.

Having a three-acre fenced yard was great for Duke to roam and get some exercise, but it took way too long to search right about now. Raid walked along the perimeter of the yard to the right while Khloe did the same on the left side. He could see her through the trees as they systematically searched. But with every second that passed, and Duke didn't respond to either him or Khloe calling his name, the more dread welled up inside him.

He'd almost lost the big lug a few months ago. He wasn't ready to lose him now.

It wasn't until he reached the back corner of the property that fear *really* sank in.

A tree had fallen onto the fence, crushing it underneath the massive weight. Duke could have easily gotten out of the enclosure, especially if he caught an interesting scent from outside the yard.

"Khloe!" Raid yelled.

He saw her jogging toward him—and the worry on her face when she caught a glimpse of the crushed fence. "Oh no! He got out?"

"Looks like it," Raid said tightly as he turned back toward the house.

"Duke! Come back!" Khloe yelled almost frantically.

"Khloe, come on, we need to make some phone calls then head out and see if we can find him," he told her.

"We're kind of close to the road," Khloe said with tears in her eyes. "He might've gotten hit."

Raid had already thought about that, but didn't want to bring up the possibility. "Don't borrow trouble. You know as well as I do that bloodhounds can go for miles and miles and miles when they're on a scent. And when they do finally lose it, they look up and wonder where the hell they are. Duke's a great dog, but he's not exactly the brightest. He's been on hundreds of searches through the woods around here, though. I have every confidence that he'll be able to use his nose to get back to a place that's familiar to him. In the meantime, we need more eyes than just ours. I have to call everyone."

"Yes!" Khloe said, impatiently wiping her face of the tears that had managed to fall. "You call the guys and I'll start getting in touch with others around town."

Raid nodded. Everything he'd told Khloe about Duke

was the truth, but that didn't mean he wasn't still terrified for his dog.

They burst into the house and headed straight for their cell phones. Raid called Ethan first.

"Hey, what's up?" he asked as he answered.

"Duke got out of my yard. He's been gone anywhere from an hour to an hour and a half. I need help looking for him."

"Shit, all right. I'm just finishing up a job now and I'll head out as soon as I can. You need me to call anyone else?"

"Thanks. And yes, if you can let Rocky and Zeke know, I'll call Drew, Brock, and Tal."

"Got it. We'll get the word out, Raid. We'll find him. It's not like Duke is a stranger in these parts."

Raid knew that, and was counting on it. If someone around town saw Duke by himself, they'd certainly know something was up and grab hold of him until Raid could get there. And if a local saw him on a trail in the woods, surely they'd wonder what he was doing out there alone.

"Thanks. My number's on his collar, so hopefully if someone finds him, they'll call."

"They will," Ethan said. "We're on this. Later."

When Raid hung up, he heard Khloe speaking with Harry Grogan, asking him to spread the word.

He hated this. Wanted to be out there looking for his dog, but he knew the more people who knew he was missing, the better chances Duke had of being brought home. He dialed Drew's number.

Ten minutes later, it felt as if they'd called everyone they knew in town. Khloe had spoken with everyone she could think of, even swallowing her pride and calling

Ziegler's office and letting them know to be on the lookout for Duke. They'd informed enough people that the gossip network of Fallport would be in full swing. Everyone would be looking for the bloodhound.

That should've made Raid feel better, but the dread that had formed in his throat was threatening to choke him. He was having a hard time thinking about anything other than Duke lying injured somewhere. Or scared and alone in the forest. Or hungry.

He'd thought it was bad when Duke was bloating and in surgery, but he'd been in good hands back then. In Khloe's hands. Being lost was almost worse. The not knowing where he was or if he was hurt was excruciating.

For the first time, Raid understood a little more of what Tonka had gone through when Garcia was torturing Steel and Dagger. Their dogs had been smart and deadly, as well as affectionate and their best friends. Thinking about the pain and confusion they'd gone through as Garcia hurt them, and when their masters did nothing to stop it, was its own form of torture.

"Raid, snap out of it!" Khloe ordered gently. "What's the plan? Where do you want to search first? Should we take separate cars?"

"No!" he exclaimed a little too harshly. Then he took a deep breath. "No, we stick together." He wasn't so far lost in his panic to forget there was a reason he and everyone in their group were keeping an eye on Khloe.

For a moment, Raid wondered if Duke's being missing had anything to do with either one of their pasts, but he dismissed it. He'd seen the crushed fence. That tree hadn't been tampered with. It had fallen on its own. It was just bad luck.

But he also wasn't dumb enough to let Khloe go off on her own.

"Okay, your car or mine?" she asked.

"Mine," he said. He needed the control of being behind the wheel. But his Expedition was also bigger. Duke barely fit in the back seat of Khloe's Bug.

Raid didn't miss Khloe grabbing her "go-bag" as she called it. The bag filled with medical supplies so she could help an injured animal en route to her clinic, if need be.

Pushing away the thought of Duke needing emergency medical attention, Raid grabbed his keys and headed for the door.

At first, they drove slowly up and down the road that went by his house with their windows down so they could call Duke's name. When that didn't work, Raid pulled into the parking areas for the hiking trail nearest his house. Both he and Khloe got out and yelled Duke's name. Again with no results.

It was possible Duke headed toward town. He'd been there often enough and probably even remembered getting food from people here and there. So they drove into town, going down every street, hoping and praying to see Duke trotting down the road looking pleased as punch at his adventure.

But there was no sign of him.

Forty minutes later, Raid was struggling not to let panic overwhelm him. The guys had checked in periodically, and no one had seen hide nor hair of the wayward bloodhound.

"Maybe we should head back to your house and see if he's there. He could've found his way back because he was hungry. You know, backtracked his own scent."

It wasn't a bad idea, but the more Raid thought about being in his house without Duke, the more his stomach hurt. He could still remember the first days he'd brought home the abused and neglected puppy who'd been thrown out like trash. Duke had quivered and cowered every time Raid went near him. But with a lot of patience, and food, he'd eventually come around. And become completely loyal to Raid.

No, Duke wasn't as smart as Dagger had been, or vicious. He wouldn't exactly tear the throat out of someone on command, but Raid had been content working hours and hours with Duke on tracking human scent. And now he was missing. Disappeared as if without a trace.

Khloe's phone rang, scaring the crap out of him.

"Hello? Really? Oh my God, thank you so much for calling! We're headed in that direction right now! Yes, I'll let you know. Bye!"

Raid turned to ask who it was, but he didn't need to bother when Khloe began speaking excitedly.

"That was Sandra. She said someone called the diner and said they saw Duke! He was near the trailhead for the Eagle Point Trail. I guess the person said they tried to get him to come to him, but Duke ignored him and trotted off."

Raid floored the Expedition. He wasn't surprised Duke wouldn't go to a stranger. He'd never really learned to like many people...Lilly and Khloe were exceptions. He tolerated men, but Raid suspected he'd been abused by one as a puppy, so he'd never really learned to trust them completely.

The Eagle Point Trail was one of the toughest in the

area, and not too far from his house. It made sense that Duke would be hanging around there, as he'd been on many searches starting in that very parking lot. He prayed Duke would stay put long enough for them to get to him.

"Did Sandra say who the person was? Why did they call her and not one of us?"

"She didn't. Just that it was a guy, and he said he spotted a bloodhound that didn't look like a stray, and he thought maybe someone would be looking for him. She thinks he was a tourist. He mentioned having the diner's number because it's one of the only places in town that does takeout."

He wasn't wrong. Hell, Raid knew the number by heart. He'd bought his fair share of meals from the diner, especially before he and Khloe got together.

Raid definitely broke the speed limit as he raced toward the trailhead. Every minute it took to get there was torture. He just wanted his dog back.

They pulled into the Eagle Point Trail parking area and saw three vehicles in the lot. There was a man Raid didn't recognize standing next to an older-model Oldsmobile. That had to be the guy who'd called in the sighting of Duke. A black Jeep and a Honda Civic sat in spaces across the gravel lot, their occupants nowhere in sight. They were probably on the trail.

Raid pulled into an empty spot and was out of the car like a shot. He and Khloe walked toward the man.

"Did you call about my bloodhound? You saw him?" Raid asked bluntly, not wasting time with polite greetings.

"I did. He was over there," the man said, turning and pointing into the trees.

Raid and Khloe turned to look where the man was

pointing. Raid cupped his hands around his mouth and yelled, "Duuuuuuuke!"

"Um, Raid," Khloe said in a strange tone of voice.

He was entirely focused on trying to see any kind of movement in the forest. "Duuuuuuke. Here, boy!"

"Raid!" Khloe said more forcefully.

Still distracted, Raid absently glanced at Khloe—and when he did, his blood froze for a completely different reason. All thoughts of his missing bloodhound disappeared in a flash.

The man who'd greeted them had pulled a gun and had it pressed against the back of Khloe's head. She had her hands up, as if to show she was unarmed.

"What the fuck?" Raid growled.

"You're going to do what I say, or I'll blow her brains out right here," the man said.

"My phone is in the car," Khloe said quickly. "Raid's too. Take them. Hell, take the car, the keys are still in the ignition," she pleaded.

But Raid instinctively knew he wasn't there to rob them. He wasn't Pablo Garcia; this man was a tall Caucasian. But there was absolutely no doubt in his mind that he worked for the drug lord.

He'd been unbelievably stupid. Too concerned about Duke to think clearly. He'd been running around like a chicken with its head cut off and Garcia's man had taken complete advantage.

"I don't want your fucking phones," the man informed Khloe. "You. Walk very slowly to my car and get in the trunk," he told Raid.

Khloe inhaled sharply at the man's demand. Her eyes were huge in her face and all the color drained from her cheeks as she stared at Raid as if waiting for him to get them out of this. But with that gun pressed against her skull, Raid had few options. He had no doubt the man wouldn't hesitate to shoot. If he was working with Garcia willingly, he had absolutely no compassion, no humanity.

He hesitated too long. Without a word of warning, the man took the gun away from Khloe's head, pointed it at Raid, and pulled the trigger.

Pain immediately exploded in Raid's right leg. By some miracle, he managed not to crumple to the ground.

The sound of the gunshot was muffled, and Raid realized there was a homemade silencer at the end of the barrel of the gun. As soon as he had the thought, the gun was pressed back up against Khloe's head. Her temple this time.

Khloe stood there, trembling in shock and fear, trying to catch her breath.

"I said, walk over to my car and get in the trunk. Unless you want the next bullet to be in her brain," the man said calmly and clearly.

Knowing he had no choice, and hating that he'd put Khloe in this situation, Raid did as the man ordered and backed toward the vehicle.

"Raid, don't..." Khloe begged.

"Yeah, Raid. Don't," the man mocked. "Please let me kill her. It's been a while, and I'll take great pleasure in doing so. I've had to be in this fucking town for weeks watching you two. There's nothing I want more than to end you both. You're the only one I've been ordered to deliver alive, but I'm thinking she's a great way to control you. Now—get the fuck in."

The trunk had been unlatched already, and Raid lifted

the lid, eyeing the interior dubiously. He wasn't sure he'd even fit.

His thigh throbbed where he'd been shot. Raid didn't think his femoral artery had been hit, but he was still bleeding profusely. "Let her go," he pleaded, not ashamed at all to be begging this monster. "She has nothing to do with this. Garcia wants me, not her."

"Get in," the man repeated.

With literally no other choice, Raid did as ordered. His mind spun, attempting to figure out his options. His friends were all out and about looking for Duke. Surely they'd have heard about the call to the diner, or would at some point. They'd find him, he knew it with every fiber of his being. But would it be in time?

As soon as he was lying awkwardly inside the trunk, the man shoved Khloe hard. She went down to the gravel on her hands and knees, and he swung his foot, kicking her in the side. "Now you. Get in."

"What? No!" Raid exclaimed.

The man merely pointed his gun at Khloe again. "Get in or you're dead."

Khloe moved quickly, getting to her feet and approaching the trunk. She didn't hesitate, lifting a leg over the bumper and climbing into the tiny space with him.

Without another word, their captor reached out and slammed the lid, shutting him and Khloe into the pitch blackness.

Raid could hear Khloe breathing too hard and too fast. He did his best to wiggle around to give her some more room, but it was no use. There wasn't a spare inch in the trunk.

Wrapping an arm around her, Raid pulled her against him. She managed to turn so they were face-to-face. Their legs were intertwined and every time she moved against him, fire shot down his leg from where he'd been shot. But Raid ignored the pain. It was the least of his worries at the moment.

The vehicle started and began to move. He could feel Khloe crying against his chest and every tear felt as if it burned his skin as they soaked into his shirt. *He'd* done this. This was his fault. She was in this situation because of *him*.

They both jerked in surprise when loud music suddenly filled the trunk. The man driving had put on some heavy metal and turned the volume up as loud as it could go. Raid's head immediately began to throb.

He felt Khloe take a deep breath. Then another. Then she shifted, and he felt her lips first against his cheek, then his ear. "Is there an emergency release lever?" she practically yelled.

She'd gotten control over her emotions, and Raid couldn't have been prouder.

"I don't know," he replied, hoping she could hear him.

She apparently did, as she wiggled around, turning so her back was to his chest once more and doing her best to feel all around them. Newer cars were made with a glow-in-the-dark release in case kids got stuck in a trunk, but no matter how hard they fumbled around in the dark, they couldn't feel anything that might help them escape the dire situation they'd found themselves in.

Raid tried to pry off the back of the taillight, but found it had been screwed in with some heavy-duty hardware.

The man who'd forced them into the trunk had definitely planned this abduction.

Khloe turned again, and Raid was impressed she was able to maneuver at all. When he felt her hand on his thigh, he jerked and couldn't stop the loud curse that left his lips when she found where the bullet had entered his leg—and clamped down hard.

"Sorry," Khloe said over the music, but she didn't let go.

To distract himself, Raid did his best to try to figure out what direction they were being taken. They'd turned right out of the parking area, toward Fallport. They'd slowed down a few times and stopped once, probably at the stoplight on the edge of town, before accelerating onto what Raid knew had to be the road that led toward the interstate.

Fuck, the asshole had driven straight through Fallport. Probably right past people who were looking for Duke. Past their friends.

The music was a smart touch. He and Khloe couldn't exactly communicate effectively, and if they pounded on the trunk or yelled for help, no one would hear them.

Raid clenched his teeth as Khloe did her best to examine his leg through touch. Even with the cramped space and darkness, she was extremely efficient. He had no idea what she was doing, but eventually, he felt something tighten around his leg.

A tourniquet. He realized it was his belt. The wound was so painful, she'd taken off the belt without Raid even realizing it.

He needed to pay far better attention to what was happening. He'd spaced out because of the pain, and the damn throbbing in his head to the beat of the music thumping all around them, but if he was going to think of a way to get them both out of this alive, he needed to concentrate.

It was several moments before Khloe scooted forward and he felt her lips against his ear once again. "That will stop the bleeding, but if we remove it, it'll start again. I have no idea what your leg looks like. Until I get some light, I won't be able to tell what we're dealing with. I don't know if this is good or bad news, but there's no exit wound."

Raid nodded, the gun was probably a smaller caliber since the bullet didn't go all the way through his leg. He wasn't thrilled about the tourniquet, but the alternative was losing so much blood, he would be completely useless to defend himself or Khloe.

"What are we going to do?" she asked.

Raid stiffened. He'd been dreading that question. He honestly wasn't sure what they *could* do. And he didn't think she'd want to hear the only answer he had—wait and see.

"Raid?" she asked.

Raid wrapped his arms around her and held her tightly as he bent his head so he could speak directly into her ear. "I don't know, Khloe. God, I wish I had a better answer for you, but I don't. We have to wait and see what this asshole has planned for us and go from there. But if you have a chance, you need to run. Get as far away from me as you can."

He felt her stiffen against him and knew without her having said a word that she wasn't happy with that plan.

"I know. It sucks. But that asshole wasn't wrong. The

only reason I got in this trunk is because he was threatening you. If you aren't around, he can't use you against me."

She trembled, and he felt her lips move against his throat.

"I hate this."

He could easily read her lips.

"I know."

They lay against each other for what seemed like forever, but was probably only about twenty minutes or so. They seemed to still be headed east. They should've reached I-81 by now, but they hadn't turned north or south as far as Raid could tell. So that meant they were likely headed for the coast. In the direction of Norfolk.

More time passed. It could've been an hour, it could've been six. In the pitch black of the trunk, it was impossible to tell. Raid was sure every minute probably felt like an hour as his mind raced, creating and discarding scenarios for when they were finally released from the trunk. But he knew no matter what he devised, all it would take was another gun pointed at Khloe's head for any plan to go to hell. He couldn't—*wouldn't*—risk her life.

As he wondered yet again how long they'd been in the car, music blasting through his skull, something occurred to him. He squeezed Khloe. "Hey!" he shouted in her ear. "Are you wearing your watch?"

She nodded against him.

"You can make calls from it…right?"

Her head came up so fast, she almost knocked into his chin. She thrust her arm between them. A small light glowed from the face of the smartwatch. Not enough to illuminate the interior of the trunk, but enough that they could both read the display.

Raid was shocked to see that nearly three hours had passed since their abduction.

"Oh my God, yes! Why didn't I think of that?! I don't need my phone to make a call! I thought it was an unnecessary expense to buy the cellular version instead of the wi-fi one, but it's come in handy when I'm working. I don't have to stop and find my phone to respond to texts or calls!"

She was babbling, but Raid didn't blame her. He could only hear every other word or so because of the blaring music, but he understood what she was saying.

"Who should I call?"

"Rocky," Raid said without hesitation. Any one of his friends would move heaven and earth to help him and Khloe, but Rocky had heard the entire story of what happened with Garcia all those years ago. Yes, he'd explained the situation to all the guys, but he and Rocky had a more in-depth conversation about Garcia when Khloe had asked him to come to his house to talk.

"Call Rocky," Khloe said after hitting a button on the phone—but nothing happened.

"Try again," Raid urged.

She did, with the same result. "The music's too loud. It can't pick up my voice."

"Take a breath, Khloe. It'll work. It has to."

She did, and this time before she hit the button to activate the computer chip to dial a number, she took the watch off her wrist. She cupped it in her hands between them, then dipped her head.

Raid couldn't hear her say the command to call Rocky

this time, but apparently it worked, because her head came up and she held the watch up against Raid's ear.

He didn't know if this was going to work or not. The music was so loud around them, he wasn't sure Rocky would be able to hear a word he said. But the fact that a call was coming in from Khloe's phone with such loud music on the other end should clue him into the fact that something was very wrong.

"Khloe? Where are you?"

As soon as he heard Rocky answer, Raid brought Khloe's hand down to his mouth. She understood and cupped her hands around it as he prayed his friend would be able to hear him.

"This is Raid. Khloe and I are in a trunk of a white Oldsmobile. We're using Khloe's smartwatch to call. Garcia's man got us and we're headed east. Call Tex to track us. I've been shot, but for now the bleeding's under control. Whatever happens, make sure Khloe's safe."

He brought Khloe's hand back up to his ear and strained to hear anything on the other end. But all he heard was the screaming of what apparently passed for music as it echoed around the trunk.

"Did he hear you?" Khloe asked.

Without a word, Raid picked up her hand and wrapped the watch band around her wrist. He wasn't sure if Rocky had heard a damn thing. He hoped and prayed he'd heard enough to know something was very wrong. He trusted Rocky. He'd get with the others and they'd use every resource to find them. Of that he had no doubt.

For now, all he and Khloe could do was wait. And try not to panic. They had no control over where they were going, over what would happen in the near future. They had to conserve their energy and be ready for when the car stopped. Because that was when the real fear would kick in.

Raid wasn't looking forward to coming face-to-face with Pablo Garcia again, but in a way he was glad it was happening now, and he didn't have to spend months, years, looking over his shoulder. His only regret was that Khloe had gotten swept up in the coming storm.

Taking a deep breath, Raid did his best to calm himself down. He needed to be at the top of his game if he was going to get Khloe out of this. He resigned himself to dying, but he'd do whatever it took to save Khloe's life. If he could take Garcia out with him, he'd save Tonka and his new family from having to go through anything like this in the future.

Satisfied with his decision to sacrifice himself, even if leaving Khloe would be the hardest thing he'd ever done in his life, Raid held her even tighter. He was counting on his friends using their military skills and contacts to get to them, but if push came to shove, he was more than ready and willing to do what it took to rid the world of the evil that was Pablo Garcia. One way or another.

* * *

Rocky looked up at his brother, Ethan.

"What? Was that Khloe? What'd she say?"

Rocky merely shook his head as his blood ran cold. Something was wrong. Very fucking wrong. When he'd seen Khloe's number on his screen, he was momentarily relieved. Tal and Heather had gone out to the Eagle Point Trail parking area after hearing about the Duke spotting, and they'd found Raid's Expedition—but no sign of Raid, Khloe, or the dog.

Their phones were still in the vehicle and the keys were in the ignition. Two very bad signs.

A couple of hikers had come off the trail while they were there, and they'd not heard anything unusual and hadn't seen anyone else the entire time they'd been on the trail.

After quickly searching Raid's house, Heather and Tal had called everyone else, and they'd all gathered at Rocky's house, where they'd been ever since. They'd reached out to various locals to find out if anyone had seen Khloe or Raid.

The women were in the other room, stressing the fuck out, and Rocky and the rest of the team were trying to figure out their next steps. It was one thing for Duke to disappear, but now that Raid and Khloe were gone as well, they knew something bad had happened.

Rocky had been leaning toward the Mather brothers having something to do with whatever the fuck was happening, and they'd been planning a search for Jason and Scott so they could be interrogated, when Rocky's phone rang.

When Bristol had been kidnapped, Rocky installed a recording app on his phone. He'd done it in case whoever had snatched Bristol called with a ransom demand, and he was never so glad as he was right that moment that he hadn't bothered to delete the thing.

He fumbled a bit, trying to find the app and then click on the right buttons, but when he did, he took a deep breath and played the phone call from Khloe back to the five men standing anxiously around him.

All they heard was the loud sounds of some sort of heavy metal song playing.

"What the fuck is that?" Drew asked. "Is that supposed to be music?"

"Why would Khloe be listening to that? It doesn't seem her speed," Brock said.

"Wait, play it again, Rocky," Zeke ordered. "And turn it up."

Rocky pressed the volume button as high as it would go, then played the phone call he'd received once more.

"Again," Zeke said when it cut off.

Rocky wanted to ask him what he was hearing, but he simply did as asked.

After a third replay, Zeke stood up. "We need to get this to someone. Someone who can strip out the music."

"You hear something?"

"Yes. There's a voice under there," Zeke confirmed.

"Holy shit," Tal said. "Is it Khloe?"

"I can't tell."

"Wait, how can Khloe be calling if we found her phone in Raid's car?" Drew asked.

Everyone was silent a moment before Brock said, "Doesn't she have a smartwatch?"

"Fuck! Yes. She does," Ethan said. "Lilly was making fun of her for waving her arm around to trick the thing into thinking she was walking. I guess Khloe didn't like that it vibrated every hour to let her know it was time to get up and walk, so she'd wave her arm around instead."

"Can it be tracked?" Rocky asked.

"I don't see why not. If it's using cellular data, it should be pinging off cell towers just like a regular phone would," Ethan said.

The men stared at each other for a heartbeat before they moved.

"I'll call Tex," Drew said.

"I'll call Rex," Ethan said.

"I'll get a hold of Simon," Zeke said grimly.

"And I'm calling Tonka," Rocky told his friends.

"His partner from the Coast Guard?" Ethan asked.

"Yes. He told us what happened and why he got out of the Coast Guard, but we had a long conversation about the asshole who'd hurt him and his partners. If this isn't the Mather brothers, Khloe and Raid are in deep shit. We have to warn Tonka that he could be in danger as well. Also, he may have a guess as to what Garcia might have planned. He spent the most time with the psychopath."

"Let's do this," Ethan said in a clipped tone. "Raid's always been there for us. No way in hell are we letting him or Khloe down."

CHAPTER NINETEEN

"I was able to strip out the music...the song's 'Butcher the Weak' by Devourment, by the way," Tex said in a grim tone. "Fucking horrible lyrics. Full of violence and gore... more than usual. Anyway, you'll want to hear what's left. Here it is."

Rocky and the rest of the group leaned in as they stared at the phone in the middle of the table. Tex had come through in a big way. As soon as he'd gotten the recorded call from Rocky, he'd started working on separating the sound files. They heard Raid's voice as clear as day. It was obvious he was stressed, but his voice was even and calm, his sentences succinct.

"This is Raid. Khloe and I are in a trunk of a white Oldsmobile. We're using Khloe's smartwatch to call. Garcia's man got us. We're headed east. Call Tex to track us. I've been shot, but for now the bleeding's under control. Whatever happens, make sure Khloe's safe."

"Shit!" Zeke swore.

The swear words the others used were far more colorful and brutal.

"What did Tonka say?" Ethan asked Rocky.

"He said he was getting on a plane as soon as he could arrange it," Ethan told his friends. "He also assumed with Pablo being extradited, his only choice for entering the country is via boat again, so Raid and Khloe will likely be taken to someplace on the coast."

"But we don't know where they're ultimately headed," Tal said in frustration.

"Raid was right, they're headed east," Tex broke in. "The cell service sucks in southern Virginia and there are large dead spots that have little to no reception. But the last place Khloe's watch pinged—good job on thinking about tracking her through it, by the way—was somewhere along Route 58 near Emporia."

"So heading to Norfolk then," Ethan said.

"That would be my guess," Tex confirmed.

It was dark now, around ten at night. The women were all still at Rocky and Bristol's house. No one wanted to go home knowing Khloe and Raid were in trouble. Duke was still missing, which also didn't sit well with anyone, but at the moment, all their concentration was on figuring out how to find and rescue Khloe and Raid. They'd have to leave finding Duke to the good people of Fallport.

No one wanted to even think about the possibility that whoever took Raid and Khloe had killed the dog. Had lured them to that parking area by taking Duke, getting his targets to a place where he could kidnap them with no witnesses.

"There haven't been any pings for an hour. My guess is that the guy is laying low somewhere. Waiting for a specific time he's supposed to rendezvous with Garcia," Tex said.

"Is that good or bad?" Brock asked when no one said anything.

"Both," Tex said. "Good in that it gives us more time to mobilize our resources. More time for Tonka to get here from New Mexico. Good in that if there's a plan in place, Khloe and Raid are probably safe from this guy because Garcia wants them alive. Bad in that Raid and Khloe have been in a cramped space for hours and are probably terrified. Not to mention Raid was fucking *shot* and could be bleeding out in that damn trunk."

Everyone was silent for a moment, thinking about the worst-case scenarios their friend could be experiencing. Then Ethan asked, "You'll let us know the second you get another ping, Tex?"

"Of course," the former Navy SEAL said, sounding a little annoyed by the question.

"Good. We know plenty of people who live in and around Norfolk," Ethan went on.

"I've also got my Green Beret friends," Zeke added.

"My state police contacts can monitor the roads," Drew said.

"And I've still got contacts at Border Control," Brock threw in.

"Right, we're all on this," Ethan agreed. "We didn't spend a good part of our lives learning all there is to know about protecting our country to let some asshole drug dealer come in and snatch our friends out from under our noses. We need to get on the road. We can plan along the way."

Everyone murmured their agreement and prepared to

head out after Tex disconnected. No one fucked with one of their own.

* * *

Khloe's head hurt. Bad. The songs all sounded the same and the deep bass throbbing for hours was almost as bad as any torture she could imagine. All she wanted was two seconds of silence. Okay, more than two seconds, but she'd go with that for now.

The car had stopped moving about ten minutes ago. She and Raid had both tensed, waiting for the trunk to open, for more guns to be pointed in their faces, but nothing happened.

For whatever reason, their captor had stopped and didn't seem in any great hurry to get going again. It was nerve-racking, and while Khloe tried to rest to calm herself, it was impossible. She'd also tried to make more calls, but they were in some sort of dead zone and none of her calls or attempted texts went through.

She'd done her best to check on Raid's leg, but he grabbed her hand and told her not to worry about it. It wasn't exactly safe to leave a tourniquet on for hours, but unlike what most people thought, he wouldn't lose his leg as a result. And the alternative was to take it off and have him start bleeding again, so she did as he wished.

The fact of the matter was, Khloe was scared and just looking for something to distract herself. She thought about what had happened to Raid and his friend Tonka, and their dogs, and the idea of being delivered to a man who enjoyed torturing both people and animals alike was terrifying.

Raid had called her brave for going through what she had in the past, but she certainly didn't feel brave. Though one thing she did know—there was no way she was going to leave Raid in this Garcia person's clutches if she got a chance to run. No way was she going to leave the man she loved to die alone. If this was their time, it was their time.

But surely they could think of something that would help them get out of this. They'd gotten that call through to Rocky, and she clung to that, although neither had any idea if he'd been able to hear Raid.

And the longer she lay there, the more stressed and worried Khloe got. She couldn't help the tears that leaked out of her eyes. She didn't want to be a crybaby, but she figured at a time like this, it was probably acceptable.

She felt Raid's arms tighten around her and she buried her nose into his neck. He'd been her rock. She had no idea how he'd been able to remain so stoic. She wanted to talk to him. Wanted to hear his rumbly voice. But the damn music prevented them from having any kind of real conversation, which she was well aware was the point.

She took what solace she could in the warmth of his body against her own, the comforting feel of his beard on her cheek...

Miraculously, she must've fallen asleep in Raid's arms, because she jerked awake when she felt the vehicle moving once more.

Lifting her wrist between them, she was stunned to see it was almost two in the morning. Somehow she'd slept for three full hours! Shifting so she could speak into Raid's ear, she asked, "How do you feel?"

"I'm okay," he told her.

Khloe's frustration mounted. He wasn't okay. How *could* he be okay?

The longer they drove, the angrier Khloe got.

Raid had been shot and needed medical attention.

They'd been kidnapped.

They were smushed in the trunk of a car going who the hell knew where.

The damn metal music hadn't stopped for even a minute since they'd left Fallport, and she had a headache from hell.

And they still didn't know what happened to Duke!

It was too much. And she was more than ready to fight back.

Yes, she was scared shitless, but the anger was stronger.

It was another half an hour before she felt the car slowing down. They'd made quite a few turns recently, and she prayed that they'd finally made it to their destination, wherever that was. She wanted to talk to Raid about a plan, about what they were going to do once they got out of this damn trunk, but it was impossible with that damn music.

Khloe had visions of springing from the vehicle like in the movie *The Hangover*, when Mr. Chow leaped out of the trunk of the car completely naked. But that wasn't happening. When the lid finally opened, Khloe *did* try to move, but she found her entire body felt like one big cramp. All she could do was lift her head just high enough to see out of the trunk.

Besides, coming face-to-face with the barrel of a gun didn't exactly inspire her to be Superwoman. Not only that, but Raid kept a firm grip on her arm, warning her not to do anything impulsive.

Her man knew her well. They hadn't had to talk for him to know without a doubt that she wanted to do something. Wanted to protect him in any way she could.

The man waiting for them wasn't anything like Khloe imagined in her head. He was well-groomed. Had brown hair that looked as if it had been styled recently. He wore a pair of khaki pants and a polo shirt. His shoes were leather and looked expensive. All-in-all, he looked...normal. Nothing like the deranged drug dealer she'd thought of in her head. Not that she knew what a deranged drug dealer looked like. But it wasn't this.

But no matter what kind of clothes he wore, or how widely he smiled...his cold, dead brown eyes told Khloe all she needed to know. He wasn't going to take any shit from them, and he would take great delight in hurting them if they tried anything.

"So nice to see you again, Mr. Walker. And I'm pleased that you brought a friend with you," Pablo Garcia said. His voice was even and calm with only a hint of a Spanish accent.

Khloe awkwardly climbed out of the trunk when the man motioned for her to do so, her ears ringing from the cessation of sound after so many hours. Garcia's voice sounded as if it was coming through a long tunnel.

Not wanting to look at the gun in his hand, she turned to help Raid climb out of the trunk. If her muscles were sore and hurting, his had to be even more so.

His olive-green cargo pants were stained red from the thigh down to his ankle on his right side, but he stood next to her as if he hadn't been shot hours earlier and didn't still have a bullet lodged in his leg.

"I wish I could return the sentiment, but that would be a lie," Raid told their captor.

Garcia laughed. A maniacal sound that grated on Khloe's nerves and made her extremely uneasy. Intellectually, she'd understood Raid when he'd told her that Garcia was psychotic, but hearing about it and experiencing it in person were two completely different things.

"Where are we?" Raid asked in a cold tone.

"Norfolk," Garcia said easily enough. "This is where you're from, right, Ms. Moore...sorry...Watts?"

Khloe nodded slowly.

"Well, I'm sorry we won't have time to visit any old friends of yours. We've got more interesting things planned. Please, after you," he said, gesturing with his pistol for them to walk ahead of him.

Khloe didn't want to do anything this man asked of them, but when three other men climbed out of nearby cars, she realized they didn't have a choice. It seemed as if they were in some sort of parking area. It was dark, with only one streetlight shining dimly across the lot, and she couldn't see any other people. The nearest buildings were rundown, riddled with broken windows, and seemed deserted. If she had to guess, they were in some sort of industrial area that wasn't used anymore.

Taking a deep breath, she could smell the ocean, that briny smell of salt, fish, and seaweed the water gave off.

"Khloe," Raid whispered as they began walking in the direction Garcia had ordered. "When you get the chance, run."

She almost snorted, but held off at the last minute. "Run? There's not a chance in hell I'd be able to get away from all four of them," she hissed. "In case you forgot,

Alan tried to run me over and my leg doesn't work the way it used to."

She probably shouldn't have been so blunt, but she was stressed way the hell out. If Raid thought she was leaving him behind to be killed by Garcia, he was so wrong.

Raid's jaw ticked as he limped along beside her.

"It's okay. We're gonna get out of this," she reassured him. She had no idea if that was true or not, but she desperately needed to believe it.

As they walked toward some lights in the distance, she realized where Garcia was herding them. Her nose had been right.

Several abandoned docks stretched into the water beyond an equally dilapidated warehouse. A lone boat was tied to the nearest one. It wasn't much to look at. To her, it looked like one of the lobster boats she'd seen on a reality TV show, except much lower-end. It was about twenty feet long, had a small wheelhouse, and a lot of ropes and barrels and other miscellaneous crap strewn across the deck.

Raid stopped in his tracks and turned to Garcia. "No," he hissed.

Garcia laughed again. "Sorry, my friend, but yes."

"I'm not getting on a fucking boat with you," Raid barked.

Garcia moved faster than Khloe expected. He lunged toward her with murderous intent and for a second, her life flashed before her eyes.

He brought his pistol up and jammed it against her forehead.

"You *are*," he insisted. "Or Ms. Watts's brains are going to be splattered all over both of us."

Khloe couldn't take her eyes off Garcia. He was staring at Raid, challenging him. Daring him to call his bluff. She could feel herself sweating, even though the air was chilly here by the water. Her mouth was dry as a bone and she couldn't swallow.

Raid had grabbed her hand when they'd started walking, and she was digging her fingernails into the skin on the back of his hand but couldn't make herself let go. She was frozen in fear. The feel of that gun against her skin was obscene, and it was all she could do to suck in air.

The standoff lasted only seconds, but it felt like a lifetime to Khloe.

Raid must've nodded or otherwise let Garcia know he'd do what he wanted, because the gun lowered and the drug dealer turned his attention to her. "Sorry about that," he said insincerely. "Now, if you'd please continue walking, we can get our *pleasure* cruise started."

Khloe was shaking so hard she didn't know if she could put one foot in front of the other. She'd seen movies, read countless books where the heroine was plucky and sarcastic and strong as hell. She felt like none of those things right now. The anger she'd felt earlier had completely disappeared. All she felt now was pure, unadulterated fear.

They were going to die. And this man was going to make sure they suffered before he finally killed them. Despite knowing if she stepped onboard the boat, they were doomed, she had no choice but to do just that.

The only redeeming factor in this situation was that Raid was with her. She didn't want to die. She'd finally found a man she could picture herself spending the rest of her life with, she had a group of men and women she felt were true friends, and she was getting back on her feet professionally. But it seemed as if what she wanted meant nothing. Not when a psychotic man was holding them hostage, seemingly hell-bent on torturing the man he blamed for his incarceration.

She and Raid were a lot alike. They were both introverts, sarcastic, liked animals...and both had people blaming them for their own bad decisions. She would've laughed, but she didn't have it in her.

She stepped over the side of the boat and held onto Raid, steadying him as he did the same. Garcia joined them onboard, as did one other man. The two men left on the dock quickly released the lines and before she knew it, they were on their way.

Garcia stayed on the back deck with them, always pointing that damn gun, and the other man went into the wheelhouse to drive.

"Rain's coming. It's going to get cold. I suggest you sit and get comfortable," Garcia said conversationally. "We have a ways to go to reach our destination."

"And where's that?" Raid asked.

Khloe didn't think Garcia would respond, but to her surprise, he seemed delighted Raid had asked. "Back to where we were first introduced," he said with a smile that didn't meet his eyes. "I've got the exact coordinates where you stopped my boat. It didn't seem fair to me that you missed all the fun the first time, so I thought we'd recreate the scene, this time while you're conscious, so you can participate. Pity I don't have your mutt to play with...but I've got something better." His gaze swung to Khloe, and she shivered.

Raid was so tense next to her, she was afraid he was

going to break in half. Somehow he managed not to respond to Garcia's taunt, but Khloe knew it was only a matter of time before he broke.

Garcia wasn't wrong, it was cold as his buddy in the wheelhouse gunned the engine and the boat roared off into the blackness of early morning. The winds were high, making the ride rough, extremely choppy. The waves were rolling and as they continued through the water, the rain they were promised began to fall.

Khloe and Raid huddled together against the side of the boat, doing their best to brace themselves as the vessel slammed down onto wave after wave.

At one point, Raid picked her up and settled her on his lap. She protested immediately. "Raid, your leg!"

"My leg doesn't hurt and is the least of our worries," he told her.

When put like that, Khloe had to agree. She wrapped her arms around him and held on tightly. She buried her nose into his neck and tears came to her eyes. God, was this going to be the last time she was held in his arms? The last time she felt his thick beard against her skin? This *sucked*. Big time.

"This is good," Raid murmured into her ear as he bent over her, trying to block at least some of the wind.

Khloe's brows furrowed. Good? How in the hell was their situation anything *close* to being good?

"It's two against two," Raid went on.

"They have guns," Khloe mumbled into his neck. It was noisy here on the deck with the rain, wind, and waves, but nothing like the damn music in the trunk of the car they'd had to deal with.

"They're coming, Khloe. We just have to hang on until they get here."

She knew who "they" were. Their friends. The confidence Raid had in them was reassuring. She nodded against him.

Garcia had never stopped talking, taking great pleasure in explaining in minute detail all the things he was going to do to them. How he was going to torture her just like he did poor Dagger and Steel. It was hard to block out his words, but Khloe much preferred to concentrate on the man holding her.

"They're gonna get here in time," Raid said once again in a low, rumbling tone.

Khloe didn't know if he was trying to reassure *her* or convince himself. She believed in their friends, but she wasn't sure they'd be able to figure out where they were in time. If they'd be able to prevent Garcia from carrying out all the awful things he was threatening.

Yes, as Raid had said, the odds were technically even, now that it was Garcia and his buddy against the two of them, but she wasn't sure she would be much help. And Raid was wounded. And, as she'd pointed out, they had guns.

But...she and Raid had determination on their side. And love. Surely love could overcome evil. It did in the movies.

Khloe winced. That was the dumbest thought in the history of the world. Movies weren't real. They were fake. Scripted. She and Raid were flying by the seat of their pants here. And the bullets in Garcia's gun were real, not simply flashbangs. If they were going to make it out of there, they'd have to work together. Stay on their toes. Take whatever opportunity presented itself to act.

The words were easy to think, much harder to actually do. The farther they got from shore, the harder it was not to panic. It was the middle of the night, it was raining like hell, and they were trapped onboard a small boat with a psychopath. Love was going to have to work pretty damn hard to win the day.

CHAPTER TWENTY

"They're at a small industrial boat dock in Norfolk," Tex said as soon as Ethan answered the phone. He and the rest of the team were nearing Norfolk after speeding the entire way. They'd set out as soon as they could, despite not knowing exactly where Raid and Khloe were, thanks to the shitty cell service. They'd known the direction, and that was enough.

"I need the exact address," Ethan clipped.

"Already sent. Has Tonka landed?"

Ethan took a deep breath. He had to stay calm. It had been a while since he'd been on a mission like this one. Once a SEAL, always a SEAL, but he couldn't stay disconnected this time. Not when it was Raid and Khloe's lives on the line. "Yes. He's working his Coast Guard connections and as soon as he has more information, he'll be ready."

"Good. I lost their location once they headed into the ocean, because there aren't any towers out there, obviously. But I did some research and while this might be a long shot...I think they could be headed to the same spot where the shit went down with Tonka, Raiden, and Garcia."

Ethan nodded. Tex's conversation was on speaker inside Rocky's Tahoe. He, Rocky, Zeke, and Drew were in this vehicle, while Brock and Tal were following behind them in Talon's Explorer.

"I think that's a pretty good bet," Rocky confirmed. "From what I gathered from Raid, Garcia's a psychotic son-of-a-bitch and it wouldn't surprise me if he wanted to go back to where he feels his injustice started in order to finish things with Raid."

"You have the coordinates, Tex?" Zeke asked.

"Of course. I'll send 'em to Tonka. Guys?"

"Yeah?" Ethan responded for all of them.

"Be careful. This Garcia is highly unstable. He wasn't actually released on account of good behavior, but more to get him the hell out of the country and out of the US's hands. He was constantly causing problems behind bars and it's believed he killed two men with his bare hands while incarcerated. Nothing could be proven though."

"We will," Ethan said. "Tonka's got a plan. Know any Night Stalker pilots, by any chance?" he asked the Navy SEAL turned fairy godfather to men and women around the world.

Tex chuckled. "It just so happens that I know a hell of a good team."

"I'm thinking we could use their help, considering where Raid and Khloe are currently located. Raid was shot hours ago. We'll need to get him to a hospital ASAP."

"Good idea. I'll give them a call and they'll be on standby. Just keep me informed."

"Will do. Thanks for your help, Tex."

"Talk to you soon," the man on the other end of the line said before disconnecting.

"He really doesn't like to be thanked, does he?" Drew asked.

"No. Floor it, Rocky," Ethan said. "They've got too much of a head start. We all know that Garcia isn't bringing our friends to the middle of the ocean for a tea party."

The vehicle surged forward as Rocky raced toward the industrial dock near where Khloe's watch had last pinged.

* * *

Raid couldn't remember ever being this scared. Yes, he could admit that he was terrified out of his mind. But he wasn't letting any of his emotions show on his face. That was what Garcia wanted. He reveled in fear. In pain.

He could feel Khloe's heart beating frantically against his chest as he clung to her. The farther away from shore they went, the lower his heart sank. It was the wee hours of the morning, pitch black, they were in the middle of a storm, and Garcia was going to torture Khloe in order to make Raid suffer.

But...he had a plan.

It was risky, and there was a high probability he would fail, but he'd do whatever he could if it meant giving Khloe a chance to escape this asshole.

He was going to bum rush Garcia and go from there. He'd probably get shot, but maybe he could hold on long enough to wrestle the gun from Garcia and shoot both him and his accomplice. Maybe. It depended on whether or not Garcia got a lucky shot off and hit him in the head or the heart.

The thought of leaving Khloe alone and helpless in their clutches made him want to throw up. Raid didn't like feeling this powerless. If this was one of his D&D games, he'd probably take all kinds of risks with his decisions. But this wasn't a game. It was real life and Raid desperately wanted to live.

He had no idea how much time had gone by since they'd left the dock when the boat finally began to slow. Looking around, Raid couldn't see anything but the driving rain in the lights from the back of the wheelhouse. The boat bobbed up and down fairly violently as it finally came to a stop in the rolling waves.

"We're here!" Garcia crowed. "The fun can start! The last time I was here, the weather was quite different. Do you remember?"

Raid glared at the man and made no attempt to move from where he and Khloe were huddled against the side of the boat.

"I asked, do you remember?" Garcia yelled, shooting a round into the air.

Khloe jerked in his arms, and Raid found he hated this man more than ever.

"I remember," he told him. Every muscle in his body was tense, ready to act. He just needed to wait for the exact right moment.

Garcia smiled. "It was a sunny day. There were a few clouds in the sky, and the ocean was as calm as glass. The whimpers and cries of those mutts echoed across the water so deliciously."

Hatred welled up within Raid so hard and fast, it was

all he could do not to leap up right then and charge the man. His muscles tensed to do just that when he glanced into the wheelhouse and saw the second man resting with his back against the wheel, smiling. He needed to be smart, wait until both men lowered their guard. They already thought they had the upper hand. Raid just needed to wait a few more minutes.

"Stand up," Garcia ordered, punctuating his order by pointing the gun at them once more.

Raid slowly nodded. He wanted to give Garcia the impression they were completely cowed. He also needed to stall. Wanted to give the cavalry time to get to them. He had every confidence they'd figure out where they were and would save Khloe. The alternative was unthinkable.

"I need you to get up," Raid told Khloe as gently as he could.

He heard her whimper, but she moved, swinging one of her legs off his lap so she was on her knees next to him. She lifted a hand and grabbed hold of the railing, using it to stand. He saw her wobble a bit, but she stiffened her knees, spread her legs for more stability, and caught her balance.

She was being so brave, and Raid had never been as proud of anyone as he was her at this moment. Khloe held out a hand to assist him, and Raid took it gratefully. When he was on his feet, he leaned against the railing behind him for balance. The boat was really rocking and visibility was shit with the darkness and the rain.

A new plan occurred to him at that moment.

Because he was so tall, the railing hit him beneath his ass. If he wasn't careful, he could easily be knocked overboard by one of the tall waves buffeting the boat...

"Come over here," Garcia ordered Khloe.

She didn't move.

The man sighed. "I see you both are going to be pains in my ass. Are you deaf? I *said*, come. Over. Here," he growled.

Khloe squeezed Raid's hand and did as ordered. She shuffled across the deck, arms out, looking like a drunken sailor as she attempted to walk without falling into the pitching seas. When she got close enough to Garcia, he reached out with his free hand and grabbed her around the throat.

Khloe's hands immediately went to his, trying to pry his fingers off her, but he merely laughed. Raid took a step forward, and Garcia did the one thing that would keep him docile. He pointed his weapon at Khloe's head once again.

"She's ugly," he said conversationally, staring at Raid. "And old as fuck. I bet her pussy's all shriveled up and dry as a bone. Still, I went a long time without pussy, and what I've had since getting out hasn't exactly been thrilling. I'm gonna enjoy taking her for a spin while you watch. And there won't be a damn thing you can do about it," Garcia said. "Not unless you want me to put a bullet in her brain. Then again, that might be the kinder choice. Watch her suffer...or let her die?"

He cackled, and the sound wound down Raid's spine like fingernails screeching on a chalkboard.

There was no fucking way he could stand there and watch Khloe be raped by this animal. He met her gaze and read the same thought in her eyes. Knew she'd rather die than be touched by this man.

Garcia ran the barrel of the gun down Khloe's cheek as

he leaned in, keeping his gaze on Raid, then licked her face where the weapon had just been.

Then without warning, he roughly shoved Khloe away from him. She went flying across the deck and landed hard on her ass.

"Get back here," he ordered, as soon as she landed.

Khloe didn't hesitate, and Raid was in awe of her bravery. She managed to get to her feet once more and stumbled back toward their captor.

This time when she was within reach, Garcia grabbed her arm and motioned for his henchman to come forward. "Hold her while I get her clothes off," he ordered.

Raid lunged forward, fists clenched. Yet again, Garcia raised the pistol and held it against Khloe's head. "Don't move, lover boy. Unless you want to see her brains splattered all over the deck."

Raid's jaw tensed. The situation was going downhill much faster than he'd hoped. He had to move! But that gun pressed to Khloe's head terrified him. The only thing worse than watching her get abused at this monster's hands would be seeing a bullet go through her skull. He needed Garcia to lower that fucking gun!

"Good boy. Sit. Stay," Garcia mocked with a laugh. He turned his attention back to Khloe. And the woman he loved more than life itself wasn't going to make violating her an easy task. Both Garcia's and his lackey were struggling to hold her as she fought them with everything she had.

Every single muscle in his body tense, Raid waited for Garcia to lower or drop the gun in his fight to restrain Khloe—

Sudden movement in his peripheral vision had him glancing right for a split second.

What he saw had him thinking they might—just maybe—get out of this fucked-up situation after all.

A screech had him focusing back on Khloe. One of the men had managed to rip her shirt, and it was now hanging off one shoulder.

Garcia had lowered the gun, body twisting to try to hold a bucking and fiercely pissed-off Khloe.

It was time.

"Let her go!" he yelled loudly, startling the other men enough for them to pause what they were doing and glance over at him. "In a few minutes, you're going to have more to worry about than a petite woman kicking your ass." Raid pointed to the right...

At the lights from several boats in the distance, converging on them at an extremely high rate of speed.

Both men turned to look where he was pointing, stunned at the sight, and Raid didn't hesitate. He ran toward Khloe, grabbed her wrist and yanked—hard.

The move surprised the men even more, allowing Raid to easily wrench her out of their grasp.

Even as their captors lunged toward him, Raid threw himself toward the side of the boat. His high center of gravity doing what he knew it would—plunging them both overboard when he hit the rail.

He regretted not being able to give Khloe any warning. It was crazy, throwing themselves into the ocean in the middle of a storm, in the dark, but anything was better than letting Garcia use her as a hostage.

Raid had time to take a deep breath before he hit the water flat on his back, keeping a tight hold on Khloe. They tumbled in the rolling waves for a moment before he got his bearings and his head popped above the water. He wrapped his arm around Khloe so she wasn't ripped away from him in the waves. He knew if they were separated in this kind of weather, he might never find her again.

The water was cold, and it took a split-second for Raid to catch his breath. When he did, he looked at Khloe. Her hair was plastered to her head, waves were crashing over them, she clung to his shirt with a compulsive grip—and blinked up at him in shock.

"I'm hoping you're a good swimmer!" Khloe said quickly, doing her best to keep from swallowing the sea water.

"Best in my class," he reassured her. "You?"

"Mediocre at best," she admitted.

"I've got you," Raid told her confidently. The violent waves had already moved them several yards away from the boat, but it didn't really matter. Garcia and his henchman were racing around the boat frantically, trying to get it started to get the hell out of there before they were captured.

"You saved us," Khloe said, tightening her hold around his waist and not taking her eyes off him. He could feel her trembling, but he was enormously proud of her.

His leg hurt like hell, but he hoped the salt water would actually go a long way toward cleaning the wound. He used his good leg and his free arm to keep both their heads above the water.

As if she could read his mind, she gasped. "Oh, shit, I didn't even think about your leg! Do you think the blood is gonna attract sharks?"

Raid couldn't help but snort. "I think the little blood

that's still seeping from the hole in my leg is the least of our worries right about now."

"Find them!" Garcia yelled at his lackey. He'd clearly abandoned his plan to run and was standing at the railing of his boat, scanning the water with his gun at the ready, obviously trying to find where he and Khloe had gone.

"We have to get out of here!" the man shouted back from the wheelhouse.

"*No!*" Garcia screamed, but the man ignored him. He finally got the engine started and the boat was just starting to turn when the small fleet finally converged on their location.

The look on the drug dealer's face when he realized he was fucked—*again*—was priceless. Rage, frustration, hatred...all of those emotions and more twisted his expression.

He quickly lifted his weapon and started firing rapidly, not at the boats around him, but in the general direction Khloe and Raid had fallen into the water.

Someone—Raid didn't know who, but he was incredibly thankful for their good aim—shot the pistol out of his grip, blowing his hand off in the process.

That was the last thing Raid saw before a boat blocked his view of the man who'd kidnapped and planned to torture both him and Khloe.

"If you wanted to go for a swim, I'm thinking you could've found a better time and place for it," a familiar voice said as another boat carefully eased closer.

Raid was never so relieved to hear Ethan's voice as he was right that moment.

"Well, you know, I'm always one to do what you least expect," he quipped back.

The waves hadn't abated. If anything, they seemed to be even angrier than they'd been earlier. It took a bit of maneuvering, especially since the cold water had wrecked Raid's coordination, but he managed to hand Khloe over to the two men leaning over the boat, reaching out for her.

It took three people to lift him out of the waves, and once onboard, Raid collapsed on the bottom of the boat next to Khloe. The smile on her face as she stared at him was something he'd never forget.

"It's over?" she asked.

"It's over," Raid confirmed.

Khloe came up on an elbow, ignoring the men hovering around her, trying to wrap her in an emergency blanket. "Did they get him?"

"He's not going anywhere," Zeke reassured her.

Raid sat up and took the blanket from Zeke. Khloe's shirt was hanging off her body where it had been ripped and her skin was so pale from the cold water, he was concerned that she would go into shock if she didn't get warmed up. He wrapped the blanket around her even as she looked up at Zeke and began to ask questions.

"No, is he dead? Did they kill him? Because if not, he's going to come back! Like a bad penny. Which is such a weird saying. Why are pennies bad? It makes no sense. Anyway, they need to kill him. Shoot him. *Something*. Because he's not going to stop coming after Raid!"

"He's not going to be a problem," Tal reassured her.

Raid looked up at his friends. They were surrounded by several military men—Navy SEALs, by the look of them. Ethan and Rocky had obviously called in people they still knew in the service to help. A quick look around confirmed a couple Coast Guard boats bobbing in the water as well, no doubt courtesy of Tonka.

Tal—just as badass as any Navy SEAL, but a UK version—got down on one knee next to Khloe. Her lips were blue, and Raid wanted to tell everyone to move their asses. Get back to shore so Khloe could get some medical attention. But no one seemed in any big hurry to leave the area, which confused him.

"Tal—" Khloe began.

"Tonka's over there," he interrupted, speaking quietly. "And he's not happy. We all have no doubt that after he was done with you and Raid, he would've moved on to Tonka, his family, and the animals he tends to at The Refuge. Trust me, Garcia's not going to be a problem in the future."

Khloe frowned. "Will Tonka get in trouble?"

Damn, Raid loved this woman. She'd just been through hell and she was worried about a man she'd never met. But he knew without a doubt that she cared about Tonka simply because he was a friend of Raid's.

He reached over and grabbed her hand. "No," he said firmly. He had no idea what the plan was, or what was happening on Garcia's boat, but if Tonka was here, no way was the drug dealer going to end up anything but dead.

As relieved as Raid was that he and Khloe were alive and out of Garcia's clutches, he couldn't help but think of one more thing that had been stressing him out. "Duke?" he asked Ethan, his voice cracking. If Garcia had been behind his bloodhound's disappearance after all...if he'd hurt him...

"Safe," Ethan quickly reassured him, before Raid's

thoughts could go any further into the dark place where they'd been heading.

"Thank God!" Khloe breathed.

Overwhelmed with emotion, all Raid could do was nod at his friend in relief.

Before he could ask any questions about his dog or anything else, Raid heard a familiar sound over the wind and rain. Looking up, he saw an unbelievable sight. Through the raging storm, an MH-60 Knighthawk helicopter was approaching.

"What the hell?"

"That's your ride out of here," Ethan said with a grin. "Tex called in some favors and you've got two of the best Night Stalker pilots at the controls of that baby."

"We figured it would be the fastest way to get you both to a hospital," Rocky explained.

"I'm guessing you wouldn't object to getting that tourniquet off sooner rather than later," Brock added.

Raid couldn't feel his leg at this point. After the pain from the bullet wound, the tourniquet, and the cold water, it was pretty much dead weight. But he couldn't drum up the concern that he might lose it, or at the very least lose some function. He was alive. Khloe was alive. That was all that mattered.

The Knighthawk hovered directly over the boat, and the rain, whipped even faster by the rotor blades, stung as it hit Raid's face. He turned to Khloe and protected her as best he could from the wind and stinging rain.

He let his friends wrap them up and insisted on Khloe being lifted first. When it was his turn, Raid looked at the six best friends he'd ever had. They accepted him as he was, had come to his aid when he needed them most, and that was the best gift he'd ever been given. "I knew you'd come," he told them, feeling mushy and lightheaded.

"Yeah, yeah, yeah," Ethan said. "We'll talk at the hospital after they patch you up. Try not to get into any trouble between here and there."

Raid smiled and stared up at the helicopter as he was lifted into the air.

Once inside, he quickly moved next to Khloe, then the door was shut.

The medics hovered over them as they hooked up IVs and did their best to make them comfortable as they headed toward the mainland and a hospital.

Raid had a thousand things running through his head, but all he could think of was how crazy the pilots of this chopper had to be. Neither he nor Khloe were critical, although they hadn't known that, and they'd flown out in a hellacious storm to make their journey to medical help faster and more comfortable.

Turning his head, he saw two men sitting behind the controls, talking to each other and laughing as if this was a routine pleasure flight instead of an airlift in dangerous conditions.

The Army Night Stalkers were the best pilots in the military. They went places no other sane pilots dared. They worked hand in hand with special forces of all branches, evacuating teams when needed, as well as inserting them. They worked natural disasters at home and abroad and were generally the rock stars of the piloting world.

"You guys are insane," he said through the headset one of the medics had placed over his ears.

The pilot turned and grinned, giving him a thumbs up.

The copilot also turned in his direction with a smile on his face. "On behalf of Casper, who's your pilot on this little jaunt, and myself—I'm known as Pyro—we're happy to have you onboard our chopper. We got a call from someone you probably know. Tex?"

Raid nodded with a grin.

"Yeah, well, good ol' Tex asked if we were up for a little flight to pick up two of his friends. And if you know him, then you also know that no one says no to Tex. So here we are."

"I owe you," Raid said.

"Like hell you do," Casper told him. "From what we understand, the country owes *you* a huge debt for getting a scumbag like Garcia off the streets. Just hang on, we'll have you to the hospital in a jiffy."

"Are you gonna hover and have us shuttled through a window in the hospital, or are you gonna land like normal pilots do?" Raid joked.

Both pilots burst out laughing.

"You want to go through a window? We can make that happen," Casper said.

"I'm thinking landing on the heliport is good enough. We've had enough excitement for one day," Raid told them.

Both men gave him a thumbs up this time, then turned their attention back to the instruments.

Relaxing for the first time since waking the previous morning, Raid reached over to the gurney next to him and took Khloe's hand in his once more. She was getting some color back in her face and her lips weren't quite as blue as they'd been before.

She squeezed his hand, as she stared over at him. "I love you," she mouthed.

"I love you," Raid returned without hesitation.

The last twelve hours or so had been harrowing, and he never would've wished anything like that on Khloe, but he couldn't help being proud of her...and relieved she'd been with him. All he could think about was getting back to Fallport and living the rest of his life with her by his side.

* * *

Finn "Tonka" Matlick was as calm as he'd ever been. He hadn't expected to be in this situation, but now that he was, he was composed and focused.

Pablo Garcia, the man who'd made his life a living hell, was currently lying on the deck of his boat, bleeding from the stump that was his missing hand...and crying and begging for a doctor. But no doctor would be coming for this piece of shit.

No, the only thing in his future was death.

Tonka didn't know what strings Tex had pulled, and he didn't care. All he knew was that this man had to die. He wouldn't stop coming for him and Raiden. Even if he went to prison once again for kidnapping and attempted murder, he'd eventually be released, and once again they'd have to worry about looking over their shoulders.

Tonka wasn't leaving this boat without ensuring Pablo Garcia was no longer a threat.

The Navy SEALs who'd assisted with the takedown had already left with the man who'd been driving the boat. He'd be interrogated about any accomplices and would then end up in federal prison to rot. There was only one boat left bobbing in the ocean along with Garcia's. And the two men who were waiting for Tonka on the other vessel had been briefed on the situation.

Tex swore they could be trusted, and Tonka had no reason to think his old friend was lying.

He squatted next to Garcia, studying him with narrowed eyes but not saying a word.

"*What?* What are you looking at? Hurry up and take me back to land! I need a fucking doctor!" Garcia barked.

"Not happening," Tonka said after a long moment of silence.

"What? What do you mean? I need help!"

"No, you don't. You need to die. The world will be better off without you in it."

Garcia's eyes widened. "You can't! That's murder!"

Tonka chuckled, but it wasn't a humorous sound. "That's rich, coming from you." Then he stood and walked over to a pile of rope and an anchor lying on the deck. He calmly grabbed the pile and brought it over to Garcia.

"What the fuck? Stop! No!" Garcia cried, attempting to avoid Tonka's hands. It was no use. Within seconds, Tonka had zip-tied Garcia's ankles and wrists together. Then he began to tie the long rope to his body as well.

"Please! Let's talk about this!" Garcia blubbered. "I've got money. I can make you rich! Don't you want that stupid ranch of yours to prosper? I can make that happen!"

"You know what I want?" Tonka asked in a flat tone.

"Anything! I'll give you anything."

"I want my dog Steel back. I want the hours I listened to you torturing him and Dagger back. I want to be able to go to sleep and not see their begging eyes in my dreams. Can you give me all that?"

Garcia stared at the man who would be his executioner, not uttering a word.

"I didn't think so," Tonka said with a shrug, continuing to knot the rope.

"You won't sleep ever again with killing me on your conscience!" Garcia told him desperately.

Tonka chuckled. "You're wrong. I'll sleep like a baby. You know why?" He didn't give him a chance to speak. "Because I'll know you're not around to hurt anyone else. You won't be able to torture another animal for the fun of it. You won't be here to count your money when someone gets addicted to the drugs you make and distribute."

"If you do this, you'll be as bad as me!" Garcia swore.

"No one's as bad as you," Tonka said, his voice hard. "And I've got a woman who knows all my secrets...and loves me anyway. You know what the last thing she said was, before I headed out here? 'Find him and kill him.'" Then Tonka looked him dead in the eye. "I'm gonna sleep like a fucking baby, you son-of-a-bitch."

With that, he dragged a screaming Garcia to the edge of the boat. "You thought throwing Dagger and Steel overboard when they were still alive was *funny*. Let's see how you like it."

And with that, Tonka hefted Garcia's body up and over the low railing, throwing the anchor attached to his body by the rope after him.

Tonka didn't stick around to watch. He turned and signaled to his ride that he was ready to be picked up.

Right before leaving the boat, he overturned a large can of gasoline that was sitting in the corner of the deck. Once safely onboard the other vessel, he aimed a flare gun and shot at the drug dealer's now-empty boat. It immediately went up in flames, despite the rain that was still falling.

In half an hour or less, there would be nothing left of the boat. The report would state that it caught fire and sank with Pablo Garcia still onboard. There would be no questions asked, courtesy of markers Tex was owed.

Tonka didn't look back as they headed to Norfolk. He had a plane to catch and a family to return to.

"That was for you, Steel," he whispered after closing his eyes. "You and Dagger can finally rest in peace."

CHAPTER TWENTY-ONE

Khloe sat on Raid's couch with a blanket around her. Raid was at her side, as he'd been from the second he'd been released from the hospital. The bullet had been removed from his leg and the doctor was amazed that more damage hadn't been done. He had a good amount of rehab to go through, but he'd been reassured that, with a lot of hard work, he'd be able to get back on the trails as a member of the Eagle Point Search and Rescue team before too long.

Khloe had recovered fairly quickly from the entire ordeal, except now she felt as if she was always cold. Raid had turned the heat on in his house, despite it being the middle of summer, and it didn't matter if it was set at seventy-one or eighty-one, she still felt chilled. So he'd bought a ton of throw blankets and was constantly wrapping her up in them whenever she sat down.

She'd spent a lot of the last week cooking for them and making sure the house was clean. Raid wasn't able to help much, which seemed to frustrate him to no end. He wanted to be up and moving immediately, but Khloe reminded him that, from her experience, he'd need time to get back to his normal self.

The best thing about coming home to Fallport was being enthusiastically greeted by Duke. Raid had cried when he'd seen his furry friend and wasn't even embarrassed that everyone had seen him blubbering at the sight of the bloodhound, safe and sound.

All of their friends had come over today to celebrate Raid and Khloe—and Duke, of course—being home and in one piece. And to gossip.

"All right, someone needs to *finally* tell me where the hell Duke was and what went down after Khloe and I went missing," Raid said.

Just over a week had passed since that awful night, but he and Khloe had been busy with Raid's short hospital stay, getting resettled, and generally healing both physically and mentally from their ordeal. They'd begged their friends for a bit of time before they all converged, which meant they'd yet to hear the story of how the bloodhound was found. They'd both been content just having him by their side. Now, it was time to hear about everything that happened after they were kidnapped.

Instead of lying on his bed in the corner, Duke had climbed up onto the couch. He sat to one side of Raid, his head in his master's lap, while Khloe was snuggled up on Raid's other side.

Their friends were on every available piece of furniture in the living room. Chairs from the table had been brought in as well, and most of the rest sat on the floor around the couch. Tony was entertaining Marissa out in the yard. Zeke and Tal were standing at the sliding back door, keeping an eye on them as they played.

Looking around, Khloe got a little teary eyed once more. Never in a million years would she have expected to have found a group of men and women who would come to mean so much to her. She was a lucky woman, and she knew it.

"Right, so as you know, once word got out that Duke was missing, the entire town was on the lookout," Caryn explained. "Shortly after Garcia's goon called the diner to report the false sighting, a couple was taking a walk in Raymond Ziegler's neighborhood."

"They heard the most ear-splitting howling coming from his house," Bristol said, picking up the story. "They said it sounded like an animal was being tortured in there. So they did what anyone would do in that situation—they called Simon."

"Simon went to the house, and by that time, a crowd had gathered," Elsie said excitedly. "The police chief knocked on the door, and no one answered. But the howling got even louder. He sent Miguel over to Ziegler's clinic to ask what the hell was going on."

"Ziegler, obviously sensing the shit was about to hit the fan, lied his ass off," Brock added. "Said he had no idea what they were talking about. Which is about the stupidest thing he could've done. If he'd simply confessed right then and there, he might still be in business instead of fleeing town with his proverbial tail between his legs."

Khloe smiled at the image Brock's words evoked.

"To make a long story short," Lilly said, "Simon broke into Raymond's house and they found Duke in a guest bathroom."

"Duke doesn't do well in locked rooms," Raid said dryly.

Everyone laughed.

"Yeah, obviously. He'd shat all over the room and walked in it," Bristol said with a grin. "When Simon opened the bathroom door, Duke bolted out and practically ran the poor chief over. Then, to show his appreciation for being free, Duke zoomed around the house, making sure to get his poopy pawprints all over everything."

"I learned the hard way when he gets stressed, he tends to lose his bowels," Raiden said after everyone had stopped laughing. "The only thing I can figure is that his first piece-of-crap owner kept him locked up. He hates being shut in rooms by himself now."

"Well, as relieved as everyone standing around Ziegler's house was to see Duke, they were also pissed. Everyone wanted answers," Rocky said. "I swear, by the time Simon and most of the onlookers arrived at the clinic, it was practically a mob. When asked, Ziegler said he'd found Duke wandering along the road and picked him up to keep him safe."

"Riiiiight," Finley said sarcastically. "Picked him up, didn't tell anyone—like *Raid*—that he'd found his dog, locked him in his house, then went to work as if nothing was wrong."

"Not saying anyone believed his story, just what he claimed," Rocky said with a grin.

"People were so appalled that Fallport's resident veterinarian had basically kidnapped one of the town's heroes, they started canceling their appointments at Ziegler's clinic," Lilly said. "By the end of the day, he'd basically lost all his clients."

"Last I heard, he went to stay with his brother for a while up near DC," Tal said.

"Good riddance," Heather said with a good deal of heat...for *her*. "I think this town has had enough kidnappings, no matter if it's people or animals."

"Definitely!" Bristol said fervently.

Everyone agreed.

"Do you think Duke got out on his own, or do you think Garcia's guy had a hand in it?" Ethan asked.

Raid shrugged. "I don't know. Duke's never really been a wanderer, but if given a chance, and if he caught a scent, I wouldn't put it past him. In the end, it doesn't really matter. I didn't even know Garcia or someone working for him was here. He clearly took advantage of the situation and did what he'd been sent to do."

"And he's really gone? He won't come back?" Finley asked.

Raid paused for a moment before nodding. "He won't ever be an issue for me or Tonka, or those we love, ever again."

"Because his boat went up in flames and he was caught in the fire," Elsie said dryly, clearly skeptical.

"That's right," Raid said with a straight face.

Khloe knew what really happened because Raid had told her late one night in the hospital, when it was just the two of them. He admitted that while he couldn't have done what Tonka did, he didn't condemn him. Garcia had put Tonka through hell, and it had affected every part of his life since. He was also very grateful for his friend for making sure he and Khloe would be safe from here on out.

"Well, good riddance," Caryn said. "And the same goes

for Doctor Ziegler too. Khloe...are you going to be able to keep up with the increase in business?"

Khloe shrugged. "I'm gonna try. Afton and my other vet techs have been lifesavers. They've been able to do most of the routine things, like shots and checkups. The more serious issues they leave for me or my new partner. That friend of mine from Norfolk is already doing a wonderful job of holding down the fort."

"The timing of her accepting your offer was damn perfect," Bristol agreed.

"So...Garcia's taken care of, Ziegler is a bad memory... what about the Mather brothers?" Ethan asked.

Khloe frowned. "I'm not sure. I haven't seen Jason or Scott lately, but I wouldn't put it past them to show up when I least expect them."

"They won't," Raid said with such conviction, Khloe turned to him with her eyes narrowed.

"What'd you do?"

"Nothing anyone else who wanted to live a nice, quiet life with the woman he loved wouldn't do," Raid said, squeezing her shoulder.

Khloe swore every single person in the room leaned forward, eager to hear more details.

"Raiden Walker, I haven't gone through what I have— being run over, going through rehab alone and scared, moving to a town where I knew no one, taking a job I knew nothing about, getting sniped at by *you* every day at work, having to sit through a trial where I felt as if *I* was the one being accused, watched my friends get kidnapped and hurt, had my secrets exposed to everyone in town, falling in love, being kidnapped, and *finally* feeling as if I can breathe and really start a life with the person I was always meant to be with—only to have to worry about you being arrested and thrown in jail for doing something illegal to the asshole and his brothers who are harassing me for no good reason!"

Her voice had risen throughout her little freak-out, but Khloe didn't care. She was serious. She felt as if things in her life were *finally* falling into place, and the last thing she wanted was to have Raid get in trouble because of her.

Raid laughed, as did his friends—the male ones—and it infuriated Khloe all the more. She sat up, intending to give Raid another piece of her mind, but he tugged her back against him.

"Shhhh. Don't get worked up, Khloe. I'm not ashamed to admit that I had grand plans for Alan and his brothers. A plan that included using a contact in Colorado to get word to some people behind bars with Alan...the kind of men who'd make sure he understood you were off-limits. And if he didn't call off his brothers, his life in prison would become even harder than it already was."

"And?" Khloe demanded when Raid paused and didn't say anything else.

"Turns out, we didn't have to do anything. My guy's contacts in prison didn't even have time to make their point before Alan Mather did what he does best—pissed off the wrong person. He was killed six days ago when he stupidly took on a high-ranking gang member who was serving time in the same cell block. From what I understand, he was stabbed in the heart and he bled out in minutes."

"Holy crap!" Khloe whispered.

"What about his brothers?" Elsie asked. "Won't they be even more pissed now?"

"I was worried about that too, but the gang member has plenty of friends outside the prison, and they apparently delivered their own message to the brothers. Khloe and Fallport are off-limits unless they want to end up the same way as Alan did," Raid said with a shrug.

"Why would some random gang care about Khloe?" Heather asked. "No offense intended," she said quickly, after she realized what she said could be taken the wrong way.

"It's okay, I wondered the same thing," Khloe reassured her.

"I don't think it's Khloe so much," Raid said. "Details about his case, and why Alan had it out for you so badly, got around the prison...which is what Alan and the gang member were 'discussing' when he died. Apparently, even some of the most hardened criminals have pets they love. I can only guess they're willing to go out of their way to protect those who help them."

"Wow," Caryn said. "I'm not sure whether to be impressed or freaked out."

"Impressed," Finley said firmly.

"Right, so, there shouldn't be anyone else lurking in the shadows to try to hurt you," Lilly said decisively. "And that goes for the rest of us too...unless anyone wants to share anything? Now's the time. Anyone got any exes who might want to stalk them? Any business deals that went bad and now they're in the crosshairs of a monster? Maybe a connection to the Russian mafia we don't know about?"

Everyone laughed and shook their heads.

"Good. So the most stressful thing we have to worry about is not working too hard. And maybe Bigfoot storming into town, pissed off because his peaceful existence in our mountains has been disturbed."

Ethan rolled his eyes, but everyone else laughed.

Khloe listened to the banter between her friends with a smile on her face. *This* was what she'd always wanted. Friends she could laugh with, cry with, and count on beyond a shadow of a doubt.

Raid leaned over and kissed the top of her head, and Khloe looked up at him.

"You good?" he asked quietly.

"I'm great," she told him.

"Will you marry me?" he blurted.

Khloe stared at him for a heartbeat. "What? *Seriously?*"

He blushed. "Yeah. I hadn't actually planned to do this now, but I love you so much, and I figured if I asked you when you were feeling mellow and happy, you'd be more likely to say yes."

"You have got to be kidding me. You actually think I'd say no?"

Raid shrugged.

Ignoring their friends, Khloe rose to her knees on the couch. She badly wanted to straddle Raid's lap, but with his leg still healing, that wouldn't be smart. She put her palms on his cheeks and leaned in.

"I love you, Raid. So much it scares the shit out of me. If you hadn't been with me in that water, I would've given up even in the few minutes before the cavalry arrived. You make me want to be a better person. You make me a *stronger* person. The way you look at me makes me feel as if I can do anything. Be anyone. I want to be Anise to your Bjorn. I want to conquer gnolls and ogres, and cast magical spells, and live happily ever after."

She heard Lilly shushing everyone, but she ignored their audience.

Raid didn't say anything for a heartbeat—then he grabbed her waist and yanked, dipping her backward over his lap. Duke grumbled as he was jostled, but when he realized Khloe's face was within reach of his tongue, he took advantage of the situation.

Khloe shrieked as Duke gave her a tongue bath. She was still laughing when Finley came to her rescue and pulled Duke off the couch.

Raid hovered over her, face inches from her own. One of his hands supported the back of her head while the other was wrapped around her waist, keeping her steady.

"Was that a yes?" he asked.

Khloe grinned. "Depends."

Raid frowned. "On what?"

"On whether you're going to make me put on a big, poofy white dress and suffer through a formal wedding."

Relief shone in Raid's eyes. "You can have any kind of wedding you want. As long as you're my wife when it's all said and done, I don't care."

"I want a party. A *big-ass* party. Celebrating life. Mine, yours, Duke's, and everyone's," Khloe told him. "We've all been through some pretty gnarly stuff in the last year, and I think we need to let loose and celebrate the fact that love triumphs over evil."

She heard everyone clapping and cheering around the room, but Khloe only had eyes for Raid.

"Deal," he whispered. "I never thought this would be my life. That someone as amazing and beautiful as you would ever choose me."

"I choose you, Raid. Today, tomorrow, and every day after that."

"I love you."

"And I love you," she returned.

They kissed as their friends began planning Fallport's party of the century.

EPILOGUE

Khloe sat at a large table on Bristol and Rocky's back deck and smiled at the absolute chaos all around her. There had been countless ups and downs in the last fifteen years, but she wouldn't change a thing.

Rocky and Bristol had built onto their house, expanding the barn, the deck, putting in a pool, and adding three bedrooms to their already perfect house. This was the go-to place for everyone to hang out. In the summer, Khloe was here just about every day, in between shifts at her vet clinic. Because there were now three vets in the area, no one was overwhelmed with patients, and each of her colleagues had plenty of free time to enjoy life in Fallport.

There had been Pickleport festivals, Bigfoot expos, Bristol Wingham-Watson art shows, and a lot of laughter and smiles.

Elsie and Zeke's second-eldest son was currently attempting to wrangle the younger children as they ran around the yard as if they'd just been injected with straight-up caffeine pills. Finley and Brock's oldest daughter was inside watching *Frozen IV* with some of the other kids. She'd volunteered not because she enjoyed the animated movie, but because she could flirt with her boyfriend via text while the kids she was supposed to be watching over were distracted.

Khloe was amazed she could remember all the children's names. There had been so many additions to their group over the years, it felt as if they were running a daycare most days.

Elsie and Zeke had four between them, plus Tony; Rocky and Bristol had one...Samantha had been a surprise to them both, and even though they hadn't even been sure they wanted children, Sam was a blessing they couldn't live without. Drew and Caryn hadn't wanted kids of their own, but they were always babysitting the littles and volunteering to take the older kids on camping trips, as well as entertaining them at the firehouse, where Caryn spent a large portion of her time.

Brock and Finley had ended up with three, and Tal and Heather had two biological children, in addition to Marissa, who was currently off at college with goals to become an FBI officer specializing in finding kidnapped and missing children.

And then there was Lilly and Ethan. It had taken two long, frustrating, often heartbreaking years for them to conceive again...but after having Brandon, it seemed as if she'd been pregnant nonstop. Every year for the next five, she'd gotten pregnant. The girls had made merciless fun of Lilly, often saying they couldn't remember what she'd looked like without a baby belly.

Khloe and Raid had talked about it a lot, and in the

end decided maybe having kids wasn't in the cards for them. They were both over forty when they married, and neither really wanted to be in their sixties with children still in school.

But life had a funny way of blowing well-laid plans to smithereens.

She'd been in Richmond for a veterinarian conference, relaxing in the hotel after a long day, when a segment on the news had caught her attention.

It was early December at the time, the holidays approaching, and a reporter was interviewing a boy who was around ten, asking what he wanted for Christmas. His answer nearly broke Khloe's heart.

He said all he wanted was a safe place for his three sisters to sleep.

That had started a three-year-long odyssey to meet Joaquin and his sisters, to qualify to be foster parents, and to eventually adopt them. It was crazy, and Khloe was grateful every day that Raid hadn't even blinked when she'd come home from that trip and informed him that she wanted to look into bringing four children into their home and possibly adopting them.

So now, she and Raid were parents to seventeen-year-old Joaquin, fourteen-year-old Lateesha, eleven-year-old Tasha, and nine-year-old Diamond. Life hadn't been easy for the siblings, but Khloe wanted to think since coming to Fallport, it had gotten a little easier.

And Raiden, despite his worries, had turned out to be an excellent father. He was there for their children no matter what their needs were. He wasn't afraid to talk to them about their feelings, opening up to them about his own upbringing and making them feel as if they could come to him with any problems or concerns they had.

And watching him play Dungeons and Dragons with Tasha made Khloe's heart melt. The eleven-year-old was turning out to be a fierce player, and her and Raid's bond was all the more special because of their shared love of the game.

Last year, out of the blue, Joaquin had come up to her in their kitchen and given her a long, hard hug—which was very usual for the taciturn teenager—and thanked her for giving his sisters a safe place to sleep.

But today's get-together was special. Each year, they all got together and celebrated the child that wasn't with them physically, but would forever be in their hearts.

When Elsie had first suggested having a celebration for Lilly and Ethan's first child, the one who didn't make it into the world, everyone had been a little uneasy about the idea. They didn't know how Lilly would take it. But to their surprise, Lilly had cried—overjoyed that they wanted to do something for the baby she missed every single day.

So that first year, on what would've been the baby's birthday, they had a small party. Basically the women got together and drank—those who weren't pregnant or breastfeeding, that was—while the men watched over them. The parties had morphed since then into what it was today. A chance for the adults to get together and chat while the almost two dozen children ran around and enjoyed spending time with their "cousins."

"It's time," Elsie said, coming out from the house with a single cupcake in her hand. Rocky used his fingers to whistle loudly, calling everyone in from the yard. Meanwhile, Zeke appeared with the kids who'd been inside watching the movie.

Nineteen children, minus Tony and Marissa who were off at college, gathered on the deck. Elsie, Bristol, Caryn, Finley, Heather, and Khloe sat around the table, with Lilly at the head in the place of honor. Their men all stood behind their wives, supporting them silently as they always had and always would.

Elsie placed the cupcake in front of Lilly, then lit the candle.

"We want to wish Lilly and Ethan's firstborn a very happy birthday. You've never been forgotten and never will. You were wanted, and so very loved. Happy Birthday."

The words changed a bit each year, and they took turns who said them, but the sentiment was the same. That baby who never got a chance to take a breath. Who hadn't made it to his or her first day on Earth, had been wanted. Was missed. Was important.

Lilly took a deep breath and Ethan leaned down to whisper something in her ear. She nodded and blew out the candle. Then she tilted her head back and Ethan kissed her on the lips.

There was a short—very short, considering how many kids there were in their extended family now—moment of silence, then one of Finley's kids yelled, "Cake time!"

Everyone chuckled. She wasn't wrong. After blowing out the single candle on the cupcake, they traditionally all dug into a monster cake that Finley made every year. And each year she seemed to outdo the last. This one was no exception. Brock came out on the deck with a huge sheet cake in his hands. He held it up high, drawing out the moment everyone saw the cake for the first time, then he put it down with a flourish.

Khloe burst out laughing, along with everyone else. Over the years, the Bigfoot theme seemed to keep popping up...much to Lilly's dismay. She'd come to town because of the legendary creature, but claimed it had gotten old to always be seeing and hearing about him.

Finley had used fondant to decorate the cake with a giant Bigfoot. Except he wasn't hiding in the woods, as most thought he was wont to do. This one had a conical party hat on his head, a bow tie around his neck, and he was holding streamers in his hands. He had a huge smile on his face and was surrounded by squirrels, deer, skunks, and even a bear. Apparently there was a party going on in the forest that only animals were invited to.

Khloe was impressed with Finley's artistic talent. She'd gotten better and better every year since she'd opened her bakery, and her cakes were always in high demand around Fallport.

After Khloe hugged Lilly, she stepped back to let the kids have access to the table, and the fabulous cake. She felt Raid's arm go around her waist. They were both in their fifties now...closing in on sixty, and not one day in the last fifteen years had gone by without her husband telling her how much he loved her.

They both had some gray in their hair, and even though Raid complained about it, Khloe secretly thought the silver in his red beard and hair made him look even more handsome.

"You about ready to head home?" he whispered in her ear.

Khloe shivered as she turned in his arms and looked up at him. "Yes."

"I'm gonna knock your socks off tonight, woman," he said.

"Is that a threat?" she asked with a grin.

"A promise," he told her. He tightened his hold on Khloe and lifted his head until he'd caught Drew's eyes. "We're headed out."

"Go on. Have fun, you two. Caryn and I will be sure to keep your kids up until all hours of the night, fill them with sugar and crap, then bring them back tired and cranky and bouncing off the walls in the morning."

Khloe giggled when Raid scowled as his friend. "You better not," he warned.

Caryn came up and pushed Drew with her shoulder. "We won't," she promised. "Okay, they might stay up a bit later than usual, but I'll make sure to make them all eat at least one vegetable, and maybe we'll bring them to the new obstacle course behind the auto shop so they'll be more than ready to crash at the end of the night."

"Thanks, Caryn!" Khloe said. Then she blew a kiss to each of her kids, gave them the "be good" look she'd perfected, and pulled Raid toward the front of the house. "Let's go. I want to see if you can put your money where your mouth is," she teased.

"It's on, woman."

"It's on," Khloe agreed.

* * *

Two hours later, Khloe leaned forward and listened intently as the Dungeon Master spoke. Anise and Bjorn had just

351

fought a small battle with a pack of wereraccoons. Anise had taken some hits, but Bjorn had used some spells and healed her. Now they were in pursuit of the surviving wereraccoon, who had disappeared down a series of tunnels.

"You've been walking in the tunnel for about the length of a football field, there's water under your feet and it's very cold. Every now and then, something brushes against your ankles and it smells as if something died down there. A mist has formed and it's getting hard to see very far in front of you."

"Crap, I don't like this," Khloe told Raid. She turned back to the screen on the laptop and asked the DM, "Is there anything around us? Like a doorway? Or does the tunnel perhaps branch off ahead of us?"

"Roll a perception check," the DM responded.

Khloe picked up her twenty-sided die and dropped it in her dice tower. When it finally came to rest at the bottom of the box, she checked the number on the die and her perception score on her sheet. "Twelve," she informed the DM.

The DM checked her notes. "Within the range of your torch, you can't see any bends ahead. There aren't any doorways in sight either."

"So that means the wereraccoon had to come this way," Raid said calmly.

"Unless we missed a door because of the mist," Khloe scowled.

"Let's keep going," Raid said.

"Fine." Khloe turned back to the screen. "We're gonna keep walking," she told the DM.

"Okay. About forty or so yards down the tunnel, you discover a stone block on the floor."

"How well can we see it? I thought there was water under our feet," Raid asked.

"It's about fifteen inches wide and twenty inches tall. It's made out of a different material than the tunnel around you," the DM said calmly.

"Is it in the middle of the tunnel? Or against the wall?" Khloe asked.

"Against the wall."

"Can I move it, or is it too heavy?" Khloe asked, moving to the edge of her seat. Over the years, she'd really come to love D&D. There was always something different to conquer and she had to use her brain as much as her magical abilities in order to stay alive.

"Roll a strength check," the DM told her.

Khloe snatched her D20 quickly and rolled it without the tower this time. It bounced around the tray and stopped with the twenty up. "Natural twenty!" Khloe squealed. She ignored Raid's smirk. He was always amused at how excited she got while playing.

"Yes, you can push it without too much trouble."

"Okay, I want to examine the stone."

"You don't find anything out of the ordinary."

"Hmmmmm. Okay, then maybe it's a marker of some sort. Bjorn and I want to check the area for secret doors. We want to examine the walls."

"Roll an investigation check," the DM said.

"We'll let the dwarf helm this one." Raid smiled as he reached for the dice. "Fifteen."

"You don't find anything unusual along the walls."

"Shoot," Khloe said with a huff. "There has to be something here. Otherwise, the stone wouldn't be so obvious. What about on the ceiling?"

"Neither you nor Bjorn can reach the ceiling, it's about a foot beyond your reach, and several feet beyond Bjorn's."

"Ah ha!" Khloe crowed. "I bet that stone isn't a marker, it's a step! I climb up with Bjorn steadying me and start poking around on the ceiling."

The DM looked up and smiled at the camera. "You look around for a bit and suddenly a part of the roof shifts. You've found a panel that can be lifted away."

"Be careful," Raid warned.

But Khloe had played the game enough that she knew she shouldn't rush into anything. Some of the scenarios other DMs had thought up had been extremely precarious, and she'd almost died plenty of times. And it would've sucked to have the character Raid created die after they'd both spent so much time building her skills and strengths. "I open the panel very slowly and cautiously. Can I see anything?" she asked.

"Your head is still below the level of the opening, but you can see some sort of light to one side."

"How about if I lift Bjorn up so he can get a better look?"

"All right, you change places and lift him up into the space above the tunnel—"

"No, wait!" Raid exclaimed. "She boosts me up just high enough for my head to be in the opening. I'm not all the way up in the room."

"Okay, Bjorn, you see another tunnel, a lot like the one you were just walking through, but it only goes in one direction. There's a doorway about fifteen yards away, and you can see footprints leading from where your head is, to the doorway."

"Yes!" Khloe exclaimed.

Raid turned toward her and smiled. "It never fails to amaze me that you really do enjoy this," he said quietly.

Khloe put her hand on Raiden's thigh and squeezed. She'd reassured him many times over the years that she didn't play D&D just to appease him. She loved figuring out the clues and mysteries and seeing what their characters could accomplish together.

Having kids had limited the time they could join in, but when they could manage it, she enjoyed it just as much as the first time they'd played together.

Several hours later, with the mystery of the wereraccoon solved and relieved that, once more, both Bjorn and Anise had lived to face another challenge and play another game at some point in the future, Khloe couldn't stop smiling as her husband towed her up the stairs toward their bedroom.

After getting ready for bed and crawling in next to Raid, Khloe straddled him, smiling as she felt his cock growing against her ass. "You tired?" she asked.

"Does it feel like I'm tired?" Raid retorted, tightening his hands on her waist.

"Just checking," she said as she moved down his body, another smile growing on her lips.

An hour later, she snuggled into Raiden's side as she tried to catch her breath. Raid might not be able to have more than one orgasm in a single lovemaking session anymore, but he took great pride in making sure *she* was satisfied at least twice.

"Raid?" Khloe asked.

"Yeah, sweetheart?"

"I love you."

"And I love you back," he reassured her.

"What time is Caryn bringing the kids home tomorrow?"

"No clue."

"I should get up and check the schedule, see when the kids need to be where," Khloe said, making a move to get up.

"No," Raid said, shaking his head. "It's late. We're comfortable. The dog's sleeping. We can check the schedule tomorrow. Go to sleep, Khloe."

She smiled. "Fine."

"Fine," Raid echoed.

It didn't take long for his breaths to even out and his grip on her relaxed.

Thirty minutes later, Khloe was still awake. She should be sleeping. It *was* late, and their kids would be wound up tomorrow, wanting to talk about how much fun they had with Aunt Caryn and Uncle Drew and explain in minute detail all the fun things they'd done.

Sighing, Khloe slipped out of bed and picked up her warm, fuzzy robe she'd dropped on the floor before crawling under the covers earlier.

She padded over to the window and looked out across the dark landscape. There was a full moon tonight and as a result, Khloe could see all the way down their driveway to the road, and the forest beyond, where Raid had spent so much time.

Instinctively, Khloe looked to the left, to the corner of their room that Duke had occupied for so many years. He was gone now, he'd died peacefully in his sleep, but not a day went by that Khloe or Raid didn't think about him. He'd never be replaced, but the coonhound they'd acquired not long before Duke's death was doing her best to fill the big shoes he'd left. She was still learning how to be a search dog, but her energy and enthusiasm had helped her find half a dozen lost hikers already.

But Callie was still no Duke. She loved getting pets, loved people, but preferred to sleep in her crate, her safe space, rather than in the room with her and Raid. It had taken some getting used to at first, but they'd both eventually adjusted to her personality.

Khloe stood at the window, thinking about how lucky she was for a long while...before frowning as something caught her eye. She leaned forward, her forehead practically touching the glass, and tried to figure out what the hell she was seeing.

In the distance, between the trees on the far side of the road, stood what looked like...a person. No, not a person. Maybe a bear?

But bears didn't walk on their hind legs.

Khloe blinked and shook her head before squinting and trying to come up with a reasonable explanation for what she was seeing. The...thing in the woods turned toward her for a moment, looking in the direction of the house, before disappearing into the trees.

"What are you looking at so hard?" Raid asked a split-second before he wound his arm around her and rested his chin on the top of her head.

Khloe turned and looked up at her husband with wide eyes. "You wouldn't believe me if I told you."

"Try me."

"I'm pretty sure I just saw Bigfoot."

Raid's lips twitched. "Yeah? Maybe it was a wereraccoon."

"Don't laugh at me, Raid. I know what I saw!"

"Uh-huh. I'm thinking your brain's stuck in D&D mode. Come on, come back to bed. It's super-late now, and we're gonna have to be up way before we're ready when Caryn returns with our munchkins."

She let Raid lead her back to bed, loving how he always snuggled up against her when they were under the covers. His arm went around her, and he kissed her gently behind the ear. "Sleep, sweetheart."

"I really *did* see Bigfoot," she told him, wanting him to believe her so badly.

"Let me guess...at least eight feet tall, black and brown hair, walking along the edge of the road?"

Khloe came up on an elbow and turned to stare at Raid. "Yes!"

"I've seen him too," he told her, completely nonchalantly.

"Oh my God, Raid! Why haven't you said anything before now?" she asked.

He shrugged. "I feel bad for him. Ever since that show aired all those years ago, he's been hunted relentlessly. I figured I'd give him a break."

Khloe lay back down and snuggled into Raid's chest. "Yeah...I get that. But still! You should've told me!"

"Would you have believed me?" he asked sleepily.

Khloe wanted to say yes, but she wasn't sure if that was completely the truth.

"I love you, Khloe. Only *we* could be having this conversation as if we're talking about seeing Davis, the way he used to creep around in the forest."

Her husband wasn't wrong. Davis Woolford, the formally homeless veteran, had moved to Washington, DC, and had managed to become one of the many bakers working in the White House. He came back to Fallport now and then, and everyone was overjoyed to see how successful he was now. He'd gotten into therapy, had married, and he now had two children. He was as proud of Fallport as Fallport was proud of him. He'd left his troubles behind him and made a life he was proud of.

"I can't believe I just saw Bigfoot," Khloe whispered.

"I can show you something else big and hairy," Raid told her.

Khloe giggled and shoved an elbow back into his belly.

Raid chuckled in return.

"Raiden?"

"Yeah?"

"I love you."

"It's a good thing, since you married me. Now shush and let me get some sleep."

Khloe grinned and sighed in contentment. She fell asleep in her husband's arms...dreaming of Bigfoot joining forces with Anise to take down Saltborn the Stone Giant, who'd overtaken the troglodyte scouts and come to slaughter their hunting party.

* * *

Thank you for reading the Eagle Point Search & Rescue Series! I loved every second of writing it and being in small-town Fallport was a joy! Next up for me, I'm going back to where I started...active-duty Navy SEALs! The first book, *Protecting Remi* features not only an ocean rescue, but a kidnapping as well (both things I love writing because it allows the heroine to be scared, yet strong. Doing what she can to help herself survive with a little help from the Hero!) Thank you all for your support and read on!

Want to talk to other Susan Stoker fans? Join my reader group, Susan Stoker's Stalkers, on Facebook!

Also by Susan Stoker

Eagle Point Search & Rescue Series

Searching for Lilly
Searching for Elsie
Searching for Bristol
Searching for Caryn
Searching for Finley
Searching for Heather
Searching for Khloe

The Refuge Series

Deserving Alaska
Deserving Henley
Deserving Reese
Deserving Cora
Deserving Lara
Deserving Maisy (Oct 2024)
Deserving Ryleigh (Jan 2025)

SEAL of Protection: Alliance Series

Protecting Remi (July 2024)
Protecting Wren (Nov 2024)
Protecting Josie (Mar 2025)
Protecting Maggie (TBA)
Protecting Addison (TBA)
Protecting Kelli (TBA)
Protecting Bree (TBA)

Game of Chance Series

The Protector

Rescuing Sadie (novella)
Rescuing Wendy
Rescuing Mary
Rescuing Macie (novella)
Rescuing Annie

Delta Team Two Series

Shielding Gillian
Shielding Kinley
Shielding Aspen
Shielding Jayme (novella)
Shielding Riley
Shielding Devyn
Shielding Ember
Shielding Sierra

SEAL of Protection Series

Protecting Caroline
Protecting Alabama
Protecting Fiona
Marrying Caroline (novella)
Protecting Summer
Protecting Cheyenne
Protecting Jessyka
Protecting Julie (novella)
Protecting Melody
Protecting the Future
Protecting Kiera (novella)
Protecting Alabama's Kids (novella)
Protecting Dakota

Badge of Honor: Texas Heroes Series

Silverstone Series
Trusting Skylar
Trusting Taylor
Trusting Molly
Trusting Cassidy

Stand Alone
Falling for the Delta
The Guardian Mist
Nature's Rift
A Princess for Cale
A Moment in Time- A Collection of Short Stories
Another Moment in Time- A Collection of Short Stories
A Third Moment in Time- A Collection of Short Stories
Lambert's Lady

Special Operations Fan Fiction
http://www.AcesPress.com

Beyond Reality Series
Outback Hearts
Flaming Hearts
Frozen Hearts

Writing as Annie George:
Stepbrother Virgin (erotic novella)

ABOUT THE AUTHOR

New York Times, *USA Today*, #1 Amazon Bestseller, and #1 *Wall Street Journal* Bestselling Author, Susan Stoker has spent the last twenty-three years living in Missouri, California, Colorado, Indiana, Texas, and Tennessee and is currently living in the wilds of Maine. She's married to a retired Army man (and current firefighter/EMT) who now gets to follow *her* around the country.

She debuted her first series in 2014 and quickly followed that up with the SEAL of Protection Series, which solidified her love of writing and creating stories readers can get lost in.

If you enjoyed this book, or any book, please consider leaving a review. It's appreciated by authors more than you'll know.

www.stokeraces.com
www.AcesPress.com
susan@stokeraces.com

facebook.com/authorsusanstoker

x.com/Susan_Stoker

instagram.com/authorsusanstoker

goodreads.com/SusanStoker

bookbub.com/authors/susan-stoker

amazon.com/author/susanstoker

9 781644 993842